Other books by Leonard Maltin

Leonard Maltin's Movie Guide (released annually)
Leonard Maltin's Family Film Guide
Leonard Maltin's Movie Encyclopedia
The Great American Broadcast
The Great Movie Comedians
The Disney Films
Of Mice and Magic: A History of American Animated Cartoons
The Art of the Cinematographer
Selected Short Subjects
The Little Rascals: The Life and Times of Our Gang (with Richard W. Bann)

Leonard Maltin's

MOVIE CRAZY

PRESS™
Milwaukie

Portions of this book originally appeared in issues of *Leonard Maltin's Movie Crazy*.

Photo credits and acknowledgments: Warner Bros., Metro-Goldwyn-Mayer, 20th Century Fox, Universal Pictures, Paramount Pictures, Columbia Pictures, RKO Radio Pictures, Republic Pictures, The Walt Disney Company, CBS, Lou Valentino, Edward Bernds, Ray Bradbury, Richard H. Kline, Richard W. Bann, Jack Mathis, Cole Johnson, Mark Johnson, Delmar Watson Photography Archives, Academy of Motion Picture Arts and Sciences, Jimmy Lydon, Alexander Courage, Rudy Behlmer, Miles Kreuger, Peter Mintun, Roy H. Wagner, Michael F. Blake, Brent Walker, and Robert S. Bader.

Please note that while every attempt has been made to identify the copyright holders of the material published herein, some omissions or errors may have occurred. Please send any corrections to the publisher at the address listed for correction in subsequent reprints.

M Press
10956 SE Main Street
Milwaukie, OR 97222

mpressbooks.com

Book design by Tony Ong

ISBN 978-1-59582-119-5
First M Press edition: January 2008

10 9 8 7 6 5 4 3 2 1

Printed in U.S.A.

Dedicated to the memory of William K. Everson
Scholar, Teacher, Mentor, and Friend

TABLE of CONTENTS

INTRODUCTION

I have a long history with fanzines, a breed of publication that has all but vanished in the world of websites and blogs. That well-traveled road in my life has led to the book you hold in your hands, but it started with *Film Fan Monthly,* a fanzine founded by the late Daryl Davy in Vancouver, Canada, in 1961.

Film Fan Monthly was a journal for people who collected 8mm and 16mm movies—not video, mind you, but prints of films. As a budding collector and nervy would-be expert, I wrote to Daryl and offered my services to review new 8mm releases. I didn't tell him I was thirteen years old until he'd accepted my first article; he then told me he was nineteen. There was no money involved; this was a labor of love.

Two years later, Daryl told me that he no longer had time to put out his monthly publication, but hated to see it fold after five years of hard work. He asked if I wanted to take over his magazine, and I eagerly agreed. The purchase price was $175, for which I would inherit his four hundred subscribers, mostly in the U.S. and Canada but also around the globe. Because he had $400 in the treasury, I received a check for $225 and his mailing list. That's how I became a magazine publisher. I've never had a better deal since.

I was thrilled to kiss my mimeo machine goodbye and bring the layouts to a local printer. What's more, I could now publish photographs for the first time. In May of 1966, my humble bimonthly publication *Profile* was incorporated into *Film Fan Monthly*, and I started downplaying the collector angle in order to focus on film history. Every issue reflected my personal taste: the first cover featured my hero, humorist and actor Robert Benchley. Before long, I was receiving submissions from other film buffs and talented writers who were seeking an outlet—and didn't mind not being paid.

I wrote, typed, edited, laid out, published, stuffed, and stamped *Film Fan Monthly* from 1963 through 1975. Warren Dressler became my business partner, and, when he went off to college, my father took over as "circulation manager." When I started out, I was in high school and the magazine consumed my every thought. Nine years later I was newly married, paying rent, and working professionally as a writer—the thrill of turning out my own monthly magazine had become something of a burden. I brought an end to *FFM* and received an outpouring of letters from readers who felt a real connection with the magazine.

That, more than anything, is what I missed in the years that followed: a sense of personal communication with like-minded people. I was lucky enough to sell a series of books to various publishers, but the book projects didn't have the immediacy of the magazine. Being a publisher was also the ultimate power trip, a real spoiler for a freelance writer. I've rarely had the same degree of freedom in the professional arena since.

From time to time, I thought about reviving *Film Fan Monthly* in some form, but always talked myself out of it, not wanting to deal with deadlines, printers, or the post office ever again. Then, in the spring of 2002, I embarked on a research expedition at the Warner Bros. Archives at the University of Southern California and stumbled onto one of the greatest scoops of my life. When I got home, I checked the index of every book I owned about Orson Welles; not one of them mentioned the fact that he came close to directing and starring in the 1942 film adaptation of *The Man Who Came to Dinner* for Warner Bros. It would have been his second film, following *Citizen Kane*. Think what this might have meant to Welles's career. At the very least, it would have given him an ally in the person of Jack L. Warner . . . but it was not to be.

I was certain that this nugget of information was worthy of an article in a major magazine. I actually sold the idea to *Vanity Fair*, which later killed the piece because they had just run an excerpt of Steven Bach's Moss Hart biography and felt that mentioning *The Man Who Came to Dinner* a month or two later would seem redundant. I tried other publications but no one was terribly interested. A friend at the now-defunct *Premiere* agreed to run a very brief précis-like version of the story.

I decided there was only one course of action: to return to my roots and go back into the fanzine business. This time around, I wouldn't have to do all the dirty work myself. My intrepid computer coach, Jeanne McCafferty, turned out to be an excellent editor and a pretty fair layout artist as well. She found a capable printer who was also able to take on the task of mailing. And I was back in the magazine business.

I set myself a quarterly publication schedule, thinking that the slower publication pace would be livable; I was wrong. But when I finally sit down to generate a new issue, I feel a surge of energy and purposefulness. I love exploring movie history, especially without anyone looking over my shoulder to second-guess my ideas or make me doubt the topics I've chosen.

Leonard Maltin's Movie Crazy has a rather modest circulation, but my readers are true believers, fellow movie nuts who enjoy unearthing odds and ends from the silent film and early talking era as much as I do. Their letters and e-mails encourage me to keep going. (A remarkable number of them used to subscribe to *Film Fan Monthly*!)

The newsletter enables me to make use of my collection of movie stills, which I began amassing at the age of twelve. I also draw from my collection of movie memorabilia, an addiction that started somewhat later on and received an unexpected boost when I got married to someone who loves this stuff as much as I do.

As much as I enjoy having a vehicle to print interviews I conducted decades ago, it's just as exciting to find new interview subjects today. From the time I worked on *Film Fan Monthly* to the present, I've had a particular interest in spotlighting people and films that don't get the attention they deserve. It's not that I don't love the great stars and movies of the Golden Age, but there are many places where you can read about them and too few opportunities to learn new information, or discover worthy unsung films.

Another reason this journey has been so pleasurable is that it has given me reason to tap into a network of friends around the world who share my passion. If I have a question about animated cartoons, I know where to go. If the topic is early talkie musicals, I have many sources to consult. It's a kick to be able to draw on the vast knowledge of my friends and colleagues, who are always willing to share. What they know can't be found in any library, let alone on the Internet.

That's why I want to offer my deepest thanks to Jerry Beck, Richard W. Bann, Miles Kreuger, George Feltenstein, Rudy Behlmer, Stacey Behlmer, Howard Green, Robert Bader, John Scheinfeld, Ron Hutchinson, Peter Mintun, Lou Valentino, Kit Parker, Keith Scott, John Cocchi, Mary Harris, Marvin Eisenman, the late Jack Mathis, the late Joe Grant, Marvin Paige, Michael Feinstein, Mark Cantor, Joe Adamson, Patricia Tobias, Shel Dorf, Jon Burlingame, Antoinette and Delmar Watson, Bob Thomas, Bob O'Neil, Gloria Stuart, John Leifert, Kirk Crivello, Anthony Slide, Alex Hassan, Roy H. Wagner, Mark Evanier, Robert Tieman, Dave Smith, Scott MacQueen, James V. D'Arc, Mike Mashon, Mark Cotta Vaz, Schawn Belston, Cole Johnson, Bill Blair, Michael Schlesinger, the folks at the Academy of Motion

Picture Arts and Sciences, and the Warner Bros. Archives at USC. I must add special thanks to my savvy readers who regularly send in additions and corrections, which I was able to incorporate into the articles for this publication.

I owe a special debt to my wife, partner, and soulmate Alice for allowing me this indulgence. And I doff my hat to Jeanne McCafferty for her diligence and attention to detail as she shepherds each issue of *Leonard Maltin's Movie Crazy* through to completion.

Finally, I am grateful to Mike Richardson, the President of Dark Horse Entertainment—another man who follows his dreams—for offering to publish this assemblage from my first five years of publishing *Movie Crazy*. He put me in the very capable hands of Robert Simpson and Victoria Blake, who have shown tremendous care and respect for me and my musings about film.

I think the best way to describe my latest publishing venture is to say that it makes me feel like a kid again. It take me back to the time when I first fell in love with movies, and that's a very happy place to be.

LEONARD MALTIN

Chapter 1
DISCOVERIES

THE MAN WHO *ALMOST* CAME TO DINNER

Orson Welles was just twenty-five years old when he made movie history with his debut feature, *Citizen Kane*. Even dilettante film buffs know that.

But until now, the aborted plans for his second film have never been revealed in print. This intriguing footnote to film history has eluded Welles scholars for nearly sixty years.

I wish I could claim that I unearthed this nugget by dint of diligent research, but the truth is, I stumbled onto it quite by chance in the Warner Bros. archive at the University of Southern California Cinema-Television Library.

I had requested files relating to the 1941 film version of *The Man Who Came to Dinner*, hoping to learn why and how the great John Barrymore had, toward the end of his life, come to make a screen test for the starring role of Sheridan Whiteside. This had piqued my interest ever since I found an original 35mm nitrate print of that test in the film collection of the Museum of Modern Art, years ago.

I never did learn the genesis of that test, but I uncovered more undiscovered pages of Hollywood history than I'd ever anticipated . . . including the fact that Orson Welles very nearly came to direct and star in the picture.

But I'm getting ahead of my story . . .

The brothers Warner believed in writing things down. No one would have accused the former Pennsylvania nickelodeon owners of being especially literate, but Jack and his siblings believed so strongly in the importance of the written word that, during their long tenure, all studio stationery bore this motto: "Put it in writing. Verbal communication causes confusion."

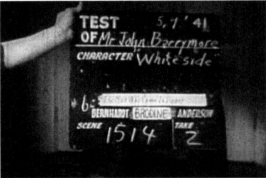

Frame enlargements from John Barrymore's unsuccessful screen test.

Thanks to that edict, film students and researchers today can follow a remarkable paper trail at USC on any Warner Bros. movie, actor, or filmmaker. There are handwritten notes from Bette Davis to J. L. explaining why she will not report for work; a letter from Errol Flynn, on location for *The Adventures of Robin Hood*, complaining bitterly about his ill-fitting wig; and detailed, incisive memos from longtime studio production chief Hal B. Wallis telling errant directors how to improve their footage. Many of the best exchanges were published in Rudy Behlmer's revelatory book *Inside Warner Bros.*, but that collection is just the tip of the iceberg.

When I opened the bulging folder concerning *The Man Who Came to Dinner*, I found several neatly organized files. Each one contained studio inter-office correspondence, tracking the progress of the film on a day-by-day basis, from the moment Warners committed to making a movie from George S. Kaufman and Moss Hart's hit Broadway play. The still-hilarious comedy tells the story of a lordly drama critic (based on the real-life, acid-tongued Alexander Woollcott) who is forced to spend several months at the home of a small-town businessman and his wife after breaking his leg on their front steps. By reading the memos in chronological order, one is drawn into a daily drama almost as interesting as the play itself.

The most surprising discovery was that Monty Woolley, the Yale professor-turned-actor who became an overnight star on Broadway as Sheridan Whiteside (and eventually starred in the movie) was not considered a shoo-in for the part. What's more surprising is who might have taken his place . . . and who campaigned for the role.

Charles Laughton, already an Oscar-winner for his unforgettable portrayal in *The Private Life of Henry VIII*, agreed to make a screen test to prove he was right for the part of Whiteside. Several days later, his agent, Bert Allenberg, wrote an eloquent letter to Hal Wallis, explaining that Charles felt he hadn't quite captured the part in that test, as it takes him at least a few days to sink his teeth into a characterization. In the letter, Allenberg admits that he's heard Wallis is considering a younger man for the role, and writes in protest, "The part calls for an eccentric. It's a man produced once in a generation; an Oscar Wilde, a Bernard Shaw, a Charles Laughton." Apparently this plea fell on deaf ears.

John Barrymore was tested in May of 1941. He had cast his lot with the Warner brothers when they were still struggling producers in the mid-1920s, and enjoyed great success in such films as *The Sea Beast* (an adaptation of *Moby Dick*) and *Don Juan*. By the mid-1930s, the virile and versatile actor had experienced a breakdown, grown puffy, and descended from the ranks of leading men to become a supporting player, unable to memorize dialogue and wholly dependent on blackboards to recite his lines.

Perhaps it was *auld lang syne* that led the studio to give him a try; we'll never know, because there is no documentation to tell us how his screen test came about. All that survives is a May 9 memo from director Kurt (Curtis) Bernhardt to Wallis, explaining that the second half of the test is better than the first (in which "he is mugging and hamming a lot"), because Bernhardt figured out the right way to position those blackboards just outside of camera range. He adds that any given scene has to be shot "in bits, rather than in one round, which, for him, is physically impossible."

Wallis replies tersely the next day: "WILL FORGET ABOUT JOHN BARRYMORE FOR *THE MAN WHO CAME TO DINNER.*"

Watching the surviving test reel, one can see that Barrymore would have been wrong for the part. His vitriol is too intense; he lacks the light touch that makes Kaufman and Hart's sarcastic dialogue so funny. (Think of Nathan Lane, the latest actor to play the part in the recent Broadway revival.) A year later, Barrymore was dead.

On March 17, a casting roster was prepared at the studio, listing possible actors for each leading role in order of desirability. Making such lists was common practice; old hands who helped prepare them would not only cite the most appropriate, but also the most practical choices first, then add pie-in-the-sky candidates further down each column.

For Sheridan Whiteside, the three names listed as likeliest contenders were: Alexander Woollcott, the acerbic columnist and radio personality who inspired the character of Whiteside; Monty Woolley, who played him on Broadway; and Clifton Webb, the Broadway musical-

Orson Welles in a rare photo on the set of Citizen Kane, *where he discusses Joseph Cotten's old-age makeup with his longtime makeup artist Maurice Seiderman (at right).*

comedy performer who had yet to make his name in Hollywood. (A decade later, he would have been considered typecasting for Whiteside, but in 1941 he was an unknown quantity to movie audiences. When his name was suggested for the role of Waldo Lydecker in *Laura* just a few years later, 20th Century Fox chieftain Darryl F. Zanuck, who'd seen him on stage, was aghast that someone so obviously gay would even be considered for the part. Zanuck reportedly exclaimed, "He flies!")

Just below these three names were another group of possibilities: Orson Welles, Frank Morgan, John Barrymore, Robert Morley, Charles Laughton, Laird Cregar, Lionel Barrymore, Thomas Mitchell, Adolphe Menjou, Jack Benny, and Bob Hope.

The last section was more pro forma, showing little regard for good casting but keen awareness of star power: Cary Grant, William Powell, Melvyn Douglas, Fredric March, Robert Montgomery, Fred MacMurray, Ray Milland, Franchot Tone, Douglas Fairbanks Jr.

Hal Wallis wanted to test young, portly character actor Laird Cregar (who went on to costar in *The Lodger*, as Jack the Ripper, before his untimely death in 1944) but Cregar was busy shooting two films at once at 20th Century Fox, his home studio, and was unavailable.

Veteran actor Charles Coburn, who would win an Academy Award in 1943 for his vibrant performance in *The More the Merrier*, refused to make a test. He must have felt that forty years in show business constituted his proving ground for any part. (In fairness, Coburn was known for playing mostly serious roles and hadn't yet acquired the screen persona of a lovable old codger. In the Warners 1942 soap opera supreme *Kings Row* he was the cruel doctor who amputated Ronald Reagan's legs.)

Humorist-turned-performer Robert Benchley was willing to test, and was put on film in a sample scene. There is no recorded reaction to his work in the Warner Bros. files, but since his screen persona was one of affability, not acidity, he may have been a poor choice to begin with.

Producer Max Gordon sent a telegram to Wallis suggesting Groucho Marx for the part, while an agent pitched the studio chief on former

Warners star Warren William (who was sometimes referred to as the poor man's John Barrymore).

On Friday night, March 28, 1941, Hollywood newcomer Orson Welles had dinner at the home of Jack Warner (a majestic estate on the west side of Los Angeles now owned by David Geffen). That night, Warner scrawled a series of notes in ink on the back of a piece of paper; the paper survives in the USC library. The next day, he had a secretary type up the notes.

They reveal that J. L. offered the part of Whiteside to Welles, who also expressed interest in directing the film. Their conversation got down to specifics: Welles insisted on having the renowned James Wong Howe as his cinematographer (and not, interestingly, the man with whom he collaborated on *Citizen Kane*, Gregg Toland), and approved Warner's choice of studio-contractee Ann Sheridan for the role of actress Lorraine Sheldon. Welles had in mind young stage actor David Burns for the part of Banjo, and, wrote Warner, "He talked about Stanwyck, Goddard, and Lombard as the Secretary. I spoke about DeHavilland," referring to Olivia, of course, who was part of the Warner Bros. stable.

The finished film: Monty Woolley with John Ridgely, Grant Mitchell, and Billie Burke.

If Welles were not to direct, comedy master Leo McCarey was his first choice, but the next day—before Warner had his memo typed up—he called and said he'd actually prefer Howard Hawks. For starring in the film, Welles would receive $100,000. If he also directed, he would be paid an additional $50,000. Welles told Warner that night that he was getting $125,000 a picture from RKO, as well as 20 percent of the net profits. (Not mentioned, but certainly present in Welles's mind, would have been the participation of makeup artist Maurice Seiderman, who had credibly transformed the twenty-five-year-old into a bald, jowly old man in *Citizen Kane*, and on whom Welles relied for most of his career for a now-legendary series of putty noses.)

To plug this newly discovered information into the carefully documented Welles chronology, *Citizen Kane* was finished and would have its premiere one month after the meeting with Warner. Welles may have still been putting finishing touches on the picture, but was essentially between projects. Welles had been wooed to Hollywood by RKO chieftain George Schaefer with an unprecedented contract that gave the boy wonder carte blanche *and* the coveted right by him during the now-famous movie industry firestorm that surrounded *Kane*'s release.

It would require Schaefer's okay for Welles to work for Warner Bros., or anybody else, but Schaefer was not immediately reachable.

Monty Woolley, seated, recreates his most famous role for a 1954 live television production of The Man Who Came to Dinner; *with Bert Lahr, Buster Keaton, and ZaSu Pitts.*

Warner and Welles stayed in touch, and Welles even telegraphed J. L. to say how eager he was to make *The Man Who Came to Dinner* a reality.

On April 8, Schaefer was told of the potential deal, and responded as any reasonable man would: he said no. Why, having lured Welles to Hollywood in the first place, and subsidized his on-the-job learning process, would he have allowed his young genius to make a film for a rival studio?

Warner telegraphed Welles at the Ambassador Hotel in Manhattan to say that he had just had a telephone call from Schaefer, who "told me emphatically" that he could not give permission. Warner closed, "Love to Dolores from Ann Myself," referring in telegram shorthand to Welles's paramour of the moment, beautiful screen star Dolores del Rio.

Jack Warner's second choice was even more unlikely than Welles: Cary Grant.

What led to this decision is unclear. Grant had never played a snide or curmudgeonly character on-screen—and in fact, never did. But he was a box-office star, and was more than willing to take on the challenge of Whiteside.

(Grant made only a handful of films for Warner Bros. over the years, but J. L. must have been an avid admirer. Years later, he reportedly wanted Grant to play Harold Hill in *The Music Man*, and then wanted him for the role of Henry Higgins in *My Fair Lady*. In both cases, he was persuaded to do as he had done in 1941, and stick with the parts' Broadway originators.)

The studio wasted no time in pursuing the busy actor. On April 9, Hal Wallis sent word to "tie him up." For starring in *The Man Who Came to Dinner*, Grant would be paid $125,000, but the actor stipulated that his entire fee should be funneled directly to British War Relief, Hollywood Chapter. (Grant's agent, it was noted, would still get his 10 percent.)

Everything seemed locked in place, until the matter of Grant's schedule came up. This deadlock led to a telephone conversation between Warner and Sam Briskin, the no-nonsense production executive for Columbia Pictures, where Grant was then making *Penny Serenade* with Irene Dunne.

A transcript of the conversation in the USC file shows Briskin being properly deferential to Warner but delivering bad news just the same: Grant was so heavily committed, to several studios, that there would be no way of clearing him on a timely basis to make *Dinner*. For its part, Warners was loath to delay filming, wanting to strike while the Broadway iron was hot. (The studio encountered Broadway-related problems twice during that same decade. Frank Capra filmed *Arsenic and Old Lace*, with Cary Grant in 1941, but the studio was forbidden to release it until the play finally closed. By that time, in 1944, Capra was working for the U.S. Army Signal Corps, and leading lady Priscilla Lane had retired from the screen! Later in the 1940s, the seemingly endless run of *Life with Father* prevented Warners from getting its film into theaters before 1947.)

So it was that in early June, Warners contract director William Keighley went to New York to film Monty Woolley in several scenes from the play. There was some fear that Woolley had lost his freshness in the part, but Jack Warner was delighted with what he saw. Plans to also test Alexander Woollcott (who had performed the role on stage by this time) were abandoned.

On June 6, 1941 Warner wrote to Hal Wallis that he thought Woolley was "excellent" in his test. His only decree was to have him trim his moustache and lighten his beard to look more blond than gray. The studio executive also hoped that having the original Broadway star would help persuade Bette Davis to play his long-suffering assistant. "You can see how strong the part of the secretary would measure up, and naturally Davis would play it straight," he concluded.

The die was cast. Monty Woolley, who was born to play the part of Sheridan Whiteside, immortalized his Broadway performance on-screen. Character actress Mary Wickes accompanied him in the transition from stage to film, in the hilarious role of the much-maligned nurse Miss Preen. The balance of the cast was made up of Warners regulars like Bette Davis and Ann Sheridan, and such reliable freelance players as Grant Mitchell, Billie Burke, and Reginald Gardiner, with Jimmy Durante as Banjo, the life-of-the-party buffoon inspired by Alexander Woollcott's real-life friend Harpo Marx.

On New Year's Day of 1942 *The Man Who Came to Dinner* debuted at the Strand Theatre in New York, not far from where the play originated.

By that time, *Citizen Kane* had opened and established Orson Welles as a force to reckon with in filmmaking. He immediately dove into several other projects, none of which would come to fruition as he planned. He supervised and appeared in *Journey into Fear* while working simultaneously on *The Magnificent Ambersons*, which he adapted and directed, but the latter film was taken out of his control after a disastrous audience preview. Welles was already in South America planning a multi-episode feature film about the culture and people of Argentina and Brazil, and was unable to return to Hollywood on a timely basis to fight for his picture. It was the first of many setbacks in a checkered directorial career.

Film historians have played the game of what-if about Welles's career for years—but this discovery adds a particularly relevant point. If Welles had starred in and directed *The Man Who Came to Dinner*, he might have had a sure-fire box-office hit under his belt, and that in turn might have won him the clout to make other, more personal projects. He might have been forgiven an occasional career detour. He also might have forged an alliance with Jack Warner, a powerful man who could have come to Welles's rescue at different junctures. Instead, after the *Dinner* plans went askew, Welles never worked for Warner Bros.

Monty Woolley became an overnight star, at a time when it was still possible for character actors to carry a major movie vehicle. One year later he was nominated for an Academy Award as Best Actor in the tailor-made wartime parable *The Pied Piper*.

In 1954, Woolley reprised his star-making part for a network television presentation of *The Man Who Came to Dinner*, with Merle Oberon, Joan Bennett, Margaret Hamilton, Bert Lahr as Banjo, Buster Keaton as the local doctor, and ZaSu Pitts in the role originated by Mary Wickes. (A copy survives in the collection of the Museum of Television and Radio.) And in 1972, fifty-seven-year-old Orson Welles, now bearded and portly, had his chance to play Sheridan Whiteside in a Hallmark Hall of Fame production of the play that aired on NBC. Lee Remick and Edward costarred, with Mary Wickes repeating her original stage and screen performance as the nurse.

I remember watching that telecast, and thinking that Welles had drained all the fun out of Whiteside. He seemed genuinely venomous; there was no twinkle in his eye.

Just like John Barrymore a generation before.

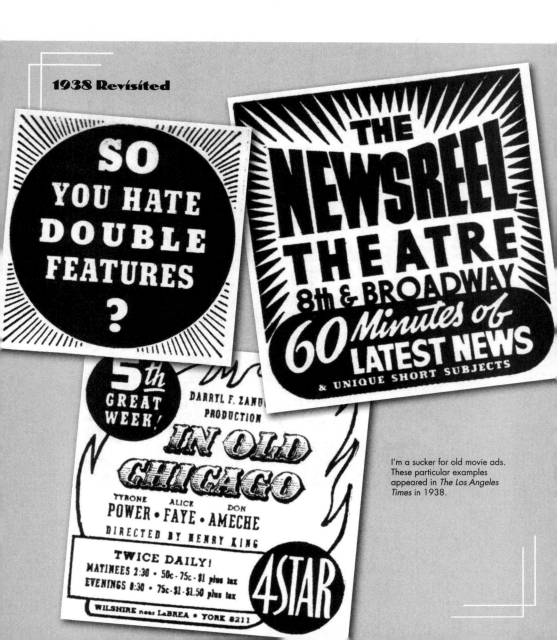

I'm a sucker for old movie ads. These particular examples appeared in *The Los Angeles Times* in 1938.

Conversations:
ROBERT YOUNG

After spending an afternoon with Robert Young and his wife Betty one day in 1986, I came home and told my wife, "That was the most candid and interesting interview I've ever done." Yet this is the first time it has ever appeared in print.

Robert Young was a ubiquitous figure in American life for six decades . . . in movies, on radio, and most successfully on television in two hugely popular, long-running shows, *Father Knows Best* and *Marcus Welby, M.D.*, and in an equally durable series of commercials for Sanka. (There was also a short-lived TV series between his two hits, *Window on Main Street*.)

A mutual friend put me in touch with the actor, who wasn't enthusiastic about doing an interview. "After all, I'm retired," he told me on the telephone. "Usually you do this sort of thing when you have a movie or a TV show to promote." He listed other reasons why he didn't want to talk about his career, but I kept my mouth shut, and before long he said he supposed if I really wanted to, I could come out to see him at his home in Westlake Village.

He and his wife Betty couldn't have been more gracious, although I will admit he was crustier than I expected. It didn't take long for me to see that he had harbored deep insecurities throughout his career. I asked if it was exciting to travel to England to make films in the mid-1930s and he responded that he thought he was being exiled. He told me how he sweated out the annual pickup of his contract at MGM—for fifteen years—always certain that he was going to be dropped. (After a number of years, he finally asked studio executive Eddie Mannix why they prolonged his agony by waiting until the last night of

Robert Young, in one of his best roles, with Van Heflin and Hedy Lamarr in H. M. Pulham, Esq. (1941).

the year to send notice of his renewal. Mannix said, in all seriousness, that if they didn't protect themselves that way, they could be left holding the bag if an actor got into some sort of scandal during those last few weeks!)

He had already "gone public" about his longtime battle with alcoholism, which seemed to dovetail with the self-doubts he discussed in our interview. It was some years later that he spoke about his bouts of depression, and the chemical imbalance that led to a suicide attempt in 1991.

None of that was on my agenda: I wanted to seize the opportunity to talk about his career, which he'd rarely discussed in any detail. His wife Betty not only participated in our conversation, she asked more questions than I did! She enjoyed drawing him out on certain subjects, and correcting some of the details in his stories. They had met in high school, and had been married fifty-three years at the time of our interview.

Incidentally, Young did not spend the rest of his days in retirement. He made several movies for television, including *Mercy or Murder?* (1987), in which he played Roswell Gilbert, a real-life senior citizen who put his wife out of her suffering and stood trial for murder as a result. It was exactly the kind of meaty, three-dimensional dramatic role he coveted for so much of his career.

Our conversation consumed several hours' time, yet only began to scratch the surface of his resumé. I wish I'd had a chance to go back and ask about the many films we didn't get to discuss. But I hope you will agree that, in the famous words of Spencer Tracy in *Pat and Mike*, "what there is is cherce." We began by discussing his salad days as a contract player at MGM, where he began working in 1931.

YOUNG: I got this call: Mr. Mayer wanted to see me. Well, gee, if he wants to see you, it means one of two things: either he's going to tell you you're doing a great job, which is very, very unlikely, or you were going to get fired. Or there's something wrong. You know you're in big trouble, you're going to face a cut, or something. So I was really shaking, literally shaking. And they had an interesting technique. He'd let you sit out in the waiting room for twenty or thirty minutes. You'd just fry out there, have a heart attack. And the woman that he had as his personal secretary, Ida Koverman, she wasn't even looking at me. She was cold as a chunk of ice. So you sit there and die forty thousand times. Finally the word comes and you get up and you almost fall flat on your face. Now, in the office, it's a half-hour walk from the door to the desk, you know. There's a little figure sitting behind the desk. You get there and you don't sit down until you're told to sit down. "Bob," he says, "I've been thinking about you, and watching your work." I wait for what follows—nothing, no comment. He says, "A couple of things I think that you should do, for your career, and for us." Well, I came right up to the edge of my seat. This was interesting. Always eager to learn, always wanted to improve. He said, "Put on a little weight and get more sex."

Robert and Betty Young on a night out in 1942.

I said, "Mr. Mayer, I don't know how to do either one of those!" I'd been trying to put on weight for years and years and years. I weighed the same for, I don't know, twenty years. Built like Jimmy Stewart, you know. "And as far as getting more sex is concerned, how do you do that?" "Well," he said, "You live at home, don't you?" And I said yes. "With your mother?" I said yes. He said, "I think you should have your own apartment. And then I think you should get yourself a valet. You know, a houseboy." I said, "Who needs a houseboy?" He said, "That's a front; you need that kind of thing. Japanese preferably. White coat, black trousers." I said, "What would I do with it?" He said, "He could greet the people at the door and serve the drinks." I said, "That's not gaining any weight," and he said, "No, but it's a front, it's what the [reporters and columnists] see. The front. Also, you should go out to Mocambo and Ciro's, and take a different girl each night. We've got a whole stable of girls here. Mary Carlisle, Madge Evans . . ." Golly, I can't even remember . . .

It sounds so funny now as I tell it. You think, oh, it could never have been like that, but seriously, it was. This was his idea. I don't say that there was anything particularly wrong with it. The more macho image. God knows Clark Gable came right through the screen. This is what they wanted. And I represented, I don't know what, the boy next door or something.

BETTY YOUNG: You did all right. Whatever it was you had.

YOUNG: Yes, by the grace of God.

BETTY YOUNG: Don't knock it.

YOUNG: I'm not. But, that's what they wanted. I think the ultimate extreme was when they hired [Robert] Taylor, who was perfectly capable as an actor, but he was so damn handsome, that he, like Tyrone Power, looked almost feminine. He was what you might call a beautiful man. Not a handsome man, but a beautiful man. He was a wonderful, wonderful person. And a good actor, too. But they were also looking for the, you know, the Clark Gables and the Spencer Tracys and that sort of thing. And I was somewhere in the middle there somewhere. I was neither one nor the other. I think most of the time they were trying to figure what the hell I was, because casting is a big thing with them. And they just followed you might say the public's taste, as it were, in

Young and Claudette Colbert in I Met Him in Paris (1937).

typecasting. If they responded to you as a nice guy, you could be the worst sh*t in the world, and from that time on, that's what you're going to play: nice guys. You could bellyache and squawk and say, you know, I have to exercise my talent, I have to stretch as an actor, it was a lot of crap. And they knew it was, but that's what you played. Or you make a hell of a hit like Bogart did in *The Petrified Forest*, and from that time on he was never without a gun in his hand, you know?

MALTIN: So what was it like being a contract player; did you feel like an indentured servant?

YOUNG: Well, I didn't know any differently. It was, like the saying goes, the only game in town. You couldn't freelance. You could freelance if you wanted to be independent and free of that kind of control and starve to death. So I got the apartment. Little Japanese houseboy. Whole bit. Followed the front. To the letter. I said, "Betty, I won't be able to see you for awhile. Just weekends." She said. "Oh? How's that?" So I told her about this situation with Mr. Mayer. She said, "That's very interesting. When this has all blown over, if it ever does, give me a ring. But in the meantime . . ." I said, "Wait a minute, this is for my career, I'm just doing this for my career. By orders of God. And you're telling me to defy this person and say no, I won't do it? Just for us? Why don't you understand? This is my whole goddamn career that's at stake." She said, "That's your problem. You won't get me to play that kind of a game. That's the way you want to go, that's up to you." Well, I sweated that out for about a week. And finally . . .

BETTY YOUNG: You tried it for six weeks.

YOUNG: Did I? Really?

BETTY YOUNG: So he finally went in to Mayer, and somehow or other he said, "I can't see that this kind of life is going to improve my acting. I'll just have to take my chances on my talent, not on how I live daily."

YOUNG: So it was, in a way, a good thing because we realized that we had to make a decision: Which way is it going to go— their way or our way? Not that ours was so defiant. But anytime that the two collided, we had to go our way because, as far as we were concerned, our whole future life depended on it.

Young with Tom Brown, James Stewart, and Lionel Barrymore in Navy Blue and Gold (1937).

MALTIN: It seems as if the minute MGM signed you, they loaned you out.

YOUNG: After I'd left [Metro], somebody in publicity, a friend of ours, got curious and decided to tabulate the number of films I'd worked in, in those fifteen years. And it came out seventy-eight. That was a hell of a lot of films in that length of time. Thirty-eight of the seventy-eight were off the lot. They always ask ten times more than they paid you, so I figured they've made money. It didn't cost them anything. But it was all right because all of it basically was training.

MALTIN: And you did some good pictures off the lot.

YOUNG: Also, at Metro I was considered a so-called "featured player." That's a question of which side of the title your name goes on. When I was loaned out, to Paramount, for example, to work on a picture with Claudette Colbert and Melvyn Douglas, they put my name above the title, along with Colbert's and Melvyn Douglas's.

MALTIN: Someone who worked within the studio system—but maintained his independence—was King Vidor. Tell me about working with him on *H. M. Pulham, Esq.*

YOUNG: Oh, he was wonderful. He was the nicest man. King did something that I didn't know about till after it was all over. I had a lot of respect for him as a director, for his accomplishments, *The Crowd* and God knows how many others. [When] I was given a part in *H. M. Pulham, Esq* [it] threw me for awhile. And I pored over [the book by J. P.] Marquand for weeks and weeks and weeks, trying to figure out what the hell he was writing about. I got more and more caught up in the character, and the more I did the more I realized what a remarkable role this was for me. I mean, not only in length, but in dimension, different levels, going from a young man in World War I to a middle-aged, white-haired man . . . a big challenge, a hell of a challenge. And King Vidor, oh my God. I thought, what am I going to do?

What I was told was that he stood against the entire studio. It was his choice that I play the role. And everybody got in the act. Those that had some say all lined up, literally, and said no. And he said, "Well then, I won't do it." They didn't want to say too many derogatory things about me, but they said, "You can get this one, you can get that one . . ."

BETTY YOUNG: They kept saying you were too young, you looked too young.

YOUNG: Anything they could think of that would somehow diminish my attractiveness to King. King had his mind made up. I don't know why he did it, to tell you the truth. I was baffled when I was told about it. I said, "Oh, you're just telling me that to make me feel good." [And someone said] "Go ask King if you don't believe me." So I finally muscled up enough courage to ask him. I went to King and I said, "I've been told that you put up a pretty good fight for me to play the role," and he said, "That's right." I said, "Did you ever have any regrets?" He said, "Not once." I said, "What do you think about the end result?" He said, "Just exactly the way I thought it would be." Well, it was nice to hear.

MALTIN: It's such a mature film. As you said, it's so much more intelligent and mature than most of the stuff that was being made.

YOUNG: Well, yes, I hadn't played anything like that since I'd left the stage. All I was playing was these flip, light comedy [parts], that kind of thing. I'd been playing things like *Married Before Breakfast*, and *The Bride Wore Red*, these brilliant things. It was a really great challenge to an actor; some of them were unbelievable. I often said to Betty, if I could make anything out of this, I deserve an Oscar.

BETTY YOUNG: He played a football player and a baseball player. He damn near got killed playing the USC football team.

YOUNG: Oh yes, my athletic days. Never threw a baseball, never threw a football. Of all the people in the world, they cast in that picture, *Navy Blue and Gold*, Jimmy Stewart and me and Tom Brown. I said, "You'll never get this released. The first day it plays, the laughter you'll be able to hear for twenty-five city blocks. And the exhibitor's going to pull the film out of the projector and that'll be the end of it." That damn thing is still playing and people come up to me; they say, "I saw you the other night in *Navy Blue and Gold*. Boy, was that some picture." You'd think they were An-

napolis graduates.

BETTY YOUNG: Ray Bradbury has seen it nineteen or twenty times. He said that he played hooky from school to see it.

YOUNG: Yeah, it was down at the Wiltern theater. It was an awful joke to me; I used to look at Betty and I'd think, either these people are fruity or I am— there's something wrong here. Until finally it kind of dawned on me, gradually: that's the

Young with Spencer Tracy and Walter Brennan in King Vidor's *Northwest Passage (1940)*.

magic. They didn't see that I was one hundred and thirty-five pounds; I was a lunging, crushing fullback. It took me a long time to realize that it wasn't the actors so much, or the script, or the camerawork, or the director, it was the audience. The audience made the magic, made it possible. Of course, granted, all these mechanics of it made it possible to give the audience the opportunity.

MALTIN: You worked with King Vidor again on another great film, *Northwest Passage*, and so much of the action seems real. Was it?

Young with Wallace Beery and Marie Dressler in Tugboat Annie (1933).

YOUNG: Yes. We shot at McCall, Idaho. We weren't wearing buckskin, we were wearing suede, or something like that, to approximate bucksin. We grew our beards. We weren't allowed to wash our clothes, and we went through mud and slime and . . . oh, unbelievable. It kept getting worse, and then we'd hang these things out at night and they would turn sour. If you got on the downwind side you couldn't stand it; you'd faint. [It would] make you throw up, it was so bad. There were about seventy-five or eighty of us, plus another hundred townspeople that they dressed up.

MALTIN: What about that incredible sequence crossing the river?

YOUNG: The human chain?

MALTIN: Yes.

YOUNG: They did it by cuts. They never did show that human chain all in one chunk, clear across the river. I don't think anyone's particularly aware of it. That's what I call the magic. They showed the establishment of it, coming from the other side, and leaving the shore and so forth, then a different angle; it linked up with that side like Hands Across America, not seeing that this wasn't hooked up to anything. And in the audience's mind, they supplied the picture of the total human chain across the river. But true, there was a certain reality in the sense that we were in the terrain which was not unlike the Hudson River Valley, where it was supposed to have taken place. The clothes we wore were real, the muskets we carried were authentic—I don't think anyone ever fired one, probably would have blown his head off if he had—but they were genuine muskets that they used in that period.

MALTIN: Do you think that that comes through in terms of your performance? Do you react differently being in the real surroundings?

YOUNG: Oh sure.

MALTIN: What was it like working with Spencer Tracy?

YOUNG: He was marvelous; I liked him very much. He was a little bit quiet; we didn't have a backslapping, howling with laughter kind of relationship, [but] he was very friendly; he was a lovely, lovely man. He endeared himself to my heart the first day we were there. We were in this renovated camp which had been unused for about twenty years, so you can imagine what kind of shape it was in, right on the shore of Lake Payette, in McCall, Idaho. So they stuck up a service tent and the caterer brought the tables and chairs and the stove and everything else in there. Well, we went to breakfast, or whatever the hell the first meal was that we had there, and Spence stood up, threw the plate clear across the tent.

BETTY YOUNG: They had powdered eggs.

YOUNG: Oh, it was awful. He went right to the unit manager [and] said, "When you correct the situation, I'll be back. I'll be on the set. Otherwise, don't bother me. Don't even talk to me." Well, you don't think the telephone wires didn't get hot the next day. I don't know how the hell they produced it that quickly, but the next day there was a new unit manager. It was the most incredible transformation you ever saw. Overnight, there was a complete transformation; we had the most divine food. We were eating like Spago's, choice steak . . .

BETTY YOUNG: They didn't have frozen food in those days, you had to really . . .

YOUNG: No, beautiful steaks, fresh vegetables, so I went to this guy, his name was Charlie something, and I said, "How in the hell did you manage this?" And he kind of smiled. He said, "I was a road manager for a circus for about twenty years." I said, "But how did you get this done?" He said, "I called Salt Lake City. I said, you got a good chef there? Yep? Send him up. Metro-Goldwyn-Mayer, that's the magic word."

MALTIN: But it took Tracy to do it.

YOUNG: All Tracy said was fix this and then I'll be back. And walked out. No shouting. I watched him and I thought to myself, man that's great. That's power.

BETTY YOUNG: Like Norma Shearer.

YOUNG: Oh, Norma Shearer used to break me up. She always smiled. And it wasn't a false smile; it was a lovely, sweet, gentle, smile. They would ask her something, "Miss Shearer," or "Mrs. Thalberg," something

Who's Best!

I think Robert Young is one of the bet-ter romantic comedians of Hollywood. He can "put over" a fast bit of repartee with charming effec-tiveness. I hope M-G-M is grooming him for juicy parts.

Robert Young

—Helen G. Foster,
2635 Sedgwick Ave.

NOTE: You haven't seen Bob at all until you see him in "The Bride Wore Red."

they wanted done, and she would just smile and say no. And that was all. And you could just feel the other person [thinking], there's nothing you can do. What do you do, argue? She just smiled, and said no. And that was it. Bingo. Took care of the whole thing.

MALTIN: People talk about how you could never see Tracy's technique, and that was his magic. What was your observation?

YOUNG: It might be easily covered with one word in quotes: "natural." He was very intuitive, and whatever he did, he just always came out right. Directors never talked to him. I mean, what's the point in talking to him? Tracy, sort of, almost unconsciously, knew more about how that scene should be played than the director did. And that's one of the reasons I think he and Katie [Hepburn] got along so well. I think she acts very much that same way. She just acts from something inside, that's intuitive, instinctive, whatever you want to call it.

MALTIN: When you worked with her it was very early in her screen career, and she was thought kind of odd at that point.

YOUNG: She was. But even then you could feel, you could sense that she was her own person. In those days, they all came out of the same drama school. Not Katie. There was no mistaking that this was a very unique personality.

BETTY YOUNG: Anybody that's original is criticized as much as praised.

YOUNG: They broke the mold when they made her. Same way with Tracy. I think they were ideally cast together. As I think Reagan is ideally cast as the President. Best role he's ever had in his life. It beats George Gipp.

MALTIN: Did Marie Dressler make an impression on you when you made *Tugboat Annie*?

YOUNG: Couldn't help it. She was really lovely, a wonderful person. She'd come up the long hard way, and she was very, very grateful. And she wouldn't take any nonsense from this baboon, Wallace Beery. [Dressler had worked with Beery before, in the 1930 hit *Min and Bill*.]

BETTY YOUNG: When you're doing a scene and [the other actor is] off-camera, he's supposed to be quiet. Well, [Beery] was always doing movement.

YOUNG: Anything to distract you. She straightened him out the first day. She said, "Look, you silly sh*t, you pull one more thing like that on me and I'll have your head on a platter like John the Baptist, with a personal note to L. B. Mayer." And she was so huge, she looked like she could do it. He said okay, he got very cowed, and then he was like a little boy being very careful that mommy didn't catch him with his hand in the cookie jar. No, he really behaved himself on that one. I realize that his other thing was just an act: anything to destroy the other actor, anything to spoil it for them. But he couldn't do that with Marie.

BETTY YOUNG: She was sort of protective of you, too.

YOUNG: Oh, she was wonderful. She wouldn't let him do that to the crew members, anybody. [As for Beery] I developed

On the set of Secret Agent (1936): Madeleine Carroll, Peter Lorre, Alfred Hitchcock, and Robert Young.

a loathing for this man that almost ended my career. I was always ending my career. And Betty again came to the rescue. I came back to the hotel room one night after doing a scene and I said, "This is as far as I can go. I just have to phone my resignation."

BETTY YOUNG: He had to hug and love him.

YOUNG: He played my father. It was called *West Point of the Air*. I was supposed to be a young cadet in the Army air corps, and he was a mechanic, just a grease monkey. And there was some kind of a conflict, I've forgotten what it was, but anyway, there was a very emotional scene. The boy had to cry a little bit and plead with his father and so forth. When [Beery] couldn't think of a line, he rubbed his face and went, "Awwwmmmmm." After the two-shot, which went miserably—it was horrible, just little pieces of it were usable—the director then went to the over-shoulder shots. [Beery has] got his script [but] he drops it on the ground and when he picks it up, he goes to the wrong page, and for my cue he's not reading the right line. I'm supposed to be standing there crying. And I was building up on the inside; the pressure was so enormous I thought, I'm going to scream any second. I'm going to say, "You sh*t, you ignominious dumb bastard," every name I could think of. He

was the most insensitive, the most inhumane . . . [That night] I said to Betty, "Honey, I can't, I won't . . . Life is too short. Why should I screw around with that baboon? I can't work with him." She said, "Do you suppose Metro-Goldwyn-Mayer is going to have superimposed on a frame a sentence which says, 'Mr. Young's performance was due to the fact that he lost his temper because of Mr. Beery's behavior?' Who's going to explain that performance of yours? Because you're the one that's up there on the screen, and you're not looking like your heart is breaking for your old father. That's going to show."

Betty and Robert Young return from their sojourn in England on the Aquitania.

If there's one thing about the camera, it sits out there and says, "Don't get cute. Don't get fancy. Don't think that you can play a scene with your mind down at Von's Market." Because they can see it right in your eye.

MALTIN: So you survived it.

YOUNG: I survived it, again, with Betty helping. I got back on the set the next day and I thought, my best way of getting even is to give a performance that's better than his.

MALTIN: Talk to me about radio a little.

YOUNG: Well, I loved [radio].

BETTY YOUNG: The studio tried to get in the radio business, and they had a show called *Good News*, which was an hour show that had everybody on it. Meredith Willson was the orchestra [leader], and they tried everybody to be master of ceremonies, and nobody could do it but Mister Young, and he got it . . . He had a show with Frank Morgan and Fanny Brice.

YOUNG: Well they both at least had had stage experience. But some of the screen actors were dreadful, just dreadful. They didn't know what the hell to do with their voice; they'd never acted with their voice before, as an instrument, so they tried to do it with their face. Well, can you see anything over the air with a radio broadcast? As a result, it was just absolutely nothing. So then we'd work with radio actors, who were trained; they could do nine dialects in fifteen seconds, and [the movie people] looked like jerks, absolute jerks; it was an embarrassment.

BETTY YOUNG: Don't forget too that this was live. Radio was live and with an audience. When Joan [Crawford] did a show with Bobby, she finally took her shoes off, and then she took her clothes off, she didn't want any makeup, then she had the audience canceled. Do you remember?

YOUNG: She couldn't stand the presence of the audience there because she would be performing in front of an audience, and she had never done that before. Even though she was facing a microphone, and she wasn't doing a play, she couldn't stand it, so she had the audience dismissed. They sent the audience home.

BETTY YOUNG: Gable couldn't do it.

YOUNG: Their voices would quake, they would get so nervous. The first show I did, when I got this *Good News* assignment on a kind of a trial basis, they ran every contract player they had through it to see who was going to end up with it. And I ended up with the job. Soon as I started on kind of a steady basis I was very much aware of the skill of the radio actor.

BETTY YOUNG: And you had terrific training too.

YOUNG: I thought to myself, I'd better be very, very careful because these are sharp cookies. I don't want to make too big a fool of myself; I'd better watch what they do. Or listen to what they do, and try to catch on.

BETTY YOUNG: The movie stars overacted a lot on radio.

YOUNG: Well, they're so used to working in front of a camera. Now they're working in front of a microphone. A microphone can't see a goddamn thing.

BETTY YOUNG: But you had terrific voice training, and Bobby has a God-given voice to begin with. I know about it. We were all working to place our voices, and Bobby would get up and speak, and that was it. He just was born with it.

YOUNG: You have to use your voice like a musical instrument on radio, you see? You've got to use it just exactly like a musical instrument.

MALTIN: So you just took to radio.

YOUNG: I loved it. Of course, I loved acting. It didn't make any difference to me whether I was on the street corner, or in somebody's

basement, or in front of a camera, or up on the stage, or in front of a microphone, as long as I was performing or playing a role, I was happy as a clam. It didn't make any difference; I could do it in the living room all by myself. So it was just another medium to me. It was exciting. I think I would have had a wonderful time in a circus, as a clown.

MALTIN: What was it like when you went to England? Tell me about that experience.

YOUNG: [The studio] was a nine-story building. I was used to these big sound stages. I said, "What the hell is that?" and they said, "That's the studio." The first floor had all administration offices, the second floor was the prop shop, the third floor was the makeup, and one of them was a soundstage. I said, "What keeps this thing from caving in and crushing the eighth floor?" And he said, "Oh, it's propped up right." They had to bring the scenery, which they built on another floor, up a freight elevator in the back of the building. Shortly after that they built a hell of a big thing . . . so they have a studio very much like Hollywood. But at that particular time they didn't have the space, and they didn't want to be too far away from downtown London. Well, it was a funny experience; it really was strange.

BETTY YOUNG: It was a much slower pace and they served tea, four o'clock.

YOUNG: It was very casual, very casual.

MALTIN: How did they regard you?

YOUNG: Well, I was playing American in the Hitchcock thing. They wanted a kind of person who you might say was blatantly American. Unmistakably American. That was the so-called hidden gimmick [in *Secret Agent*]. [On the way over] one of the officers on the ship interrupted a ping-pong game and said, "You're wanted on the telephone."

BETTY YOUNG: This was unheard of in those days.

YOUNG: I said, "What did you say?" He said, "This is from London." I think he's pulling my leg. I think I'm going to get to the phone, some drunk down in the bar downstairs in the casino is calling me on the ship intercom or whatever. Well, I got to the phone, and it was Hitchcock. You know that wonderful mouthful-of-hot-mush voice of his? He says, "Just wanted to say hello." And I said, "Oh, thank you. Mr. Hitchcock. Thank you very much." Almost dropped the phone. It was his way of saying "Welcome," but he wasn't waiting till we hit the shore, he was saying it to us while we were still on the ship. Which I thought was very nice. Then we were invited to visit him in his office, which is downtown Lon-

Frank Borzage's Three Comrades *(1938): Young, Franchot Tone, and Robert Taylor.*

don somewhere. When we got there, Hitchy was sitting behind his desk and Peter Lorre was in the room with him. So Peter Lorre stood up and Hitchy introduced us and he said, "Would you like some tea?" We said we'd love it. So the four of us sat there and chatted. Hitchy started asking questions about restaurants in Chicago and Salt Lake, and residences and new developments in Texas, and so forth, and I said, "How do you know these things?" He said, "I expect to go to the States one of these days and I just want to know as much about them as I can." At any rate, Lorre was making some jokes now and then, which were just about as morbid and ribald as the characters he played on the screen. Finally, he finished his tea, and Hitchy asked if we'd like some more, and we said no. So [Lorre] went to the window, opened it, and threw his cup and saucer out onto the street. Well, Betty and I looked at each other and I thought, that's a little bit of English humor . . .

BETTY YOUNG: Or that's the custom.

YOUNG: Finally, Hitch got up, walked over, dumped his cup and saucer out the window and came back and [kept] right on talking. Finally, Betty and I finished our tea and we just leaned forward and put the cup and saucer on his desk. He looked so disappointed.

BETTY YOUNG: We found him to have a great sense of humor. And he was quite a wine connoisseur.

YOUNG: [When we dined at his home] I think we had seven or eight different wines with the meal and the butler came around with this beautiful cedar-lined humidor, with crusted silver and carvings. He was passing it around, and as he passed Betty, Betty just touched his arm. Well, the butler damn near dropped the humidor and he quickly glanced at Hitchy, and Hitchy nodded, in that funny, Buddha-like way of his, so Betty took the cigar. Now the conversation just stopped. So Betty took it, very casually, and carried it through beautifully. Gradually they picked up the conversation, but in the meantime they're all watching this way, out of the corner of their eye, sure that she was pulling their leg. But she carried it through, and chewed the end off, got it all prepared and puffed down, the butler held the lighter for her. By way of explanation she said to Hitchy, you know, "In the south, some women smoke pipes," which is true, but not cigars. Finally I think it was about the third puff, some of it got in her eye, and she began to cough a little bit.

BETTY YOUNG: Because I'm not a smoker anyway.

YOUNG: The cigar itself defeated her joke. But, for a moment, just a moment, at least, Hitchy was really hooked. And he loved it, he just loved it. He congratulated her afterward for a superb performance.

BETTY YOUNG: He came to our house for dinner when he first came to America. I'd been talking about a southern dinner, which he didn't know anything about, so I had fried chicken, and spoon bread and mustard greens and hominy and everything that I could think of. But what Hitchy wasn't used to was having two or three martinis before dinner.

YOUNG: I don't think he was used to having any. I think he drank sherry.

BETTY YOUNG: Champagne cocktails and sherry. So he wanted to be the gallant guest.

YOUNG: Well, it was the thing to do. Americans drank gin.

BETTY YOUNG: He had two or three and went to sleep and missed his whole dinner.

YOUNG: Just conked out on the couch. Hit him like a sledgehammer. Well, he was inclined to sleep anyway. He used to sleep in the theater.

MALTIN: Did he direct you very much?

YOUNG: No, he didn't. I didn't suspect this, or notice at the time.

It was said later that he didn't have much respect for actors; he would have been happy if he could draw them like Disney does. But he was a brilliant, brilliant man, as far as staging a scene is concerned. And he had been an art director so he would draw. He had a big artist's pad, and the night before he would sketch out the setup, the exact camera angle, just exactly what he wanted. He'd hand this to the cameraman in the morning and they never talked for the rest of the day. He choreographed a film. Well, he did the same thing with the actors. He would move them around, just like puppets. Marionettes. He'd move them around and tell us what to do. How you read the lines was sort of

immaterial to him in a way. He never looked at the actor; he'd always look at the script girl. And if she nodded, it meant the dialogue was correct. Then he had an ear for timing. If it was too slow, he would just ask you to speed it up a little bit. If it was too fast, he'd ask you to slow it down a little bit. But other than that, there was very little communication with him at all as far as between the actor and the director.

BETTY YOUNG: I think this is what perhaps disturbed stage actors because they didn't get that direction from a motion picture director.

YOUNG: No. As a matter of fact, damn few motion picture directors ever talked about characterization, motivation, the emotional level of the scene. Hitchy wasn't too far away from that, although he had a more sensitive feel, I think, for whether the scene was right. He couldn't exactly tell you what was wrong with it, but he knew when it was wrong, and he'd make you do it again until he was satisfied that it was right.

Top: Robert Mitchum and Young in Crossfire *(1947), directed by Edward Dmytryk.*

Bottom: The camera captures Young and longtime MGM director Richard Thorpe in a pensive moment during production of Joe Smith, American *(1942).*

MALTIN: Did you enjoy playing a bad guy for a change?

YOUNG: Well, actually, in the playing of it, he wasn't. So the more naively and innocently I played the role, the better, because that fooled the audience. So it was a cinch to play; all I did was play the same thing I played last week in Hollywood.

MALTIN: Did you get any response to it back here?

YOUNG: Not at the time. But since then, yes, a lot.

MALTIN: Do you remember any kind of feedback when you came back to Hollywood from having done that?

YOUNG: Well, for one thing, it didn't set my career back, and I thought it would.

BETTY YOUNG: No, but Bobby said, "You see, they don't want me," because they loaned him for a second one over there.

YOUNG: Oh yes. We were not quite finished with the Hitchy picture, and somebody came to me and said, "By the way Bob, they've loaned you for another picture. It immediately follows this one." Well, I went right through the roof. I stormed and raved around for days, accomplishing absolutely nothing, except it did get a lot of steam off my chest. We had left this twenty-two-month-old baby, because we were going to be gone six or eight weeks, we thought. Now I've got a whole, brand new picture stretched out in front of me. And who the hell is Jessie Matthews? So after I got through storming and raging and yelling and stamping my feet, Betty, God love her, who had been through this, said, "There isn't anything you can do about it. Why don't you just go ahead and do it and have a good time? Maybe she'll be fun, we can't tell. She's very popular from what I hear." Well, obviously what happened is I cooled down eventually and then I met [Jessie] and I was charmed completely, by her and her husband, Sonnie Hale, and we had a delightful time except it stretched out to damn near six months.

We did have a fascinating experience: Jessie and I were leaning on the grand piano, between takes. They were making a new setup, and we were just leaning on the flat end of the grand piano. [She was] a wonderful girl, delightful girl.

BETTY YOUNG: We saw her not too many years ago. . .

YOUNG: . . . At her home, she lives on a little farm. We just sort of broke up the conversation, sauntered away from the piano, and hadn't gone from here to that chair, when one of those flood lights that weighs a ton . . . Somehow the guy lost his balance and let go of the lamp, and it went right through the top of the grand piano! Took the whole top of the grand piano and almost went through the floor. I don't know that it's possible to reproduce that sound. I don't think I'll ever get that sound out of my head.

The last day of shooting, we wrapped it up at two o'clock in the afternoon, and we were already packed. We were on our way to Southampton to meet the ship and take off, so if there had been a scratch on the film, or it had come back from the laboratory in some way flawed and they needed a re-take, I was two hundred miles at sea, they couldn't have done a damn thing about it. But we were so anxious to get home.

Metro did come through. They said, in return for your doing two in a row like this, and accommodating us, they extended to us an invitation: a holiday on the continent, for six weeks. But we were anxious to get home. And as soon as we got home, by the second or third day, we might just as well have never been away. Except the child had changed so much. They change a lot at that age.

MALTIN: That must have been tough.

YOUNG: [It was] tough. But Betty, God love her, at the very beginning, we talked about marriage and family, she sort of indicated to me this was the order of her priorities: the two of us, as a unit, then the children—the family, the children and us—that's number two, and number three is the job.

MALTIN: Are there any directors who do stand out in your memory for having taken a little extra care with you?

YOUNG: Yes, there were a few. Out of thirty-five or forty, I'd say there were about five. That's not to belittle the directors or their ability, their craftsmanship; they were brilliant experts in mechanics, the moving of the camera, the mood, but in the actual dealing with the actors' emotional levels and that sort of thing, I don't think they knew what the hell they were doing so they didn't say anything.

BETTY YOUNG: They weren't like stage directors.

YOUNG: No, I had come from the stage and I was so accustomed to sitting around a table and talking, dissecting the character, going way back to his birth, and whether the parents quarreled or had a divorce or something. You make it up, but it begins to reveal inside the actor's mind a person, a real living person. This is the person you become when you start the play. Otherwise you just say, "You're angry on this line," but there's nothing behind it. So an actor's pretty much put on his own in film.

MALTIN: Can you give me any exceptions to that?

One sheet poster for They Won't Believe Me! (1947).

YOUNG: Yes, Eddie Dmytryk, who did *Crossfire*; Eddie Goulding, who did *Claudia* . . .

BETTY YOUNG: Who did *Enchanted Cottage*?

YOUNG: John Cromwell was an actor and became a screen director. Oh, he was magnificent. Well, that was just a lead pipe cinch. One, we had the best love story that's ever been written, and two, wonderful people to work with: Bart [Herbert] Marshall and Dorothy McGuire and Millie Natwick and John Cromwell, so that was one of those films I hated to see end. I wanted it to go on and on and on. It was such a joy to do.

BETTY YOUNG: Who directed the picture with Helen Hayes?

YOUNG: *Sin of Madelon Claudet*?

BETTY YOUNG: Yes.

YOUNG: Oh, [Frank] Borzage.

BETTY YOUNG: He was pretty good too, wasn't he?

YOUNG: Very good, Frank was a very good, a sentimental slob but he was a lovely, lovely man.

MALTIN: You also worked for Dorothy Arzner once, didn't you?

YOUNG: Yes. Rather severe. And disciplined. Sort of noncommunicative, but very capable. I had a lot of respect for her . . . after I got over the shock of it being a woman.

MALTIN: It was so unusual then.

YOUNG: Well, not only unusual, it was never heard of; I mean, the mere idea of it shows you how this macho male chauvinism [was at that time].

MALTIN: Another director I have to ask you about is Fritz Lang, with whom you worked on *Western Union*.

YOUNG: Oh, I hated his guts. He was a two-timing bastard as far as I was concerned. He committed what I call an unforgivable sin. He designed a shot up in Kanab, Utah, a seventy-five-foot dolly track, and the cameraman, Eddie Cronjager said it would take them damn near a whole day to build that dolly track. Anyway, he's dollying with three guys on horses. In the first place, how do you get the dolly up to speed, in order to keep up with the horses? So I think we screwed around about three or four more days. We finally got it so he's got a quick cut of three guys on horses, going like a bat out of hell. One is covering up the one in the back, which is kind of bad for the camera angle; too late to correct that, simply because he insisted. Well, the phone began to ring. I think it was Darryl Zanuck himself who called and said, "You've got to cut out this ridiculous wasting of time and money; the shot wasn't worth it." Lang said, "Well, actually, it was Mr. Cronjager. Mr. Cronjager thought it would be very effective." It was the most outrageous lie you've ever heard, and Cronjager just sat there, and looked at us, and we looked at him. This was a caucus we were having in one of the cabins. We got up and just walked out of the room. So, finally this guy came out, I think he was from the production office, and said what's going on? Why did you walk out? We said, "It happened to be Mr. Lang's idea, not Cronjager's. We were standing right there when he said it."

Three of the easiest guys in Hollywood to get along with: Randolph Scott, Dean Jagger, and me. By the end of the first week, none of us were speaking to Fritz Lang.

BETTY YOUNG: He certainly was a friend of yours for the rest of his life.

YOUNG: Who, Fritz?

BETTY YOUNG: Eddie.

YOUNG: Oh, Eddie. God love him, yeah. He shot our independent film, the one Gene Rodney and I made called *Relentless*.

MALTIN: Another one of those larger-than-life figures I wanted to ask you about was George Arliss.

YOUNG: I only worked with him the one time, in *House of Rothschild*. I didn't have much to do with Arliss, as far as the scenes were concerned. He had a valet, and he had it in his contract: four o'clock, straight out. This guy would stand there with this great big watch, it was like a railroad watch with a spring cap on it, watching it like this, and the director's watching this guy—he's not watching Arliss, he's watching this guy, see? Four o'clock. One time he did it right in the middle of a take, walked right out of the set. [The man] said, "Mr. Arliss?" He said, "Oh, thank you, Joe, thank you so much. I'm so terribly sorry, terribly sorry," and off they went. And that was it. But he was wonderful. He was incredible, he was a brilliant, brilliant, brilliant actor. Wonderful actor. One of the things that I got a big kick out of was the opportunity to work with these people, because it was unlikely that I would have made it on Broadway with them, but I did get to work with them in front of a camera, and however little it was, it was a brush with nobility. I never worked with Olivier, but I worked with some pretty damn good ones, and it was a wonderful experience. One of the things that I enjoyed about *Welby*, we had a new guest star every week, and we did two hundred and seven of those things, that's a lot of guest stars. And some of them were pretty damn good. Some were pretty damn awful, too.

MALTIN: You did a nice one with Dolores del Rio, I remember.

YOUNG: She was so beautiful, she was so wonderful. I remember looking over one time, and I thought to myself, it wasn't very respectful to tippytoe around her [but] I think she's asleep. And she slept. Her eyes closed. Finally, the assistant comes and she says, "Miss del Rio? We're ready now." She said, "Okay." And she said, at the end of the day, "I'm not tired, because I've been meditating." Meditating, yeah.

MALTIN: How and why did you finally leave MGM?

BETTY YOUNG: He built up a radio audience and he was doing all the work and they were collecting the money. So he asked for his dismissal from the studio and Mayer offered him five years with no option. Which is a terrible, hard thing to turn down.

YOUNG: Oh, that was murder. I was talking to Mayer on a Friday afternoon; I almost fell out of my chair. So I fell back on my old dodge and that was, "I have to talk it over with Betty; I really can't decide right now. Is it all right if I let you know Monday?" He said, "Certainly, let me know anytime." Well, we both sweated that weekend, and I said, "What do you think I should do?" And Betty said, "I think you should do what you want to do. What you want to do?" I said, that's the reason I'd went to all that trouble to get the release—it took me about six weeks, I had to canvass that whole goddamn administration building. There was a block there somewhere, and I didn't know where it was. When I finally found it, it turned out to be my best friend. Or the one I thought was my best friend. He was the one that refused to vote yes on the dismissal, the release.

MALTIN: Who was that?

YOUNG: Benny Thau. So I said the same thing that I said at the very beginning when I asked for the release: I think I can do better freelancing. All the guys that went to war, my career didn't change, and now they're all back. If it didn't change with them away, it's not gonna change with them back, so I think I can do better on the outside by myself. But I was still shaking when I walked into Mayer's office on Monday. We weren't being defiant, we weren't being indifferent, or daring, we just did these things and then I'd always wait for the roof to fall in. It never did. I don't mean that I broke ground. Well in some respects: the fact that I, in a sense, defied the deity and the sky didn't fall on me. Others said, "Well, Young got away with it, why the hell can't we?"

BETTY YOUNG: It was just second nature for Bobby. That's what really got him into TV. Because he did *Father Knows Best* on radio for six years first.

MALTIN: One of the best films you did as a freelancer was *They Won't Believe Me*, where you got to play a heel, for once.

YOUNG: It was a good film [and] I enjoyed it. It was kind of fun; there's an O. Henry twist on the end.

BETTY YOUNG: Bobby felt that, many times, they didn't accept him in a part like that.

MALTIN: Oh no, you're very convincing in it.

BETTY YOUNG: It was very good; it was at a time when RKO changed hands and it just lacked advertising. The picture got lost.

YOUNG: I always remember, my beloved partner Gene Rodney—my business partner as well as a very dear friend—said he would never have to explain a hit.

MALTIN: It's true, isn't it? Still true.

YOUNG: Spend the rest of your life ducking a flop. And what's the difference between the two? Who the hell knows? What's the secret? There is no secret. Nobody knows.

BETTY YOUNG: What was it Gene used to say about the public?

YOUNG: Don't think you can fool the public because they can't tell you what's wrong . . . except they know that it isn't right. That's what I said about actors: Watch what you're thinking. Don't let your mind wander, because a shade will come right down and the camera will see it—even the director will miss it, sitting right alongside the camera. He won't see it; the camera will see it.

BETTY YOUNG: The camera can also pick up insincerity.

YOUNG: Oh, in a second.

FLASHBACK

Hollywood movies have always entertained the world, but each country has traditionally taken its own approach to advertising and promotion. At first glance, this might seem to be a vintage movie ad, no more. In fact, it is the cover of a program book from the Paramount Theatre in Manchester, England from 1933. Note the ad copy, which has a distinctive British flavor . . . including a non-prudish approach to the movie's sex appeal!

PERSONAL FAVORITES

I couldn't publish a newsletter without spotlighting two special people: my wife Alice's favorite actor (who ranks pretty high on my list, too), Ronald Colman, seen here (left) in a wonderful publicity shot for *A Tale of Two Cities* examining a miniature guillotine with his director, MGM's prolific Jack Conway. Colman certainly had a run of great parts in the 1930s, and great speeches to read with that mellifluous voice. Sydney Carton's final soliloquy is perhaps his finest moment on screen.

Then there is my personal heartthrob, Thelma Todd, seen here in a rare photo with former silent-screen comedy star Monty Banks, who directed her in a cute British musical comedy, *You Made Me Love You* (1933). Incidentally, the Italian-born Banks (real name Mario Bianchi) later married British singing sweetheart Gracie Fields, and even directed Laurel and Hardy, in *Great Guns*, during a brief World War II sojourn in Hollywood.

STILL LIFE

Summertime is the perfect time to gaze back over the years at lovely Jean Parker, who posed more often in bathing suits than any actress I can think of! Here's the original caption that accompanied this 1937 Whitey Schafer photo, which offers no explanation of the contraption in which she's posing. A breeze-blocker, perhaps?

TO SWIM OR NOT TO SWIM:
And Jean Parker, bright-eyed, dark-haired Columbia star, is trying to make up her mind. It's such fun to sit on a big rock and dream and yet the surf looks so inviting! What to do? The lovely Miss Parker is one of the most ardent seashore addicts in Hollywood, spending many a leisure hour on the beach, frolicking in the surf, swimming far out to sea, or just relaxing in the sunshine.

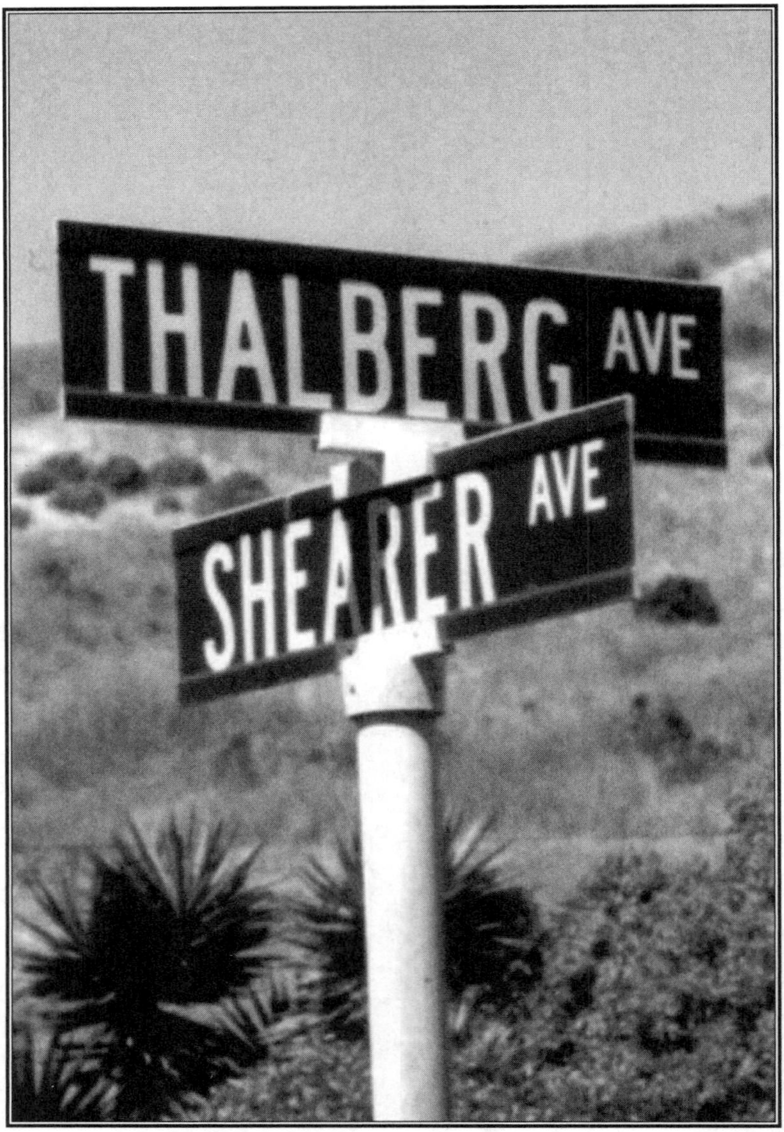
THALBERG AVE
SHEARER AVE

MOVIETOWN, U.S.A.

It's not uncommon for cities to name streets after favorite sons and daughters. In recent years, famous people ranging from Martin Luther King Jr. to Duke Ellington have been honored in this fashion. The cities of Palm Springs and Palm Desert offer a parade of familiar names on its signposts, from Gene Autry to Buddy Rogers to Frank Sinatra.

It's more unusual to find instances of stars from the silent film era having been celebrated this way during their lifetime . . . and even more uncommon to see a thoroughfare named after movie studio executives who were largely unknown to the public.

That's why the town of Cayucos, California is so striking, and why it poses such a special challenge to any historian.

In 1928, developer Harry E. Jones Inc. filed papers in the country courthouse at San Luis Obispo, proposing a new subdivision of the Rancho Morro Y Cayucos called Morro Strand, in which every street would be named for someone associated with Metro-Goldwyn-Mayer studio! Not only was there to be a

MAP OF
MORRO STRAND
UNIT NO. 1

A SUBDIVISION OF A PART OF LOT 40
OF THE RANCHO MORRO Y CAYUCOS

SAN LUIS OBISPO COUNTY, CALIF.

Surveyed by BURCH and BECK Civil Engineers
Scale. 1 inch = 100 feet   April 1928

Detail of developer's map filed in 1928.

Greta Garbo street, but another for Louis B. Mayer. Not only would Ramon Navarro have his name on a postal address; so would Eddie Mannix!

I discovered this movie-themed community through the good graces of Mary Harris, who presides over the San Luis Obispo Film Festival. It was Mary who found the developer's plans reproduced here. But so far, neither she nor I have been able to uncover the reason for this movie-crazy map. Neither local historians nor the very helpful librarian in town had an answer; neither did a historian at Hearst Castle, just up the road a piece. Roger Mayer was kind enough to check the MGM studio files, to no avail; his longtime secretary, June Caldwell, who had worked for Eddie Mannix in his later years, was unfamiliar with the town.

The Hearst connection might prove fruitful. There is an historic inn in Cayucos that has photographs from the turn of the twentieth century when it was a way station for travelers heading up the California coast. William Randolph Hearst's father may have stopped here when bringing travelers to his expansive property. In the mid-1920s, W. R. and Louis B. Mayer formed a personal and business alliance, which led to

Top: Still united by zip code: Buster Keaton and Marceline Day in MGM's The Cameraman *(1928).*

Middle and Below: Notice that the studio execs earned premium placement on the oceanfront streets.

MGM producing and distributing Hearst's Cosmopolitan productions (mostly starring Marion Davies) for many years.

Still, that doesn't explain naming a street after Metro's Harry Rapf, let alone actors like William Haines and the less-than-iconic Marceline Day.

With that, I throw down the gauntlet to the ambitious and the curious, to discover the origins of Cayucos's movie-themed development. In the meantime, it's just plain fun to turn off California Highway 1 at Chaney Drive, and explore the quaint seaside community.

Some of the intersections are particularly apt: Irving Thalberg intersects with his wife, Norma Shearer. John Gilbert occupies a street sign alongside his *Big Parade* costar Rene Adoree. Part of the hillside development was never completed, however, so Keaton Boulevard and Barrymore Avenue never came to be.

Others may name streets for television hosts and country music performers in years to come, but I doubt that any municipality will ever match Cayucos for capturing one famous movie company's leading lights in quite this way.

Follow-Up:
Florida's Movie Town

No one has been able to solve the mystery of why Cayucos, California adopted the names of MGM personnel for its roadways some eighty years ago. However, Lisa Bradberry of St. Petersburg, Florida wrote to us, saying, "I thought you might be interested to know that Sun City, Florida, located twenty-five miles south of Tampa, also has street signs named for actors, directors, and studios of the silent film era. As a film buff and member of the Florida Historical Society, I enjoy digging up obscure facts about Florida's recent history. Researching the history of Sun City's street signs is a recent project. Today, Sun City is a small community of mobile homes, an RV park, and a golf resort; but in 1925, it was developed to be a movie studio city. Most of the streets are still there as designed in the plans, with some more accessible than others."

Streets are named for such stars as Charlie Chaplin, Lon Chaney, Mary Pickford, Harold Lloyd, John Barrymore, Norma Shearer, Gloria Swanson, and Lillian Gish. Today's residents might recognize those

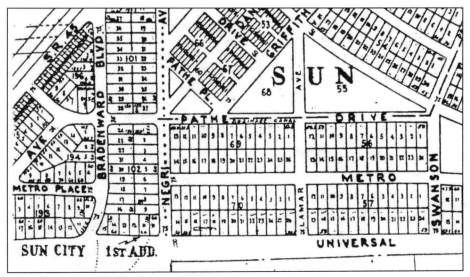

names, but they may be less familiar with the inspirations for (Betty) Bronson Way, (Thomas) Meighan Drive, (Alla) Nazimova Ave, or (Olga) Petrova Circle. Silent film aficionados will be happy to learn that Betty Blythe, Viola Dana, Priscilla Dean, Barbara LaMarr, Pola Negri, Mary Philbin, Irene Rich, Milton Sills, and Alice Terry are all immortalized on the byways of Sun City. (It's not clear which Talmadge was being honored, so we'll assume the founding fathers meant to recognize both Norma and Constance, and maybe even Natalie.) The town is also home to Fairbanks Park and Pickford Park.

There are streets named for D. W. Griffith, Thomas Ince, Marshall Neilan, and King Vidor, along with Studio Boulevard and other streets named for Hollywood studios. Many of those names still dominate the movie industry, but only movie buffs would fully appreciate roads named for Christie, First National, and Pathé.

"Florida's Moving Picture City" was founded in 1925 (before Cayucos, we should note) when Florida was at the peak of its real-estate boom. The developers hoped that their town would become a genuine movie colony, but that never came to pass. Our thanks to Lisa Bradberry for passing along this wonderful discovery.

STILL LIFE
In the 1930s, the elegant Argentinean movie magazine Cinegraf delighted in publishing photos of Hollywood stars perusing its pages.

Thelma Todd (above), Miriam Hopkins, and even Popeye were among those recruited for such poses. Would that Movie Crazy could do the same today!

ART CORNER

James Montgomery Flagg is best remembered today as the man who created the Uncle Sam "I Want You" poster in 1917. One of the most celebrated illustrators of the twentieth century, Flagg also had a long association with Hollywood.

As early as 1916 he accepted commissions from movie studios: he rendered a delicate and beautiful profile portrait of leading lady Mae Murray for the Paramount Pictures house organ. He even wrote a handful of short subjects in the teens, promoted on the strength of his name, including a series for Paramount (with such comedic titles as *Hick Manhattan* and *The Immovable Guest*), and another for the Edison company called *James Montgomery Flagg's Girls You Know*.

In the 1930s he took on a great deal of movie work, including an entire year of *Photoplay* magazine covers in 1937, and the poster art for Frank Capra's *Lost Horizon* that same year. In 1951 he published a collection of his caricatures, with accompanying anecdotes, called *Celebrities*, but his movie-inspired art is seldom recognized alongside his more famous poster work. Herewith, a small tribute.

1. The cover of Paramount's Picture Progress magazine from 1916 2. This portrait of Ann Harding was used to publicize her 1933 movie Gallant Lady. 3. Flagg's Lost Horizon artwork was used for a variety of posters and even this sheet music. 4. Popular artists Russell Patterson, John Lagatta, and Flagg (who actually resembled Uncle Sam) sketch Metropolitan Opera star Gladys Swarthout in 1933.

Chapter 2
SILENTS AND SOUND

SILENT SABOTAGE

In 1996, Dustin Hoffman agreed to host the Los Angeles Chamber Orchestra's annual fundraiser, a showing of Charlie Chaplin's *The Kid*. I interviewed Hoffman a short time later and asked what he thought of the evening. He said, with great earnestness, "You know, we in the movie business should be ashamed of ourselves, because we've always made fun of silent films. The cliché is that the acting is broad and exaggerated, but the truth is that it's incredibly subtle."

Thus, one of our greatest actors—named for a silent-film star, Dustin Farnum (pictured, opposite)—made a discovery that millions of others have yet to learn about a great period of moviemaking. But Hoffman also pointed out the chief culprit in perpetuating silly and damaging clichés about silent movies: Hollywood itself.

It's human nature to make fun of the past as we move forward. Hairstyles and fashions of the 1980s are considered campy today. The almost universal use of color in recent years has made black-and-white movies and television shows seem antiquated to many people. The coming of television decreed a slow death for radio, although no one in the audience found anything lacking when listenership was at its peak in the late 1940s.

Planned obsolescence has been part of the American way of life since the industrial revolution. Anyone who uses a typewriter in today's computer generation is considered quaint, at best. Audiocassettes are now seen as yesterday's technology, just as the videocassette is being supplanted by the DVD.

So it was that just a few years after the birth of talkies in 1927, Hollywood seemed to have made a concerted effort to reshape people's thinking about silent film; in doing so, it eradicated both memories and perceptions of the silents' power to move and inspire an audience. In an effort to embrace modern and forward thinking, Hollywood turned an art form into a joke.

Original caption from May 27, 1936: "Film players who worked for the old Essanay company. . . gathered at a Stars of Yesterday program given by the Riverside Breakfast Club today." First row: Vic Potel, Bryant Washburn, Dot Farley, Edwin August; back row: Ralph Lewis, Jack Richardson, Walter Long, Creighton Hale, William Austin.

Pete Smith produced and narrated a series of MGM short-subjects called Goofy Movies beginning in 1933. He transformed silent-film dramas into broad comedies, using sarcastic narration and non-sequitur interpretations of the actors' dialogue. A decade later, Richard Fleischer created a similar series for RKO called Flicker Flashbacks, drawing on some of the earliest, most primitive silent shorts as raw material.

"I came across some of the old movies while I was working at RKO Pathé News in New York, and found them to be so outrageously awful that they were truly funny," Fleischer recently recalled. "They used painted backdrops, phony costumes, and unintentionally ludicrous overacting. I made a narration soundtrack that accompanied the film; while the action on the screen remained the same, the narrator was describing something completely different. We recorded the films with (intentionally) the worst movie music ever made. The series was a great success and my career was made."

Of course, these early films bore scant resemblance to the polished works of the 1920s . . . and nothing is so sacrosanct that it can't be spoofed. Yet, without meaning to, movies like this came to represent all silent films to some viewers, especially at a time before television and home video offered alternatives.

Another problem was the industry changeover to sound speed, twenty-four frames per second; silents were shot at varying speeds, but most often at 16 fps. This made almost any silent film (except for some comedies) look sped-up, and often absurd. Even today, most audiences believe that people moved in a herky-jerky way in the pre-talkie era. Many otherwise savvy documentarians don't even bother to adjust the speed of silent newsreel footage, despite the fact that digital technology makes this incredibly easy to do.

Fortunately, there were moments when the movie industry did do justice to its earlier achievements. MGM reissued *The Big Parade* and *Ben-Hur* in the early 1930s with music and sound effects. Paramount honored its past in a pair of short subjects called *Movie Milestones* (1932), which presented great scenes from such silent classics as *The Ten Commandments* and *Old Ironsides*. (In fact, the only surviving footage of Lon Chaney's memorable performance in *The Miracle Man* is the excerpt included in that short.) And in 1939, William S. Hart filmed a moving speech about

One of D. W. Griffith's finest actors, Henry B. Walthall, as he appeared with Will Rogers and Berton Churchill in John Ford's *Judge Priest* (1934).

his career and his devotion to the West that served as a prologue for the reissue of his 1925 silent epic *Tumbleweeds*.

That same year, The March of Time produced *The Movies March On*, an admirable capsule-history of motion pictures that treated the subject with great respect. John Nesbitt celebrated the precious images of the twentieth century captured (and preserved) on film in his MGM short subjects *The Film That Was Lost* (1942) and *Forgotten Treasure* (1943), entries in his popular Passing Parade series that made use of the Museum of Modern Art film archive.

But on the whole, Hollywood seemed to believe that whatever had been achieved in the silent era should and could be topped in talkies. In 1930, Columbia produced a remake of the 1921 classic *Tol'able David*. Cecil B. DeMille made his third version of *The Squaw Man* in 1931. Later in the decade, Fox produced remakes of D. W. Griffith's *Way Down East* and its own blockbuster hit *Seventh Heaven*. Almost without exception, those remakes made little headway with audiences; today, they are mostly, and justly, forgotten.

Comedy producer Hal Roach was considerably more successful in remaking and recycling silent comedy shorts with Laurel and Hardy, Charley Chase, and Our Gang, reasoning that audiences wouldn't remember the originals—or perhaps believing that they would welcome "modern" versions of the ideas executed in the dear, dead days of silents. Indeed, Laurel and Hardy's most celebrated short, *The Music Box* (1932), which won an Academy Award, was a reworking of their 1927 comedy *Hats Off*.

Overnight, some actors were regarded as "old-timers." By 1935 it was a novelty to gather veterans of the silent era for reunions, or cast

Mack Sennett hams it up as two former employees, W. C. Fields and Frank Capra, offer him his honorary Oscar in 1937.

them for the sheer novelty value of their presence, as Paramount did in *The Preview Murder Mystery* (1936) and *Hollywood Boulevard* (1936). Robert Florey, a film buff as well as a filmmaker, directed both of these B-movies, which featured Francis X. Bushman, Maurice Costello, Rod La Rocque, Franklyn Farnum (no relation to Dustin), and Conway Tearle, among other 1920s stars.

Yet many actors whose careers dated back to the very beginnings of motion pictures continued to work steadily throughout the 1930s and forties without anyone turning it into a stunt. (Think of Wallace Beery or Lewis Stone, just for starters.) Henry B. Walthall, the "little Colonel" of Griffith's *The Birth of a Nation*, worked up until his death in 1937, often in prominent supporting roles. Others learned to adapt: such silent-film directors as Del Henderson, Oscar Apfel, and Wilfred Lucas became character actors in talkies.

While filming *Tarzan's New York Adventure*, Johnny Weissmuller was standing on top of a circus wagon, waiting for cameras to roll on a scene in which he is pursued by a group of burly roustabouts. He made eye contact with Elmo Lincoln, who had starred as the screen's first Tarzan in 1918 and was now one of these roustabout extras. Lincoln called out over the crowd, "Save your money, Johnny! Save your money!"

One place silent film stars found a haven was Republic Pictures. Check the cast lists of most Republic serials and you'll find such names as Monte Blue, Herbert Rawlinson, and William Farnum (Dustin's brother) in key supporting roles. Many of them were former matinee idols, and had the enormous benefit of stage experience.

Frank Coghlan Jr., the beloved Billy Batson of *The Adventures of Captain Marvel*, told me: "In our serial we had Bryant Washburn, who was a major star in the silent days, and Jack Mulhall, who played opposite some of the biggest leading ladies in the business. If you recall the first episode, when I meet Shazam the mystic, that was Nigel DeBrulier, who played Cardinal Richelieu with Douglas Fairbanks in 1921, and then repeated that role with Fairbanks in *The Iron Mask*. Here was a 'class act' actor doing a half-day bit, and he did it superbly." Why did Republic cast these veterans so often? "You'd get a person who was a good actor to start with, and budget-wise you got a guy who could do it in one take, which was very important on a busy schedule like we had."

There was some irony in the fact that Republic took over the Studio City facility that had been built by silent-comedy legend Mack Sennett in 1928. "When I first went out there [in 1934]," recalled Republic director William Witney, "Mack Sennett was still wandering around the halls, and I got to know him. He was a delightful, beautiful man [but] broken. It broke my heart. The prop rooms were there, [and] all the little cars: the one that the Keystone Cops used to drive between the street cars and the long, narrow one that came out the other end. The Keystone Cop uniforms were there in the prop rooms. All that stuff was still at the studio and they threw it all out."

In a 1941 episode of Paramount's short-subject series *Hedda Hopper's Hollywood*, Hedda has a happy reunion with silent-film star William Farnum. She screens a 1916 film they made together, *The Battle of Hearts*, for her son Bill and some of his friends. In the midst of a dramatic scene, someone shouts, "Boy, is that corny!" and Bill responds, "Don't tell Mother; she thinks it's good."

Most people had no choice but to grin and bear this kind of wisecrack. For Buster Keaton, good humor was a matter of survival. Many of his jobs from the 1930s to the end of his life called on him to represent the silent-film era (he was one of the "waxworks" in Billy Wilder's *Sunset Blvd.*), even though the skits he was often called on to do were Sennett-type slapstick that had nothing to do with his own unique brand of humor. (It's not clear exactly when the fiction began that Keaton worked for Sennett, but this misinformation was repeated ad nauseam for decades.)

In 1939, Buster co-starred with Alice Faye in a sequence recreating a silent comedy—and the throwing of the first custard

Cecil B. DeMille is flanked by Raymond Hatton and Jack Holt, who starred in his silent films of the teens, at a 1930s Hollywood gathering.

pie—in Darryl F. Zanuck's *Hollywood Cavalcade*, a romanticized Hollywood history with a central character inspired by D. W. Griffith, Cecil B. DeMille, and especially Mack Sennett, Zanuck's onetime boss.

Another Sennett veteran, Malcolm St. Clair, directed the entertaining segment, which pegged Keaton forever as a pie-throwing expert. Ironically, except for his debut film with "Fatty" Arbuckle, one can search in vain for such a gag in Buster's silent screen career, just as historians have come up short trying to find "definitive" Sennett slapstick scenes. As a result, countless documentaries and TV shows have made witting or unwitting use of mute footage from the 1935 Warner Bros. short *Keystone Hotel* (1935), which expertly recreated the mythological Keystone Cop chases and a massive pie-throwing melée, passing it off as an authentic Mack Sennett silent comedy.

Hollywood continued to distort—or at best, romanticize—the silent-film era in such films as *The Perils of Pauline* (1947), a purported biography of silent serial heroine Pearl White directed by George Marshall, himself a veteran of the silents; *Valentino* (1951); and the wonderful *Singin' in the Rain* (1952), which focused on the awkward transition to talkies.

And, of course, Gloria Swanson created an indelible archetype as Norma Desmond in *Sunset Blvd.* (1950). She was so persuasive that she spent the rest of her life trying to convince people that she wasn't like the madwoman she portrayed.

One of the first people to attempt to change public perception of silent films was Robert Youngson. He mined the Pathé newsreel library to craft a series of wonderful historical short-subjects in the late 1940s and 1950s, and a feature-length documentary, *Fifty Years Before Your Eyes*. In 1957 he produced a re-issue version of Warners' 1929 feature *Noah's Ark* with music and narration; a year later he made his biggest splash with a theatrical feature called *The Golden Age of Comedy*. (On a personal note, I remember my parents taking me to see this film at the Guild Theater on 50th Street in New York City, where a standee of Laurel and Hardy with Jean Harlow was perched on the sidewalk outside. To say that this film changed my life would be a mild understatement. A year later I got to enjoy Charlie Chaplin's greatest films in their 1959 reissue from Lopert Films.) Youngson continued to make silent-comedy compilations for the rest of his life.

In 1960–61, Paul Killiam's *Silents Please* introduced silent films and stars to even more people on ABC television. (Imagine a series of silent movies being aired on network TV today!) Both Youngson and Killiam took a lot of heat for tampering with films and adding often-distracting narration. Yet had they not given exposure to these films when they did, it's hard to say just when a new generation would have had the chance to discover these movies, in any form.

In 1961, NBC aired David L. Wolper's *Hollywood: The Golden Years*, a loving tribute to the silent-film era narrated by Gene Kelly, with beautiful and evocative music by Elmer Bernstein. It spawned two follow-ups and the thirty-nine-episode series *Hollywood and the Stars*, and served as a training ground for documentary talent, including the late Jack Haley Jr.

In 1962, Harold Lloyd's *World of Comedy* brought highlights of the silent comedian's greatest films back to theater screens. (I saw it on a double-bill with Billy Budd in Hackensack, New Jersey.) Lloyd appeared on TV with Steve Allen and Johnny Carson to promote the film, and the excerpts he brought along invariably wowed the studio audiences.

Buster Keaton and Alice Faye in Hollywood Cavalcade (1939).

Kevin Brownlow's groundbreaking book *The Parade's Gone By*, published in 1968, captured the magic of that period and its great personalities, and his subsequent thirteen-part documentary *Hollywood* (made in collaboration with the late David Gill) brought the era vividly to life. Anthony Slide launched a wonderful publication called *The Silent Picture*, and David Shepard made rare titles available to collectors during his tenure at Blackhawk Films (as he continues to do on video). Other film scholars, distributors, and archivists have done yeoman service ever since.

Yet, even today, we see silent newsreel footage at accelerated speed. The canard of John Gilbert's "high-pitched voice" is still, astonishingly, repeated even though it should have been laid to rest decades ago. And a blurb for Simon Louvish's new book *Keystone* insists that Buster Keaton was a Sennett employee (though Louvish himself does not make the claim.)

But all things considered, this is a golden age for silent-film lovers. There are more 35mm showings with live music (ranging from piano to pipe organ to full orchestral accompaniment) then ever before. Pristine copies of silents both famous and obscure are being released on DVD, with scholarly background-material and essays. Now, even enthusiasts who don't live near museums or archives have access to rare films of this period.

It's just a shame that it took this long to undo the damage done to the era's reputation by Hollywood for so many, many years.

Conversations:
MARY BRIAN

She played Wendy in the silent-film version of *Peter Pan*. She was a regular guest at Pickfair and San Simeon, and starred opposite such leading men as Gary Cooper, Cary Grant, and James Cagney. She became a friend of the New York literati when the literati migrated to the Garden of Allah in Hollywood. She later married George Tomasini, who became Alfred Hitchcock's favorite film-editor, and she socialized with Hitch and his wife Alma. She spent much of World War II meeting and entertaining our soldiers overseas. After leaving acting behind, she taught herself to paint, and she spent many years creating beautiful portraits in oil.

Her name is Mary Brian, and her life was certainly more interesting than many of the ingénue parts she got to play onscreen. An active woman into her nineties, she turned down requests for interviews and appearances in her later years, but with some encouragement from her longtime friends Tony Slide and Robert Gitt, and the approval of her surrogate nephew Stuart Erwin Jr., she allowed me to spend several mornings taping her recollections.

Our conversation was broad-ranging, and I asked a number of questions about the community of Toluca Lake, where I now live. The only subject that was off-limits was her age.

"People say, 'How old are you?' and I say, 'How old would you like me to be?' I say, 'It's negotiable, you know.'"

No negotiation is necessary: Mary Brian is ageless.

MALTIN: When and how did you move to Toluca Lake? How did you happen to settle there?
BRIAN: Well, Dick Arlen and Bing Crosby, of course, both golfed there. And there had been a little earthquake at this time I'd been working at

Paramount, and Huntley Gordon, I think it was, owned this piece of land that we built on and he wanted to get out of here. So we bought it at a very nice price. And the lot itself, nobody could build in front of it.

MALTIN: Do you remember the address?

BRIAN: 4204 Navajo. Frank McHugh built on the other side of me, and there was just a whole big bunch of us that lived there. We bicycled and we had charge accounts up at the grocery store, and it was like a small town. I hope it never changes. Claude Binyon lived in Charlie Farrell's old house that he leased. And Bette Davis leased it for a while, and Ozzie and Harriet, when they came out; everybody had canoes on the lake, except me. Jack Oakie gave me a rowboat, called the *Mary B.* and they said, "Why didn't you give her a canoe? Everybody else has a canoe." He said, "She'll drown herself and they'll say it's An American Tragedy." But anyway, I had been given this big white Siberian husky by the district attorney of Alaska and his wife, who sent the dog down to me by boat. And that dog let out this awful little pout if I didn't take him in the boat. He always was up like a masthead, and would hiss at the swans and the swans would hiss back. But I was safer in a rowboat. Because W. C. Fields, I tell you, he was such a devil . . . he used to call across the lake. When Stuart [Erwin] used to come over, he always wanted to feed the swans and I'd give him breadcrumbs to take down at the end of the lake. The swans paid no attention, wouldn't come up. Fields would come out with a dish [and] every duck and swan came up on his lawn. And I was telling Norman McLeod, the director; he lived a couple of doors down on the other side. He said, "Don't you feel slighted. He's got his breadcrumbs mixed with rye. They get it every afternoon." But [Fields] used to get his writers in his canoe and he'd take them out for a conference on the lake; these swans would come along the side, and you know, they're quite powerful. And he would take a swing at them and the canoe went like this (*teetering*); the writers were terrified of going out on the lake because it was very precarious . . . . But he was a wonderful character.

MALTIN: You told me a funny story, too, about being at a party when George Brent was going with Greta Garbo—

BRIAN: Oh yes. Well, this was when George Brent was working at Warner Bros.; he leased a house and he was going with Garbo at the time. We were out rowing in our old clothes, always, and he would row Garbo down and she would see these people, and she had a hat and she pulled it down over her face. And if people rowed by there, she was always doing this [*tugging the hat down over her eyes*]. Jack [Oakie] came by, and we'd been asked up to the Binyons for dinner. So we rowed down and there was a little hedge between the Binyons' house and Charlie Farrell's old house, where George Brent was staying. We were all having such laughs and fun, but she was looking to see what such laughter and fun was coming from. Jack looked over and said, "Make Greta stop peeking at me." And he pulled his hat down.

MALTIN: It seems as if it was a very social group of people that you worked with: Richard Arlen and Buddy Rogers and Jack Oakie and Stuart Erwin and you were all friends. You weren't just co-workers.

BRIAN: We were real pals. I'll tell you the reason, when I say Gary [Cooper] and Dick and Buddy and Jack—they were like a closed club, except for me, because I was on location with them all the time. And we went out to the [Paramount] ranch, and I think we probably used the ranch more than anybody

Gary Cooper—with ubiquitous cigarette—chats with Mary, George E. Stone, and Charles Bickford on the Paramount lot during production of Song of the Eagle (1933).

else. And you know, we had no freeway going out there at that time, so we had to start at a very early time in the morning. It was a long, hot trip in the summertime, and we would be out there until the light left. So we all got to know each other very well; on location, you know them more than you do just on a set in the daytime. And I had done *The Virginian* out there with Gary and Dick. Dick and I did several Zane Greys, *The Light of Western Stars*, and all of these things, and they had the same sort of character guys; they were fun and they were family, too. We'd all chip in, and they would go over and buy steaks and baking potatoes, and Gene Pallette loved to cook, so he would have this big barbecue that he was making in-between scenes, and he did beans and roasted potatoes in the ashes. We would always stay after the sun went down and have dinner there together, because by that time it was so late that we were all hungry. And anyway, we could sit around and swap stories.

MALTIN: Eugene Pallette obviously liked to eat.

BRIAN: Oh yes. As a matter of fact, every few days, he would say, "Mary, will you stop on the entrance to the Cahuenga pass, from Hollywood, there's an old Mexican there and he makes Texas tamales"—those little tamales. He said, "Get me a dozen." I would stop and buy this whole thing for Gene Pallette. And he'd sit right down there and eat them all himself. He loved to eat, loved to cook, and he was a good cook.

But, we would be out there for the whole day, and it's not like when you have maybe a couple of scenes and you work for a long time during the day. I always had old clothes, so I'd go and take my costume off, and we'd go on a ride. And we'd ride all over the place; it was fun. And then I had to learn to ride side-saddle, you know, for the costume thing. I remember one time Gary was supposed to [help me up]; I'd put my foot in his hand, and he'd lift me up for the side-saddle. We hadn't rehearsed it yet, because we were used to being around the horses. He was so strong in doing this, he pitched me over on the other side of the horse! I was slightly scratched and bruised, but we had the light and we had to keep going.

But we always had things that we enjoyed doing together. And I know Dick's wife, not his first wife, but his second wife; if we'd go to a party—there used to be a lot more parties at people's houses—she was telling me somebody said, "Where's Dick?" She said, "He's the other bookend—on the other side of Mary." Because, you know, we'd all get together and just swap things that had happened to us.

Original caption: "MADE-UP IN CHINA —Mary Brian has a colorful Chinese makeup box in her dressing room at the Paramount studios in Hollywood. It is made of very light teak wood and has three drawers filled with odd powder jars and mixing bowls." Photo by Gene Robert Richee (billed as such, and not as Eugene).

I was one of the boys. After I'd done *Peter Pan*, I was kind of an in-between age. I certainly wasn't a cuddly young girl and I wasn't a leading lady. And so I was always with the boys, with the writers, sat around with them, and not with the ladies so much who sat in the shade and had a parasol. They just took me for granted, and I didn't realize at the time how fortunate I was, because all the rest of the years there were so many times that I was included and they'd say, "Oh come on, Mary," and I would go with them. [*Laughs*]

MALTIN: Did every woman fall in love with Gary Cooper?

BRIAN: Oh, yes. You couldn't help it. I tell you—he was beautiful, to start with. But he never felt self-important. Never. When he'd see dancers, he'd say "Oh, I wish I could do that." You know? There were so many things that he was not envious about, but just was in awe of. And I saw him through [his affair with] Lupe [Velez]. Lupe was a character. She used to go to a party, and she would say, "If they do such and such, I'm going to do this (to her)," and we'd say, "Well, what did she say?" "Well, I haven't talked to her, but if she did that . . ." [*laughs*] It was always, "If she did," she was in trouble.

MALTIN: She was ready for a fight.

BRIAN: [*Laughs*] And came to a sad end . . . the last person that I would have imagined would have done it [commit suicide]. But Gary's mother and father were great friends of my mother. And it was kind of funny, because when I worked with Gary, Gary was very tall, as you know. And sometimes when it was a two-shot, they had to make a little platform for me to stand on, so I wouldn't be in one corner and he would be up here. His mother was a very handsome woman, and tall. And my mother was about my size. They looked like Mutt and Jeff.

MALTIN: So, did you know people like Herman Mankiewicz then?

BRIAN: Oh, yes. As a matter of fact, Joe Mankiewicz, we used to all eat at the same table, most of the guys and myself. We had a game going with matchsticks, you know, you keep building the thing and whoever [broke down] the building had to pay for everybody's lunch. So we were always so careful. Joe Mankiewicz was always in that. I used to be invited to Herman Mankiewicz's house; I got invited to an awful lot of things that nobody else got invited to, because most of the wives never felt like I was anyone that was inching in on their territory. And I know that when I went out, I had just taken it for granted that we all went out for dinner, and most of the other people were not that curious about what was going on in the city.

MALTIN: Who do you think set the atmosphere at Paramount that made it so social and so enjoyable?

BRIAN: Jesse Lasky. He had a big beach house down at Santa Monica and he entertained quite a bit. And all of the contract players got asked and he had special news people come there. And his wife, who was quite a good artist, seemed to enjoy it. Zukor spent most of his time in New York. He didn't come out too often, so he had parties that were given for him [when he did]. I was so lucky, I had such good friends.

MALTIN: And you appreciated it, too.

BRIAN: Well, I really did. I thought that all of our life, even up to [recent] years, Buddy [Rogers], if he was playing at Lakeside, he'd stop every once in a while just to see how I was doing . . . all the guys. It's not that you're doing a picture and then you forget it.

MALTIN: That's a wonderful feeling of continuity.

BRIAN: It was. And you know, not only the guys, but Esther Ralston. She and I were friends, all my life. Glenda Farrell, all my life . . . not all my life, but many, many years of my life. And I cherished that.

MALTIN: What was it like to go to an evening at Pickfair, for instance?

BRIAN: It was wonderful. Their house was a comfortable house; it was filled with wonderful things that they had collected and people had sent. It was like an English house, comfortable and charming and not overpowering. And I loved to go; there were always interesting people. Mary Pickford had such a wit and if she was in full swing, she could really keep people entertained. And I got in on the tail end of Douglas Fairbanks, too, because the second picture I did was with Doug Fairbanks Sr. So we'd known each other all those years. He was a real charmer, wonderful man. And of course, Buddy [Rogers] in later years . . . Buddy and I go back to the very beginning.

MALTIN: Would they be huge dinner parties or intimate at Pickfair?

BRIAN: Well, every so often, when they had visiting nobility or something, they were rather formal and rather loud. And if it was in the summertime, they spilled over onto the lawn. Otherwise, they were small, I would say twelve or fifteen, something like that. They had a table that was big, and everybody sat and swapped stories. Did you ever see their house?

MALTIN: No.

BRIAN: Well, when you came in, they had a stairway, but there was a

room off to the left that she made into a Western room, and she got an old bar that went the length of the room, and had Western pictures. If there were not too many people, that's where the party started. But it was really the place that you loved to go because you were comfortable when you were there. Because I used to go up to the Hearst ranch and that, of course, was impressive. Really impressive. [Pickfair] wasn't like that, and it didn't attempt to be.

MALTIN: Mr. Hearst had rules, didn't he?

BRIAN: Yes. He had rules. I tell you, the parties that he

Mary Pickford entertains Fuzzy Knight, Joel McCrea, and Johnny Mack Brown.

had up there, if he didn't have rules, it would have gotten to be a madhouse. You could get up anytime that you wanted, but breakfast was served only to a certain time. When he had meals, you must be on time. And they've always laughed about the ketchup bottles; well, it was such a long table that there was no passing things around. Usually we all dressed for dinner, but it wasn't that formal.

MALTIN: How would you receive an invitation to go there?

BRIAN: They would usually call you. The secretary would say, We are going to have a group of your friends and they would love to have you come and join them, for the weekend or whatever length of time they wanted you for. And we would go up on a train and they would have cars that would [take us to] the Glendale Station. We were met by limousines at the other end of the line. It was interesting, because you would go through fences and you were stopped there because they had certain animals that they didn't want to mix with the next group of animals. They had a wonderful, wonderful zoo; I was there when, I don't know if it was a giraffe or some exotic animal was going to give birth. But they had leopards and tigers and all kinds of things. It was fascinating. The first time that I went there I was barely out of my teens, I think, so you could imagine how impressed I was.

They always were talking about all of the treasures that he had and that he didn't even know what he had. I don't think that's true, because he saw that I was interested in paintings, and he took me into this tremendous room where he had famous, wonderful paintings, and he explained them all to me. He was so interested that I was interested in the things that he had collected. He was a very gracious host. I'm sure he must have been a very strict boss, but in his own castle, he was a lovely, lovely host. He explained where he had gotten these paintings, what [the painters] had done, just to me; of course I was just absolutely flabbergasted, not only from the treatment but from the paintings that they had there.

A lovely portrait of Marion Davies.

In later years, I was asked to Wyntoon, which was their getaway, if you can say getaway from the castle, which was up on a river, on sort of the border of California and Oregon.

MALTIN: I've heard that's a spectacular place, too.

BRIAN: Lovely, just lovely. But very much more informal. There were different cabins and things, and not all people ate at the same time.

MALTIN: What was Marion Davies like?

BRIAN: Fun. She really enjoyed life and was probably the most informal person that you would ever want to know. Did so many good things you never heard about. Funded things, and as you know, I'm sure, when he got into some bind financially, she put up the Warwick Hotel. And everyone that used to go to the ranch, when they went to New York, we always stayed at the Warwick. Not only out of loyalty—nobody asked us to do this—but there were always people that we knew from the ranch, and it was like an old boarding house, almost. But she had her little dolls and she would laugh; she was fun.

MALTIN: I've never heard anyone say an unkind word about her.

BRIAN: No. She wasn't unkind and she was a good, homey hostess. You know, not formally "we'll do this." If you were there and were a regular goer, you were family. Which was wonderful. And, of course, they had a motion picture room, with all these big plush, luxurious chairs. You could sit there in great luxury and watch the picture. But nobody wanted their picture to be shown there, because all of the remarks that'll be made, you know, in fun. You never know what the people are going to say, you know, to make a joke out of whatever the thing was.

MALTIN: That's funny. [*Both laugh*]

BRIAN: But when they had a big, big party . . . now I think one of the biggest ones I went to, George Bernard Shaw was out here and, of course, everybody wanted to meet him. You were very fortunate if you were asked up there for that weekend. He and his wife were there, so the single girls all had sort of a dormitory. It was funny, but we got all the service. All of the little guest houses were each done in a certain style, and filled with wonderful antiques. And if you were there when it was just a few people, why you stayed in one or whatever one that was selected. And you were living in such luxury.

MALTIN: Did you get to meet Mr. Shaw?

BRIAN: Oh, yes. As a matter of fact, in the room that was back of the long dining room, they had a fireplace, not the entrance fireplace, but this one, and he and his wife were sitting there and talking with Mr. Hearst and the ones of us that were so interested, you know, would sort of sit around and cock an ear to hear what he was saying. I wish I had some great quote that I heard him say, but it was interesting—

MALTIN: Just to be there—

BRIAN: Yes.

MALTIN: So then would you come home late Sunday night?

BRIAN: Well, if you were working, you did. And some people went up on their own, in their own cars. But most people went up on the train, because it was fun to do it that way, because there's visiting back and forth. And if you asked to stay longer and were not working, some often did that. Then it was just a few people there; it was really a time that you could look and see some of the wonders that he had there.

MALTIN: What an experience.

BRIAN: It was wonderful. They'll never have that kind again, I'm sure. Nobody ever could afford this kind of living.

MALTIN: Was it tough to come back to real life again?

BRIAN: No, it wasn't. I was always glad that I had a simpler life to live. The other's a little too rich for your blood, as a steady streak. Like too much chocolate.

MALTIN: Since you started out at Paramount, and you were there such a long time, was it disorienting when you'd have to work at another studio?

BRIAN: Well, they loaned me out a great deal, so I'd been working at some of the other studios. When my contract was up and I went out on my own, that was a big deal, because I had always had a nest at Paramount. It was difficult, because you get used to people taking care of a lot of things; that doesn't happen when you're freelancing, because nobody there is looking after your interests.

MALTIN: I imagine after a point, you knew everybody. You knew all the crew—

BRIAN: Yes, and their wives when they'd come on a location. Everybody was like a big, informal family.

MALTIN: I see that pretty early on, you were loaned out to MGM to make *Brown of Harvard*.

BRIAN: Oh, yes. That was about the fourth or fifth picture, with Jack Pickford and William Haines. And it was entirely different at the MGM studio. They trained their people; they had dancing lessons and singing lessons and it was a whole different ball game there, which I think was wonderful. But if you were under contract to Paramount, you worked six days a week, most every week. You'd just get up and you had to go to work. I think when you're enjoying what you're doing, it never seems like a hardship. When we were doing *Peter Pan*, we

had hours you can't believe because we were doing the pirate ship off of San Pedro, and we had to be out there when the sun was up. And we were [also] shooting at the studio; when we'd come back and we were shooting in the nursery, they would say, "You can get in bed and take a nap," because every time that they had you fly in another direction, it was a long wait, so we just took naps in our own beds! I just thought this is the way you made pictures. So nothing was a surprise to me after that. I just thought, "Oh, it's crazy hours, but that's fine. " But a lot of people, particularly stage people, found this completely disconcerting.

Mary as Wendy (in her film debut), Betty Bronson as Peter in Peter Pan (1924).

MALTIN: It was your baptism of fire then?

BRIAN: Yes.

MALTIN: Do you have any recollections of Anna May Wong, who played Tiger Lily?

BRIAN: Yes, of course, she went over to the Santa Cruz Islands to do a lot of stuff over there, too. She was a beautiful lady, but she stayed very much to herself. I'll tell you who on the picture I liked tremendously: Ernest Torrence, who played Captain Hook. You know, he was a villain [on screen], but he was such a charming man. Charming man.

MALTIN: So you were seventeen, I guess, or sixteen?

BRIAN: I think maybe, around fifteen, sixteen, seventeen. In the beginning, the studio wanted to make me younger, and then they wanted to make me older, because I was playing older parts. So it was already embellished.

MALTIN: Did you enjoy living in New York while you were there working at the Paramount Astoria studio?

BRIAN: I loved New York, yes. Spent almost as much time there as I did here.

MALTIN: Would you stay in Manhattan and then commute out to the studio?

BRIAN: They had a hotel where they kept most of the [contract players]. The Sheraton Hotel in New York. It was a nice hotel. They had a swimming pool in the basement and Esther [Ralston] was there a lot of the time, and she and I were friends up until she died. In the beginning [when I first went to New York] I would feel self-conscious, naturally. And wondered if your slip was showing; you think you're the focus, you're in the spotlight. Well, I found out very quickly that all of these other people, they were all feeling very insecure in their own way. And I thought, they're worried about themselves, they're not worried about me, I'm not in the spotlight. Now there are two kinds of people: one that's very sad that they're not in the spotlight [*both laugh*] and the other kind that feels like it gives you freedom. You're not the center of the thing and you can observe and do a lot of things that you can't if you are in the spotlight. I enjoyed that and I became at ease with whatever I was doing because I knew I wasn't the focus of everybody's attention.

MALTIN: What are your recollections of Richard Dix?

BRIAN: Well, that was my first great infatuation. I met him in the Long Island studios, and of course, he was a big star. I did a couple of pictures with him and he used to take me out. I guess that was the first time that I'd been around to the theaters and oh, it was heaven. [*Laughs*] But, you know, I wasn't really quite ready for that, I think.

MALTIN: I wonder about some of the comedy directors; it seems as if some of them consciously tried to keep a light touch on the set. Is that true?

BRIAN: Well, Eddie Sutherland, who was known as The Little Iron Man, was married many, many times, once to Louise Brooks. And Eddie came from a New York theatrical family, so he sort of knew this business, aside from being a comedy director. He was so helpful to me because, in the very early times, I was a teenager. And he would say, "Come over here to Uncle Eddie," and he never embarrassed me in front of people. Some say, "Don't do this" and "You shouldn't do that." And he'd sit me down and say, "You know, if you did this, wouldn't it be kind of fun if you'd do this . . ." Always good suggestions, always kind and not embarrassing in front of people. He loved to play practical jokes and he loved to play them on me. They were never cruel jokes. So he had just married again and I had grown up quite a bit. I was doing a picture with Jack Oakie, and it was a rather deep set, and there was a stairway coming down, so we were away from the director and he brought his wife over to kind of show her how he directed pictures. Jack said to me, "That's Eddie's new wife." Eddie started directing and he said, "Mary, come down the steps and when you do . . ." And I turned and I said, "Eddie, you never talked to me like that before . . ." and threw my arms around him. He got red in his face and finally said, "Mary, you win." And his wife, finally, found out how we were always swapping jokes on each other. But he was a good, good director, because he knew what he wanted. At one point, Eddie leased [a house in the Toluca Lake neighborhood] when he was going with Loretta Young. And that didn't work out, and Eddie was a very social man. Now, we'd known each other since my beginning, so he would say, "Mary, are you doing anything? Let's go down and have dinner," and there was a place on Sunset Boulevard, I'm trying to think of the name of it. Really good eating place. So I said, "Sure." This wasn't like a date. Meanwhile, some of his pals, like Benchley, Charlie Butterworth, Dwight Taylor, they were all living at the Garden of Allah. And they would call him and say, "What are you doing?" This would be on a Sunday night. So, when he'd come pick me up, he said, "A couple of the old pals are calling, let's go by and pick 'em up at the Garden of Allah." So there were five of us and we'd spend the dinner hour; if I had to get up [the next morning], why they'd take me home and then they'd go on their way. But I got to listen to Benchley and all of these guys, because I was taken for granted in another sort of circle.

MALTIN: Did you try to keep up with their drinking? I would think not.

BRIAN: No. [*Laughs*] I was a Coca-Cola drinker, and they put up with that. As I say, sometimes they went on [afterward]. The only time that I ever met Scott Fitzgerald was with them. I had come by with Eddie to get some of the other chums, and Fitzgerald was staying at the Garden of Allah—not for very long, but he was there. So we all went in; they were trying to persuade him to come with us. And he was trying very hard not to do that, and he didn't do it. But it was fascinating to meet him.

MALTIN: Directors again . . . Gregory La Cava.

BRIAN: Oh! Well, you know, in the beginning, Paramount did almost as many pictures in New York, at the Long Island studio [as they did in Hollywood], and I can't tell you how many trips I made back and forth between here and New York. And when I first went back there, nobody was dating me, and I got to see more of New York than I ever did any other trip later on. W. C. Fields was in New York and they got La Cava to direct *Running Wild*, and I did that picture.

Sheet music for a forgotten song from The Man I Love *(1929).*

He was a very imaginative and vital kind of director . . . and was in on the writing. I didn't get to know him personally; it was later on when I was married to George [Tomasini], because they're both Italian, and George knew Gregory La Cava and he used to ask us out down to his beach house. He wasn't working very much at the time, but we'd all just sit around, and I liked him. He was always full of novel ideas.

MALTIN: Someone else I wanted to ask you about is Raymond Griffith. You only worked with him once.

BRIAN: Yes. As a matter of fact, it was called *A Regular Fellow*. I was charmed by him. He was a writer and he was an actor; he could do comedy or anything. I was very impressed with him. And he was very nice to me. We used the lake to the left of my house as a location, when there were practically no houses there. We [also] used a lot of the sets that are now Forest Lawn. You know, that used to be part of our location before they had the [Paramount] ranch; well, they had the ranch but they didn't use it that much. This was close in [to Hollywood], you know, and they built some very fancy sets over there. I know we used some of those sets that were supposed to look like a foreign kingdom. And we shot quite a bit of it there. He was a very nice, very kind man. He wasn't as informal as the group that I knew later. But he couldn't be nicer.

Now, Herbert Brenon was the one that selected me for Wendy [in *Peter Pan*]. And so I guess he always kind of felt responsible for me. He was the kindest man, wonderful man.

MALTIN: And he used you in a number of films.

BRIAN: Oh, yes. And as a matter of fact, for *The Little French Girl*, we went to New York and we went on location to Bermuda, which couldn't have been nicer. But he really did do more coaching for me than anybody, because he knew I had never done anything when I came out here.

MALTIN: Would a director like that talk to you while the scene was going on, in the silent days?

BRIAN: Yes. But he also made you learn your lines.

MALTIN: So even for a silent film, you were learning dialogue?

BRIAN: Yes. Well, the thing was that he had been working with Pola Negri and Gloria Swanson and apparently, he was a very strict, very distant director. He was always so helpful to me, because he felt that he had got me into it. So I think a lot of the directors didn't insist on doing lines. But he did. Because he felt if he was doing a book, that the lines were important. And if anybody ever read lips from the audience, you could see what they were saying. And I don't think that was a standard thing, but he did it.

MALTIN: Now, you must have been the only cast member of *Beau Geste* who didn't have to go to Arizona.

BRIAN: No, I didn't go—

MALTIN: —because all your scenes were at the beginning of the story—

BRIAN: Yes. They had a wonderful cast. Ronald Colman, Neil Hamilton, Ralph Forbes. And, of course, it was really a man's picture. I was lucky to be in it.

MALTIN: Great movie.

BRIAN: You know, they made it several times later. I think ours is pretty good in comparison. And I used to be asked up to Benita and Ronald Colman's. They had a charming place that went up to Summit. Usually mostly English [actors] but I was lucky to be included. I was so lucky, I had such good friends.

MALTIN: I haven't asked you about Victor Fleming.

BRIAN: Oh . . . one of my favorite directors. Wonderful man. Wonderful. Of course, we were all out on location for *The Virginian* together, when we went to Sonora. And this was one of the first pictures that they ever tried to do in sound, when they were getting this tremendous background noise. And he got some wonderful shots of the background for a western, which you should do, [and] you can't do it in a box. He was serious when he needed to be, but he had a funny sense of humor. I think the good directors at that time knew that our hours were so long and tedious, that they must give us time to play a bit, and to have our own jokes and things. And if they rode us too hard, you'd get a very stubborn cast. He was always ready for good things to happen, funny things to happen. And yet when he was serious, he was so good about what he did. I was terribly fond of him.

MALTIN: Would a good director like that fire you up? Inspire you . . . ?

BRIAN: He did.

MALTIN: What about William Wellman?

BRIAN: Well, you know, of course he was always known as a wild man.

MALTIN: Right. Wild Bill.

BRIAN: We were doing his prizefight story, and a couple of times, he was a little rough. But he would come and find me and sort of say, "You know, I didn't mean that . . ." He and I finally got along so well but in the beginning, he was always testing, to see how much I was gonna [take] before I would blow up or something. They were shooting down at, I guess it was the Second Street gymnasium, where they had all of the fighters. And he said, "You should come along. You're not in the scene, but come and see what the background is," 'cause I was supposed to be married to Dick. So I asked my brother to take me to the fights. And he says, "I don't want to do that. I know you; you're gonna get in the middle of this and they're going to have bloody noses and they're going to fall down and you'll want to go home." And I said, "Oh no, no, I really have to, 'cause Wellman had said he wanted me to come and see the fights." So very reluctantly, he took me to the fights. We walked in the door, here were all the fighters that I'd met down in the gymnasium, and they were standing and saying, "Hi, Mary!" [*Both laugh*] A big reception. Wellman and I became very, very good friends. But he sure tested me; he would poke and pull and do all kinds of things to get a certain reaction. And he'd get it.

MALTIN: Do you remember your first reaction to the idea of sound?

BRIAN: Well, I'll tell you: Buddy [Rogers] and Dick [Arlen] and our whole little gang, we were all terrified 'cause we kept saying, "Your voice doesn't sound like your voice." And they were going to make tests of us. And I remember Dick came back and he was jubilant and he said, "You know, it was fine, we can do it." And they gave me a play, at least it was a long dialogue from a play, and I learned it, with great trepidation. And I think John Cromwell, who had been on *The Virginian*, directed me. (He was a stage director; they got a lot of stage directors at that time, because they knew that they had dialogue and they were going to need extra help). And luckily, it turned out all right. But we were terrified.

MALTIN: Once you got past that test, was it still difficult to work in sound?

BRIAN: Oh, yes, because it was so much preparation before, and you must not speak close to the next dialogue that somebody else was doing; you know, they had to have that space. It really was a chore, because there was no easy way. And they had a big box that they sat in and looked out at you. [*Laughs*] No, it wasn't an easy time. You had to be adaptable.

MALTIN: Do you remember the microphone being hidden in flower vases or things like that?

BRIAN: Oh, yes. And the thing was that they didn't accommodate you with the microphone, you accommodated yourself to wherever it was. Had to sneak up to wherever it was and speak . . . It was awful. I guess it was such a novelty for the audience that they put up with all of that.

MALTIN: Did they ever make you take speech lessons, elocution or anything?

BRIAN: No. That was what I was saying. At Metro-Goldwyn, they always had classes and this and that. Paramount never did, they just put us in there and you sank or swam.

MALTIN: I remember reading a story about the terrible fire that burned

Mary and her pal (and Toluca Lake neighbor) Richard Arlen pitching horseshoes.

the first sound stages, and everybody had to work all night because they couldn't shoot with the surrounding noises during the day. Do you remember that?

BRIAN: Yes. And a lot of good film was lost. Some things we had to do over. Some things they never replaced. Yes, that was quite a catastrophe.

MALTIN: Do you remember working through the night at that time?

BRIAN: Do you know, it never seemed that bad at the time. I think about air conditioners; we think we can't live without them. But we worked with the same hot sun that we have today; there was no way of getting around it, so you did it and you never thought about it. Well, you thought about it but there was no solution to it. And it's amazing what you do and put up with, when there isn't any solution.

MALTIN: Now, you had no acting training.

BRIAN: No.

MALTIN: When talkies came in, you were working in some cases with trained stage actors like Fredric March. Were you intimidated at all by that?

BRIAN: I wasn't intimidated; I was impressed. There is a difference. Because he and Florence [Eldridge], when we did *The Royal Family* in New York, used to all go out to the theater and have dinner together, and it was a very nice relationship. And he didn't try to impress you or make you feel like you aren't one of the chosen few.

MALTIN: I love *The Royal Family.*

BRIAN: I thought it was a wonderful picture, whether it's too dated now or not.

MALTIN: No, I don't think so. If you have any knowledge of the Barrymores, it's just such great fun to watch.

BRIAN: It was great fun to do.

MALTIN: And you actually met Ethel Barrymore?

BRIAN: Oh, yes. She was interested to see who was going to play her, and she came out to the studio. The two of us eyed each other; she was nice.

MALTIN: And she seemed to have a good sense of humor about it?

BRIAN: Oh, yes. She wasn't indignant about it. I don't know how the other Barrymores felt about it, but Ethel Barrymore, I think, was not a prude.

MALTIN: And did you like George Cukor?

BRIAN: Oh, yes.

MALTIN: *The Royal Family* was one of his first films.

BRIAN: Yes. He had Cyril Gardner, who was one of the head editors at Paramount, with him [to deal with] all the technicalities. But I thought it was a good film.

MALTIN: Tell me about making *The Front Page*.

BRIAN: Now, that is one of my favorites, and I'm not talking about how it was received, and it was received very well. But you can't believe what it was like working on that picture. We rehearsed it like a stage play, for two weeks, before we even started shooting. And we started with Louis Wolheim [who had just starred for director Lewis Milestone in *All Quiet on the Western Front*] doing Adolphe Menjou's part, which sounds like the funniest switch that anybody could possibly make. But the thing was that we started about noon instead of early in the morning, because all of these characters that were playing the reporters were accustomed to working on the stage, and it was hard for them to get up early and be funny that time in the morning. So we started about noon, and broke for dinner. It was like a long table in the boarding house, and it was wonderful food. You were free to go out and eat on your own, if you wanted to, [but] nobody wanted to because the stories that went on with that cast of characters—everybody was trying to get in that last word. And then we worked until about midnight.

MALTIN: Wow.

BRIAN: But the thing was we knew what we were going to do 'cause we rehearsed. Some of the scenes that I wasn't in, Milestone would have

The four faux Barrymores: Henrietta Crosman, Fredric March, Mary, and Ina Claire in The Royal Family of Broadway *(1930).*

them call me and I said, "Are they doing that scene?" "No, they just thought you wanted to be in on this." And I did want to be in on it . . . [so] I would go over. Of course, Pat O'Brien was wonderful; I stood in for Eloise when he got his marriage license. But it was a switchover when we went from Wolheim to Menjou. And it was a wonderful switch.

MALTIN: Was that because Wolheim took ill?

BRIAN: Yes.

MALTIN: Do you remember how much you had to reshoot? Was it quite a lot?

BRIAN: Well, not too much, because it was kind of spasmodic; he had done some of the scenes. He was great in it; everybody thought he was wonderful. And yet when they went to Menjou, he was perfect for the part.

MALTIN: I don't think I've ever heard anybody talk as fast as Pat O'Brien does in that movie.

BRIAN: Well, this was the first time that they had allowed actors to overlap. That was a no-no. Also, censorship, as you know, at the end, when he picks up the phone and he says, "That S. O. B."

MALTIN: That was so clever, when the bell of the typewriter carriage covers up the word.

Mary with Pat O'Brien in The Front Page (1930).

BRIAN: Yes. And they got away with that.

MALTIN: That was produced by Howard Hughes, wasn't it?

BRIAN: Yes, and he used to come once in a while, but he always would be off the set, sort of peeking around. He was being very self-effacing. And he and Milestone would talk every once in a while, but he wasn't telling him how to do this.

MALTIN: Tell me about Lewis Milestone.

BRIAN: A darling man. Darling man. As a matter of fact, on my birthday he went down and got these three rings that had been in his family, and there were two diamond circlets and a sapphire, and I always wore them for good luck after that. I have them in the safety deposit box.

But he was a darling man. And knew how to keep up the tempo. He let people do the thing that they knew how to do: when you get a Walter Catlett and all of these people who were funny in their own right, and we were at such a fast pace, that they'd never been really allowed to do before. Because you could step on people's lines, 'cause he kept the pace up.

MALTIN: The only person who could talk as fast as Pat O'Brien was Lee Tracy, and you worked with him in *Blessed Event*.

BRIAN: He was fast. And of course, he was playing Walter Winchell and I was just his girl Friday. And when we finished the picture, we'd been invited to the President's Ball. And we were on the plane going back, and Florence Lake was with us; we were flying and we ran into this awful, awful weather. We were just tipped from one side to the other, and they said, "We can't get there, we're going to have to put down in Chicago." Which we did, and we missed the ball entirely. And the only time we could catch a plane was very, very early in the morning and we all came out and Lee Tracy looked at his watch and said, "They always told me that I was missing the best part of the day by hating to get up in the morning." He said, "I was always right—I hate it." But he was so glib and so fast, and he was fun to work with. Yes, I liked him.

[Author's Note: Mary Brian passed away in December 2002. I feel very fortunate to have known her.]

ART CORNER

These portraits of square-jawed Jack Holt and fresh-faced Janet Gaynor are reproduced from original artwork prepared for a Los Angeles newspaper in the early 1930s. The artist is Hy (Henry) Goode, and the paper was probably the *Herald-Express*. These are strictly representational pieces, but they do capture the two personalities quite well, and remind us of a time when newspapers used illustrations as much as photographs on their entertainment pages.

Those
CHARLIE CHAPLIN FEET

Words by
Edgar Leslie
Music by
Archie Gottler

"Those Charlie Chaplin Feet"
Featured by
BAILEY & COWAN
"The Banjoker and The Songster"

MAURICE ABRAHAMS MUSIC CO.
1570 BROADWAY
NEW YORK

H. Mathews.

MUSIC AND THE MOVIES

The Sounds of Silents

When Jennifer Lopez released her first recording, having established herself as a movie star, there was much ado about her crossing over from one facet of show business to another. Over the past decade, moviegoers (and film critics) who had no awareness of hip-hop have been obliged to familiarize themselves with such rap stars as Queen Latifah, LL Cool J, and Snoop Dogg as they pursued acting careers onscreen.

These are just the latest manifestations of a dynamic relationship that has existed between the movie world and the music business since the beginning of the twentieth century. Our popular culture has changed, the technology has been reinvented many times over, but the relationship remains as vital as ever.

In the earliest days of nickelodeons, beginning in 1895, illustrated song slides were very popular, representing what we might call today a multimedia experience. Pianist extraordinaire and musicologist Peter Mintun explains, "Although they were not moving pictures, there were some film stars from Fort Lee and New York City who made extra bucks posing for these (Norma Talmadge and J. Farrell MacDonald are two). There were rival song-slide makers in New York and Chicago, mass-producing around thirteen sequential slides per song, which were projected while a 'live' singer and accompanist introduced the song to the audience. The objective was to give the projectionist time to prepare the next film, and sell sheet music. Trade magazines, such as the earliest moving picture publications, even gave reviews to the slides! The makers of the slides placed ads in the magazines advertising what their latest songs were.

"Some singers made a living going from nickelodeon to nickelodeon, with their rented slides. Generally, the first slide was similar to the sheet music cover, and the last slide had all the lyrics to the song. The singer would encourage the audience by saying, 'Now, all join in on the chorus!'"

Incidentally, one young man who earned spare change by singing along with these slides in Atlanta, Georgia was Oliver Hardy.

Music was an integral part of the American home at this time, with the parlor piano occupying roughly the same position of importance that video-game consoles enjoy today. The burgeoning piano population created a gigantic sheet music industry; just as today's hit songs and music videos have a finite shelf life, there was a constant demand for new and novel songs customers could purchase at the local five-and-dime store and play at home.

"Between World Wars I and II sheet music sold far better than records," says Mintun. "It was cheaper, and the idea back then (today we would say concept) was that everybody in your household, plus the relatives and neighbors, could benefit from having this sheet music passed from house to house, porch to porch, canoe to canoe. As my old friend Edna Fischer (composer of the 1929 song 'Some Day Soon') used to say—and she was born in 1903—'We didn't have "hit records" in those days. We had hit songs!'"

In their tireless efforts to produce songs with wide and novel appeal, the earliest denizens of Tin Pan Alley seized on the latest trends and fads. Singer and music scholar John Leifert has found a song from 1910 called "At the Ten-Cent Picture Show." Two tunes from 1912 were inspired, superficially at least, by the phenomenon of movies: "She's Only a Moving Picture" by C. E. Dittmann is a moralistic ballad about a woman who forsook true love for money, leaving beauty on the surface (like a movie star, we presume) but nothing inside: "She's only a moving picture, still beautiful to see/ Her heart was sold for shining gold, she longs but to be free . . ./ She's only a moving picture, for her heart is cold and dead."

"Mister Moving Picture Man" by George R. Moriarty and J. R. Shannon offers a more wistful, metaphoric ode to motion pictures: "Oh Mister moving picture man/ I've heard about your great big plan/ You're going to show the angels in the skies so blue/ If that's so, my Mamma's in the picture too."

Obviously, these songs had little if anything to do with movies per se, but before long the changing patterns of American life were reflected in lyrics like this one for "They're All Going into the Movies" by Thomas S. Allen, billed as the "reel" song hit of the country when it was published in 1914. Here's the verse: "A few years ago there was no such a show as the movies/ But now it's not so for the best people go to the movies/ It used to be fifty and seventy-five and though there is no one to blame, the old moving picture is now quite a fixture and that's where the nickel got fame."

This is the chorus: "They're all going into the movies, how they rush for that five-cent seat/ How they fall for that picture sheet/ First the leading man woos her, then the villain pursues her/ They're all going in to the moving picture show."

Since even the "best" people were going to the movies in the teens, clever songwriters identified social trends that rang a familiar chord with sheet-music buyers. In 1919, Ernest Dunbar and Leon Rundell wrote "Meet Me at the Movies Dear" in which a plaintive would-be Romeo sings, "Every time I call, your father meets me in the hall and we don't get a chance to love at all/ So won't you meet me at the movies dearie, I'll be waiting there for you/ I will hold your hand and we can spoon to beat the band, just like the movie actors do . . . / I would rather go where the lights are always low, so meet me at the movies dear."

The same sentiment was expressed in an even snappier number, "Take Your Girlie to the Movies (If You Can't Make Love at Home)" by Edgar Leslie, Bert Kalmar, and Pete Wendling. Among its messages: "There's no little brother there who always squeals/ You can say an awful lot in seven reels," and "Tho' she's just a simple little ribbon clerk/ Close your eyes and think you're kissing Billie Burke!" There's even a touch of topical (but dark) humor in the line, "Pick a cozy corner where it's nice and dark/ Don't catch influenza kissing in the park," although it was surely wishful thinking that a movie theater was safer from infection than a public park!

Love and romance were key ingredients in many hit songs, and here, particularly, the growing cultural influence of movies could be felt. "Hank" Hancock and Tom McNamara penned a song in 1915 called

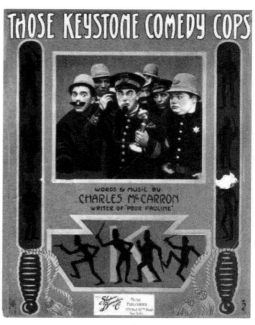

Thousands of pieces of sheet music were published in the 1930s for songs that didn't become hits from films that didn't become classics . . . but as these examples show, they're still fun to look at.

"I Want to Be Loved Like the Girls on the Film." A year later Roger Lewis and Ernie Erdman wrote a song that supposedly expressed a young woman's yearning for "The Moving Picture Hero of My Heart," but this one was much more specific than its predecessor:

"You've got a look like Henry Walthall in your eyes, You're so romantic/ You make me think of Francis Bushman by your size, You're so gigantic/ You've got a Charlie Chaplin smile, that keeps me happy all the while/ You've got the strength of Broncho (sic) Billy in your arm, When you embrace me/ And like a Keystone Cop you'll save me from all harm."

One major player not mentioned in that song turned up in another, similar song published four years later, "I Want a Caveman (Like William Hart, the Movie Star)" by composer-publishers Kendis and Brockman.

Not only did those stars appear in the lyrics; their pictures appeared on the cover. Music publishers had quickly realized that featuring famous faces on their sheets would enhance their sales appeal, whether or not the stars had anything to do with the songs. (John Bunny and Mary Pickford appeared—without identification—on the covers of two low-priced folios called *Album of Photo-Play Music* in 1914, even though none of the generic themes inside had any direct relation to their films.)

The first movie celebrity to become a star of sheet music was Pearl White, the cliffhanger queen who became a household name in the 1914 serials *The Perils of Pauline* and *The Exploits of Elaine*. Wasting no time, Charles McCarron and Raymond Walker wrote a paean to Miss White entitled "Poor Pauline," which enjoyed genuine if fleeting success in 1914: "Poor Pauline, I pity poor Pauline/ One night she's drifting out to sea/ Then they tie her to a tree/ I wonder what the end will be." Naturally, the sheet music was adorned with an eye-catching photo of the star.

Nothing succeeds like success, so later that year Charles Ebert and Howard Wesley wrote "Elaine My Moving Picture Queen." This one also featured a photo of White on the cover, with a facsimile autograph, and a legend that would adorn scores of other music sheets for years to come: "Dedicated to Pearl White."

Who could blame a sheet-music customer for being confused when yet another song, the aforementioned "They're All Going into the Movies" had a picture of the star on the cover, inscribed, "My Official Song—Pearl White."

This flurry of movie-generated music stirred the competitive juices of both publishers and song-smiths. In 1915, Edgar Leslie and Archie Gottler scored a hit with "Those Charlie Chaplin Feet," its cover featuring the man who had soared to world-wide popularity in just one year's time, as well as the vaudeville duo that introduced the song, "Bailey & Cowan, The Banjoker and The Songster." The lyrics were jaunty and typical of this now-familiar genre: "There's a funny man I know/ Who gets all the people's dough/ He works in a movie show/ Mister Charlie Chaplin . . . / Tips his hat to every dog and cat/ And when he starts to hop with one foot up/ You'll tumble from your seat."

Chaplin chronicler Gerald McDonald estimated that at least twenty songs were written about the comedian that year alone, including Jerome Kern and Schuylar Greene's "That Chaplin Walk," which appeared in the Broadway musical *Nobody Home*.

But Chaplin had the last laugh when one year later he formed the Charlie Chaplin Music Publishing Co., headquartered at Blanchard Hall in Los Angeles. Its symbol was a three-leaf clover with a C on each leaf. The venture was more than a mere investment for Chaplin; it was an outlet for him to pursue his musical ambitions. Each piece of sheet music featured the star's face as few fans would have recognized it, out of character and makeup; he was not the Little Tramp, but rather the composer and lyricist of "There's Always One You Can't Forget," described as a "slow waltz," and "Oh! That Cello," the cover of which depicted him playing his favorite instrument with an intensely serious expression on his face. There is no record of how successful Chaplin was in this endeavor,

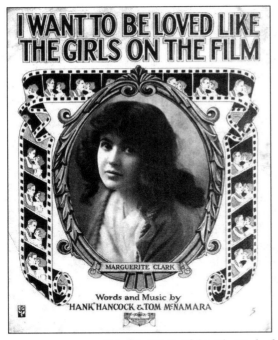

I WANT TO BE LOVED LIKE THE GIRLS ON THE FILM

MARGUERITE CLARK

Words and Music by
HANK HANCOCK & TOM McNAMARA

but the lyrics to "Oh! That Cello" indicate that he was wise not to abandon his screen career ("I love that fellow/ Who plays that Cello/ His Music so appealing/ Into my heart come stealing . . . / Oh! Memories that burn and pain/ Play that Cello for me once again").

Soon movie fans could see their favorite stars at any sheet-music store display. The songs were "respectfully dedicated to" or "inspired by" everyone from Roscoe "Fatty" Arbuckle and Mabel Normand to Douglas Fairbanks and Jackie Coogan. Some were actually derived from film scores, like the instrumental "Natu-Rich" from Cecil B. DeMille's pioneering feature *The Squaw Man* in 1914 or the published themes from D. W. Griffith's *The Birth of a Nation* one year later.

Records were also making inroads into the movie world. In 1925 the Pathé company sent out ingenious mini-records to promote their serial *The Green Archer*, inviting patrons to "hear Pathé's famous serial stars talk to you." At a time when moviegoers were completely unfamiliar with the stars' voices, this must have been exciting.

An entrepreneurial New Yorker named Robert B. "Pat" Wheelan issued a series of Talk-O-Photo discs, with autographed portraits of the stars printed on one side and a recitation embedded in wax on the other. Again, imagine the thrill (or possible disappointment) of hearing a voice one had only imagined before. The roster of stars included Gloria Swanson, Lew Cody, Mary Miles Minter, Bert Lytell, H. B. Warner, and Clara Kimball Young. (When film and theater historian Miles Kreuger happened upon these discs in the early 1960s, he whimsically looked up Wheelan's name in the Manhattan telephone directory and found him still alive and well. The onetime record producer revealed that the operation was actually intended to promote his photography studio.)

In the 1920s, the link between movies and music grew closer. "Oh Susanna" was a folk song in the public domain, but a 1923 piece of sheet music proclaimed, "as sung in *The Covered Wagon*," giving that epic western a nice piece of publicity. Movie studios recognized the promotional value of sheet music—much as movie marketers do today with music videos—and arranged for songs to be specially written, with the film's title and star featured as prominently as the name of the actual song on the front cover. Thus, there was "Dear Old Daddy Long Legs" from Mary Pickford's *Daddy Long Legs*, "Smilin' Through" from the Norma Talmadge movie of the same name, "Freshie" from Harold Lloyd's *The Freshman*, "Song of the Volga Boatmen" from Cecil B. DeMille's *The Volga Boatmen*, and scores of others. Hollywood theater impresario Sid Grauman was credited for the lyrics (and Victor Schertzinger the music) for "Just an Old Love Song," the theme from Douglas Fairbanks's *Robin Hood*. There was

even a song connected to Buster Keaton's *Go West* called "She Doesn't," with words by Walter Winchell and music by Jimmy Durante and Chick Endor about the benefits of having a girlfriend who's a cow!

Ironically, the most celebrated theme from a silent film enjoyed an entirely new life when Joseph Carl Breil and Clarence Lucas's "The Perfect Song" from *The Birth of a Nation* became the theme for the hugely popular radio (and later television) show *Amos 'n Andy*.

The final step came in the late 1920s when, in a supreme bit of irony, silent movies spawned a series of bona fide hit songs. This was not unprecedented—the theme for Mabel Normand's 1918 comedy feature *Mickey* was quite popular, and is still sung by barbershop quartets today—but the idea really caught on in the waning days of silents. "Charmaine" was written as a theme for Dolores del Rio's character in the smash hit *What Price Glory* (1926) by Lew Pollack and one of the deans of silent-movie music, Erno Rapee, and went on to become a standard. By the time the same duo wrote "Diane" for Janet Gaynor's *Seventh Heaven* a year later, audiences heard the song on a synchronized

Movietone soundtrack; it, too became a hit, as did "Jeanine, I Dream of Lilac Time," introduced in 1928's aviation saga *Lilac Time*. Even in theaters that weren't yet wired for sound, the strains of those melodies were played by the pianists, organists, and orchestras that accompanied the silent features.

Another enduringly popular instrumental, "Jealousy," was written and published in Denmark by Jakob Gade as a love theme for Fairbanks's *Don Q Son of Zorro* (1925). As Rodney Sauer, silent-film music scholar and guiding force of the Mont Alto Motion Picture Orchestra, points out, "It was immediately embraced by salon and dance orchestras, picked up by the Boston Pops, lyrics were added in the 1950s, and it has entered the consciousness of the world as perhaps one of the most recognizable tango melodies."

The coming of sound opened a new chapter in the saga of movies and music . . . while radio, seen at first as a threat to theater attendance, became instead the best publicity vehicle for movies (and movie songs) ever invented.

To hear one of the best of all silent-movie songs, listen to Howard Johnson and Joseph Santly's 1920 composition "At the Moving Picture

Ball" as sung by Maurice Burkhart. In addition to clever rhymes about movie stars ("Douglas Fairbanks shimmied on one hand, like an acrobat/ Mary Pickford did her toe dance grand, and/ Charlie Chaplin with his feet, stepped all over poor Blanche Sweet/ Dancing at that moving picture ball") the song drops the names of such producers as Thomas Ince, Jesse Lasky, and William Fox. But the best couplet of all is "Every girl, a handsome looker, had a dance with Mr. Zukor."

I Love to Sínga

The marriage of movies and music was consummated in the late 1920s with the arrival of sound. Talkies made it possible for musical entertainers to reach a far greater audience with a single filmed performance than they could in a year of trouping from one town to another. When Warner Bros. needed stars to appear in its earliest Vitaphone short subjects, it looked no further than the rosters of acts headlining Broadway shows, vaudeville theaters, and opera stages.

By 1929, Paramount and MGM had joined Warners in recruiting well-known performers for their talkie shorts, including many who were top-selling recording artists: Ruth Etting; Rudy Vallee; Eddie Cantor; Cliff "Ukulele Ike" Edwards (shown on previous page); Van and Schenck; Billy Jones and Ernie Hare (The Happiness Boys); Eddie Peabody; Roy Smeck; and the bands of Ben Bernie, Red Nichols, and Ben Pollack. Literally hundreds more big names and small-timers committed their acts (or their latest recordings) to film in this brief boom period.

The Victor Talking Machine Company even established a film studio for a short time in a church adjacent to its Camden, New Jersey recording complex. There, a series of one-reel shorts was filmed for release by Columbia Pictures in the 1929–'30 season under the umbrella title Columbia Victor Gems. Most of these films are lost, but one important title has turned up in recent years: *Jimmie Rodgers, The Singing Brakeman*, part of the Yazoo compilation "Times Ain't Like They Used to Be," now available on DVD.

As in the silent era, songwriters wasted no time chronicling the phenomenon of sound in such topical tunes as "I Can't Sleep in the Movies Any More" (1928); "My Brother Makes the Noises for the Talkies" (1929); "Since Vitaphone Put Talkies on the Screen" (1929); and best of all, "Ever Since the Movies Learned to Talk" (1928), by Walter O'Keefe, Bobby Dolan, and James Cavanaugh, which Eddie Cantor interpolated into the score of his Broadway hit *Whoopee*.

Just as songs of the teens reflected public sentiment during the nickelodeon era and the birth of the movies, this ditty managed to capture Hollywood's tumultuous transition to talkies, and moviegoers' response, with such lyrics as:

> *When the hero sings "Asleep in the Deep"/ He sounds just like Little Bo Peep/ Ever Since the Movies Learned to Talk . . .*
>
> *And when Emil Jannings opens his mouth/ You'd swear he was raised in the south/ Ever Since the Movies Learned to Talk.*
>
> *When a dark-eyed dame with a foreign name/ Starts to talk in doing a scene/ We all know she's from Buffalo/ and her Christian name is Levine . . .*
>
> *Tho' the hero's big still ev'ryone knows/ He makes ev'ry stitch of his clothes/ Ever Since the Movies Learned to Talk.*

References to talkies abound in songs of the period. In "Would You Like to Take a Walk?" Mort Dixon and Billy Rose wrote, "Ain't you tired of the talkies?/ I prefer the walkies." DeSylva, Brown, and Henderson had a bona fide hit with the sweet ballad "If I Had a Talking Picture of You," warbled by Janet Gaynor in the delightful 1929 Fox musical *Sunnyside Up.*

Gaynor was just one of many stars of dubious musical ability who suddenly found themselves thrust into all-talking, all-singing, all-dancing extravaganzas, many of which were deadly. For every Cliff Edwards (who introduced moviegoers to "Singin' in the Rain" in *The Hollywood Revue of 1929*) there was at least one silent-film star trying to put over a musical number of considerably lesser quality. For every *Sunnyside Up* there was a lumbering all-star revue that every studio felt impelled to provide, to show the world that its stars were ready and willing to take the plunge into talkies. (British comedienne and mimic Florence Desmond skewered several Hollywood stars in her famous 1933 record, "Hollywood Party," with a particularly funny send-up of Janet Gaynor.)

Late in life Walter Pidgeon recalled in a delicious, if possibly apocryphal, story that one theater owner put a notice on the poster for the actor's then-current film, "Walter Pidgeon positively does not sing in this picture."

No wonder the musical boom went bust within a year's time. Universal took a bath with its outlandishly expensive 1930 musical *King of Jazz,* featuring Paul Whiteman, and MGM put its ambitious Technicolor feature *The March of Time* on the shelf. Musical feature films were, for all intents and purposes, dead, and remained so for several years.

But music was still alive and well in the short-subject departments of the major studios. E. Y. Harburg wrote lyrics for such Paramount one-reelers as *Office Blues* (1930) with Ginger Rogers, which contains the unique couplet "I'm so cynical/ you're rabbinical." Later in the 1930s, Sammy Cahn and Saul Chaplin were part of the Vitaphone short-subject staff in Brooklyn. Composers and lyricists were even spotlighted on camera in a number of shorts singing and playing (or at least introducing) their hit songs, including Rodgers and Hart, Nacio Herb Brown and Arthur Freed, Johnny Green, Sammy Fain, and Mack Gordon and Harry Revel. Even a less glorified Tin Pan Alley tunesmith like the prolific Cliff Friend had a one-reeler all to himself.

Warner Bros. was motivated to finance producer Leon Schlesinger's Merrie Melodies cartoons because every one featured a song owned by one of the studio's giant music publishing firms.

Cartoon producer Max Fleischer went one step further, commissioning original songs for many of his Betty Boop, Popeye, and Color Classics cartoons. House tunesmiths Sammy Timberg and

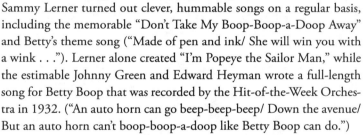

Sammy Lerner turned out clever, hummable songs on a regular basis, including the memorable "Don't Take My Boop-Boop-a-Doop Away" and Betty's theme song ("Made of pen and ink/ She will win you with a wink . . ."). Lerner alone created "I'm Popeye the Sailor Man," while the estimable Johnny Green and Edward Heyman wrote a full-length song for Betty Boop that was recorded by the Hit-of-the-Week Orchestra in 1932. ("An auto horn can go beep-beep-beep/ Down the avenue/ But an auto horn can't boop-boop-a-doop like Betty Boop can do.")

As if the coming of sound and the impact of the Depression weren't enough to deal with, Hollywood faced another daunting challenge at this time: competing with the free entertainment now being provided by radio. Radio's popularity soared in the mid-1920s, and reached a peak with the arrival of *Amos 'n Andy* in 1929. It was said that one could walk along a street in any town and follow their nightly broadcast coming through every household window. Some theaters even piped the show through their speaker system, in a desperate attempt to keep moviegoers from staying home.

Not every studio demonized radio as a dreaded competitor. Warner Bros., for instance, worked both sides of the street. Warner films of the early

1930s carried a slogan in their opening credits that read, "Brunswick Radios used exclusively," plugging another subsidiary of WB. (In the 1931 Barbara Stanwyck movie *Illicit* there's even a shot of Barbara Stanwyck turning on a radio console, with a lingering closeup of the Brunswick logo!) Another studio, the newly formed RKO Radio Pictures, was a consolidation of several interests, including the Radio Corporation of America, which owned NBC. It was no coincidence that the first radio personalities to warrant their own feature-film showcase were NBC's *Amos 'n Andy*, who starred in the 1930 film *Check and Double Check* for RKO.

By the mid-1930s, however, Hollywood began to see that radio could be a partner as much as a competitor. When films like *Love Me Tonight* and *42nd Street* resuscitated the musical genre in 1932, songwriters found themselves busier than ever, and radio helped promote their tunes—as well as the films in which they were introduced. This in turn promoted sheet music. Record sales took a nosedive during the depths of the Depression, but sheet music was still affordable at the neighborhood five-and-dime, and sheet music covers were essentially mini-posters that promoted the movies (with four or six separate songs from each

This shot from the 1929 Vitaphone short "The Jazz Rehearsal" reveals an orchestra playing "live" on the set, a practice limited to the early-talkie era.

score multiplying those images on display). This was synergy long before the word was coined.

It's astonishing how many movie-generated songs were published during this period. Someone even thought it was worthwhile to issue Max Steiner's music cue "King Kong March," heard in the classic movie as eager New Yorkers make their way into the auditorium to see the *Eighth Wonder of the World*. And as in the silent era, no one in the movie or the music business disparaged the potential of a tie-in song for a dramatic film. Hence "Farewell to Arms," which displayed a picture of Gary Cooper and Helen Hayes on its sheet-music cover, was "dedicated" to the film of the same name, though it was never heard on the soundtrack. And if you find an original 78 rpm pressing of the popular 1937 song "Gone with the Wind," you'll see that it's "dedicated to the film," even though the movie wouldn't be released for another two years.

(With all this activity, it's equally puzzling why some movie songs were never published. Musicologist and performer Peter Mintun has recorded Harry Warren's "Love Theme" from *42nd Street*, but amateur pianists never had that opportunity in 1933. Sam Coslow and Arthur Johnston wrote a snappy song for the 1932 Nancy Carroll movie *Hot Saturday* called "I'm Burning for You," but it was never issued as sheet music; nor was a funny throwaway number introduced by Jack Oakie in *Sitting Pretty* and addressed to Thelma Todd: "Blond, Blasé, and Beautiful.")

A separate category might have to be made for the songs introduced by comedian Charley Chase in his Hal Roach two-reelers of the 1930s. Chase loved to sing, and he introduced dozens of ditties in his Hal Roach two-reel comedies of the 1930s. Novelty songs like "Aunty's Got Ants in Her Pantry," and "Oh, Desdemona!" never had a life outside of those shorts; only one was published, in 1931, the peppy tune "Smile (When the Raindrops Fall)."

Yet producer Hal Roach was way ahead of the major studios when it came to background music. A parade of jaunty, unforgettable themes were played over and over again in the Laurel and Hardy, Our Gang, and Charley Chase shorts from 1930 onward, adding zest and humor to these films.

The Roach music was a source of frustration to fans for decades. Who wrote those memorable themes, and why were they never issued commercially on records? T. Marvin Hatley, composer of Laurel and Hardy's theme, "The Cuckoo Song" (also known as "Ku-Ku" and "Dance of the Cuckoos") and "Honolulu Baby" from *Sons of the Desert*, was feted many times by the Sons of the Desert in Los Angeles, but he wasn't the man responsible for most of that early 1930s music. And how did Hal Roach have the foresight to fill his modest comedy shorts with wall-to-wall music years before the Big Boys of Hollywood realized how much scoring could enhance their feature films?

Hal Roach historian Richard W. Bann explains that the producer used his experience in silent films to point the way. "Audiences were accustomed to hearing music performed live in movie theaters during the silent era, so there was never a question of should the comedies have music or not. Roach went to so many previews that he knew sometimes the live theater accompaniment wasn't up to the standard he wanted. He liked the idea that now he would be able to control both the video and audio components of his films' presentation.

"Roach, who could play several musical instruments, prided himself on having music and sound in his pictures before MGM did. He never hesitated on getting sound, and went right after it as soon as he could, as soon as it was practical, as soon as the technical aspects had been conquered. But his real genius was in subverting sound to the visual style of comedies he was making. Sound was intended only as an adjunct to his visual comedy style, not as a substitute for any part of it. Even when talking pictures came in he tried to tell his people he didn't want them emphasizing sound effects instead of visual gags, the way others were doing.

"The day after he saw *The Jazz Singer*, Roach did his own study and came to the conclusion that the Victor Company 'had the best sound.' In 1928, as soon as he made his deal with Victor to add sound to his pictures, he sent his top editor, Dick Currier, back East to Camden, New Jersey to select stock music from the library held by Victor. When RCA became involved, they contributed the services of LeRoy Shield, who supervised the NBC Orchestra in Chicago, which I believe happened at the outset of the 1930–31 release season. Shield was never an employee of Hal Roach Studios, but came out whenever Roach sent for him to write and record cues to be used as incidental background music to score the various series. Roach always held Shield in high regard."

So do all of us who love these comedies. In the 1980s, bandleader and musicologist Vince Giordano started playing medleys of Hal Roach music with his Nighthawks band, to the delight of listeners who grew up with Laurel and Hardy and *The Little Rascals* on television. Then a Dutch film buff named Piet Schreuders commissioned a multi-CD project involving the notation of all available Hal Roach cues, and matching the instrumentation exactly. These discs, by the Beau Hunks band, have been a source of joy for film buffs around the world.

By 1934, it was evident to the Academy of Motion Picture Arts and Sciences that a category for Best Song was overdue. As part of the seventh annual ceremony, the Academy named "The Continental" from *The Gay Divorcee* the first recipient of the Best Music (Song) award, over

two competitors: "Carioca" from *Flying Down to Rio* and "Love in Bloom" from *She Loves Me Not*. Astaire-Rogers films dominated the field for the first few years; MGM also had two nominated songs in 1936 ("Did I Remember" from *Suzy*, and "I've Got You Under My Skin" from *Born to Dance*) and that, apparently, was the last straw for rival studios. In 1937, the Academy changed its rules and requested each company to submit one song, and one song only, for Oscar consideration. This must have caused great consternation at Paramount and Fox, but it opened the door for undistinguished, and unmemorable songs from Hal Roach's *Merrily We Live* and Walter Wanger's *Vogues of 1938* to be nominated alongside the work of Irving Berlin (who worked for two different studios that year, and thus had two songs in the running, "Change Partners" from RKO's *Carefree* and "Now It Can Be Told" from 20th Century Fox's *Alexander's Ragtime Band*). There were five nominees in 1937, ten in 1938, four in 1939, nine in 1940, and so on. After thirteen nominated songs made the cut in 1945, the Academy decided to limit the candidates to five every year, based solely on merit . . . and not a moment too soon.

If the great movie songs of the 1930s and 40s had only been heard on screen, they might not have burrowed their way into the public consciousness. It was their continual performance on radio that cemented the popularity of so many tunes that are now considered standards. *Billboard* magazine kept track of airplay on a weekly basis, at a time when all music heard on network shows (and on many local stations) was live, not recorded. Instead of hearing the same record dozens of times, as one does with a hit nowadays, listeners encountered the song in dozens of different renditions, by vocalists, choral groups, pianists, and orchestras.

No wonder the whole country was practically whistling "Please" or "A Fine Romance" in unison. (Or even, for that matter, "I Love to Singa," which Al Jolson introduced in *The Singing Kid*, and Tex Avery immortalized in a Warner Bros. cartoon.) One thing is certain: movies would have been the poorer without the wonderful songs they brought to life in the 1930s and forties, and so would we.

Hollywood on the Record

Stars of the silent era often appeared on sheet music covers, but hardly any made commercial recordings; those few that did, like William S. Hart, mostly performed recitations.

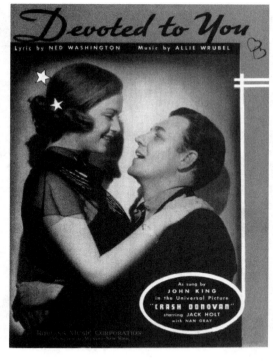

Imagine how surprised audiences must have been to learn, in the earliest days of talkies, that some of their favorite stars had good singing voices, including: Gloria Swanson, who introduced "Love (Your Spell Is Everywhere)" in her 1929 debut talkie *The Trespasser*, directed by the song's co-writer, Edmund Goulding; Pola Negri, who introduced the hit song "Paradise" in her 1932 vehicle *A Woman Commands*; and Bebe Daniels, whose first sound film was the Ziegfeld musical *Rio Rita*, and who introduced "You're Getting to Be a Habit with Me" in the 1933 classic *42nd Street*.

But it was a newcomer to Hollywood, Al Jolson, who ushered in the talkie era, and became the first of many stars, like Bing Crosby and Maurice Chevalier, to enjoy simultaneous success in movies and on records. In fact, the titles of many of Crosby's early two-reel comedies (*One More Chance, Please, Just an Echo*) were taken from his hit records, a choice early example of show-business synergy.

So great was the appeal of records as home entertainment that one didn't even have

Inside the record label:

★ ★ ★ ★ ★
Five Great Stars
NOW AVAILABLE
On Special Recordings Made Exclusively For
FAMOUS RECORD CO., OF NEW YORK, N. Y.

★ (1) FRANCHOT TONE—Popular, romantic Hollywood idol brings you the grandeur,
the stirring message of the famous "England, My England" hit from his motion picture, "Lives of a Bengal Lancer."

★ (2) LUISE RAINER—The wistful and
charming star of many great motion pictures records the tender pathos of her
great performance as Anna Held in the
picture, "The Great Ziegfeld."

★ (3) JOHN BARRYMORE—The famous
actor of stage, screen and radio is at his
very best in his own stirring version of the
famous "Hamlet" soliloquy.

★ (4) ILKA CHASE—One of the great
comediennes of our time records an all
time laugh and fun in her uproarious version of "The Picnic."

★ (5) JOE E. BROWN—You'll howl at the
performance of old big mouth as he relates
the laugh-laden adventures of the cat and
the drunken mouse.

Like this recording, each of the five new Famous Film Star Records is a complete special performance in itself, with an introduction by the famous radio
announcer, Del Sharbut, and appropriate incidental music. Each record has on
it a beautiful, autographed picture of its star. Send $1.00 for any three to

FAMOUS RECORD CO.
Box 3246, Madison Sq. Station
New York, N. Y.

Manufactured by R. C. A. Manufacturing Co., Inc., Camden, N. J., U.S.A.
Pat. Pending, The Talking Book Corporation of America, Inc.
New York, N. Y., U. S. A.

Labels on discs: ILKA CHASE IN THE PICNIC; JOE E. BROWN "MOUSIE"; LUISE RAINER AS ANNA HELD FROM THE GREAT ZIEGFELD; FRANCHOT TONE SAYING "ENGLAND MY ENGLAND" FROM LIVES OF A BENGAL LANCER

More Famous Wax: A few of the many records Famous Record Co. produced.

to sing to appear on "wax." A novelty outfit called Famous Record Co. hired John Barrymore to perform the soliloquy from *Hamlet* for one of its picture discs, some years after he played the role on Broadway.

The concept of soundtrack albums took considerably more time to establish itself in this country. Walt Disney was a pioneer in this field, as Victor's set of 78 rpm records of the songs from *Snow White and the Seven Dwarfs* may technically qualify as the first movie "soundtrack" to be marketed to the public, in 1938. (Decca released its own *Snow White* album which bore no relation to the Disney soundtrack, and did the same for *Pinocchio* two years later, but for that set they were able to hire Cliff Edwards to recreate his role as Jiminy Cricket.)

The *Snow White* album was followed a year later by a popular four-disc set of songs from *The Wizard of Oz* featuring Judy Garland and the Ken Darby Singers, but this was newly recorded, and not taken from the actual movie soundtrack. And again, this was a collection of tunes with no instrumental music from Herbert Stothart's background score.

Many classic films of the 1930s—including *Oz, Gone with the Wind*, and Charlie Chaplin's *City Lights and Modern Times*—wouldn't receive proper, full-length soundtrack treatment until many years later.

While some composers of background music began to receive public recognition in the 1930s, that didn't necessarily translate to the recording field. Bing Crosby had a hit record of Alfred Newman's "The Moon of Manakoora" from *The Hurricane* (1937), for example, but that was a song (with lyrics by Paramount studio work-horse Frank Loesser), not an instrumental. (Incidentally, Newman had written the melody as a recurring theme for Douglas Fairbanks's *Mr. Robinson Crusoe* five years earlier.)

No composer was introduced to the American audience with greater fanfare than Erich Wolfgang Korngold. He was even featured in the elaborate promotional trailer for *A Midsummer Night's Dream* (1935) along with the man responsible for bringing him to Hollywood, the eminent director Max Reinhardt. Three years later, Korngold's magnificent score for *The Adventures of Robin Hood* was previewed on a special half-hour NBC radio network program hosted by Basil Rathbone. But fans still couldn't purchase the music on disc.

Sabu records his narration for the ground-breaking album of music from The Jungle Book (1942). Drapes are being used as sound baffling.

It was another European émigré who would be the first to have his music sold in 78 rpm gatefold-album form. Having followed his cinematic mentor Alexander Korda to Hollywood from London, Miklós Rózsa prepared a special version of his score for *Jungle Book* (1942) with the Victor Symphony Orchestra, featuring narration by the movie's endearing star, Sabu. The liner notes on the twelve-inch album (featuring three discs) declare, "Those who listen may plainly hear the chuckle of the bear (as interpreted by the bassoon), the trumpeting of the elephant tribe (through the trombone passages), and the merry senseless chatter of the monkey people as the orchestra ensemble breaks into shafts of glittering melody. So descriptive is the music that instruments clearly assume the character of beast, mood, or environment. Consequently, throughout the entire score, the music is as clearly identifiable as a painted picture."

A year later, multi-disc sets of background music from *For Whom the Bell Tolls* by Victor Young and *The Song of Bernadette* by Alfred Newman further established the concept of the soundtrack album. (There was also a set featuring Vicente Gomez playing his Spanish guitar themes from 1941's *Blood and Sand*, a less conventional, but still notable, early example of a recorded film score.)

In 1945, Miklós Rózsa again made history when his haunting, evocative score for Alfred Hitchcock's *Spellbound* was released on ARA Records, with liner notes that put each theme into its dramatic context, even explaining the use of the Theremin, "that fascinating electronic instrument played by hand motions toward and away from a metal rod. This is the first time that a Theremin has been used in a motion picture score supported by a full orchestra."

"That was a turning point," recalls film music historian Miles Kreuger. "It was an album you had to have." The music from *Spellbound* enjoyed great popularity; in what may have marked another first, its themes were even published as a piano-solo.

In retrospect, the most unusual aspect of the *Spellbound* recording may be its enthusiastic endorsement by Hitchcock. In later years the director was said to have disliked the score, but on the inside cover of the 78 rpm album he wrote, "The growing importance of music in motion pictures . . . cannot be overestimated, for through the medium of sound, the intelligent composer has a device by means of which he can actually create within the hearer some of the emotion visible on the screen. I believe that those who see *Spellbound* will agree that Miklós Rózsa has composed a score which utilizes the medium of auditory appeal to an extraordinarily high degree of effectiveness."

The success of Rózsa's album may have been responsible for changing the course of the entire record business in America, for in 1947 a number of albums of dramatic-film scores were issued: Dimitri Tiomkin's *Duel in the Sun* (performed not by the composer but by Arthur Fiedler and the Boston Pops), David Raksin's *Forever Amber*, Alfred Newman's *Captain from Castile*, Victor Young's *Golden Earrings*, and Rózsa's *The Red House*. In 1947, MGM decided to launch its own record label with a tie-in album for its all-star musical *Till the Clouds Roll By*, "recorded directly from the soundtrack of the MGM Production," a designation applied to many subsequent releases, including Miklós Rózsa's two-disc recording of his music from *Madame Bovary* in 1949.

SPELLBOUND CONCERTO

PIANO SOLO

COMPOSED BY
MIKLOS ROZSA

For Mrs. Marian Dealers with many thanks and best wishes
Miklos Rozsa
1947

from the
ACADEMY AWARD WINNING SCORE
of the
SELZNICK INTERNATIONAL PICTURE

SPELLBOUND

directed by
ALFRED HITCHCOCK

produced by
DAVID O. SELZNICK

COMPLETE $1.00
THEME   .60

CHAPPELL
& CO., INC.
RKO BUILDING
ROCKEFELLER
CENTER, N.Y.

Although too-seldom mentioned in the same breath as Rózsa or New-man today, Victor Young had name recognition as a bandleader, composer ("Sweet Sue"), and radio and recording artist long before he joined the Paramount Pictures staff in the mid-1930s and became a prolific composer and conductor of movie scores. A gifted purveyor of melodies, he dominated the 1940s in the field of movie tie-in and title songs with such hits as "Stella by Starlight" (from *The Uninvited*), "Love Letters," "My Foolish Heart," "The Night Has a Thousand Eyes," "Golden Earrings," and "Delilah" (from *Samson and Delilah*), most of which went on to become standards and favorites of jazz musicians. He earned twenty-two Academy Award nominations, but won his only Oscar posthumously, for the score of *Around the World in 80 Days*. Another of Young's greatest scores was given new life after his untimely death, when Ray Heindorf conducted a recording of *For Whom the Bell Tolls* for the newly formed Warner Bros. record label. The memorable album cover featured an exquisite closeup color photo of Ingrid Bergman.

Over the years, Victor Young worked with a number of lyricists, including Ned Washington, Edward Heyman, Sammy Cahn, and Peggy Lee (remember the title song from *Johnny Guitar*?). The words for "Golden Earrings" (1947) were penned by Paramount's newest song-writers-in-residence, Jay Livingston and Ray Evans, who had gotten their big break the year before when they were willing to take on an assignment everyone else turned down.

Livingston and Evans had been hired by the studio on a provisional basis, and supplied songs for some of Paramount's Technicolor two-reel musical shorts of the mid-1940s. Then came *To Each His Own* (1946), a classy soap opera starring Olivia de Havilland.

As Ray Evans recalls, "Charles Brackett [the screenwriter] got the title from some old English poem and refused to change it. Paramount's publicity department said, 'No one knows what that title means; how can we sell it?' So they asked the music department if they could get a song written with that title; if they could get it played on the air a few times, it might help them sell the movie. Every reputable songwriter at the studio turned it down, including Victor Young, who did the score [and said] 'We don't want to write a song with a dumb title like that!'

"We had just been hired at Paramount, low men on the totem pole, and they asked us if we could do it. Brash and young, we said 'Sure,' and every company turned our song down. Then one day we picked up *Billboard* and a review of a new record by Eddy Howard predicted it would be a hit, and it was. In several weeks in 1947, of the ten best-selling records in the U.S., five were different versions of 'To Each His Own,' a record unequaled ever since. It made us 'big' and we would have won another Oscar if it had been in the movie, only it wasn't. It was an advertising ploy, out of PR desperation."

Almost every movie song seems to have a story that goes with it. Livingston and Evans were delighted to write an original song for Billy Wilder's *Sunset Blvd.*, especially since Wilder had them appear onscreen to perform it in a party scene. But Wilder had second thoughts and at the last minute cut the song, having the songwriters "loop" their previously shot footage with just a line or two of parody lyrics for "Buttons and Bows." The discarded song, an insider's view of working life in Hollywood, was called "The Paramount Don't Want Me Blues," and it did get published by the studio's Famous Music division . . . but moviegoers were denied a set of lyrics that dropped names like Dore Schary and Jimmie Fidler.

Gregory Peck records "Lullaby of Christmas" at Decca with radio stalwarts Carleton Young, William Conrad, Eleanor Audley, Anne Whitfield, and Lou Merrill. Partly hidden at top left is the famous painting placed in the studio by founder Jack Kapp, to which he added the caption, "Where's the melody?"

Livingston and Evans went on to win three Oscars for other songs that did appear in movies: "Mona Lisa" was sung by Nat "King" Cole in a forgettable Alan Ladd movie, *Captain Carey, U.S.A.* "What Will Be, Will Be (Que Sera, Sera)" was introduced in *The Man Who Knew Too Much* by another of the stars who managed to top both box-office and recording charts at the same time, Doris Day. And "Buttons and Bows" was sung by Bob Hope in his comedy hit *The Paleface*.

But unlike Cole and Day, Hope didn't have the hit platter on this bright novelty number. Dinah Shore's record spent twenty-five weeks on the *Billboard* charts, including ten weeks in the number one spot. (As was customary in those days, many artists could enjoy success with recordings of the same song; "Buttons and Bows" did well for a variety of singers ranging from Betty Garrett to Gene Autry.)

That didn't stop Bob Hope from making records, but despite his enormous popularity, he never had a solid hit. (He nipped at the charts a few times, with Shirley Ross on "Two Sleepy People," from the 1939 film *Thanks for the Memory*, with Bing Crosby on the title song from *Road to Morocco*, and with Margaret Whiting on a 1950 tune called "Blind Date.")

It became clear that the public had final say when it came to deciding which musical performers they enjoyed watching onscreen, which they liked best on radio, and which they were willing to pay money to play on their Victrolas over and over again. Gene Autry and Roy Rogers were the top singing cowboys on screen, and had long recording careers, but Roy seldom cracked the Top 10, while Gene had a series of hits, including his unexpected success with such family-friendly holiday songs as "Rudolph the Red-Nosed Reindeer," "Peter Cottontail," and "Frosty the Snowman." Dinah Shore, who had many popular records and long-running success on radio and TV, never scored as a movie star.

Some actors did find satisfaction, and a degree of success, in the field of spoken-word recordings, and in dramatized plays that were essentially radio shows on disc. In the years just prior to the introduction of long-playing albums, these 78 rpm sets enjoyed considerable success. Lionel Barrymore's annual radio performance of Charles Dickens's *A Christmas Carol* was a natural for this medium. Barrymore also read *Ali Baba and the Forty Thieves* for MGM Records. Blessed with one of the greatest speaking voices of the Twentieth century, Ronald Colman was another obvious choice to read poetry, as well as narrate and/or star in adaptations of *A Tale of Two Cities*, *A Christmas Carol,* and other classics.

Decca Records hired some of radio's most capable writers and directors, including George Wells (longtime writer of Lux Radio Theatre), Nat Wolff, and the team of Jerome Lawrence and Robert E. Lee, to supervise a series of "star" recordings, usually with Victor Young supplying the musical accompaniment. These were written, rehearsed, and recorded just like network broadcasts, with supporting casts drawn from the ranks of Hollywood's best radio actors.

Among the recordings: *Alice in Wonderland* with Ginger Rogers, *The Littlest Angel* with Loretta Young, *The Cask of Amontillado* with Sydney Greenstreet, *Cinderella* with Edna Best, *The Count of Monte Cristo* and *The Snow Goose* with Herbert Marshall, *Moby Dick* with Charles Laughton, *The Pied Piper of Hamelin* with Ingrid Bergman, *Rip Van Winkle* with Walter Huston, *The Selfish Giant* with Fredric March, *The Man Without a Country* with Bing Crosby as narrator and Frank Lovejoy as Philip Nolan, and *Treasure Island* with Thomas Mitchell.

Orson Welles appeared on several Decca releases reading great poetry, but also appeared in his own adaptation of Oscar Wilde's *The*

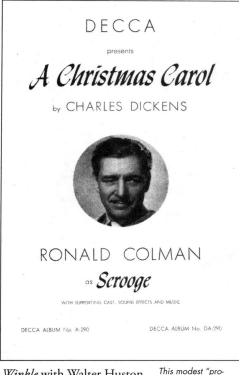

DECCA

presents

A Christmas Carol

by CHARLES DICKENS

RONALD COLMAN

as *Scrooge*

WITH SUPPORTING CAST, SOUND EFFECTS AND MUSIC

DECCA ALBUM No. A-290   DECCA ALBUM No. DA-290

This modest "program" was enclosed with the 78 rpm recording of the Dickens classic.

Happy Prince with Bing Crosby. Decca hired Walter Huston, Fredric March, Brian Donlevy, Agnes Moorehead, and Pat O'Brien to join the busy Bing Crosby in a series of readings about the history of America called *Our Common Heritage*. (Moorehead, not as big a "name" as some of the others, nevertheless was featured in Decca's 78 rpm recreation of her signature radio performance in *Sorry, Wrong Number* by playwright Lucille Fletcher.)

Other record labels responded with occasional forays into this kind of material. Columbia Masterworks commissioned an elaborate adaptation of Robin Hood which gave Basil Rathbone the unique opportunity to play the swashbuckling hero rather than one of the villains.

Perhaps the greatest, and most unusual, opportunities for movie stars came with the post–World War II baby boom–related growth of children's records. It was natural for stars with proven family appeal like Danny Kaye and Jerry Lewis to make records aimed specifically at children (both on 78 rpm and the new "unbreakable" 45 rpm discs) but many other less likely participants dived in as well, including John Garfield ("Herman Ermine in Rabbit Town"), Ruth Chatterton ("The Revolt of the Alphabet"), Claude Rains ("Bible Stories for Children"), James Stewart ("Winnie the Pooh"), Gloria Swanson ("Joey the Jeep"), Jack Carson ("Willie and Hannibal in Mouseland"), and Frank Morgan ("Gossamer Wump"). With the aid of special material, Gene Kelly, Rosemary Clooney, Tex Ritter, and others recorded songs and musical stories exclusively for the younger set.

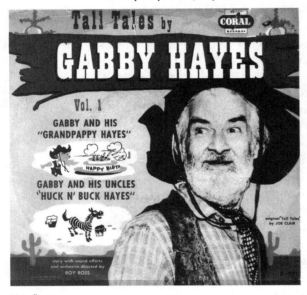

Virtually every movie cowboy made records for children in the 1950s. Our example above is this Coral Records release featuring the beloved George "Gabby" Hayes.

Capitol Records' Alan Livingston (brother of songwriter Jay) put his company on the map in the arena of children's records when he created the character of Bozo the Clown, and hired the original voice of Goofy, Pinto Colvig, to personify the red-nosed character for a hugely successful series of albums (most of which had read-along pages bound into the jacket). Capitol also recorded Hopalong Cassidy adventures and multi-disc albums featuring Woody Woodpecker and all the Looney Tunes stars (performed by the great Mel Blanc, who had a great singing voice, and accompanied by the music of the great Billy May). The entire line of Capitol kiddie records bore a seal that they were "Bozo-approved"—even "The Story of Jesus" (read by Claude Rains), which wouldn't seem to need the endorsement.

There were many record labels devoted exclusively to children's entertainment (Cricket, Peter Pan, et al.), none more prominent or successful than Little Golden Records, which thrived in the 1950s and sixties with its six-inch, yellow-vinyl discs, distributed (unlike most mainstream records) in toy stores. While the Golden catalog had dozens of original songs and stories, it also had tie-ins with several cartoon studios, including Disney, Warner Bros., Terrytoons (the source of Andy Kaufman's "Mighty Mouse" record act), and Hanna-Barbera, although artists like Mighty Mouse's singing voice Roy Halee and Elmer Fudd's alter ego Arthur Q. Bryan were rarely credited. (In fact, they often used sound-alikes for their New York–recorded releases instead of the "original cartoon voices" heralded on the covers.) In time, a variety of stars including Bing Crosby, Roy Rogers and Dale Evans, and The Three Stooges all recorded material especially for Little Golden Records.

This 1942 promotional recording enabled Dari-Rich customers to play two preview scenes of Reap the Wild Wind on their phonographs at home.

While television began to erode the dominance of radio in the early 1950s, nothing, it seemed, could or would take the place of records in the American home. Bing Crosby licensed a "Junior Juke" record player for children that looked like a miniature jukebox. A novelty company called Hollywood Film Guild sold tinseltown tourists an album called *Hooray for Hollywood* that enabled the user to synchronize a series of 35mm slides with a "soundtrack" on a double-sided record. (They called the process "Cinevision Talkies.")

Advertisers (including movie studios) used records for special promotions, even binding cardboard-backed discs into popular magazines in the 1950s and sixties. Sheet-music sales continued to be strong, if not what they were in the 1920s and thirties, and these, as always, were sparked by tie-ins with the movies. It's astonishing to see what lesser efforts warranted publication well into the 1960s.

Bob Hope hits the road to promote his latest Capitol release.

And like the aforementioned MGM and Warner Bros., virtually every studio started its own record label in the 1950s, including Walt Disney, 20th Century Fox, Columbia, and United Artists.

The production of original musicals waned with the gradual decline of the studio system in the 1950s, but the title song became more popular than ever. It was the decade of hits like "Love is a Many Splendored Thing" and "Three Coins in the Fountain." Asked which came first, the music or the lyrics, the voluble Sammy Cahn invariably responded, "The phone call," explaining that no one ever set out to write a song called "Three Coins in the Fountain" until hired to do so.

There is one dramatic instance of a song—without lyrics—turning an offbeat movie into a household name. Viennese zither virtuoso Anton Karas's theme for *The Third Man*—which the film's American co-producer David O. Selznick wanted to replace—became a fluke success, catapulting the musician into the international limelight and rousing tremendous interest in a somewhat offbeat film.

At least one title song made its mark long after the movie for which it was written had come and gone. Alfred Newman composed a beautifully evocative theme for *Street Scene* in 1931, when there was little awareness of instrumental music in movies. The theme later became a staple at Newman's longtime home, 20th Century Fox, and served as main-title accompaniment for seemingly every New York–based movie to come from the studio in the 1940s and early 1950s (from *I Wake up Screaming* to *The Dark Corner*). In 1953, Newman conducted his theme with the Fox orchestra on screen as a Stereophonic sound prelude to *How to Marry a Millionaire*, and issued a 78 rpm single—more than twenty years after the piece was composed.

The 1950s were a peak time for pop vocalists, and they were all heard on movie soundtracks singing often-forgettable title songs. (Just how many westerns did Frankie Laine introduce?) It's amusing to watch *Somebody up There Likes Me* and observe that Perry Como gets a single-card credit in the main titles in letters as big as Paul Newman or Robert Wise. By asking a friend from Paramount to do him a favor, producer A. C. Lyles got to put a special highlighted box in the advertising for his 1960 Allied Artists release *Raymie* proclaiming that the title song was sung by Jerry Lewis.

Even John Wayne had a hit record, in a manner of speaking, with a title song. In the first scene of his smash hit movie *The High and the Mighty*, Wayne is seen (and heard) whistling the melody of Dimitri Tiomkin's memorable theme. The melody (with lyrics by Ned Washington) went on to become a hit for a number of artists, and composer Tiomkin even had a modestly successful single . . . though as music-trivia buffs know, it was Muzzy Marcellino doing the whistling for Wayne.

Unsung Heroes:
ARTHUR Q. BRYAN

Some are born great, some achieve greatness, and others have greatness thrust upon them. Arthur Q. Bryan spent most of his busy show business career as a supporting player, just outside the limelight, yet he brought to life one of the most indelible characters in movie history. He was the voice of Elmer Fudd.

Although this vocal assignment lasted for twenty years, it was just a small part of Bryan's overall career.

He was born on May 8, 1899 in the cradle of show business, Brooklyn, New York, and his timing was good, because he came of age at the same time as radio. By the time Arthur reached his twenties, there was a living to be made in this new mass-entertainment medium, and he longed to be one of radio's top tenors.

Instead, he found work as an announcer, beginning in 1923 at station WEAF, where he auditioned for the soon-to-be-legendary radio voice Milton Cross. He still pursued his singing ambitions, and appeared with various quartets, including The Sieberling Singers. But Bryan enjoyed greater success as an announcer, and in 1929 he filled in for his friend Norman Brokenshire, one of the top men in the field, when Brokenshire took ill. In 1932 he took a job at WCAU in Philadelphia as announcer, writer, and producer, but continued to work in New York, appearing on shows with such stars as Jack Pearl. It was around this time that he developed the voice that would win him fame in animated cartoons.

In 1938, Bryan traveled to California on vacation and decided to stay. He became a regular on a popular series at KFWB called *The Grouch Club*, a half-hour show about life's little annoyances. The series was written by Nat Hiken, the comedy genius who later gave us *Sergeant Bilko*, and hosted and co-created by Jack Lescoulie, who achieved greater fame

Arthur is the Little Man about to be chastised by William Bendix in The Grouch Club short No Parking.

a generation later on television's *Today* show. Someone at the parent company Warner Bros. obviously liked the show and commissioned a series of six one-reel short subjects, which provided Arthur Q. his first experience in front of the camera. One would never know that from watching such hilarious shorts as "The Great Library Misery," in which our poor, set-upon hero attempts to take out one particular book in a series of escalatingly absurd vignettes. Bryan's roly-poly physique seemed to match his nebbishy character quite well. (He wasn't always fat; he once recounted that he weighed a mere 135 pounds when he started out in New York, but later ballooned to a hefty 240.)

Because KFWB shared space with Leon Schlesinger's cartoon studio, the animation directors often hired voice talent they heard on the air, including announcer Robert Bruce and *Grouch Club* host Lescoulie (who did a great Jack Benny imitation in many Warners cartoons). Bryan's performance as the "Little Man" of *The Grouch Club* prompted Tex Avery to hire him for a featured role in "Dangerous Dan McFoo." This was the first appearance of the character that evolved into Elmer Fudd.

Elmer Fudd was a perfect marriage of voice and personality. The bulbous fellow in such funny cartoons as "McFoo" and my favorite, "The Hardship of Miles Standish," had started out as an animated equivalent of radio comedian Joe Penner named Egghead. But Egghead, like Penner, could be strident at times, and when Avery changed voices he found a new direction for the character. Something in Bryan's performance suggested vulnerability. In *Miles Standish*, a standoff with a band of marauding Indians is interrupted when a missile breaks through Priscilla Alden's cabin. Miles/Elmer steps outside and says, with great seriousness, "Who bwoke that window? Somebody's gonna have to pay for that gwass!" The formerly savage Indians back off, like kids in a stickball game who've been accused of window-smashing. The gag wouldn't pay off if not for Bryan's comic conviction in the delivery of his lines. (The film also makes excellent use of his vocal skills as he delivers a singing telegram set to the tune of "You Must Have Been a Beautiful Baby.")

Over the next few years, Elmer Fudd came into focus just as Bugs Bunny did, through trial and error. Chuck Jones's 1940 cartoon "Elmer's Candid Camera" is an important stepping stone, with Elmer using a camera instead of a gun to stalk his quarry (and still wearing a derby hat and starched collar, like Egghead). Avery's "A Wild Hare" (1940) is recognized as the first genuine Bugs Bunny cartoon, but it also represents the flowering of his comedic adversary ("Be vew-wy quiet—I'm hunting wabbits"). Elmer is certainly the dumbest hunter who ever picked up a shotgun, but he's nothing if not determined.

Interestingly, Mel Blanc started working in Warners cartoons two years before Bryan, and came to them through the same route, KFWB. But as Bryan began to gain recognition on network radio shows, he was actually paid more than Blanc for his work at the Schlesinger studio! (Payroll records show that in the early 1940s, Bryan got $75 per recording session—triple the usual daily rate for voice work—while Blanc received $65 a week, every week. Blanc had signed a contract in 1941, but Bryan continued to work on a freelance basis.)

Arthur Q. moved from local radio to big-time shows like *Texaco Star Theater*, *Burns and Allen* (where he was a regular for one season), *Blondie* (as Mr. Fuddle), and Dick Powell's *Band Wagon*, where he performed in Fudd-ese as "Waymond W. Wadcwiffe." By the 1940s he was one of that elite corps of actors who could work multiple shows in one evening, and be heard a dozen times or more in the course of a week.

He was best known for his running parts on *Fibber McGee and Molly*, in the fairly "straight" role of Ol' Doc Gamble ("Take off your shirt, McGee!"), and as Floyd the barber on Fibber's spinoff show, *The Great Gildersleeve*. An NBC publicity biography from 1943 describes him as "quick-witted, jovial, easygoing," qualities which certainly helped to ingratiate him with the radio community. He later had extended runs on *The Al Pearce Show*, *The Charlotte Greenwood Show*, *Major Hoople* (in the title role), *Red Ryder* (as Roland "Rawhide" Rawlinson), *Forever Ernest*, and *Nitwit Court*. He also made guest appearances with Jack Benny, Bob Hope, Jimmy Durante, Eddie Cantor, Red Skelton, and countless other stars.

Like other character actors, he also benefited from the anonymity that radio afforded, and often played dramatic parts as well. He appeared on sixty-six episodes of *Lux Radio Theater*, including adaptations of such movie hits as *His Girl Friday, Knute Rockne, All American, Young Tom Edison, The Whole Town's Talking, They Drive by Night, A Tale of Two Cities, The Champ,* and *A Star is Born*. He even played an Irish sprite in an episode of *Favorite Story*.

In 1947 he moved to New York for one season at the request of his old *Grouch Club* colleague Nat Hiken, who was writing a series for Milton Berle. (Berle even reprised the library skit, taking Arthur's role.) He returned two years later for a running part on a short-lived Ethel Merman variety show, and briefly hosted an early TV game show called

Arthur with Eve Arden and Robert Rockwell in a 1953 episode of television's Our Miss Brooks.

Movieland Quiz, broadcast locally in Philadelphia. Back on the west coast, he replaced Ed Begley as Lieutenant Walt Levinson on Dick Powell's popular series *Richard Diamond, Private Detective*. (There's an amusing Christmas episode in which Bryan plays the Ghost of Christmas Present in a variation on Dickens's *A Christmas Carol*, written by the show's creator, Blake Edwards.)

Over the years he took small roles in two-reel comedies and such feature films as *I Stole a Million* (1939), *Little Accident* (1939), *Devil Bat* (1940), *Grand Central Murder* (1942), *Larceny, Inc.* (1942), *The Dark Horse* (1946), *Road to Rio* (1947), *Samson and Delilah* (1949), *Here Come the Nelsons* (1952), and *The Lieutenant Wore Skirts* (1956). He even starred in "The Golfer's Lament," one of the three-minute musical shorts called Soundies that played in jukebox-like machines in the 1940s. But like many of his busy radio colleagues, it took a fair amount of juggling to balance movie jobs with continuing commitments on the air.

Through it all, he continued to work as Elmer Fudd, occasionally doing other incidental voices as well (like the irate hotel guest in Chuck Jones's *Pest in the House*, with Daffy Duck). He also appeared as Elmer on children's recordings for Capitol and Golden Records. Listen to his performances in such classic shorts as "The Old Grey Hare," in which he portrays a doddering, aged Elmer, still trying to catch the wascally wabbit, or "Rabbit Seasoning" ("Isn't she wuv-wy?"), and you'll hear a great comic actor at work. And try to imagine such great musical cartoons as "The Rabbit of Seville" or "What's Opera, Doc?" without the benefit of his vocalizing.

Mel Blanc's son Noel recalls, "He was very musical, a great singer just like my father. My dad could sight-read anything, and even do harmony, and Arthur was the same. I don't know if he had perfect pitch, but he always got the right note, and that's rare."

In the 1950s, as network radio began to fade from the scene, Arthur appeared regularly on television (he plays Desi Arnaz's nightclub boss in an episode of *I Love Lucy*) and did both on and off-screen work for Warners' Joe McDoakes shorts. Then he took to the road and did theater work. Radio and TV personality Gary Owens met him around this time and remembers him as "a very convivial man, very kind. He looked a lot like Elmer Fudd, only bigger."

When Mel Blanc became an important asset to Looney Tunes and Merrie Melodies, he agreed to give up other cartoon work in return for sole voice credit on screen. This is part of the reason that Bryan's name isn't better known, though that had nothing to do with Blanc's regard for his colleague.

"He and my father loved working together," says Noel Blanc. "That's why when he died, my father felt funny about doing Elmer. He never liked doing someone else's voice, but in this case he really didn't want to do it."

As a result, following Arthur Q. Bryan's death on November 30, 1959, Elmer Fudd's appearances were few and far between. Warners hired character actor Hal Smith to imitate the voice, and others have tried it over the years, but it's never sounded quite right. As Noel puts it, "Arthur *was* Elmer Fudd."

In other words, this genial, hard-working, unsung hero achieved something very few people can claim. Arthur Q. Bryan was literally irreplaceable.

[*Author's Note: My thanks to Keith Scott, John Cocchi, and Jerry Beck for their help with this section.*]

Chapter 3

LIFE IN HOLLYWOOD

Conversations:
JIMMY LYDON

When I was very young, a local television station scheduled a Henry Aldrich movie every Saturday morning at 8:00. I couldn't wait for my weekly dose of Henry and his mis-adventures in this cheerful series of B-movies. When I revisited them years later I was pleased to find that my first impressions were accurate: they were entertaining, unpretentious, and slickly made.

They also had the perfect actor in the leading role. Jimmy Lydon was extremely likable, and held his own onscreen with a formidable roster of youthful costars and seasoned character actors.

I never dreamed that the day would come when I would spend an entire day with the very same Jimmy Lydon—now Jim—chatting and exchanging stories. (We took a "work break" to record material for the commentary track that appears on the DVD release of *Island in the Sky* (1953), which gave him his best adult role, as John Wayne's aerial navigator.) His wife Betty Lou couldn't have been more welcoming to me and my wife Alice.

Through the years, Lydon became an active member of the actors' fraternity in Hollywood, through his membership in the fabled "Irish Mafia," as well as the Screen Actors Guild. He was vice president of the Masquers Club and has many colorful stories about his fellow thespians. In fact, he became a legal guardian for veteran actor Robert Armstrong (who achieved immortality as Carl Denham in *King Kong*) and took care of him until his death in 1973, at the age of eighty-two. Although he always wanted to be a director, Jim loved being part of the acting fraternity.

Lydon continued acting, mostly on television (*The Rockford Files*, *M*A*S*H*, and *St. Elsewhere*, and commercials for everything from Mc-Donald's to the Massachusetts State Lottery) through the 1980s, but he is proudest of his work behind the camera. He directed episodes of *Hawaii Five-O*, *The Six Million Dollar Man*, and *Simon and Simon*, produced a great deal of episodic television, and then concentrated on post-production. He worked closely with William Conrad at Warner Bros. on a series of tightly budgeted feature films in the 1960s, and received associate producer credit on Gordon Parks's feature *The Learning Tree*.

In recent years, film buffs and scholars have discovered and lauded *Strange Illusion* (1945), Edgar G. Ulmer's low-budget, modern-day retelling of *Hamlet* in which Jimmy starred with Warren William and Sally Eilers. (Along with other Ulmer films, it is available on DVD from All Day Entertainment.) Because Jimmy has been interviewed about this film a number of times I thought I would avoid redundancy in discussing it here. For the same reason I've omitted the portion of our interview that dealt with William A. Wellman's *Island in the Sky* (1953). You can hear me with Jimmy (plus William Wellman Jr. and Darryl Hickman) on the commentary track of the Paramount DVD.

But let's not get ahead of ourselves; we'll start at the very beginning.

MALTIN: How did you come to the notice of William K. Howard?
LYDON: I did a musical in New York in 1938 called *Sing Out the News* for Moss Hart and George S. Kaufman, and we took it to Philadelphia for three weeks to try it out. By this time, I have enough background that I have an agent in New York, which is rare for kid actors. Mr. William K. Howard, who was a great motion picture director-producer-writer, comes to New York to make a documentary-type motion picture about a young boy who never has a break and who winds up in the electric chair.

Mr. Howard comes to New York and he wants a kid actor for this lead in his picture and my agent says, "You've got to see Jim; he's in Philadelphia." He said, "Get him." So you know, we were dark on Sunday, and I got on the train in Philadelphia and came back to New York. I met my mother at Pennsylvania Station and we walked across town, to save the money, and we took a bus up to his sumptuous two-story apartment on Fifth Avenue somewhere. And I met the most fascinating, the kindest man I've ever met in my life. He must have known I was scared green, 'cause my knees were shaking like tambourines and he said, "Jim, take this. Sit down over there and get familiar with the script." We sat on the couch and he was talking to my mother; he was Irish and my mother was Irish. I guess he knew when my knees stopped talking, so he said, "You ready?" I said, "Yes, sir," and he said, "Come on, sit next to me." So I sat down next to him and he said, "I'll do all the other parts and you read Frankie." And I read about seven or eight pages of the screenplay and he said, "That's enough. When do you get back from Philadelphia?" I said, "A week from Thursday, sir." He said, "Fine, we'll start the picture the following Monday." And that's all he said. No money discussed, no nothing. I got back on the train to go back to Philadelphia with the lead in the first film I was ever going to make. I had the first half of the film as the boy and Wallace Ford had the last half as the man who gets electrocuted.

MALTIN: How did Howard make you comfortable in front of the camera?

LYDON: He was so kind, because at that time, I was doing the play in New York. I was getting up at six o'clock in the morning, having a quick breakfast, jumping in the subway and going over to 5th Street and 35th Avenue in Long Island City. It was the middle of winter, it was colder than Johnny-be-darned. Then I'd go down on the set and this man would just very gently teach me what I had to know. He'd say, "You see that microphone up there, Jim? That man on that boom, he has to have that microphone in front of you and up above out of the camera range every time you talk. You don't have to worry about that; that's his job. It'll always be there, don't worry about that." He said, "What I'm trying to tell you is motion pictures are different from the stage. If you have to whisper in the stage, you have to make the audience believe you're whispering; you have to reach underneath the balcony and up to the second balcony with the whispers. In motion pictures, if you whisper, you whisper. If you scream, you scream, if you cry, you cry, because you can't lie to a camera. I can put that camera anyplace I want, I can put it up on the roof, under your arm, wherever I want." And he said, "The difference between acting in motion pictures and in the theater is in the theater you must act. In motion pictures, you don't dare act. You have to do every scene as if it were actually happening the way it should happen." And it was a wonderful lesson from this very kind man.

Jimmy Lydon (and friend) in his first Hollywood movie, Two Thoroughbreds (1939).

You'd have to ask who was the director on one of his sets because he was so quiet and so dignified. If he wanted to talk to you, he'd say, "Come on, sit next to me." And almost whispering, he'd tell you one at a time these little things. He never told an actor how to do anything; he'd always suggest. He'd say, "What do you think? You think maybe if you got up there and walked over to the mantelpiece and put your elbow on the mantelpiece there, that that might work?" And you'd say, "I don't know sir, I'll try." Pretty soon, you'd think it was your idea; that's how he directed film. And I've never forgotten him. I went under contract to him and when the twelve-week layoff was over he had to start to pay me. He'd spent too much money, he didn't have any money to pay me, so he sold my contract to RKO and [the contract of] a man called John Farrow, who was a writer. Farrow and I came to RKO as a kid actor and a writer. Farrow wound up at Paramount as a big-time director, and I started making films for RKO.

MALTIN: Was the first feature you made in Hollywood *Two Thoroughbreds* [1938]?

LYDON: That's right, with Joan Brodel, who became Joan Leslie. A real redhead, and so was I; I was a real redhead, too.

MALTIN: You'd had this wonderful, warm introduction to moviemaking with William K. Howard. What was it like working with less skilled or less gentle directors . . . or were you lucky? Did you meet nice people?

LYDON: Well, no. I was not any luckier than anyone else as far as directors went; some of them were very good and some of them were truck drivers. But, the first one I shall never forget, because we were friends until he died. His name was Jack Hively. Jack was a cutter at RKO with a couple of other people who became directors, too, Eddie Dmytryk and Robert Wise. Jack Hively was a young man; he was about thirty-two and I was about sixteen. He was a great big man, about six-two and he weighed about 210; a big, big, strong man. I met him in the producer's office. We're going to make a boy-and-a-horse picture together and he looked at me and he said an expletive and "Mmm-mmm. Kids, horses and dogs," which is the worst thing a director could ever get. He started to laugh and I started to laugh and we became great friends. We made the picture in twenty-one days. We finished on time and on schedule and it turned out very well.

MALTIN: What did you think of Joan? She had been doing bit parts in movies.

LYDON: She'd done a couple of bit parts, but this was the first halfway decent part she'd had; she was so sweet and so nice and we're still great friends today. I was pretty scared, because I'd made [only] one film and I didn't know anything. I learned very quickly. There's a great saying in motion pictures that is very true: if you don't know how to do something, go and ask somebody who's done it how to do it and they will tell you, and they'll tell you for free. But if you try to bluff your way through and you're wrong, they'll figuratively cut your throat. Because you're costing them money. Jack Hively and certain other directors of that era taught me very well. All I ever wanted to be was a director like my friend William K. Howard.

MALTIN: When you moved to California, did any of your family members come with you?

LYDON: My mother came with me originally and then all the family came to California, except my second-oldest brother, who was married; he was a mechanic in New Jersey. They couldn't find any work, because the Depression was still all over the country. I was the only one in the family working and shortly three of my four older brothers joined the National Guard. On December 7, 1941, we got into war with Japan and December 8, the National Guard was now the United States Army. In April of the following year, they were sent overseas and their first assignment was Guadalcanal. So once again, I was all alone with the younger part of the family and my mother and father.

MALTIN: Where did you live when you came out here?

LYDON: We lived in Wally Ford's mother-in-law's house on Van Ness Avenue. She had a big family and they were all married and off now and she had one son left who became a wonderful, Academy Award–winning art director for *Sayonara* and things like that.

MALTIN: What was his name?

LYDON: Edward Southern Haworth. We lived on North Van Ness Avenue. We had two bedrooms there and she had one and Teddy had one.

MALTIN: Practically walking distance to the studio.

LYDON: Well, all I had to do was go right down Gower Street and I was there, yes.

MALTIN: After *Two Thoroughbreds* you went on to *Tom Brown's School Days* and that film had a really interesting cast.

Lydon and his friend Freddie Bartholomew in Tom Brown's School Days (1940).

LYDON: *Tom Brown's School Days* was, as you know, a very famous 1800s novel about English public school life, which is private school [as we call it], and about Dr. Arnold, who revolutionized the vicious British gentry schooling system through this young boy Tom Brown. Now, the only kid in the world that should have played Tom Brown was Freddie Bartholomew. He was English, he was the right age, and he was a famous movie star. But Freddie wasn't under contract to RKO; I was [*laughs*] so I played Tom and he played East, the second lead in the picture.

I thought that Freddie would hate me for the rest of his days and you know, we became great friends and we were friends right up until the time he died in 1992.

MALTIN: Looking at the cast list for *Tom Brown*, besides Freddie, there's Gale Storm, whom you worked with quite a bit, and Billy Halop . . .

LYDON: They were the only other Americans in the whole picture.

MALTIN: And further down the cast list, I saw Charles Smith's name; this was before he costarred with you in the Henry Aldrich movies.

Lydon with George Bancroft in Little Men (1940).

LYDON: Charlie Smith was one of the cast; he didn't have anything to do though.

MALTIN: After *Tom Brown's Schooldays*, the studio kept you in period mode, and you made *Little Men*.

LYDON: That's right, for Norman Z. McLeod, who drew stick figures of where he wanted people on the set. A lovely man.

MALTIN: That makes sense because he had been a cartoonist.

LYDON: Oh, I didn't know that. He'd draw out the set and then he'd do these stick figures of where the actors were going to be, and he used that as a kind of [guide] to tell the cameraman what he wanted.

MALTIN: Again, you had the feature juvenile part, but Jack Oakie and Kay Francis and George Bancroft were the grownup stars.

LYDON: Oakie was a fascinating man. He was like Edward Everett Horton. You know, Edward Everett Horton used to ad-lib funny, wonderful things and so did Jack Oakie. But, they didn't ad-lib anything, [really]. They wrote those things out the night before in their script, and they'd try 'em on the director and [he'd] say, "Oh, that's good, keep that in!" They were very, very smart, those fellows and both of them very nice fellows. Jack Oakie had the most amazing memory of anybody I ever knew. You'd see Jack Oakie ten years later, he'd say, "Jack Oakie— Jim, how are you?" He'd always say his name first as if you didn't know his name. A lovely man.

MALTIN: How were you selected to be Henry Aldrich, do you know? Jackie Cooper had made the first two films for Paramount . . .

LYDON: . . . and Jackie didn't want to do it anymore. Hugh Bennett had seen the picture that Bill Howard made in New York and he'd seen me in it. He thought it was wonderful. So when I was at RKO and I'm grown up and I'm sixteen now, or seventeen, and they've got to find a new guy for Henry Aldrich. He knew I was an American and he knew I'd been stage-trained. He asked the studio to get me to make a test and I [prepared for] a test for Henry Aldrich by listening to Ezra Stone's recordings. Ezra Stone had that cracked voice and he created the stage versions of Henry Aldrich called *What a Life* and a second play called *Life with Henry* with Eddie Bracken. And, of course, Ezra couldn't do the thing because ethnically, he didn't look like the boy next door, which was a pity. I went and I made a test for Paramount and I started to make the films.

MALTIN: Did they put you under contract?

LYDON: Yes.

MALTIN: Do you remember what they were paying you?

LYDON: Yes, they were paying me very well. I think I started at $850 a week. Forty weeks a year and I only worked sixty-three days a year. I wound up with twelve or fifteen hundred dollars a week for forty weeks a year.

MALTIN: Pretty good.

LYDON: For making three films a year with Hugh Bennett; he directed all of them. John Litel was the father and Olive Blakeney, who became my mother-in-law, was the mother.

MALTIN: Now, you couldn't make that up.

LYDON: No, you couldn't, it just happened . . .

MALTIN: Was it coincidence that you met Olive's daughter?

LYDON: Well, yes, but it didn't mean anything at the time because I was eighteen when I met Betty Lou and she was thirteen. And, you know, when a girl is thirteen and the guy is eighteen, that's a baby. [Years later, when] I'd been married, and very sadly, divorced in California, and I'm back in New York doing this daytime television soap opera, Betty Lou was in Bermuda, and she came back to New York. I knew her parents, Olive and Ben [Bernard Nedell], very well; they were in New York in the theater and doing stock in New Jersey in the summertime. Olive called me on the phone and told me Betty Lou was coming in and would I pick her up? I said sure. So I met Betty Lou again and now she wasn't thirteen years old. [*Leonard laughs*] She was twenty-four years old, you know; I was twenty-eight, going on twenty-nine. We fell in love and we've been married ever since, for fifty-two years.

MALTIN: That's the best story of all.

LYDON: Oh, it is for me.

MALTIN: Did you have any regrets about doing the Henry Aldrich series?

LYDON: I'd never done a comedy before and I knew that [going into a series can be] the kiss of death—even in television, it's the same way. You get so identified with a character that you don't work for a couple of years. I knew it was going to happen and it did, of course. I had a big, powerful agent at the time, the Orsatti Agency. I'd made hundreds of radio shows and five Broadway plays and a couple of plays that ran in stock. By now I'd made eight or ten pictures and I don't want to do just this series; I want to do like what Rooney did at MGM, you know, make a Hardy picture and then make another. It took me four months to make an appointment with Mr. Y. Frank Freeman, the head of the studio. I finally went in to see this great man. He was sitting behind his desk in his huge office and he said, "What do you want?" I said, "Mr. Freeman, I don't want a thing. I don't want any more money or anything else but I just want you to know that I'm a dramatic actor and I've been one all of my professional life. I want to do other films for Paramount. It's not going to cost you anything. All I do is do three films for you and you pay me all year long. Let me do other things." He said, "Are you unhappy here?" I said no. He reached into his drawer and he picked out a contract, I don't think it was mine but he said it was. He said, "I've got your contract right here. Do you want me to tear it up?" I said, no, and he said, "Get out of my office."

Finally, at the end of the [contract], they lent me out to "The Bills," Bill Pine and Bill Thomas [who had their own unit making B movies for Paramount], and I made a film with two wonderful guys, Chester Morris and Dick Arlen, called *Aerial Gunner* and to show you the curse of this thing . . . We make this picture in Arlington, Texas with the Army and fifty thousand guys in the Army gunnery school. All these things that look like money [on the screen] and it was a little, tiny B picture. And I made a big mistake. I went to the preview of the picture in Huntington Park with Bill Pine and Bill Thomas. At the end of the picture I get shot down and I'm dying all over the screen, in a very, very dramatic scene. This is the very, very end of the picture, just before the closing titles. And a little kid walked into the theater just at that time, looked up at the screen and said, "Oh, there's Henry Aldrich!" Well, the whole audience broke up. That's the curse of the series, you know.

MALTIN: One of the things about the Henry Aldrich series is they used it as a kind of proving ground for a lot of other young talent.

LYDON: Diana Lynn, Gale Storm, yes.

MALTIN: Were you aware of them trying to showcase people along the way? Did you ever have any feelings that maybe it was taking anything from you?

LYDON: Well, these little B pictures made a lot of money, not because of what they were but because the exhibitors had to take one of my films with a Cecil B. DeMille picture. And the studio had a contract list of up-and-coming actors of all kinds. They would put them in the series whenever they could fit one, and it was good training for them; it was training for everybody in those days, so I didn't mind that at all. That's how I learned.

MALTIN: Exactly. Because in the first one, *Henry Aldrich for President* there was June Preisser, Mary Anderson, Junior Coghlan, Martha O'Driscoll, Kenneth Howell, Rod Cameron, Buddy Pepper, Sidney Miller . . . the whole juvenile population of Hollywood is in that movie!

A promotional photo for Henry Aldrich, Editor (1942) with Rita Quigley, Jimmy Lydon, and Charles Smith.

LYDON: Just about, and very few of them are still with us today. I think Frankie Coghlan is still with us. He was in the Naval Air Corps, too. And he was quite a flier.

MALTIN: There was a lot of quality in those movies . . .

LYDON: They were well made. They were [done on] a twenty-one-day schedule, and that's a very comfortable schedule for a little B picture. Hugh Bennett had been a cutter and he was such a delightful man, a nice, easygoing, charming man.

MALTIN: The character people in your films were always so good.

LYDON: Wonderful.

MALTIN: Lucien Littlefield, and Vaughan Glaser, who played the principal . . .

LYDON: Oh, wonderful guy. Wonderful old guy.

MALTIN: I always liked John Litel . . .

LYDON: Just a delightful human being. I loved him.

MALTIN: He always played the square, sober type.

LYDON: Yes, and he was everything but; he was just a fun, nice guy. Like my mother-in-law, Olive Blakeney, she was so much fun. It was a delight to work with them, it really was.

MALTIN: And Maude Eburne, one of the great faces . . .

LYDON: Oh . . . one of the funniest women in the world. Maude Eburne was the character of the world, she was so funny.

MALTIN: She could make anything sound funny.

LYDON: She even looked funny.

MALTIN: I always liked *Henry Aldrich Gets Glamour* because I had a crush on Frances Gifford.

LYDON: Aw, nice gal. Very nice.

MALTIN: And then in the last film, *Henry Aldrich, Boy Scout*, they brought in Darryl Hickman.

LYDON: [In that film] I had to carry Darryl on my back. I was very tall, I say just a fraction under six feet tall, and he was short and stubby but he weighed more than I did. I had a terrible time trying to lift Darryl and carry him! Fine, fine guy; he got into production, too, years later.

One story I want to tell you about that, about people who shouldn't be in the motion picture industry. Bill Meiklejohn was the head of the casting at Paramount, and he picked up a couple of hitchhikers one time from Santa Monica, driving into the studio. They found out who he was and they said, "If you're a casting man, you ought to know the most beautiful girl in Santa Monica. She is so gorgeous she'll knock your socks off." So, he said, "Here's my card, have her call me and we'll set up an appointment." The girl called and she came in and her name was Gail Russell. Gail Russell was the most beautiful girl you ever saw, except for Elizabeth Taylor. She's going to high school and she's an artist and a very good one. And she's scared green. So they put her into the schooling at Paramount and they're teaching her something about acting and she makes a Henry Aldrich film with me. The first thing she had to do was a telephone conversation. They're on a closeup of her and I'm off-camera feeding her the lines and Hughie is directing. We start to rehearse and she can't get through the first sentence and she starts to tighten up and she starts to cry. She's really scared and really crying. Hughie said, "Take ten, everybody. Jim, come on." We got Gail by the arm and we walked her outside the soundstage and all around the studio. Both of us said, "Film is cheap . . . you get used to this. All you have to do is just try it and get comfortable . . ." She finally stopped crying and went back in the soundstage and they powdered her down and got her all set again. And she got through the first scene. Not well, but she got through it. That was the beginning of Gail Russell.

But she never got over her fears, and as you know, she began to drink very heavily. I saw stories about her, most of them totally untrue, and then she was a terrible risk and nobody would employ her anymore. She died when she was about thirty-six years old, in Westwood. There were three actors at her funeral: Alan Ladd, me, and Diana Lynn. The newspaper said she died of an overdose; she didn't die of an overdose. She died of malnutrition, caused by alcohol. She didn't eat, she drank for the last couple of months of her existence. She starved herself to death. Isn't that tragic?

MALTIN: It's so sad. Much too young.

MALTIN: Were you happy when the Henry Aldrich series came to an end?

LYDON: Yes, very much so. I knew that the minute that series was over, I was going to have a tough time finding work—and I didn't, but that's just because of luck again that I've always had. But for years, every place I went somebody would say, "Hennnry!" and I'd just want to dive under the table. I grew a moustache to get away from it and I still wear a moustache. [*Laughs*]

MALTIN: In looking at the casts of your other films of the 1940s, certain names constantly recur because you so often played with other actors in your age bracket.

LYDON: Or the B-picture bracket. [*Laughs*]

MALTIN: People make these generalizations about child actors, but everybody's situation is

Jimmy and the formidable Maude Eburne in Henry Aldrich Plays Cupid *(1944).*

different. Why do you think you came through that period so well when many of your colleagues didn't? Is it the family background, is it some sort of inner strength? Is it just good breaks? Bad breaks?

LYDON: I know what you're trying to say. I'll give you some examples, if I may. We were all studio brats; the studios controlled our lives completely. They told us who to go out with, where to go, and all that sort of stuff; they owned us like a piece of furniture. When we went to parties, the parties were fine with Rooney and Garland and Donald O'Connor and Sidney Miller and all the gang. It'd be fun until the photographers came in about 10:30, 11:00 o'clock at night and then I'd go home. Everybody then had to be "on" and that's not my bag, so I would leave. But in those days you wouldn't want a sweeter, nicer, more wholesome girl than Judy Garland. Now, a lot of people are of the opinion that the motion picture industry ruined Judy Garland and made her what she was, and that's not true at all. I think Judy Garland would've wound up the same way if she had been a hat-check girl in a nightclub. She destroyed herself; not the motion picture industry.

It's a very strange life. I happen to be very fortunate because I was the middle of those nine children and my mother was a very wise lady;

she never laid a glove on any of us. We had our own method of doing what we were told. And my mother made no distinction between her nine children, even though I was making the only living; it didn't matter. I was still supporting her until the time my mother died when she was ninety-seven years old, and I was proud of that. But that isn't because of me. If one of my older brothers had walked across the room at the wrong time and they became the actor, they'd have done the same thing. That's what it was in those days.

I'm making the Aldrich series and I've got two younger brothers and two younger sisters. And the Paramount Theatre on Hollywood Blvd. opens with Alan Ladd, who was a friend of mine, in *This Gun for Hire* and one of my Aldrich pictures. My mother takes my four younger siblings to the opening. They came out of the theater and my mother said, "Well, what do you think?" They said, "Oh, Mom, that Alan Ladd was wonderful, just great." And after a while, my mother said, "What about Jim's picture?" They said, "That's okay. But that Alan Ladd, he was . . ." So, you see, even at home, it didn't make any difference.

Back in New York, my mother would parcel out our day's work. She would say to me, for instance, "Jim, when you come home from school today"—this was before I was professional, I was maybe eight, nine years old—"I want you to do two loads of wash and make sure you do at least twenty-four of the baby's diapers." And I'd say, "Okay, Mom."

Well, that's the way it was, except for doing the dishes. We always did 'em in pairs, and it would take us a half an hour to argue as to who was going to wash and who was going to dry. My mother said, "I can't stand it. You five boys are going to do the dishes for one week apiece by yourself. Starting with you Jack, Luke, Bernard, Vincent, Jim. One week, each of you, apiece." And that's how it worked. Now, I'm in Hollywood and I'm making more in one week than my father made all year long and I still had my week of the dishes. No difference. There was no difference.

MALTIN: It explains a lot.

LYDON: Well my mother was a dear lady. She knew everything about the motion picture business but she never wanted to have any part of it, you know? Marvelous lady. So, that's the difference in my lifetime.

MALTIN: You made a couple of films with Jane Withers in the 1940s while you were doing the Henry Aldrich films.

LYDON: I made three films with Jane. The first time I worked with Jane was at Fox, in *The Mad Martindales*. I love her dearly and she me. We're still friends, a long time.

MALTIN: One of my favorite character actors is in that movie, Alan Mowbray.

LYDON: Oh, boy. Alan Mowbray was the president of the Masquers Club at one time and I was the vice president. Alan is a character of all time. Alan was a wonderful, lovely man; totally irresponsible. His wife . . . how she stayed with him, nobody will ever know.

MALTIN: Did he have a theatrical air in real life, or was that just put on when he was performing?

LYDON: Oh no; Alan was every inch a very theatrical, wonderful, fun guy. The Masquers Club at that time was a very staid old-fashioned kind of place. I came in whistling one day and Ned Sparks said, "Young man, nobody in the theater whistles; it's bad luck." So I never whistled again.

The furniture was old and huge and the whole thing was 1890 or something. Mowbray was the president and I'm the vice president and we were sick and tired of this. The father of one of our members was the president of the Hollywood Bank on Hollywood Boulevard and Highland Avenue, so we went in there and negotiated a loan of $18,000, which was a lot of money in the early forties, and we rebuilt that club. We built that bar downstairs, which was magnificent, and we had a pool, pool tables, and a restaurant and everything upstairs and we did a wonderful job for $18,000 bucks and we spent every nickel of it. And the board of directors of the club were going to impeach the both of us, because they didn't know how we'd ever get out of debt. eighteen thousand dollars, you know. But we did, and the club was wonderful for a lot of members for a lot of years.

MALTIN: So I've heard. Getting back to Jane Withers, you made a film with her at Republic called *My Best Gal* that I want to ask you about because it's one of the first movies directed by Anthony Mann.

LYDON: That's right, Tony Mann. Well, I knew Tony Mann from New York and his name was Anthony Bundesmann, which was not a very good name to have during the second World War, if you remember. Tony was a test director for Selznick in New York. I'd made a test for *Tom Sawyer* in the mid-thirties.

MALTIN: I love character people, so I have to ask you about all my favorites on that picture, like Franklin Pangborn.

LYDON: Absolute fun guy. Like all the professionals I've known, no problem at all. Always ready, prepared, and full of fun; a joy, really.

A radiant young Elizabeth Taylor and Jimmy Lydon in Cynthia (1947).

MALTIN: Fortunio Bonanova?

LYDON: Bonanova was originally an opera singer. He was all ham and a yard wide but you couldn't get mad at him, you know. He was an actor kind of fellow and he loved being an actor kind of fellow.

MALTIN: Frank Craven?

LYDON: Frank Craven had been a very successful stage actor, a very successful author—he wrote a bunch of plays, you know—and he was a consummate actor. He was a bit of a stuffed shirt but a fine, fine actor.

MALTIN: Any memories of Erle C. Kenton who directed at Columbia?

LYDON: Yes, just one. Freddie [Bartholomew] and I were making quickie pictures for the Briskin unit at Columbia, which was the Z unit. We had eight days to make a feature, and you have got to learn thirteen pages of dialogue a day. Well, Erle Kenton was a very well-known silent director as well as a quickie feature director for Columbia. He taught me some of the tricks you have to do, like for instance, if you've got a two-shot with Freddie and myself and they light for Freddie and he's looking left to right, in my closeup, I have to look right to left. But when you have an L-shaped set and you have a picture behind Freddie and he's lit, all you have to do is take him out of the set, put another picture on the wall and it becomes my set. Instead of looking left to right, I look right to left, because when they turn the film around, it's going to be okay, you see? You don't have to relight anybody and you're finished in ten minutes instead of two hours. So that was quickie directing.

Also, if you flub in a master shot, you keep right on going. When you can finish the shot, then they pounce in for a closeup where you fluffed. And that's how you do quickie films. Freddie and I had a gentleman's pact together; we wouldn't flub purposely just to get a closeup. When we flubbed, it was for real. [*Laughs*]

MALTIN: You got to work again with William K. Howard.

LYDON: Yes, and that was interesting. I told you about my beginnings and how important this man was to me. When I was under contract to him and he couldn't pay me, he sold my contract to RKO. That opened the doors for me and I owed him my professional life, I thought; at least in films, I did. When I left Paramount I made a four-picture deal with a company called Producers Releasing Corporation [PRC]. I'm to make three films for them as the leading man and the fourth film I'm to direct; I'm twenty-one years old and I thought I could do it. The first film we made with Freddie Bartholomew is a kind of a fun picture called *The Town Went Wild*. My friend Ralph Murphy directed it and it was a pretty good film; we didn't have the six-day schedules that most of PRC [had]. We made—if there is such a thing—A pictures for PRC, because we had twenty-one-day schedules.

MALTIN: How did you get that?

LYDON: Because that's the deal we made, you know, and Mr. [Leon] Fromkess who was a wonderful man, wanted to upgrade PRC. He really wanted to make decent films. That was the first one. The second one I made with Edgar Ulmer, a very brilliant man, was called *Strange Illusion*. The third one, I'm in the studio and I'm talking to Mr. Fromkess and we're going to make a film about a Marine coming home and he's in an automobile accident. He's in a taxi accident going to his hometown; he's shell-shocked and he has no memory that he's married and has a wife and his family who live in this town. Regis Toomey is the newspaper man in the town. We're talking about the picture and Fromkess said, "Boy, I don't know who to get to direct this picture, Jim."

Now, I've got to back up a little bit. Bill Howard had been a very profligate spender and he was a big boozehound, but a brilliant, brilliant man. The government had attached his beautiful home in Brentwood and all his furniture and everything else. I had a house up in the Hollywood Hills and had a drawbridge across the front of the house to get into the front door, which was on the top floor of the house—it was three stories down a mountain. You had to get in through this drawbridge, and I came home this one afternoon and there's barrels and packing cases and trunks and everything else on the drawbridge. I can't get into my house. Bill Howard [and his wife] had moved in. My mother didn't mind that, 'cause she felt, like I did, that we owed him; we owed him a whole lot.

He stayed with us for well over a year. While he's staying with us, I'm trying to get him work and I'm talking to Fromkess and I said, "I have in my house William K. Howard." He said, "Oh my, but Bill's got a reputa—" I said, "Listen, he's here in the house with me. I will take him to the studio. I'll watch him, I'll bring him home at night, I'll be here all during the preparation for this film and every day that we're shooting. I won't let him out . . ." He said, "Do you think . . . ?" I said, "I know it; he'll be wonderful." And this is his kind of film, as you know it was. Fromkess said okay.

So Bill made his last film with me at PRC. I used to let him have a little Listerine bottle for the scotch in the morning and we'd drive down to the studio. I didn't know that he'd gotten a hold of the prop man and, you know, the director is God almighty for a prop man. Well, the prop man had Johnnie Walker Black label in the prop department and every now and then Bill would have some of the stuff. One time, we were doing a very dramatic scene with Harry Shannon (from the New York days). Right in the middle of the scene Bill said, "Fine, cut, that's it, now . . ." I walked over and said, "Bill, we're only halfway through the scene." He said, "Oh. Oh, let's do that again." We shot the scene again.

I was a little nervous a couple of times but Bill did a fine job and the picture was very well reviewed. I don't know if it ever made any money, because they didn't have a great release or anything.

MALTIN: I can't think of a bigger leap than going from PRC to MGM, but that's what you did. The next two films you made were at Metro, where I don't think you'd worked before.

LYDON: No, I never had.

MALTIN: A little film, *Twice Blessed*, with the Wilde twins and Preston Foster, then *Cynthia*. What was it like going to MGM?

LYDON: First of all, you have to realize that when you come to Hollywood and you go to a studio, that studio becomes your home. At least it did in those days. The crews were all under contract to the studio, the producers, the writers, the directors, the actors were all under contract to that studio, and RKO was my home. Then I moved down the street to Paramount for years. So I was used to a big studio, but I was not used to anything like MGM. Nobody got to MGM unless all of their people were working and they had to go outside to get somebody and they did with those two films. I came to MGM full of awe for this enormous machine, Leo the Lion, and with Elizabeth Taylor who was so beautiful she'd take your breath away. But I found her to be just a fun, fun lady, crazy about animals—and a much better actress than anybody ever gave her credit for. We had a wonderful time with some old pros like George Murphy and Mary Astor. The whole thing was a very nice experience, really.

MALTIN: I've always been fascinated with Michael Curtiz, and you got to work for him when you went to Warners to make *Life with Father*.

LYDON: Let me tell you about Mike Curtiz. He had a very thick Hungarian accent, he could barely speak English, he had a violent temper, and he got to direct all of the Americana at Warner Bros. He was a very artistic, wonderful director once you got used to this very odd personality. For instance, if something went wrong, he'd stand in the middle of the set and he'd scream his head off, "Who gets the big dough? You or me?" He always had an Englishman who was his prop man for many years, Limey his name was. Limey would listen to this tirade and he'd say, "Oh, shut up Mike, for God's sakes!" He'd say, "Limey, you son of a bitch, you're fired! Get off of my set! You're fired!" Well, Limey would leave for five minutes, then come right on back, but that's the way Mike was.

We were doing *Life with Father* for months at a time. When I became a director, I could make a picture in thirty days standing on my head without even breaking into a sweat. [This picture] all happens in one house, on one sound stage with a small cast; there's nothing difficult about it at all, it's easy to shoot. It took us five months to make this picture because Mr. Warner wanted to make this the key film from Warner Bros. that year. He spent a million dollars to buy the rights to it in the first place. Nobody had ever spent that much money before. That picture cost $4.5 million, in those days, and that was a lot of money.

Anyway, I got to know Mike in the strangest way. I turned down the part in New York when I was a kid, 'cause I'm working a lot at radio

William Powell, Emma Dunn, and Jimmy in Life With Father *(1947).*

and doing these plays and things and I'm making a very good living and I get a call from Howard Lindsay and Russell Crouse. I'm about fourteen at the time. I go down to the Village to meet them and they show me *Life with Father* as a play and they want to take this to Skowhegan, Maine for two weeks of rehearsal and open the season for one week of playing to see if it's capable of bringing it to Broadway. I thought that was very interesting and very practical. Crouse was a nice, easygoing guy. Howard Lindsay was a very strict kind of fella, which was all show; he was a wonderful guy underneath. But Howard Lindsay said, "You'll get $20 a week for rehearsal," which was the normal pay for rehearsals in those days, "and $20 a week for the run of the show." I said, "Mr. Lindsay, I'm doing a daytime radio show making thirty-two dollars and fifty cents for the morning show and twenty-eight dollars and fifty cents for the afternoon show, five days a week. I'm making three hundred dollars a week in radio; I can't afford you. I'm very sorry." And I walked out.

Well now they're trying to cast the movie, and I can't get in to see 'em. I'm a natural redhead and all the guys in the cast are redhead, but I can't get in to see them at Warner Bros. because the Henry Aldrich thing is a curse. They tested I don't know how many guys and none of them worked. Finally, we get a chance to go in and meet Mike Curtiz. I walked in on the set [and] he said, "That's the boy! That's the kid I want! All the time there; why you don't take this boy?"

So I signed to make this picture and I went under contract to Warner Bros., not knowing why but I went under contract at Warner Bros. Now, we're into the picture thirteen weeks—we shot for God knows how many weeks—and they dropped my option. I was shocked, and Mike said, "What's the matter, kid?" I said, "I don't know, Mike, I must be stinkin' up your film because Warner Bros. just dropped me." He said, "What? They crazy; come with me, we call Jack right now." So up we go to Mr. Warner's office, who I worked for years later and learned to love. And Mike said, "Why you do that to this kid? He's marvelous in the picture there. You crazy or something, Jack? What the hell you do?" And Warner said, "Listen, Mike, it's my job to get this picture made for a certain amount of money. I signed Jim purposely to a thirteen-week contract so we could get him at that reduced salary. Now are you satisfied? Are you happy? I think he's wonderful, too, now get out of my office." Years later, I understood that.

But that was Mike Curtiz, who was so difficult to know but once you did, he was just a marvelous director. He had a wonderful sense of camera angles and balance and he always put a framing piece into his shot. He was just marvelous.

MALTIN: That cast is pretty imposing, too.

LYDON: Oh, yeah. Irene Dunne. We were shooting, maybe two or three weeks and I couldn't see anything. Bill Powell, of course, a marvelous actor and a wonderful man. And ZaSu Pitts. Everybody's lovely. But I can't see Irene Dunne for sour apples. Mike came over to me, said, "What the matter, kid?" I said, "I don't know Mike." I said, "I don't understand Irene Dunne." He said, "Do me a favor, kid, you come to the rushes with me tomorrow." So I see the rushes for the first time and everything is there. She had a perfect, perfect technique but you couldn't see it when you were playing with her. She was marvelous.

MALTIN: Another big movie right after that was *Joan of Arc* for another larger-than-life character, Victor Fleming.

LYDON: I've got to expound on that, if you don't mind, and realize that what I tell you now is my opinion only. Victor Fleming had been a cameraman in the silent days, and apparently a very good cameraman. Victor Fleming made some strange and marvelous pictures in his time, including *The Wizard of Oz* and he did part of *Gone with the Wind* and all these things. He was known as a very big-time director. I tell you that Victor Fleming didn't know beans about directing, because you know how he used to direct? First of all, he never had a cast that wasn't full of players with credits as long as your arm. Then he would call the cast together and he'd sit down in this chair and he'd say, "You folks

Jimmy's description of The First 100 Years, television's first soap opera: "Twenty-eight pages of dialogue every day, Monday to Friday, fifty-two weeks a year. Toughest job I ever had."

know the words?" You'd say yes and he'd say, "Okay, kick it around; I've got to go talk to so-and-so."

Joe Valentine was his cameraman on that. He'd go in the corner for about forty-five minutes and discuss it with Joe Valentine while Ingrid Bergman and the rest of us would rehearse a scene. And when we'd staged the thing and rehearsed the thing he'd come and he'd say, "Let me see this." You'd show him the scene that you'd rehearsed and staged and he'd say one of two things. He'd say, "Nah, that stinks, skate around again," or he else he'd say, "Yeah. Now Joe, we're going to be right here." That's the way he'd direct a film. Honest to God. And he got away with it for many, many years.

MALTIN: What was your impression of Ingrid Bergman?

LYDON: Ingrid Bergman I thought, and still do today, was the consummate screen actress. She knew what to do with these and these, and she was a perfect screen actress.

MALTIN: You just pointed to your hands and your eyes.

LYDON: Yes. She was a master at it, like Spencer Tracy was. I always wanted to work with her and I did; I played her brother. And we're working for this no-talent director. Ingrid Bergman is what you always wanted in an actress, a great actress—she'll rehearse with you all day long. She hasn't had an ounce of temperament, screaming or anything like that, just a perfect professional. Let me tell you about one time: she was in armor. It's aluminum, but nevertheless, it's the dead of winter at the Hal Roach Studios in Culver City, colder than a well-digger's you-know-what. It's really cold, and it's miserable. She's on the set at eight o'clock every morning ready to go and one day, she's not there—eight fifteen, eight thirty. Quarter to nine, she came on the set in the armor and everything else and she went to the director first and she apologized to the director, she apologized to the cast, and she apologized to the crew and said, "I have no excuse. My alarm went off and I turned it off and I meant to get up and I fell asleep and I'm very sorry." Now, that's a classy lady.

MALTIN: Tell me about *The Time of Your Life*.

LYDON: I knew Jimmy Cagney as a child actor in New York. Jimmy was a hoofer, as you know. In Hollywood, I knew Cagney because I was the youngest member of what they called the Irish Mafia. Did you ever hear of the Irish Mafia?

MALTIN: Yes, but I didn't know you were a part of it.

LYDON: Well, I was the only young person in the Irish Mafia, which consisted of Jimmy Cagney, Jimmy Gleason, Frank McHugh, Pat O'Brien, Allen Jenkins, Spencer Tracy (who very rarely came to anything), Bob Armstrong (who was not Irish, he was Scots), and me. A kid. Well, I'm twenty-one, twenty-two years old. I knew Jim as a very nice man and we had done a couple of public service films together. I knew his family: two of his older brothers were doctors and one of them was my mother's doctor, so we knew the Cagneys very well.

This is how Jim treated everybody. I got a call to go over and see him. He owned General Service Studios at the time; he owned the whole lot. He said, "I want you to take this home, Jim, and read it for the part of so and so and come back tomorrow at about two o'clock and let me know, huh?" I said okay. So I took the script home for *The Time of Your Life* and I read it. I couldn't make any sense out of it at all. Here's a fifty-year-old cowboy who rides a bicycle and who herds cattle on a bicycle and here's a big guy who goes out and buys all sorts of gum and all these crazy characters. I'd never seen the play. Even if I did, I couldn't have made any sense out of it, so I went back the next day and he said, "What do you think?" I said, "Jim, I don't understand a word of it. I'm sorry, I just don't understand what the hell it's all about." He said, "I didn't ask you that. Do you want to do it?" I said, "Oh, yeah, I'd love to." He said, "You got it." Never mentioned money, nothing. We shot that thing with Jimmy Wong Howe for God knows how long, forever. With Bendix and all those other folks, you know. And Jim protected that no-talent director every step of the way.

MALTIN: I've read about a famous production of *What Price Glory?* that John Ford directed. You were cast and traveled all over California with it, didn't you?

LYDON: Yes, we played San Gabriel, we played Long Beach, we played Grauman's Chinese, and then we went to San Francisco and played the San Francisco Opera House. We played the Oakland Auditorium and someplace else, I've forgotten where. We went up to San Francisco in a day coach, all of us. We slept two or three in a room at the St. Francis Hotel.

MALTIN: Who did you bunk with?

LYDON: I've forgotten now. But I dressed with Duke Wayne and Oliver Hardy. Babe Hardy and Duke and I . . . we had a dressing room for the three of us. We were finished in the second act so we took curtain calls together, the three of us.

MALTIN: What I would have given to see Oliver Hardy onstage . . .

LYDON: Oh, he was wonderful, what a lovely man, and you know, he was almost broke. They never really made any kind of money and it was too bad 'cause he was just a great, great comedian.

MALTIN: John Wayne had never appeared on stage before; how did he do?

LYDON: Well, he didn't have very much to do and he just did it because Mr. Ford asked him to; he had a few lines and he was a little nervous. He was with some real stage actors like Robert Armstrong and Wallace Ford and he held his own okay.

MALTIN: So tell me how you're related to John Ford.

LYDON: Well, I did [this] play for John Ford so he could raise enough money for the Field House he built out in the Valley for the recipients of the Purple Heart. It was a magnificent cast of people that were all working for free for Mr. Ford. During rehearsals at the Masquers Club in Hollywood he asked about my lineage. I told him my father was born in New York and my grandfather and all the family for generations back were born in County Mayo. He said, "You know something? We're

This photo accompanied Jimmy's biography in the Masquers Club program for What Price Glory? Jimmy signed it to costar Ward Bond. (Courtesy of Michael F. Blake)

cousins." I said, "Really, Mr. Ford?" He said his mother was Mary Lydon from Kiltimagh. We're second cousins.

MALTIN: Kiltimagh. What a wonderful name.

LYDON: Well, I wish it were a wonderful town. The first time I drove into town, was a great big sign over a building that said "Lydon's Bar." That was the curse of my whole family.

MALTIN: Did being related to him score you any points in terms of how he treated you?

LYDON: Not at all. Not at all. I worked for him once in a film only, *When Willie Comes Marching Home.* He always had his gang, you know, and his gang were toadies, really. They worked when Mr. Ford worked. He would pick on somebody during the production, and many times he would drive them up the wall and I guess he enjoyed that sort of thing. I was playing a flier; I come back to the little town as a big hero and the other fellow who's older than me never gets out of the town. So Ford said, "Jim, you know when people come back, especially Navy people, the thing they want is ice cream." I said, "Oh, really?" He said yeah, and then said, "We've got a scene coming up and I want you to eat ice cream. What kind of ice cream do you like?" I said, "I don't care . . . vanilla, chocolate's fine." He said, "Vanilla?" I said, "Yeah, vanilla." He said okay. So when we got to the scene, of course, it was strawberry. You know, he would do these things purposely.

I was an old-timer by that time. I'd made a lot of films and the one thing that teed him off was he had done a big master shot of the family saying goodbye to the first guy drafted in the service.

MALTIN: That's Dan Dailey.

LYDON: Right. And Ford's got this big master shot of this guy saying goodbye and he gets on a train and he goes. Now Ford's doing a trucking shot across the faces just saying goodbye, and he got to me and he stopped the camera. We were dress-rehearsing. He got off the camera and he came over and he saw I was wearing a suit and a shirt and a tie. He said, "Jim, was your tie up that high?" I said, "It was, Mr. Ford." He said, "Well, you look too damn comfortable." He unbuttoned the top button on my shirt and he yanked the collar down a little bit and he ran his hand through my hair and mussed it a little bit and he started to get back on the camera and I couldn't help it, I said, "Mr. Ford, it won't match." You could have heard a pin drop on that set. He hunched his shoulders and he took a big long pause and he turned around to me and he said, "Are you a cutter now?" and I said, "No, sir." And he didn't talk to me for one week. Not hello, how are you . . . nothing. We'd rehearse a scene together and he talked to everybody else, he wouldn't talk to me. That's Mr. Ford.

More than 20 Stories in Every Issue

MOTION PICTURE
MAGAZINE

A Fawcett Publication

OCTOBER
15¢

JOAN LESLIE
A CLOSE-UP BY
SIDNEY SKOLSKY

OUR BIG
EXCLUSIVE!   **STARS OF TOMORROW**   BY CHARLES
SAMUELS

Conversations:
JOAN LESLIE

In 1940 a pretty, adolescent girl named Joan Brodel won the leading role in a Warner Bros. short subject called *Alice in Movieland* about a girl's dreamlike experience in Hollywood: spotted on the set, given the lead in a major movie, becoming a star, and winning an Academy Award. Never was casting more ironic—or prophetic—because Joan Brodel's real-life story wasn't so different from that piece of fluffy fiction.

After several years of appearing in tiny roles, she was signed by Warners and, as Joan Leslie, co-starred with Gary Cooper in *Sergeant York*, Humphrey Bogart in *High Sierra*, James Cagney in *Yankee Doodle Dandy*, and Fred Astaire in *The Sky's the Limit*—all before she turned eighteen! (Not so incidentally, Warner Bros. reissued *Alice in Movieland* and refilmed the main titles to feature Leslie's "new" name as well as her star billing. You can see the short on Turner Classic Movies, or on the Warner Home Video DVD of *The Sea Hawk*.)

Joan Leslie has given many interviews about her career and her notable co-stars—she adds a great deal to the hour-long DVD documentary on the making of *Yankee Doodle Dandy*—but I was curious about her earliest experiences in Hollywood, and I wanted to learn more about day-to-day life as a contract player under the studio system. She was happy to oblige, although when I made the mistake of referring to her as a one-time extra she politely but firmly corrected me.

MALTIN: Can you help me understand the difference between an extra and a bit player?
LESLIE: I had lines; I had scenes in films like *Men with Wings* and that little picture at Columbia, *Military Academy*. If you have lines, you're

not an extra. And at that time, I don't think you were in the union if you were an extra. I had an agent, you see.

MALTIN: Would you go for readings?

LESLIE: Yes. I remember one picture out at Fox, for instance. [My agent] said, "There'll be others there up for the same part; it's a Jones Family series [picture]." That's all they told me. I got there and there were two or three other young ladies there, and the producer and director were sitting at their desks. We were standing in front of them and they were looking at us and they said, "We would like somebody with a Southern accent." And nobody said anything, so I said [in Southern accent], "Well, y'all, you come to the right gal. You want to talk to me?" I talked as Southern as I could come up with and that's all I needed to do, to show initiative.

MALTIN: I'm curious about the details of your working experience at this time. How were you treated when you were a bit player? Did anybody pay attention to you? When you showed up, you would report to whom and where? Were you given a call sheet [where] they would tell you what time to show up . . . ?

LESLIE: You had to sense a lot of it. When you'd go to makeup, then they'd say, it's on Stage Twelve. You go down there and report to the first assistant. You'd just look around until you found who the first assistant was; you'd feel your way out, trying not to make mistakes. Then, [it's] the second assistant [who] would call you, so you'd get to know his name. And in a nice, open way, you'd get to know people's names. I remember that when I'd come back from lunch, I'd always bring a couple of packs of gum and I'd give anybody that I'd made acquaintance of that morning a stick of gum. It was casual so that they'd kind of remember me.

On the set you just have to listen very closely, listen to everyone around you, absorb everything and try to be what they want you to be with the little bitty line that you'd have to say. If it was a good line, it would be such fun to say it with vigor, you know. In *Winter Carnival,* when they asked me what school I went to, I wasn't a college student, so I had to lie; I pretended to be a French girl and said it was the Sorbonne in Paris! And oh, they were surprised at that and let me "go" in the scene, so that was fun to do. Then [my character] said "Jeepers!" all the way through. Whenever something exciting or happy happened I would say "Jeepers!" with such vigor that it knocked them over. You're so glad when you get a line like that, that you can play with and do something interesting with. That's the way it is: you have to show your initiative, you have to show talent and availability, and still have an awful lot of luck.

MALTIN: Yes, but you had smarts, too. The way you were open and friendly and you picked up on things and followed through . . . that was smart.

Joan Leslie, left, with June Wilkins, Elsie Esmond, and Lionel Barrymore in Camille *(1936).*

LESLIE: You have to do that. It was just part of the game, though . . .

MALTIN: Well yes, but you understood the game. There may have been other lovely young girls who may have had talent but they didn't get it. Or they may have been too assertive and off-putting in that way. That's a delicate balance, I'm sure.

LESLIE: Yes, because everybody on the set is very sensitive and very with-it. Every person is there doing their job and they're aware of their importance and the importance of new people coming along, and the big guys and how they should be treated—they all know it.

MALTIN: Tell me about working in *Camille*.

LESLIE: That was an experience. You know, I was signed at MGM just to do that bit, and I was only there six months. I had one line in the picture, which was cut out. I played Robert Taylor's little sister and it was in the scene where he comes home to see his father, Lionel Barrymore, and wants to seek his approval of him going with Camille, which, of course, he never got. He came home and I was being confirmed—a very Catholic service. That was to emphasize the straight-and-narrow of his life and how it had changed when he met Camille. I had a beautiful dress to wear; they said, "You take that home and wear it around the house, because it's got to look like it's been worn." I had this one line and I had two coaches to tell me how to say it. Two! They worked with me for a couple of weeks before the shoot. I had to say, "Armand, so you did come all the way from Paris?" I had a French teacher telling me how to say Armand and an Englishman telling me how to say Paris, for about twenty minutes every day for a couple of weeks. Can you imagine that they would have coaches like that? Then that particular scene was cut out, but I had another scene and another dress and another occasion with Lionel Barrymore, in which I had no lines.

MALTIN: So, you're still visible in it.

LESLIE: Yes, visible, and I have a still picture from that. I actually was on the set one time and saw Greta Garbo. I was there to have a dress approved by George Cukor and I didn't realize I was so close to a dressing room, because this particular dressing room was surrounded by folding screens. One of the screens opened and Garbo came out and I was almost in her way and she said, "Pardon." She went onto the set and I nearly fell over in a dead faint, because I adored the ground she walked on. She was just the epitome of everything screen actors could be. She was so far advanced in makeup, too. Do you know, she was the first actress that ever wore lines over her lid? She brought that from Europe. Anyway . . . that's my story on *Camille.*

MALTIN: How about *Laddie?*

LESLIE: I had a nice part in that. That was at RKO, and it was a wedding scene, I think. We were perhaps helping the bride-to-be to dress, and giggling and saying nice things to her. Something like that.

MALTIN: *Nancy Drew—Reporter,* with Bonita Granville?

LESLIE: I had a scene in that in which she came in to talk to a reporter. I was there with two or three other girls and I had a line but I don't know what it was.

MALTIN: *Susan and God* with Joan Crawford . . . ?

LESLIE: I had lines in that and that was very interesting because it [was] a nice, long run. Rita Quigley played the daughter. Gloria De Haven had a very important part in it and I got to know her pretty well. There were some other nice young people, too, and we were all supposed to be the friends of the daughter of Joan Crawford. And they asked me if I had riding clothes and I said no. [They said] "We'll fit you at wardrobe, that's all right." So there was a scene out at their estate where all the youngsters have to ride by in the distance. I liked to ride. I was not an accomplished rider but I was a courageous rider and I happened to have gotten the liveliest horse of the bunch. It was kind of fun to ride him but he was not controllable. All we had to do was ride by and I think somebody in the front waved to the daughter as they went by. We went through several times and I sensed that I could not hold this horse. When we started making takes he got wilder than ever and he threw me and dragged me. I recall Fredric March came over and helped me up, and I was quite thrilled about that. But it scratched my face quite badly—

MALTIN: You're lucky you got away with just a scratch.

LESLIE: Yes, it was pretty scary, because that horse was very fast. If that happened later on, I'd have stopped and said, "I can't ride that horse." But I didn't. I thought, "I'll show them." But they [applied makeup over] that scratch and put me right in scenes. I think they deliberately put me in scenes where I showed in the background of scenes and fixed up my face or turned me in a way that it didn't show.

Can you spot Joan among the young people listening to Joan Crawford in this scene from Susan and God *(1940)?*

MALTIN: You mentioned *Men with Wings*, I didn't know about that one.

LESLIE: That was quite a nice break. I played Louise Campbell and Ray Milland's child and it was all about flying. I had some scenes with Andy Devine and nice dialogue.

MALTIN: And you were in Alfred Hitchcock's *Foreign Correspondent*.

LESLIE: In the first scene in that picture, I think, he's leaving on a boat [and] all of his family and friends are there to see him off. I was just one of the family, maybe a cousin or something, and we were all trying out the beds and seeing what the ashtrays look like as they panned around the room, that's all. I don't even know if I showed. But it's a good movie, and I thought Joel McCrea was just such a great actor, so sweet and so handsome. Like Cooper, you know, that quality.

MALTIN: Were you observing? Were you soaking all this in when you were on a set?

LESLIE: No, not only was I observing, but I was thinking, "I'm on my way, I'll do better, I'm going to get better parts, I will be something some time." I thought that. When I was little, at home in Detroit and going to dancing school and playing my accordion at benefits and at school and seeing Shirley Temple pictures, I thought, "I could do that." We moved to New York when I was about nine or ten and then MGM signed me at ten or eleven and I got that taste and I thought, "Mmm-hmm." [Then I went] back to New York and did modeling and radio work, all those things. Poor Mama and Dad, I wonder what they were thinking, because those were hard times. Then my sister came out under contract to Universal and she kept telling them they should have me out here because they were doing the Durbin pictures and I would fit in perfectly. Finally she brought me out, and Mama, and I started to get little parts right away.

Joan, left, poses with her sisters Mary and Betty Brodel in this 1942 Warner Bros. publicity photo.

MALTIN: Did you have a sense, at that age, of a caste system in Hollywood?

LESLIE: Automatically. In Rosemary DeCamp's book she speaks about that so interestingly, because she was always a character actress. As good as she was, she was always a character actress. She said the stars have a responsibility to be individual, interesting, even eccentric and outlandish, but important and on top of things. Everybody else has to support them. She said, "It's been great fun for me to sit back and to watch them work." It's an analysis I never heard anybody else make.

MALTIN: She had a great perspective on that.

LESLIE: She worked with everybody and she was respected by everybody, every director.

MALTIN: When you were doing a bit part and they were lighting or getting things ready for a shot, were you discouraged from talking to the stars, or was it easygoing on the set?

LESLIE: You wouldn't speak to them unless they initiated conversation. But usually the stars were very nice. Very nice to you, and helpful. Of course, they're not available, they're always being powdered or working on their lines or rehearsing or something. Any that I encountered were open and encouraging but busy with their own thing.

MALTIN: When you were put under contract at Warners, was there a ceremonial signing with the boss?

LESLIE: Oh, no. As you know, I was fifteen and Mother was there. And [the contract was for a] very, very moderate sum, and they said, "We're going to groom you, and you won't have any big parts for some [time]." Within two weeks I was testing for *High Sierra*, and I got that part. It's really amazing. Then to have the studio promote you and push you the way they did me was extremely fortunate. Raoul Walsh as a director and Bogart, all those names. It was very good. Why they thought I could do it . . . I suppose they just trusted that the director would pull me through.

MALTIN: I get the impression that there was kind of a family atmosphere for the contract people at a studio. You were working with the same people day after day, week after week, year after year. Was it like a cocoon?

LESLIE: Yes, I think it was for most of the people under contract. We saw things in the same light and we were all working to succeed and get the best dress and get the best makeup man and try to get the best role and all of that. But not with the front office and not with the executives. I've had friends in the production office but not in the front office. They were so far above us that they couldn't be bothered with actors. And, of course, J. L. [Warner] had a strong tendency to look down on actors. He had no respect for actors. A sharp businessman; he sometimes made mistakes, too, but he knew how to run that studio, didn't he?

MALTIN: Do you remember the first time you ever met him?

LESLIE: I suppose it was at a party. It'd just be, "How do you do?" I was the kid on the block, definitely younger than anybody else and that's why I don't think I ever went on a junket for Warner Bros. Alexis [Smith] did, and all the big stars I suppose did, but I was either in school or taking dramatics or taking ballet or working, because I did picture after picture out there.

MALTIN: That's what I wanted to learn about: What kind of grooming did you get at the studio? Did you have singing lessons, dancing lessons, elocution lessons?

LESLIE: They had a wonderful dramatic coach on the lot, full-time, Sophie Rosenstein. She always thought that she would become a director; she was promised that. She was the Professor of Dramatics, I think, at Washington University, or one of the schools in Washington, and she was very astute. She really made careers, for Alexis and Gig Young and Susan Peters. She helped me a lot, on every picture I ever did. She would advise me and then she'd say, "But remember, do whatever the director says. Forget whatever I have told you and do what the director says, these are only just a guideline for you." Smart. Then, after a while, she brought in a diction expert who was a teacher at UCLA and I [did] some work with him, which cleaned up my English so I didn't sound so Midwestern. It's not a difficult thing to do, if you have an ear, and most actors do have an ear. I had a good ear for accents and things like that. When people that don't know me hear me talk now, they say, "Are you a teacher?" If they don't think I'm an actress, they think I'm a teacher.

And they had a ballet teacher there who always worked on musicals; he would either be in the chorus or be an assistant to [choreographer]

Another movie, another leading man: Ronald Reagan and Joan in Irving Berlin's This Is the Army (1943).

LeRoy Prinz. They permitted him to do classes and all of us under contract would show up for classes.

MALTIN: Was there a vocal coach, too?

LESLIE: Let me think. Before *Thank Your Lucky Stars*, they had a choral and vocal group expert in the music department, Dudley Chambers, work with me one day a week, over a period of six months, and it was very helpful. It was during wartime and he helped put together a medley of songs that I could sing at the [Hollywood] Canteen or on camp tours.

MALTIN: Did you have contact with guys like M. K. Jerome and Jack Scholl? They were there at Warners for so many years.

LESLIE: Jerome wrote the music for us, and he was such a nice, unassuming guy. He worked very hard and I'm trying to think if it was he that taught me how to play "Mary's a Grand Old Name" for *Yankee Doodle*. That was an outstanding music department. When I had to play that one song, and Jimmy [Cagney] was singing, more or less standing over me, I had to practice playing it, and I did learn how to play that, chords and all, for the picture by going in at least three days a week and putting in half an hour with somebody. They wrote out the fingering for me and I practiced it at home so that I was comfortable with it. That, too, was available.

MALTIN: Would they set a schedule for you? They knew your shooting schedule and such, [but] would they say, ballet is Monday at 10:00 or acting is Tuesday at 4:00?

LESLIE: No, it seems as if these things occurred between pictures, but the piano [lessons, for example] would be on the picture schedule.

It would be casually scheduled. It was very casual and you kind of sought it out yourself.

MALTIN: Tell me about going to school while working at the studios.

LESLIE: My first year out here I was in the eighth grade at St. Ambrose parochial school. Then my first year of high school I was at Immaculate Heart High. I didn't even finish that first year when Warners signed me, so I didn't go to public school,

MALTIN: When you were in the parochial schools, were they understanding about when you would be off for a week or two and then come back?

LESLIE: Very much so, although at Immaculate Heart, I said, "Couldn't I graduate with the girls if I kept up with my studies?" And the nuns said, "You won't be able to; don't even think about it." I was really kind of miffed at that, but it's just as well because it would have been very difficult, because I worked so much of the time. I did finally take my high school exams down at the Board of Education and I passed my high school with good marks and a year of Spanish and two years of French. I don't think I did very well in algebra, not very well at all.

[At MGM] I went to school with Mickey Rooney, and Deanna Durbin was there at the time, you know, Edna Mae Durbin. After that she went to Universal. Freddie Bartholomew was also in school at that time but he was in another room with a coach who helped him retain his English accent.

MALTIN: How interesting.

LESLIE: It was a nice little school house and she was an excellent teacher. Usually [at Warners] I was working and the teacher would be with me in the dressing room. On *Sergeant York*, we had one of those canvas dressing rooms and June Lockhart and Dickie Moore and I were going to school together. They played [Gary Cooper's] brother and sister in *York*.

MALTIN: Do you remember how you felt when you no longer had to attend classes while you were working?

LESLIE: I had my eighteenth birthday on the set [of *The Sky's the Limit*, with Fred Astaire, on loan-out to RKO] and then I didn't have to have a teacher with me. It was right in the middle of production, and they continued to provide me with a teacher so that I would finish my work and graduate . . . but the limitations were off on the hours [that a minor could work], and they were very limiting. Did you know that? [The state determined] how many hours you could stay and somebody had to be with you all the time and you had to quit pretty early.

MALTIN: What was it like when you were loaned out? Did you feel odd walking onto another lot when Warners was your home base?

LESLIE: Well, they always treat you very well when you're on loan-out.

You get the best dressing room and your clothes are always done with more care and attention. Warners was such a routine kind of place. They'd pull things out of stock to put on you and say, "This'll be good; we'll let this out and we'll take this in." [If] we were doing a picture in '42, you were wearing the clothes of '40, at least. But if you went to Fox, they were dressing you like it was '45. If you were at MGM, you'd be dressed in something elegant and advanced—Adrian clothes and so on. Toward the end, I did a couple of pictures [at Warners] in which I had some nice clothes. They got some new designers. Milo Anderson put the same clothes on me in picture after picture. They didn't realize how important glamour was—only as far as Bette was concerned, or Ann Sheridan, or Olivia de Havilland. They were always shown to their best advantage. But as you were coming up the ladder it was very hard to get attention like that.

MALTIN: Did you entertain at camps during the war? You alluded to that earlier . . .

LESLIE: Oh yes, you were assigned to do that by the studio. I did a bond-selling tour with Walter Pidgeon and Adolphe Menjou and they gave serious speeches. The Epstein brothers wrote a speech for me—ten, twelve pages long—saying all these things I was supposed to say at a bond-selling tour. It ended up that I said very few things. I took off my hat and I waved and said, "The boys out there are no older than I am and we've got to support them, haven't we?" That was about my whole speech. We were in shipyards up and down the coast. Then I did a camp tour also, visiting hospitals at camps. Mother went with me. I'd sing a little bit, sometimes maybe even do impersonations.

MALTIN: Who did you do?

LESLIE: Well, I did Ida Lupino. I did that in *Thank Your Lucky Stars*. I don't know how it came off, but Mark Hellinger told me, "I want you to do your imitations in this. I want this to be a showcase for you." I did a Cagney and [was planning on doing Ida, but] he said, "The only thing is, you have to go to Ida and get permission to do it." I was very concerned about that, and I thought, well, she's a friend, I know I can talk to her, but what if she says no? What if she says, "You hurt my feelings?" So I went down on the set and I said, "You know, an impersonation is just an exaggeration of your characteristics and it isn't really like you at all, it's more like a caricature." She said, "Don't give me any of that, darling, just go ahead and do it just the way you're going to do it on the screen." So I had to do it. She laughed hysterically and said, "That's fine with me."

The
BALLYHOO EXPRESS

Today, the movie junket is a well-oiled machine—too much of a machine, if you ask me—involving a floating band of journalists who trek to New York or Los Angeles almost every weekend to screen new films and conduct brief interviews with the principals involved.

It was not always so. Once upon a time, a junket involved putting stars—not the press—on the road . . . and in some cases, having the press travel alongside the stars.

The film industry recognized early on that the stars held an incredible, magnetic attraction for both the general public and for the fans. The first important manifestation of that allure came in the teens, when such stars as Charlie Chaplin, Marie Dressler, Douglas Fairbanks, and Mary Pickford made personal appearances to sell Liberty Bonds—and throngs of people turned out to see them. This practice would be repeated and expanded during World War II.

In terms of movie-related ballyhoo, the stunt that is often cited as the first junket, or traveling show, took place in 1933, when Warner Bros. sent a train called the *42nd Street Special* across the country on a sixteen-day tour that was modestly billed as "the greatest ride since Paul Revere." The film being touted was, of course, the landmark musical *42nd Street*.

The stars on board had nothing to do with that movie; some were under contract to Warner Bros., while others were simply "available." Publicity never hurt anyone's career, and fans were happy to see any motion picture personalities up close.

Tom Mix was no longer the star he had been in the silent era, but his name still packed plenty of punch; he was accompanied on this trip by his horse King, who had a car all to himself. (Mix's legendary horse

Lyle Talbot, Bette Davis, Claire Dodd, Eleanor Holm, Preston Foster, Leo Carrillo, and Laura La Plante smile and wave as the 42nd St. Special takes off.

SPECIAL TRAIN CARRIES '42d STREET' TO RECORD

Holdovers of Warner Picture a Regular Occurrence, Despite Bank Holidays, Earthquake; Grosses Exceeding "Fugitive"

Warners' "42nd Street" special is speeding back to the Coast after a 16-day trip across the continent, making scores of stops and carrying the picture to unusual grosses due to the comprehensive exploitation achievement of S. Charles Einfeld, in charge of advertising and publicity.

Despite the bank holiday and even the California earthquake the special stirred up unusual public interest that has been re-'ed at the box offices.
' ''--'---

Louis Ambassador and eleven days at the Empire in San Antonio.

The Warner home office says the grosses are running far ahead of the business done by "I Am a Fugitive from a Chain Gang" and "Silver Dollar." Philadelphia reported fully 50 per cent greater business than done with "Fugitive." In Denver the Orpheum with eight days doubled the "Fugitive" gross. In six days at the Warner Memphis, the musical hit outgrossed the Muni hit by 55 per cent. In St. Louis, "42nd Street" ran more than double "Silver Dollar," which had held the high mark for two years. San Antonio was 100 per cent higher than "Fugitive."

New York St͞-- ͞-- Appear

Tony retired around this time, though some reports simply said he was not keen on travel.) Warner players Bette Davis (honeymooning with her first husband, Harmon Nelson) and Glenda Farrell were joined by Leo Carrillo, Laura La Plante, Lyle Talbot, champion swimmer Eleanor Holm (a recent Warners contractee and WAMPAS Baby Star), Preston Foster, Claire Dodd, and Harry Seymour. Jack Dempsey joined the troupe in Kansas City, and Joe E. Brown hopped on board in Chicago for the duration of the tour.

For sex appeal—and unlimited photo opportunities—a bevy of Busby Berkeley beauties were recruited to join the festivities, including such future notables as Toby Wing (to whom Dick Powell sings "Young and Healthy" in *42nd Street*), Shirley Ross, and Lois January.

The troupe did more than make whistle stops; there were personal appearances on theater stages in every major city. What's more, the junket bore a commercial tie-in that might impress even today's marketing mavens. General Electric cosponsored the jaunt with Warner Bros., because the *42nd Street* train carried a specially designed car featuring an all-electric "kitchen of the future," including a 1933 marvel: an automatic dishwasher.

In some respects the publicity stunt was ill-timed, but the Motion Picture Herald reported, "Despite the bank holiday and even the California earthquake the special stirred up unusual public interest that has been reflected at the box-office.

"Almost from the first day the project translated itself into increased theater attendance. The first big stop—and that was for only four hours—was Denver, but long before that, through California, Arizona, and New Mexico, crowds greeted the seven-car gold and silver train with its ten stars and dozen '42nd Street Beauties.' Then Denver. Greeted by the governor of Colorado, the mayor of Denver and civic leaders. The picture opened at the Orpheum to record business, a capacity week, and then another big first-run week at the Aladdin. In the meanwhile the train had gone to Kansas City, and at the Newman theater the picture held over for a second week . . .''

Veteran Hollywood chronicler Bob Thomas remembers the event, and says it was his father's brainchild, although Warners publicity executive S. Charles Einfeld took credit for the stunt.

To make sure everything would go smoothly, the company made a dry run with their specially decorated train. Thomas recalls, "They took the train out to San Bernardino and back. They had a bunch of stars and executives from the studio up in the first car and the drinking room, and had a gala party. My brother and I were stationed in the observation car, which was florally covered with white fans, and there were pictures of the desert on the walls. In the baggage cars there were two searchlights which would be shining into the sky as the train moved along. It rode through the orange groves to San Berdoo and back again. My brother and I sat back there, watching the groves go by and drinking ginger ale, and I told my father, 'This is the life,' little knowing that I would some time later be a patron of such junkets. He left there a year or so after that; he got fired by Jack Warner. I had my revenge forty years later, writing Warner's biography."

The Warners' train wound up in Washington, D.C. in time for Franklin D. Roosevelt's presidential inauguration—"inaugurating a new deal in entertainment," the studio proclaimed. But there was some competition in our nation's capital from the "MGM Globe Trotter Traveling Studio," an enormous two-unit vehicle that was able to appear in the Inaugural Parade, which Warners' railroad train could not. Instead, the *42nd Street* brigade boarded a special float featuring an actual merry-go-round to greet movie fans along the parade route.

Motion Picture Herald editor-publisher Martin Quigley praised the efforts of both studios in his weekly editorial. "These are activities of showmanship, whoope-te-doo showmanship, that the mob likes, which is the only showmanship that can do us much good in these days when the motion picture has the problem of selling the millions." His remarks appeared in the same issue as a sober report on the threat of free radio broadcasts to paid movie attendance in the depths of the Depression.

Not that the studios shunned radio as a publicity medium; the promotion of songs from *42nd Street* on the air played a major role in building audience awareness of the musical, and the *42nd Street Special* carried a portable broadcasting facility that hit the local airwaves in every major city along its route. A seven-minute short-cum-trailer (jointly presented by WB and GE) was released so the whole country could catch *42nd Street* fever. The train's exploits even warranted an item in *Newsweek*.

A short time later, the *Herald* ran a Warners ad promoting new studio arrival Bette Davis and her latest film. A headline blared, "The *42nd Street Special* Made Her Famous—*Ex-Lady* Will Make Her a Sensation!" As a relative unknown, Davis's exposure on the coast-to-coast junket was considered a major boost.

But the trip was not without its perils. According to a photo caption in Frederic Thrasher's 1946 book *Okay for Sound*, "Traveling across the country in the midst of a bank holiday, Warner executives and stars were forced to raid box-office cash boxes to keep the caravan rolling. Nobody had any money but everyone was optimistic for the first time since the Depression struck the nation."

It would be six years before Warners attempted something as ambitious again, for the debut of its Technicolor *Western Dodge City*. This time, S. Charles Einfeld planned a double-whammy: not just a huge world premiere in Dodge City, Kansas, but a whistle-stop junket with a trainload of stars and reporters riding from Los Angeles to the event. A live NBC broadcast would be heard from coast to coast, and Technicolor cameras would roll on location so moviegoers could witness the festivities in a short-subject-cum-trailer. (The one-reel short appears on the laserdisc of *Dodge City* and also on the DVD released in early 2005.)

On March 20, 1939, Einfeld outlined some of his plans in a letter to Jack L. Warner, boasting, "I think I can safely say this is going to be one of the biggest things that has ever been put on in the history of show business . . . We are going to have a parade and already there are five hundred horses entered and approximately forty-five bands. Add to this stagecoaches, buckboards, Indians, etc. and you'll get some idea of what a spectacle it will be . . . I figure there will be a hundred thousand people to witness the event.

"Our entrance into Dodge City is going to be sensational. Fifty miles from the town a convoy of fifty decorated planes will sweep down from the clouds and accompany the train to the depot. Five miles from town fifty masked horsemen will sweep out from the prairie, shooting guns and pacing the train."

Life magazine's photographer Peter Stackpole was among the entourage. Years later he published some of his candid pictures of the stars in his book *Life in Hollywood 1936–1952* and wrote, "Hollywood columnists, photographers, stars, publicity people, New York press, Western Union

reps, some starlets, and a few girls who just looked like starlets all joined in on the train treks, eager to see what effect the glitter of Hollywood would have on rural America. Enroute to Dodge City, Kansas, whole towns seemed to turn out, and crowds swarmed over the tracks to get a glimpse of Errol Flynn, Humphrey Bogart, Alan Hale, and others stars, who took turns plugging movies at the rear platform.

Wearing outfits seen in 42nd Street, some of Busby Berkeley's chorus girls pose for a sure-fire publicity shot. That's the unmistakable platinum blonde Toby Wing third from left.

"But the trips were too long for all those egos to be captive on one train. Near Dodge City, Big Boy Williams got in a fight with another cowboy and had to be taken off. Actors drank heavily, making good copy for the columnists. A day out of Los Angeles on the Dodge City trek, Bogart had one of his predictable fights with wife Mayo Methot. He thought she was losing too much money at cards, chased her from the bar, and ran after her through several cars. He caught up with her just as she reached their bedroom compartment and she slammed the door behind her, catching him across the eyes, and giving him two shiners. Bogart got off the train in Los Angeles wearing the darkest glasses he could find."

Longtime Hollywood columnist and entertainment editor Jimmy Starr wrote an especially colorful chapter about the Dodge City junket in his posthumously published book *Barefoot on Barbed Wire*. Relying on his own published columns, rather than strictly his memory, he reconstructed events leading up to the gala festivities of April 1, 1939. "A deal was made with Lee Lyles, assistant to the president of [the] Santa Fe [Railroad] for a special train of fourteen cars. Santa Fe was standing part of the expense for the exploitation—and a Warner movie to be called *Santa Fe*, slated for a later date. [It eventually became *Santa Fe Trail*.] Smart cookies, these movie moguls. The choo-choo schedule was this: Leave Los Angeles at 8:30 p.m., Thursday, March 30. Ten- and fifteen-minute stops were arranged for San Bernardino, Barstow, Needles, Seligman, Winslow, Gallup, Albuquerque, La Junta, and Syracuse, where two cars were added with newspaper writers from New York and Chicago. Arrival in Dodge City was at 9:00 a.m. Saturday, April 1. There was a Palace car for sixteen horses and a Pullman car for a rodeo troupe and studio technicians.

"Two extra dining cars divided seven Roomette cars for the stars and Fourth Estaters. There were two lounge cars, an observation car, and an elaborately outfitted Gay Lady Cabaret car. This is where most of the action took place. As it turned out, there was considerable action not on the official program.

"Blaney Matthews, the Warner Bros. Studio chief of police, and a dozen of his men were along as security guards and possible fight stoppers." Less circumspect than Peter Stackpole, Starr also says flat-out that there were four prostitutes along to keep the male travelers happy.

Among the stars onboard were Dodge City's own Errol Flynn, Olivia de Havilland, Ann Sheridan, Alan Hale, Frank McHugh, and Guinn "Big Boy" Williams, along with Humphrey Bogart, John Garfield, Priscilla and Rosemary Lane, Jane Wyman, Jean Parker, John Payne, Hoot Gibson, Gilbert Roland, Wayne Morris, Lya Lys, Frances Robinson, and Gloria Dickson.

Starr also recounts that the train made an unscheduled stop at Pasadena, where a teary-eyed Olivia de Havilland was taken off by order of David O. Selznick, who claimed that she was needed for wardrobe tests and story conferences on *Gone with the Wind*. Starr speculates that the producer simply didn't want her to be exploited during the rowdy junket when he had his own publicity campaign for *GWTW* coming up later that year.

But perhaps the most interesting revelation in Starr's account is how 20th Century Fox publicity chief Harry Brand attempted to steal Warners' thunder, for the greater glory of Fox and its chief, former Warners production head Darryl F. Zanuck. With less than a week to make final preparations, Zanuck's company decided to pull out all the stops for a special train junket to San Francisco at the Fair on Treasure Island. The timing and the subject were just right. Zanuck had William Randolph Hearst's Cosmopolitan Production of *The Story of Alexander Graham Bell* (1939) to sell. It was a hard sell.

"With the backing of Hearst's powerful papers, Zanuck and Brand could—and did—steal a lot of thunder from the Warner blast-away. The great Harry Brand trick was to stage the event two days before the Warner junket took off."

Fox amassed an impressive roster of talent to participate in the junket, including Don Ameche, Loretta Young, Tyrone Power, Sonja

Henie, Annabella, Cesar Romero, Linda Darnell, Nancy Kelly, Sally Eilers, Lynn Bari, Mary Carlisle, Constance Bennett, and Darryl F. Zanuck himself.

Starr details all the ins and outs of staging this coup, and then adds a punchline: while all the top entertainment reporters, editors, and photographers were enjoying themselves on a train ride up the California coast, Clark Gable and Carole Lombard chose that exact moment to elope to Kingman, Arizona. The press was scooped by the two biggest stars in Hollywood.

The success of Dodge City in 1939 inspired Warner Bros. to star Errol Flynn in another large-scale western, *Virginia City*, the following year . . . and prompted the Warners publicity department to cook up a celebrity-filled junket to rival their enormously successful Dodge City event.

So it was that at 12:05 p.m. on Friday, March 15, 1940, an eighteen-car train left the Burbank station with fifty Hollywood celebrities and two hundred members of the press onboard. The following day they would participate in an unusual dual premiere, at the Granada Theater in Reno and all three movie theaters in Virginia City, Nevada. NBC agreed to air a special broadcast from Piper's Opera House in Virginia City, while a fleet of cars, buses, and motorcycle escorts planned to shuttle the guests between the two locations where two days of festivities were planned. Errol Flynn led a parade down the main street of Reno. As with the Dodge City rail junket, this one took advantage of every stop along the way to garner publicity and spread goodwill from a truly

Stopping off in Rio Pueblo, New Mexico the Dodge City junketeers pose for cameramen. Standing: Gilbert Roland, Frank McHugh, Chief Santa Fe, Maxie Rosenbloom, Priscilla Lane, Errol Flynn, John Garfield, Jack L. Warner, Rosemary Lane, Wayne Morris, and John Payne. Kneeling: Leon G. Turrow, Hoot Gibson, Buck Jones, Lee Lyles, Guinn "Big Boy" Williams, Humphrey Bogart, Jean Parker, and Frances Robinson. (Courtesy Delmar Watson Photography Archives)

imposing lineup of stars. And while the studios were normally clannish about their contract players, when it came to these junkets they seemed to believe that star power was the most important ingredient, not studio affiliation. So, along with Warners players Flynn, Wayne Morris, Rosemary Lane, May Robson, Alan Hale, Jeffrey Lynn, Guy Kibbee, and newlyweds Ronald Reagan and Jane Wyman were Binnie Barnes (and her husband, football star and future producer Mike Frankovich), Sigrid Gurie, Gilbert Roland, the outgoing Leo Carrillo, Mary Astor (who'd score big at Warners a year later in *The Maltese Falcon*), Bruce Cabot, Pat Dane, Patricia Ellis, screen veterans Fred Stone and Hobart Bosworth, a bevy of attractive starlets, and three of movies' greatest western stars—Tom Mix, Buck Jones, and William Boyd.

Comedian Ken Murray was hired as the emcee, not only for the NBC broadcast but for the whistle-stop appearances the stars made on the back of the train platform. Citizens of Bakersfield, Fresno, Merced, Modesto, Stockton, and Sacramento, California were treated to impromptu fifteen-minute shows by some of the traveling stars. Boyd, clad in his signature all-black Hopalong Cassidy outfit, was a great hit with fans throughout the weekend.

The night of the premiere, Nevada Governor Carville and his wife hosted a ball for the visitors from movieland, and when the stars departed the next day, they continued to promote *Virginia City* with brief stops along the route back home to Burbank. They even stopped at Norden on the way home, where photographers had a field day snapping Tom Mix and other stars throwing snowballs.

By this time, Ken Murray had started taking 16mm home movies, and footage of the *Virginia City* outing appeared in his oft-repeated 1966 television special *Hollywood without Makeup*.

With the storm clouds of war on the horizon, junketeering faded from the scene in the early 1940s. After December 7, 1941, all priorities shifted toward the war effort, and travel was severely restricted. But the junket didn't die; it was reinvented for the purpose of selling war bonds. Stars took to the road, just as they had during World War I, to use the power of their popularity for a cause all Americans could believe in. (It was after a hugely successful bond drive in her home state of Indiana that Carole Lombard died in a plane crash in January of 1942.)

Perhaps the greatest junket of all time was war-related: the Hollywood Victory Caravan, which set off from Los Angeles in March of 1942—just three months after Pearl Harbor. Because it was not tied to a specific movie studio, talent was drawn from all of Hollywood to make a cross-country railroad trip with many stops along the way for parades, performances, and war-bond rallies. Stars included Laurel and Hardy, James Cagney, Groucho Marx, Cary Grant, Claudette Colbert, Bert Lahr, Charles Boyer, Merle Oberon, Olivia de Havilland, Joan Blondell, Pat O'Brien, Frank McHugh, Charlotte Greenwood, Frances Langford, Jerry Colonna, Desi Arnaz, and Faye McKenzie. In every city, the arrival of an A-list array of Hollywood stars was front-page news, and untold thousands of fans got to see their screen favorites sing, dance, and perform in comedy sketches. Some more stars joined the party when they were received at the White House by Mrs. Eleanor Roosevelt.

Gene Lester was the caravan's official photographer, and the only one to capture candid moments with the stars after hours on the train. A few shots appear in his book *When Hollywood Was Fun* (Carol Publish-

Laurel and Hardy on stage for the 1942 Hollywood Victory Caravan.

ing, 1993), but Lester wanted to publish an entire volume documenting this once-in-a-lifetime trip, and never did. (The pictures still exist, but Lester's anecdotes died with him.) The most vivid and heartwarming account of this remarkable experience appears in John Lahr's biography of his father Bert, *Notes on a Cowardly Lion* (Knopf, 1969). It's a beautifully evocative chapter about show-business camaraderie, well worth reading or re-reading. (Paramount later produced a two-reel short called *Hollywood Victory Caravan* in 1945, emphasizing its own studio roster—Bing Crosby, Bob Hope, Betty Hutton, Alan Ladd, Barbara Stanwyck, Diana Lynn, William Demarest—but also featuring Humphrey Bogart.)

At war's end Hollywood, like America, made a gradual transition back to business as usual, and personal-appearance tours took the place of the more elaborate junkets. It was obvious Hollywood still knew how to put on a good show.

June Haver remembers going on the road fairly often to promote her new movies when she was a 20th Century Fox star and George Jessel was producing such musicals as *The Dolly Sisters* (1945), *I Wonder Who's Kissing Her Now* (1947), and *Oh You Beautiful Doll* (1949). "We usually went by train, and all the places were jam-packed. In New York, we did seven shows a day, and interviews in between the screenings. We were young and energetic. There was no television, so they set up appointments for the radio. Remember Don McNeil's *Breakfast Club*? Well, I had heard that for years and I thought, do they really march around the breakfast table? At the age of fourteen, I thought that was really a corny thing to do, but when we went into the studio and it came time, everybody got up and marched around; it was really like kindergarten."

Jessel and the Fox publicists would send along any cast members who weren't otherwise engaged, and other stars as well. "Cesar Romero went on a lot of [these trips]," Haver recalls. "He wasn't in the pictures, but he was a good traveler. And," she adds with a laugh, "he liked the free trips.

"We didn't do an act or anything like that [onstage]. Jessel would introduce us, ask us a few questions . . . Jeanne Crain, myself, Phil Silvers would do a few jokes, so would Jessel, and that was it. It couldn't have been more than six or seven minutes, then the next screening would start. They wanted to empty the theater.

"They were lined up around the block, and of course you're going to be onstage at the Roxy. I'd never been to New York before, and that was so exciting. The wardrobe department would fix you up with all of their clothes, so you didn't have to buy a thing. You had a hairdresser backstage to fix you up between scenes, and it was top drawer all the way. [Going from town to town] we'd go to the races and put roses around the horse's necks, things like that . . . and I was always kissing the bald-headed mayor. They'd have parades down the main street, and we'd all sit on top of these cars and they'd put our names on the doors."

When June started making these trips she was still a minor, so her mother came along. "She had more fun than I had, 'cause she was a pretty cute dish." But Mom made sure there was no hanky-panky. "They were all afraid of my mother; she protected her little virgin virtuoso."

Haver also participated in a pair of unusual movie industry goodwill junkets to South America in the late 1940s and early 1950s that afforded many Hollywood stars the travel experience of a lifetime.

"When we got to Argentina and Brazil, we were mobbed everywhere we went. We'd sit down at a cocktail party and there'd be so many people around for autographs we'd never get to eat. I was with Pat Neal; she and I roomed together, and she was madly in love with Gary Cooper at the time. And quite a few others like Joan Fontaine, Claire Trevor, Janet Gaynor and Adrian, Walter Pidgeon, Irene Dunne, John Derek and Lizabeth Scott; there were also stars from France and Germany. The second time I went, Fred MacMurray was on the junket and we fell in love.

"That was quite an exotic experience, to be in Rio. Peron had a whole fleet of trick motorcycle riders that rode on either side of all the cars. They would [say] 'Look at this! Look at this!' And one would be standing on his head, another would be running along and he'd jump on the motorcycle, and then he'd jump down on the other side and jump up again. It's a wonder they weren't all killed, but they were putting on a show for the Americans.

"When we went, we met Madam Peron, and the second time I met her, she was on her way out; she had leukemia, and she was very, very weak. She looked like a tiny little bird. I knew that she loved St. Teresa, a French saint, and I had a really gorgeous cameo of St. Teresa that I was wearing to this reception, so I took it off and silently pinned it on her dress. She looked down at it, she had tears in her eyes. She took a medal that she was wearing of the Madonna, it was porcelain, and she gave it to me. I still have it; it's been blessed by six Popes. I've been to Rome, and I always wear it. And that's my token from Evita."

Haver also got to visit the lost city of Macchu Pichu. "You got on a little train and you went across the river and you started up on donkeys, way up the hill; they had no jeeps down there. Joan Fontaine was on a donkey and we got to a little chalet hut, halfway up the mountain, and there was this little Aztec family with a darling little girl. Joan Fontaine fell in love with this little girl, adopted her, and brought her home.

"We all stayed in the same hotel. I remember Claire Trevor was so adorable; she kept knocking on the door, saying 'Fred'—I could hear

her next door—'Can you zip up this damn dress?' And another one would come and say, 'How can I get something ironed around here?' So it was all like one big traveling circus."

Even if the days of big-time junkets had passed, some enterprising publicity departments still clung to the idea. Paramount's Pine-Thomas production unit was noted for its B movies, but in the late 1940s and early fifties the "two-dollar Bills," William Pine and William Thomas, started upgrading the quality of their product. Their publicity man, A. C. Lyles, thought some good, old-fashioned junkets would be the perfect way to promote them. Besides, films with titles like *Albuquerque*, *El Paso*, and *Streets of Laredo* seemed to invite the kind of hoopla that had made *Dodge City* and *Virginia City* so successful.

Lyles says he had no trouble recruiting Paramount stars to come along on the trip. "We'd do about twelve cities and I'd take maybe ten or twelve stars—Rhonda Fleming, Gabby Hayes, John Payne, William Bendix—and we'd go out and do four shows a day. And they did this on their own time."

Why? "They liked us, and we did a lot of things for them, and we had fun going out, and changing the shows, it was almost like Mickey and Judy saying 'Let's do a show.'

"We'd get in in the morning and do the radio shows, then we'd do the shows on stage with all the people who were in the picture. The show would be put together on the train. We'd say, 'We'll open up with Randolph Scott being introduced by a local emcee.' He'd come out and say some words and then he would introduce Gabby Hayes. Gabby would come out and do his bit, then Livingston and Evans would come out and play 'and then we wrote,' [a medley of their hit songs] then Rhonda would come out and sing, or John Payne would sing. William Demarest would come down the aisle and do his routine. It got so I could do everybody's routine and put on the shows.

"We'd leave the things on the train, and have one porter in charge. If we had laundry and things he would see that was all done and clothes pressed. We'd get on the train after the last show, it'd be 9:30, whatever, and they'd hook us on and then the next morning, a lot of times we'd be on a side track, and we'd awaken and be in the next city. The fellow in charge would have the coffee and orange juice for us, we'd dress on the train, get out, and the press would be there, and the radio people would be there, and that would be the arrival. We'd work that day and then we slept on the train every night. We only took things we'd need that day, a toothbrush or something like that.

Gabby Hayes in his civvies.

"Gabby Hayes's wife Helen was always with us; she was a tall lady in a long mink coat. She was a very elegant lady, and Gabby was a dude. He had cashmere suits, and a green Lincoln convertible. He was adorable; I just loved him.

"I would always take Gabby to the main street and walk up and down the street with him and [he attracted so much attention] it was like a twenty-four-sheet. We'd make an excuse to stop in a place, and the place would get so crowded we'd have to call the police. That would always be a front page story: 'Gabby Has to Be Rescued by the Police'."

And did the great cowboy sidekick enjoy all of this? "He claimed not to, and he'd grumble, and then he'd get to the next town [and ask] 'Where's the street?'"

Paramount songsmiths Ray Evans and Jay Livingston made their junket debut in May of 1949 when they boarded a train to promote *Streets of Laredo*. Among the stars along for the ride were Mona Freeman, Corinne Calvet, William Demarest, Don DeFore, singer Dick Foote, and Fortunio Bonanova.

Says Evans, "We wrote a song called 'Streets of Laredo' and I see in my scrapbook in Laredo, Texas they had five thousand school children massed in the streets who sang our song. It really was a big, big celebration in the city, and Paramount handled it very well.

"'Streets of Laredo' was on the charts, it did fairly well, so that would be part of our presentation, but 'Mona Lisa' was just coming out

On the road with the Hollywood Victory Caravan. Standing: Cary Grant, Risë Stevens, Charles Boyer, Desi Arnaz. Kneeling: Joan Blondell, Oliver Hardy, Stan Laurel.

and when we got to New Orleans, we met the Capitol Records representative there. He had just gotten a first collection of Nat Cole records in, so we picked those up and from that point on—in Atlanta, Baltimore, all the stations—we'd do personal interviews and give them the copy of Nat Cole's 'Mona Lisa' and ask them if they would play it. And I think that might have helped get the song started."

Livingston and Evans hit the road again for *The Eagle and the Hawk* in May of 1950 with John Payne, Arleen Whelan, and William Bendix, among others, starting in Houston and continuing all the way to Indianapolis, but had to return to Hollywood before the trip was over in order to fix a problem with the scene they had shot for Billy Wilder in *Sunset Blvd.*

Evans still harbors fond memories of his junket experiences, and understands why the crowds were always so enthusiastic. "You know, in San Antonio or El Paso or even in places like Dallas, you don't get movie stars there, a whole trainload full of them. We had our cars attached at the different trains and different railroads. There was all the liquor you wanted to drink and the best food—you ordered whatever you wanted—and in the town itself while you were there you'd be invited to parties. We were really living high on the hog, as they say."

With the rise of television and the fall of the studio system and its contract rosters in the 1950s, junkets started to fade from the scene. The term came to be redefined as bringing the press to the stars instead of the other way around, and that continues to this day.

The Associated Press' Bob Thomas, whose father helped stage the pioneering *42nd Street* junket in 1932, cites one junket of the 1950s as the most memorable of his career. "It was a picture called *Underwater!* with Jane Russell. Howard Hughes owned the RKO studio at the time, so he got a plane to take us all to Silver Springs, Florida where they were going to show the movie underwater. And as a footnote, there was a gorgeous, busty blonde, very skimpily clad, who was gotten down there by her press agents, she turned out to be Jayne Mansfield. At the junket itself she kind of overpowered Jane Russell, because she had a bigger bust, and was willing to pose in bikinis for anybody who wanted to photograph her. Jane didn't care, 'cause she didn't much like all this hoopla; she did it because she had to. But we were all given a half-hour lesson scuba diving, and then they set up a projector and a screen which was down at the lower part of the water which was very clear. They had a big loudspeaker that would carry the sound. I went down there and the picture looked pretty good, but you couldn't hear any of the sound. They canceled the movie after a reel or two. It didn't really help anyway. The picture was a bomb."

In this Age of Hype, as in the salad days of Hollywood, clever promotion can't save a bad movie . . . yet while *Underwater!* has faded from memory, the junket experience is still fresh in Thomas's mind after half a century. Maybe those publicity men knew what they were doing after all.

STILL LIFE
God bless the often-anonymous still photographers and publicists who dreamt up shots like these. If you don't know who's really sitting in the chairs on this MGM set, you get three demerits. Hint: it isn't James Gleason and Benita Hume.

At the right studio, but on the wrong set, are Lee Tracy and Una Merke

This picture was set up to show how even movie stars were "making do" with wartime restrictions in 1943. Here's the original caption: "The tire shortage means no more limousine rides to and from location, and when the cast of *City of Men* went to Columbia Ranch for a scene, director Sidney Salkow (right) took them in the studio's truck. Linda Darnell and Michael Duane, stars of the film, are on the top, while in the truck, from left to right, are Doris Dudley, Constance Worth, Glenda Farrell, Don DeFore, Margaret Hamilton, Sara Allgood, Jeff Donnell, and Leslie Brooks." The photo has an amazing immediacy to it; you almost feel as if you could walk into the frame and have a conversation with those people.

Conversations:
NOAH BEERY JR.

Noah Beery Jr. was part of a Hollywood dynasty. His father, Noah Sr., was one of the great villains of the silent screen, and a great character actor in his later years. His uncle Wallace Beery had an even longer and more impressive career, from 1913 until his death in 1949. The likable Noah Jr. (known to friends and colleagues as "Pidge") carved his own comfortable niche, first as a youthful leading man, then as a character actor, from the 1930s through the 1980s, and seldom wanted for work.

I'm especially fond of a scene in the 1930 Warner Bros. talkie *Show Girl in Hollywood* in which several real-life stars portray themselves attending a movie premiere, including both Noah Beerys. Senior tells the master of ceremonies that he's always glad to see the younger generation succeed; then his smiling seventeen-year-old son approaches the mic and chirps, "Well, my dad knows what he's talking about, so that goes for me, too."

His career included 1930s Saturday matinee fare (*Stormy, Ace Drummond*, and two *Tailspin Tommy* serials), 1940s B-movie fodder (*Hi Beautiful, The Crimson Canary, The Cat Creeps*) and wartime flag-wavers (*Gung Ho!, Corvette K-225*), 1950s westerns and adventure yarns (*The Last Outpost, Tropic Zone, Jubal, Decision at Sundown*), and throughout the decades the occasional A movie. He became a fixture on television from the 1950s onward.

He married into another famous family when he wed Maxine Jones, the daughter of western star Buck Jones; their son Bucklind also became an actor, and even worked in some episodes of his father's series *The Rockford Files.* (Bucklind's son, Noah Beery III, continues the family tradition, working behind the scenes in the television industry.) A stroke brought Noah Jr.'s career to an abrupt halt in the 1980s, although he lived until 1994.

In 1983 he and another western veteran, Ken Curtis, were hired to add color and spice to a new television series, *The Yellow Rose*, starring Cybill Shepherd. Although the series didn't last terribly long, I'm grateful that it afforded me the opportunity to meet such a lighthearted and unpretentious man. The interview, never published until now, was conducted at his home, which was filled with western art, including work by his hero Charles Russell, and some impressive pieces of his own.

MALTIN: At the risk of asking the obvious, how did you get started in the movie business?

BEERY: Well, I got started through my folks, of course, in that it was a family business and it didn't seem like there was anything else for me to do. But to answer you a little more specifically, I got started in school, 'cause in those days the public schools had these wonderful dramatic teachers and voice teachers and they'd stage the opera, and Gilbert and Sullivan. And you could get all these casting departments that the studios all had then and they'd come and see you. That's how I basically first started.

MALTIN: That's because you were going to school right in movieland . . .

BEERY: Yeah, I was in North Hollywood, which is as close to Hollywood High School as you could get and not be in it.

MALTIN: What was your father's attitude toward all of this?

BEERY: Oh, he was tickled. They all were, I think, even though they didn't especially show it. But, they were all glad to have a younger member at that time continue on.

MALTIN: Your father and your uncle had started on the stage, right?

BEERY: Mmm-hmm. Back in New York, both. And they had done musicals. Then my dad and mother came out ahead of Wally, three years, something like that. Then when he sent word to "Wal" how good the pickings were out here in Hollywood, why he came, too. Pretty soon the whole outfit was here.

MALTIN: Am I ignorant of any other family members who were involved . . . ?

BEERY: No, there was one older brother, but I'm not speaking of him in this light at the moment; he was here, too.

MALTIN: I've read that you actually visited your dad on the set of *The Mark of Zorro* and are in it somewhere.

BEERY: Oh, yeah, I used to go all the time. I was a little kid then, I don't know, five, something like that, but I got to play one of the little Mexican kids who was imitating Zorro. I was on the adobe walls after Zorro himself had passed through there. And that was my true first job, but I never counted [it] 'cause I didn't work again for fifteen years . . . which is too long.

MALTIN: Did you often visit your father on the set?

BEERY: Oh, yeah, whenever he'd let me come. All the time. And they'd take me on location with him, too.

MALTIN: Do you remember any particularly notable films?

BEERY: I remember one was a picture that he was in with Pola Negri [*The Crown of Lies*, 1926] that was [set] in the Alps or the snow country, and they [filmed] it in upper California. And I remember very well going on location on that one because of the snow and the train they used.

MALTIN: Did you go with your dad when he did *Beau Geste* in Arizona?

BEERY: Oh, yes. *Beau Geste* was the first of the great movie encampments on location, where they actually lived there.

Straight shooters: Noah Sr. and Jr.

And to go to Yuma, the United States Highway passed over what was called the Plank Road. It was a road made of wooden strips because there was no other way that they could cope with the sandstorms moving the road and all. And Paramount built their own road into the junction of the original wooden road and when my mother and I went to visit him, he came out with a whole entourage on horseback and escorted us into camp there. It was a real thrill.

MALTIN: And they built a little mini-village?

BEERY: Camp? Oh, it was more than a mini-village, 'cause I remember there were about eight hundred "Arabs," supposedly. That was great.

MALTIN: So you grew up on a movie set.

BEERY: I did; it was my life, my normal life, you know; it was just to be expected. I don't know where I would have gone if I hadn't been with them.

MALTIN: What was your first serious work and how did it come about?

BEERY: Well, it came about the way I was telling you: the casting directors would come to the different schools and colleges in the area. There was a wonderful serial producer at Universal named Henry MacRae—oh man, he was something else, wonderful. For some reason he liked me and started me doing *Call of the Savage* and *Tailspin Tommy*, all of that, and that's how I started, in the serials. I made a bunch of 'em too.

MALTIN: You also worked with your father in a couple of those, didn't you?

BEERY: Oh, yes, he did a lot of them, too, in his later professional days. We had a lot of fun.

MALTIN: What was that like working with your dad? Was it intimidating at all . . . ?

BEERY: Oh no, he was not an intimidating man, except onscreen where he was a classical deep, dark villain. But he was quite the opposite actually. It was strange at first, but he could generally iron me out pretty good the night before [so] I wouldn't make too many blunders.

MALTIN: Did your father ever resent being typecast as a villain?

BEERY: No, he loved it. He was always thinking of new ways to be mean. He liked it.

MALTIN: You got your start in low-budget films.

BEERY: Oh boy, they were lower than that. But they were great; they filled their niche completely. They wouldn't have had to be any better. If they were any better, they wouldn't be any better, you know?

MALTIN: Did you feel that you should be learning more about acting or did you just take to it?

BEERY: I just sort of took to it. I was, I hope, smart enough to realize that probably the greatest form of training I could have was the actual participation in it, even though crudely done or ineptly done. You probably wouldn't make the same mistake twice there.

MALTIN: Who did you learn from the most in the early days? Was it from the director or from watching other actors?

BEERY: I'd say from the other actors really, 'cause in the serials, the wonderful directors they had, they had very little chance to do anything except say, "Stick it here" or, "Stick it there," you know? Because they were so harassed on their time and their budget, which so many TV series still are. They don't realize what a director has to go through. He has to even sacrifice some of the things he knows are right because of the time element or the money element.

MALTIN: You grew up on a ranch, didn't you?

BEERY: Mmm-hmm.

MALTIN: So you knew how to ride.

BEERY: Oh, yeah. [It was] one advantage I had over a lot of people who would come in and had to acquire that.

MALTIN: You worked with John Wayne when you were both pretty young in *The Three Musketeers* serial.

BEERY: I hadn't even thought of that. We did that, which was very early for both of us, and then didn't work again 'til *The Trail Beyond* (1934), [from the novel by] James Oliver Curwood. My father was in that, too. And then, goodness, [nearly] fifteen years after that, *Red River*. Then after *Red River*, I never saw Duke again. [*Laughs*]

MALTIN: What were the logistics of shooting those serials?

BEERY: Well, they had twelve, fifteen episodes and you would work every Saturday night all night, which naturally meant you didn't have Sunday off. They had two or three units shooting at one time on the same vehicle. And that was, of course, their great secret of commercial success. They could get by with a lot of stuff that wasn't quite so finicky, you know?

John Wayne, Eddie Parker, Noah Beery Jr. and Sr., and unidentified actor in The Trail Beyond *(1934).*

MALTIN: I remember seeing one hilarious scene of you as Jan of the Jungle in *Call of the Savage* (1935) with the equivalent of your Jane, teaching you the difference between which berries are good to eat and which berries are poisonous.

BEERY: Oh, God . . . I could use that now. [*Laughs*] I'd love to see that. They created features out of some of them, [and they were] lousy generally. I saw that as a movie and it was one of the strangest things I'd ever seen, because as a serial, it was at least honestly bad, I mean raw and rough. But when they tried to cut it into a movie, it was something else.

MALTIN: Do you remember anything particular about *Tailspin Tommy* (1934)?

BEERY: It was a classical serial, a true little boy serial. I don't remember anything particular on it, except that [the actor who played] Tailspin, Maurice Murphy, and I became close friends for the rest of his life.

MALTIN: I think you worked just once with your uncle.

BEERY: Yes, I did *20 Mule Team* (1940). That was great. He got me that part, 'cause I wanted it. It was a good part, too, it was a juvenile. And, of course, Wally was the boss of his set. He really ran things and he always said that I was the only juvenile that ever got a closeup in a Wally Beery picture. [*Laughs*]

MALTIN: That's really funny.

BEERY: But he was great to me. Just wonderful.

MALTIN: Would you try to describe how your father and your uncle were offscreen?

BEERY: Well, my father went through two careers really, 'cause he reached his great success as a silent villain and was recognized as the peer of it and then dwindled, really, to nothing. He was always good but [had] no opportunities. Then when he got near the end, he went back to New York and landed [the role of] Boss Tweed in [the Broadway musical] *Up in Central Park* and he was superb in it. One review I always remember said that "Noah Beery played Boss Tweed with a punch and a paunch." [*Laughs*] And so it gave him a great exit from life, you know, doing what he did so well.

Wally went onto become, I dare say, one of the half-dozen giants of the business, box office–wise and every-wise. But he completely dominated his sets, even to the point of correcting writing. With it all, he was a wonderful fellow and took care of his home. He didn't believe particularly that it was his responsibility to take care of everybody, but his own, he really took care of. He was a superb person, very high sophisticate. I don't think anyone was ever more opposite to the character they were famous for portraying than he was.

MALTIN: Really?

BEERY: Completely. He was a fine dancer and a pianist and all of those things that he had mastered at different parts of his life.

MALTIN: Do you remember the first time you ever worked on a major film and did it impress you, having come from westerns and serials?

BEERY: Well, it impressed me, I know, I'm just trying to think of what it was, so . . . I did quite a few good ones. *Of Mice and Men* (1939) was the first so-called big picture I worked on, I think. It was neat. I remember they stayed [on] location right in Malibu, the Malibu Lake, over the hills. Millie Milestone—Lewis Milestone—was such a gentle and kindly person to someone like me who hadn't done much of that caliber work, you know. He was great. Then *Only Angels Have Wings* (1939) for Howard Hawks. I went on and did *Sergeant York* (1941) for Hawks, and then *Red River* (1948).

MALTIN: What was the biggest difference moving from potboilers to A movies like that?

BEERY: The great difference is in the director and what the director can do and what he has the power to do.

Howard Hawks was the peer to me and to many people, 'cause he made such wonderful product. He could handle you so well. They always said [about] Hawks was what a gentleman he was. Well actually, it wasn't that; he was that, too, of course. But he was so concerned and kindly and yet completely firm. When you'd come out in the morning to do whatever your job was that day, he made sure you knew it and then he'd let you alone, unless you did something he didn't like, at which time he would tell you. [*Chuckles*] Hawks ran his own ship, and it was good because he was so perfect at it. That's how he got that quality. And then, he had a writer's mind. I always thought he was a writer more than anything else, 'cause he could contrive these wonderful situations out of just a few lines in the script.

A lobby card for a 1944 Universal quickie with Beery, David Bruce, and Martha O'Driscoll.

MALTIN: Did he take advantage of ideas on the spur of the moment?

BEERY: Oh, yeah. He might not like it or might not take it but he would listen to it. And if he did like it, he'd use it.

MALTIN: Which of the films you made for him meant the most to you?

BEERY: Actually, *Red River* is the one everybody remembers, but the one that meant the most to me, I think, was *Only Angels Have Wings* 'cause it was a completely different part than I had ever done and I was working with Jean Arthur and Rita Hayworth, and although I was only tagging along behind, it was such a thrill. That would be the one, even over *Red River*, although I enjoyed *Red River* more.

MALTIN: Why?

BEERY: Well, I was doing exactly what I liked doing. I was acting *me* instead of acting a part, or me the way I'd like to have been [had I] lived in those days.

MALTIN: Did you have a feeling of reality on that set?

BEERY: Oh, yeah, 'cause you see that. Well, when was that made? 1948. There were old cowboys on that who'd been cowboys thirty, forty years before that. You could just talk with them and it was like throwing yourself back in time. Even the presence of a rented 1880 train that we used all the time on the siding. That was, to me, a great, fun experience whereas to other people it might have been great work.

MALTIN: What are your impressions of John Wayne?

BEERY: Wayne was a lot of fun. I always remember what no one seems to think of when they mention him and [that is] all the fun he was and the humor he had. He was just plain funny.

MALTIN: And what was Monty Clift like?

BEERY: He couldn't *spell* "horse," I don't think, when he got there. But he developed into a real [cowboy] just through study and work, and personally, he was a delightful little guy. You hear all these strange stories; I never saw anything other than just a very nice, working companion.

MALTIN: You moved to Universal on a fairly steady basis in the forties . . .

BEERY: . . . I was in and out of Universal about a dozen times. I got fired more than anybody who ever worked there, I think. They'd give you these $250 contracts, you know, for a week and you'd do everything they had, but I'd only last about six months at a time [*laughs*].

MALTIN: There was a time when you seemed to be in every movie that was coming out of the studio, you and Richard Arlen and Andy Devine . . .

BEERY: . . . and Brian Donlevy. Apropos of that, Donlevy and Andy Devine were making [a picture] and one morning the A.D. [assistant director] called Donlevy to hurry up, come to work, that he was late, and Andy said, "He'll be there as soon as they get him off the assembly line." 'Cause he had the hairpiece and the heels and the shoulder . . . [*Laughs*]

MALTIN: They were grooming you at that point then as a juvenile leading man; it was a whole different image than you'd had.

BEERY: I did one good picture, *We've Never Been Licked* (1943) for Walter Wanger. That's the one that pulled me out of the serials and everything, for a little while, anyway.

MALTIN: And did you enjoy that?

BEERY: Oh sure. I liked all of that.

MALTIN: Were you pampered at all, as the star?

BEERY: Well, there were four or five of us so you had to work for your pampering.

MALTIN: Same thing on *Gung Ho!*?

BEERY: That was a great one. That one we made down at San Clemente and in those coves there on the Marine bases [at Camp] Pendleton. There were a lot of people on that who later became very well-known, like Bob Mitchum and Pete Coe . . . and [there was] Randy Scott. We had a great group on that, and lived there in the base for about six weeks.

MALTIN: How did it happen that you took a different turn again and went from being a juvenile leading man to a young character actor?

BEERY: Well, I guess just the age basically, as you change or mature as they like to politely call it, or you become more fitted for something than something else. There was what they called in those days the sidekick, and they still have [the sidekick] although they don't acknowledge it. In nearly every low-budget picture there was a sidekick of some kind, he could be a young one like I was then, or an old one like Gabby Hayes was or something like that. And they were really a little more lucrative because there were more of them and you did more.

MALTIN: And you sure did a lot of those.

BEERY: Oh, God, I'll tell you.

MALTIN: For the B westerns, did you ever go off on interesting locations or were they mostly done close in?

BEERY: Well, they had smaller locations, but they'd go to Lone Pine, nothing like the big ones that would go to Arizona or Mexico or Canada, or something like that. But they had interesting, smaller engagements. I can remember playing an Indian in Lone Pine, sitting on my horse, waiting to attack and the people we were gonna attack were flying in. The plane was late bringing them to the location. They came in, we annihilated them, they all went back in the same day.

MALTIN: You did a whole bunch of films in the forties for Hal Roach.

BEERY: Yeah. Those were "Streamliners." We didn't do too many, four or five, but Jim Rogers [Will Rogers's son] and I did 'em, and we became close friends and have been ever since. They were forty-minute features—they were very cute. They actually were.

Noah as Jan of the Jungle (we kid you not) in the Universal serial Call of the Savage (1935).

And the main villain was a superb villain, Marc Lawrence; he's so good.

MALTIN: And they were supposed to take the place of the second feature.

BEERY: Yes.

MALTIN: Did you have any contact with Mr. Roach himself?

BEERY: No. His son, though, was a producer and the director and also a good friend. No, I never met the old man.

MALTIN: Had you ever met Will Rogers?

BEERY: No, my dad did one picture with him, *David Harum.* I never met Will Rogers.

MALTIN: But you were in *The Will Rogers* Story a few years later.

BEERY: Yeah. I did Wiley Post in that.

MALTIN: Was there a funny feeling about that?

BEERY: No, I always say anybody could have played Wiley Post. But

Mike Curtiz insisted on me for Wiley Post and I know why he did it. He was afraid that Will Jr., who was gonna do the [leading] part might not be able to deliver. Well, he did in superb style, he came through and played it. Curtiz would call me "Villy" and "Viley" and there was no need for me being in it at all, but I was in it.

MALTIN: You think he had you in mind as a backup?

BEERY: Just perhaps as a tenuous form of insurance or something. But, if you saw it, you know how great Will Jr. was in it.

MALTIN: What was Curtiz like?

BEERY: He was wonderful to me. Of course, he and my father had been close friends, and that did give me an entree to him in the friendship line, you know; he sort of gave me lots to do that wasn't required.

MALTIN: You were also in one of the pioneering science-fiction films.

BEERY: *Rocketship X-M* [1950]. I daresay that's run as many times as any feature movie ever did on TV. [*Laughs*] Just a million times. The little man who directed, Kurt Neumann, was a fine director. Had a wooden leg. He built all the sets out of spit and made this whole picture and it made a bundle. He was just wonderful and a scientist himself. I don't know what happened to him.

MALTIN: Did the content seem ridiculous to you or was it believable?

BEERY: It just seemed to me like a nice ten days' job was all. [*Laughs*]

MALTIN: Did you ever get tired of making westerns?

BEERY: No, I always got a big kick out of 'em. It was like a double life, going to work was the same thing as staying home, you know? Of course, I liked the historical part of them the best of all.

MALTIN: Is western history a big part of your life?

BEERY: Mmm-hmm. Yeah. It's my main literary engrossment, the historical part of it.

MALTIN: Who do you think was the greatest western writer?

BEERY: A. B. Guthrie. Boy, he was something else. And then, of course, the genius of all, Charlie Russell was also a fine writer, although he didn't try to predominate that. Owen Wister . . . there's a lot of them.

MALTIN: How did you get involved in western art?

BEERY: Well, as a very young kid, Russell came to Los Angeles, which was one of his strong markets in those days. And somebody gave a big dinner for him at the Biltmore and the whole art gallery there. I always remember, I went with my folks, watching Russell tell a sign language story. That got me interested in him and hence, in the art. CBS, I think it was, made a neat reel on Russell, on his life, and I got to narrate it.

MALTIN: So, when did you first start attempting to sculpt?

BEERY: I did 'em all my life . . . but that's just such a little gift.

Noah, center, joins another famous offspring, Lon Chaney Jr., left, in the serial *Riders of Death Valley* (1941) with Ben Taggart.

MALTIN: And when did you start actually displaying and selling?

BEERY: I'd say about 1965, something like that. I had very good success with them for a long time. I haven't lately because with bronzes, when you start them, you almost have to continue clear through the process of casting and retouching, or if you lay 'em down, you're liable to never pick 'em up again. Well, that means that when you're working another job, which I've been doing ever since I started with *Rockford*, I haven't been able to do any of them.

MALTIN: This brings us to TV, and there is a whole generation that knows you instantly, not from *The Rockford Files* and the things you're doing now, but from *Circus Boy*.

BEERY: I get that all the time. They say, "Oh, *Rockford*, fine and all," and then "What ever happened to *Circus Boy*?" I can almost tell their age. [*Laughs*] That was a wonderful little series. It ran three complete go-rounds, one on each network, but I never could figure out why they haven't brought it out in later years for the kids 'cause it has no date, wardrobe, or anything, and it was so cute, it'd be a wonderful show. It certainly would compare with Disney, I think.

MALTIN: That was your first brush with television, I suppose.

BEERY: Yes.

MALTIN: Was it comparable to working in B movies?

BEERY: These were half-hour shows, and we were doing them in two and a half days. So time-wise, it must have been very parallel to the B

movies, although I never quite made them that quick—in eight days, but the norm, like the George Montgomery pictures, was fourteen full good days. On *Circus Boy* we made fifty-two of 'em, I think, and they filmed two a week, or two in seven days, something like that.

MALTIN: Was it pretty grueling?

BEERY: Oh, you bet. But you never had a day that you didn't look forward to going to work; that was one of the great things on *Rockford Files*. I truly can't say that there was one day that I resented going to work on it.

MALTIN: Well, you played a wonderful character, James Garner's dad Rocky.

BEERY: I didn't make the pilot, there was another gentleman who played the part and very well, as a matter of fact. I never understood why they happened to make a change.

MALTIN: Then how many seasons did you play in it?

BEERY: Six. But every one was fun. Especially the ones I wasn't in. [*Laughs*] There were quite a few that way. You know, they write you out but that's nice, because then you don't become too oppressive to your audience, being there all the time.

MALTIN: Did you find that a bother?

BEERY: No. It was a nice character to begin with, you know, so it wasn't one that you minded being associated with. I have heard of a lot of people who are tied into something they don't like or can't stand or want to get out of. That'd be a rough situation, I think.

MALTIN: You've been working steadily since then, even on several series since then.

BEERY: My agent is Meyer Mishkin, a wonderful middle-generation agent, one of the classic ones, and he says that it's been a unique situation in that I've come off a series and gone into something good right after, whereas the norm is you have to lay by for quite a while sometimes.

MALTIN: I've read interviews with many character people who say that that's the great benefit of being a character person as opposed to being a star . . .

BEERY: Well, I think it is. It's not that there're more characters; I don't know how you'd explain it. There are more people trying for leading roles than there are for leading character roles and, of course, nearly all the younger generation all want to be Romeos and all, so it leaves a nice void there to be filled by somebody else.

MALTIN: Did you ever want to be a star?

BEERY: You mean one of the few big ones.

MALTIN: Mmm-hmm.

BEERY: I always would like to have tried it but I never especially resented not being one, 'cause actually, I think, the stuff that I've been given to do is terribly important in its own right, and while all things are relative, it's been nice.

MALTIN: Do you take yourself seriously as an actor?

BEERY: Oh gosh, no. That would be the kiss of death. I see some serious ones and to me, they're not quite as effective as some who can take it a little lighter.

MALTIN: You've made so many films, you've worked with so many people. Are there certain ones that stand out to you?

BEERY: My uncle, Dad, and Wayne always did, and Cooper. Cooper was lovely to work with. It's one of those questions where you leave out maybe the one you think the most of . . . Freddy March is one that I really liked; he was delightful.

MALTIN: On *Inherit the Wind?*

BEERY: Yeah.

MALTIN: Were he and Tracy competing, you think, on that picture?

BEERY: Oh, you bet. They were very, very respectful of each other except for one thing: Freddy March was livid because Tracy had in his contract two hours for lunch. And March only had one hour. [*Laughs*] But, as long as that's all they had to squabble with, that was fine.

ART CORNER: ACTORS AS ARTISTS

Many actors, like other creative spirits, have the need to express themselves in more ways than one. In the 1940s, Henry Fonda hosted weekly art classes that were attended by Claudette Colbert, and Van Johnson, among others. Ginger Rogers painted and sculpted for much of her life. When Gloria Stuart turned her attention to painting, the results were so good that she had her first exhibition at the prestigious Hammer Galleries.

Here are two interesting examples of gifted men and their work: James Cagney, passing the time during production of *Mister Roberts* by painting portraits of such colleagues as director John Ford and angelic bad-boy Ward Bond. Harry Langdon was a talented cartoonist who not only drew images of his screen alter ego, but sketched his co-star Nancy Carroll on the set of their 1935 movie *Atlantic Adventure*. His caricatures were also used in the main titles of the 1938 Laurel and Hardy movie *Block-Heads*, which Langdon co-wrote.

ART CORNER

Bandleader Xavier Cugat was a gifted caricaturist; he even sketched Adolphe Menjou on camera in *You Were Never Lovelier* (1942). He was also an entrepreneur, as indicated on the bonus card of Clark Gable that came with Cugat's "Nugats." Milton Caniff was just beginning his newspaper career when he drew this Joan Crawford page for the *Columbus Dispatch*. A few years later he would create *Terry and the Pirates* and leave caricatures behind for the world of comic strips. Below are the stars of *The Nitwits*, Betty Grable with Wheeler and Woolsey, as rendered by an RKO studio artist who was already pursuing an acting career as Charlie Chan's number one son, Keye Luke.

Comedic actor Don Barclay never became a star, but he was well-known in Hollywood for his delightful caricatures that hung on the walls of the Masquers Club in Hollywood. Barclay's film career peaked during its first year when he appeared in a number of Hal Roach two-reel comedies, including the memorable Our Gang short Honky Donkey (1934), in which he plays a haughty chauffeur. Most of his subsequent work in feature films consisted of unbilled bit parts. He returned to Roach to star in a pilot for a TV series that never aired called *Botsford's Beanery*. He then contributed voices to several Disney animated features, and made his final screen appearance at that studio as the assistant to Admiral Boom in *Mary Poppins*. (Thanks to Lou Valentino for these rare photos.)

Barclay presents a vivid likeness of Cary Grant to the actor (with whom he guest-starred on a 1940s Eddie Cantor radio show), who then tries to recreate the expression captured in his caricature.

Chapter 4

BEHIND THE CAMERA

Conversations:
NORMAN TAUROG

When I made my first trips to Los Angeles in the late 1960s and 1970s, I seized every opportunity to talk to movie veterans, especially those who hadn't been interviewed before. The trick was figuring out how to contact them. When I noticed Norman Taurog's name, address, and telephone number in the membership roster of the Directors Guild of America during a 1975 visit, I couldn't believe my good fortune. I took a deep breath and summoned up the nerve to call him at his home in Beverly Hills. I needn't have been nervous; he was extremely cordial and was happy to grant me an interview.

Norman Taurog! His name loomed large in my life as a movie buff, having seen it so many times onscreen, from films of the 1930s (*We're Not Dressing, College Rhythm, Mad About Music, The Adventures of Tom Sawyer*), 1940s (*Broadway Melody of 1940, Young Tom Edison, Girl Crazy, Words and Music*), 1950s (*Room for One More, The Caddy, Living It Up, Don't Give Up the Ship*), and 1960s (*Visit to a Small Planet, Blue Hawaii, It Happened at the World's Fair*). He won an Academy Award as Best Director for *Skippy* in 1931, and was nominated again for *Boys Town* seven years later.

It wasn't possible, or practical, to cover Norman Taurog's entire career in one interview. After all, he directed his first film in 1920 (*The Sportsman*, co-directed by its star, Larry Semon) and his last in 1968 (*Live a Little, Love a Little*, his ninth film with Elvis Presley). Even so, as I reread this transcript of our conversation from thirty-one years ago, I wish I could step back in time and ask about Bing Crosby, Joe Pasternak, Deanna Durbin, *Boys Town, Words and Music*, and so much more.

I was most excited about discussing the earliest days of his career making two-reel comedies during the silent era. How many people were still around to relate what it was like in those wild-and-woolly days? Mr.

Taurog had lost his sight in the late 1960s but not his gift of gab, or his memory. In this interview, you'll hear about the stars he directed, from W. C. Fields to Fred Astaire to Elvis Presley.

At the time of our meeting at his home in Beverly Hills in 1975, Taurog was extremely friendly, if a bit fragile; he had lost his eyesight a few years before. I wound down the interview only when it seemed as if it would be an imposition to continue. He passed away on April 7, 1981, by which time he had moved to Rancho Mirage in the California desert. It is still amazing for me to realize that I actually sat and talked to a man whose career was so rich and wide-ranging.

MALTIN: If you'll forgive an obvious question, how did you happen to get into movies?

TAUROG: I was an actor, saw myself on the screen, and immediately became a property man. That was about 1916.

MALTIN: Who were you working for?

TAUROG: I was working for a company called L-KO Motion Pictures. The original name was Lehrman Knock Outs. They had brought me out to become an actor, because I had been acting ever since I was four years old, when I went over and did a part in Central Park, the rear end of a deer. I happened to be a little round fat boy. In fact I played so many rear ends of animals that I thought that was going to be my career. My mother had always wanted to be an actress. In her day, that [meant] a bad woman, even if you came from a good family, so she stifled that pretty quick, [but] when I became interested in it, she became interested in helping me. I did an awful lot of stock up and around New York. I was a very young fella and I worked in *Little Johnnie Jones* with George M. Cohan. I worked for David Belasco with Mary Pickford and Ernie Truex in *A Good Little Devil*. Finally I went to work at IMP [Independent Moving Pictures] as one of the Imp Twins, and I worked with Pauline Curley. With a big company like that you were never allowed to see your dailies. So, I [never] did see myself on the screen. [And of course, on] the stage, you don't see yourself. But the minute I came out here and did one part, I looked at myself and said, "That's a little fat roly-poly and he ain't going to get nowhere." So I decided to go into the other end of it and went with what little stage experience I had, which was pretty good. I became a property man.

MALTIN: How old were you then?

TAUROG: I was seventeen going on eighteen.

MALTIN: Where did you get your first chance to direct?

TAUROG: First chance was for L-KO after being with them about three years. They were impressed and thought I'd done so wonderful they fired me. When they found out they had to pay my way home because I was a juvenile they took me back immediately because they didn't want to put out the money. They were a nice firm to work with. They gave me a chance.

MALTIN: Who did you work with there?

TAUROG: A man by the name of Dan Russell, who was one of their comedians. Alice Howell and Slim Summerville, after they had left Lehrman, Bobby Dunn, and Vin Moore were some of the actors.

I stayed around L-KO until I became a pretty good assistant director. Then Larry Semon sent for me because he'd seen a chase that I made for Henry Lehrman all by myself. So Larry Semon sent for me. At the time I was getting $65 a week from Lehrman. Semon said, "You're an awful young kid." I said, "Yes I am." He said, "How would you like to go to work with me?" and I said, "I'd like that very much." He said, "You could co-direct with me the first couple of pictures and then direct me if we got along all right." I said, "I'd like to very much." He said, "I'm going into see the Smiths; if you wait here I can get you an answer right now. By the way, what is Lehrman paying you?" And I mumbled, "Seventy-five." "Oh," he said. "Well, I may have a little problem with that. But you wait here." He went over to the office and was gone about three hours. I watched a crap game going on. Joe Rapp, Montgomery, and Rock were there. Semon came back and said, "I'm awful sorry, Norm, all they would do is give $750 for the first year and then $1,000 for the second, and $2,000 the third year." And I was numb. I said "I want to call my mother"—because I was just twenty then—"There would have to be a contract and she would have to sign it." He said, "Go call your mother."

So I called and said, "Mother, I just made a deal with Larry Semon for $750 a week." She said, "Come on home, son, it's all right. I never knew that you took a drink or so in the daytime but, you come on home." I said, "No, Mother, you'll have to sign the contract." She said, "Fine, bring it home and I'll sign it." So I went back and said, "Mother told me to take it."

He said, "You seem unhappy with it." I was in shell shock. I was asking for $75 a week; I was getting $65 from Lehrman, and I upped it $10. I said, "No, I just never had a deal go this quick." He said, "Well you better go on home and I'll have them draw up the contract and it will be at your mother's house day after tomorrow but I'd like you here tomorrow." So I said, "Good-bye Mr. Semon, thank you for everything." I had a little Chevrolet car parked there, but I ran all the way from Vitagraph to Hollywood Boulevard, got on the streetcar, and went downtown. And then realized when I got home that I'd forgotten my car! My mother said, "Your bed's turned down." I said, "Mom, it's on the level, it's on the up and up, this is no kidding." And that's what we started with.

MALTIN: How much was Semon making then?

TAUROG: $3,000 and all of his expenses: his home, servants, everything paid for.

MALTIN: Was there that much money in two-reelers?

TAUROG: Oh God, we used to spend as high as $100,000 with Larry Semon; we would get that out of the big towns alone. That's why I say he was the biggest thing there was for a guy that couldn't act.

MALTIN: What was your next move after that?

Larry Semon tees up in the aptly titled Golf (1922).

TAUROG: I met a young fella by the name of Jack White. He was only about twenty-three years old, a brilliant guy, and Director General for Henry Lehrman over at Sunshine Comedies. We became very good friends and I sat in on a couple of story conferences. He said, "Hey, you belong working on stories; you ought to be co-directing." I said, "Anytime." He said, "You could go to Sennett's, but I advise you to come to Lehrman's." So I went over and went to work for Henry Lehrman's Sunshine Comedies.

MALTIN: Who was there? Not too many of those films have survived so they aren't well known.

TAUROG: Well, Hughie Faye was one of the big stars over at Sunshine Comedies, and of course, the top man was Lloyd Hamilton, who was on his own, having just broken up with Bud, the Ham & Bud act. One of the first things that I did was take that big mustache off of him and they thought that I had gone crazy. Here the man had created a great character and I said, "Yes, but there is no expression in his face with that size mustache." Lehrman was a good scout and he said, "Let's take a chance." Once they saw a picture of Lloyd with just a straight face and that little cap and the little cutaway coat, they liked him very much. So I stuck with Lloyd pretty well and directed him.

MALTIN: Tell me about Lloyd Hamilton. I'm fascinated by him.

TAUROG: Lloyd was a sensational man; he had a great nose for comedy. He was a funny man. He didn't have to do terrifically broad gags; just a look and the way that he would react. Lloyd was a very good story man, also. He used to sit in on a lot of the stories with us. He was a big, big star in his day. My God, he was a big star.

MALTIN: How did he develop that style? He was doing something totally different when he was with Bud.

TAUROG: The character was created by Henry Lehrman, Lloyd, and a little bit of Jack White, and a little bit of me, little by little. I'm the fella that insisted on that walk, as if he always had tight underwear. Lehrman insisted on the cap because he said it gave him a boyish look, which was right. Jack White cut off the cutaway coat one day on the set with a tailor and made the short cutaway coat and the baggy pants. Of course, Lloyd discovered his own character. These were things that helped to make the character, but he was responsible for his own character.

MALTIN: What do you think distinguished gags that you had devised for different people? A gag that would work in a Hamilton film might not work for Al St. John.

TAUROG: Well, you wrote for the individual. You just didn't sit in a room and write. For instance, if we started, we'd sit in the room and maybe have three or four gag men sitting around. One would be a good story man who could hang it on the line, put the gags on, and you'd say, "We're going to do a story about Lloyd and I think I could get something funny out of him being a schoolteacher. He'd be playing with little kids and they could be smarter than he is." You start talking that way and then you develop some gags pertaining to the opposite. His bringing an apple to one of the little kids instead of the kid bringing the apple to Lloyd. When you saw the height of the man and the size of the kid . . . He came in and he would polish the apple and of course [spit] on it and polish it good and give it to the kid, that was humorous. But if the kid gave it to Lloyd, it wouldn't be nearly as humorous. Now, you couldn't do that with Hughie Faye, you couldn't do it with Slim Summerville. But you could with Lloyd because he had a baby face, flat face. So you would write for the individual.

I know when we worked with Lige Conley, who is strictly a good comedian, you had to have big gags. You had to go up on buildings and you had to do all kinds of things. You couldn't give Lloyd Hamilton big

A characteristic shot of Lloyd Hamilton from The Movies (1925), directed by Taurog's compatriot Roscoe Arbuckle.

physical things to do because they wouldn't believe it. But he could be a part that caused the physical thing and then come back and react on him.

MALTIN: Was there much improvisation?

TAUROG: Oh, an awful lot. We would write the story, get the idea [of] where we were going, how we're going to get there, and [then] you'd do an awful lot of ad-libbing on the stage. If they thought enough of you, nobody ever bothered you. Just make it funny and cheap.

MALTIN: How cheap?

TAUROG: Under $10,000 for two-reelers.

MALTIN: And how long would you take to shoot them?

TAUROG: About seven days. Sometimes five. And if they gave bonuses, I've been known to do them in three. We released through Universal when we worked with Abe and Julius Stern because they were brothers-in-law of Mr. Laemmle. And when we worked with Fox, who had the world by the tail, then we spent money because they had great faith in Lehrman.

MALTIN: Tell me about some of the people who were significant in doing the two-reelers. What kind of special effects men did you have?

TAUROG: The greatest, the greatest! They would keep those [guys working] year in, year out because every studio's special effects department was very important to them. Tremendous! Cameramen were great. In those days they didn't have motorized cameras, they all were turned by hand. A fella named Hans Koenekamp could be turning sixteen or eighteen [frames per second] and I'd say, "Koney, drop down to four, will ya? I want to get him out of the room quick." You'd see that hand go up and you'd see that bloody shutter change and you'd see everything and he's still in perfect rhythm as he came down. He had great hands. And they were really very artistic, very wonderful. I enjoyed all the people I worked with. If a fella made a mistake or anything, boy, I'd back him up to the hilt, because none of us are perfect. They're very important. The hairdresser was important, the makeup man was important.

MALTIN: Was there much competition among the comedy studios? Did you keep track of what the other guy was doing?

TAUROG: Anytime you could sneak into a preview, you were there. And if you finagled a couple of tickets, fine. If not, you just bought a ticket and went in to see the picture but stayed for the preview. Oh yes, we used to always be at one another's previews.

MALTIN: Just to see or borrow things.

TAUROG: To see, to steal, to do anything. I'll never forget, I won't mention a name in this because too many people know him. I happened to go to one of our director's previews and it didn't go well. Now, I had many pictures that didn't go well and had to be fixed, [but] this didn't go well and he wasn't a very pleasant man. So the morning I pulled in on the lot, I happened to park my car in his space. I was only in the studio I'd say about twenty minutes, and I came out and there was a big note on my steering wheel. It said, "When you learn to read, you'll read and see that this parking space belongs to," and said his name. "So kindly in the future, do not park your car in my parking space." I pulled my car out and put it toward the back of the lot and went out and got a big piece of cardboard. I put "Sorry," and used his first name, "but saw your preview last night didn't think you'd be here today."

MALTIN: How much tampering would you do with a two-reeler . . . and how many previews would you have?

TAUROG: We had as many as three.

MALTIN: Really! Just for a short.

TAUROG: Absolutely, for a two-reeler. We've taken them as far as San Francisco to preview them. Down to San Diego, thinking that no one [from the competition] would be there to see it if we got a real good one. When you came out, there they were and they'd say, "It's a winner."

MALTIN: What kind of changes did you make if it didn't seem to be working?

TAUROG: If you couldn't do it editorially, you would go and shoot a couple of scenes, or shoot what it needed. Maybe you'd talk the star into doing it for free because it would be better for his career. And he'd say, "Well I'll do it if you'll do it." Having that old ego which every one of us have, he'd say, "I'll do it." Before you knew it you were spending very much money but by God, you had a better picture. Of course today you can't do that on account of unions and things. We had no unions.

MALTIN: What kind of hours did you work?

TAUROG: I would get to the studio probably about 7:30. Shoot until about 6:00 maybe 6:30, go home, and then start Saturday morning and work straight through all night Saturday and go home Sunday morning and go to bed. And slept every bloody Sunday. That's if you were behind. If you weren't, you would do the normal Saturday up until 6:00, when we generally quit. We were shooting on the outside with the reflectors.

MALTIN: Who were the best gag writers you worked with at this time?

TAUROG: There was a fella by the name of Marty Martin who was excellent. And there was Harry Sweet who later became a director. Harry was a great, great comedy writer. Lex Neal, who worked for Sennett, then came over to work for us. The rest of the [names] don't come up too quickly.

MALTIN: Tell me about Lupino Lane.

TAUROG: Great man to work with, brilliant . . . positively brilliant. Lupino I didn't do many with, only one or two. A very creative man, and like all good English comics, a magnificent pantomimist. English

comics were the most amazing people in the world. This was their business and they were in it to succeed. They didn't want just a go at it. They would study the business. They knew the camera and the camera angles and editing. They could tell when you were lighting, whether you were lighting for the leading lady or for them. But that was pure education and their brilliant minds on comedy . . . fantastic. Especially pantomime, because they're all raised on it over there.

Taurog sets up a "thrill" shot with Lupino Lane in the Santa Monica mountains overlooking Pacific Coast Highway.

MALTIN: He was also an astounding acrobat.

TAUROG: Oh God, that thing on the lamppost that he used to do, fantastic. He was a great man to work with.

MALTIN: Did you know Roscoe Arbuckle at the time, when he was directing?

TAUROG: I knew Roscoe very well but not as a party playmate or anything. I was pretty much of a loner in the business all my life. And the people that I like, most of my dear friends, were outside of the business—doctors, lawyers. If I took a liking to a star and he liked me, we'd pal around together but I was never much of a party man.

MALTIN: What do you recall of Arbuckle at that time?

TAUROG: Positively genius. He'd think up a gag like that [*snaps his fingers*] if he was stuck . . . not steal a gag, think up one. And his sense of timing was out of this world. I don't think in the past thirty years— I quit directing in 1968 when I lost my eyesight—I've ever stepped on a set and watched other directors work, but I would love to go down and watch Roscoe because he knew what he was doing. He knew every part of the business and was a very funny man. He was a good actor too, a terrific actor and a great comic. I used to love to talk to him in the lunchroom where we could sit down and talk.

MALTIN: Did he seem embittered at the time you knew him, after the scandal?

TAUROG: No. I wasn't that close to Roscoe. If you said to me on a stack of bibles, "Do you think Roscoe did it?" I'd have to say to you, "Honest to God, I don't know." And yet I was a very good friend of Virginia Rappe because of Henry Lehrman. Now, I don't know what

Virginia was doing where they said she was, but that's all I knew. Remember, I was very young in those days.

MALTIN: I was just wondering, because it was obviously a terrible blow to him.

TAUROG: It was a blow to everybody in the industry, too. You felt so sorry for this thing that such a terrible catastrophe could happen.

MALTIN: Did you know Buster Keaton?

TAUROG: Very well. In fact, later on in life when I came back from the hospital and didn't think I'd ever work again, I went over and did a picture for AIP [*Sergeant Dead Head*, 1965] just to see if I could work. I didn't give a damn about the money. I made a picture and I used Buster Keaton in it. It was just before he died. He was still funny, still funny. I remember he said to me, "Hey Norm, I can get you a sure-fire belly laugh." I said, "How?" He said, "Let me run with the [fire] hose. When the firemen go, let me go to the end of it and let me go straight up and land down." I said, "Buster, at your age, are you out of your mind?" He said, "I won't hurt myself, Norm, I've done it for years." I said, "Go ahead and do it," and he did it. He must have gone six or eight feet in the air and let flap. I'm scared to death to say, "Are you all right, Buster?" So I went halfway in and said, "Buster?" and he said, "I'm all right."

Taurog with Baby LeRoy on the set of The Way to Love *(1933).*

MALTIN: There's one picture you did with Lige Conley called *Fast and Furious* that is just an avalanche of sight gags, mostly involving cars. It's used as stock footage whenever someone wants to show a "typical" silent comedy.

TAUROG: Is that right?

MALTIN: It turns up in TV commercials all the time because it's so well done. How did you set up scenes like that so that no one got killed?

TAUROG: In those days that's the way your mind went, that's the way you thought. Who would ask a guy to climb a building at Fourth and Spring? I think it was ten stories high; it was before they put up the bank over there. [I found a guy who did that] and I said, "I understand that you do this kind of work. How much do you want?" He said, "I'll tell ya, I usually get $100 a floor as I go up. If I do any slips and skid off the building and hang, it's $50 a skid." He said, "Nobody will get hurt. You just tell me on what floors to do the skid or what floors to make it look as if I'm going to fall." So I went back and we talked it over with the company, and they said, "How are you going to shoot it?" I said, "From across the street. We'll put up an outside rigging and we'll shoot with a longer lens and we'll follow him going up. We'll just allow enough so that you're always shooting down a little so you see the street." [The producer said] "You're crazy; I'm going to fire you, you're crazy." I said, "No, it can be done if this fella knows what he's going to do. But there's only one way I'll do it. I'll go down on a Sunday when there's nobody around and tell the police we're going to do it and let him climb one story and I'll see how he acts." He did a slip of his own and I tell you I nearly fell out of the window from across the street. He's hanging there, and climbing up he says, "How was that?" I said, "Sensational!" He said, "You want another?" I said, "No, God, let's save it."

MALTIN: Do you remember who you were doing it for and what picture?

TAUROG: Lige Conley and Spencer Bell, the dark fella that used to work with us all the time.

MALTIN: I still can't get over those car gags you used to do.

TAUROG: Oh, they were great. I used to love to do those.

MALTIN: Did you have to get permission to rope off the street or did you just go somewhere?

TAUROG: Oh yes, you always had to tell them where you were. I think it used to cost us $10 and they put that in the policemen's fund. The studio would always give them $25 or $50.

MALTIN: That's another thing that I think is marvelous about the silent comedies: you used real locations, instead of just staying in the studio.

TAUROG: A thousand percent better.

MALTIN: I want to backtrack with you for a minute to Larry Semon. His films had the biggest gags I've ever seen, just spectacular. What was the thinking behind that approach?

TAUROG: He wasn't funny; that's honest. You asked me and I tell you the truth. I loved the man but he wasn't funny. Do you remember the oil derrick thing, maybe you never saw it, [where he] swung from one oil derrick to another. We went out here in the oil fields and did it with Bill Hauber, who used to double for Larry all the time. We used to take five and six weeks to make a two-reeler [with Larry]. He would go to New York and we'd go out and make the picture. When he came back, we fit him in all the closeups. That's the truth. Bill Hauber was that close to him and that great and could "do" him that well. We would get as close a full figure [as we could].

MALTIN: And you couldn't tell?

TAUROG: No. I defy anybody to pick it out. But Larry Semon was a great cartoonist. When you said derricks, he'd say, "You mean like this?" He'd draw it out. That's the mind he had but golly, he was an unfunny man.

MALTIN: But he did work on his own gags.

TAUROG: He did, but with the help of the art director and everybody on the set. Boy, he paid money and he was a big man at Vitagraph.

MALTIN: If you worked with Semon, then you also worked with Oliver Hardy.

TAUROG: Oh yes. He was our heavy.

MALTIN: Tell me about Hardy at that time. What was he like?

TAUROG: A great mind to help contribute to gags and business and things and got along beautifully with everybody. He was a hell of a heavy, though; he used to do terrific falls.

MALTIN: Obviously, people got hurt doing those falls.

TAUROG: Very little, very little. It was well laid out by the stuntmen. When you told a man you're going to have a four-car accident, you would get the four stuntmen together and say, "Fellas, work it out the way you want it. I'll tell you whether it's possible to photograph it." And the boys would generally lay it out. Oh, they'd have a bum leg or a sprained wrist, but very seldom did we have any real casualties.

MALTIN: When you went to Paramount, did you work with the writers on your scripts, or was it more of an assembly line kind of thing?

TAUROG: No, no assembly lines with me. I always worked with the writers. Having been a frustrated half-baked writer myself, and having written many, many two-reelers and one-reelers, I always worked with the writers but never took any credit because I didn't think I deserved credit. Take somebody else's ideas and you do the backseat driving; you get enough on that card all by itself when it says: Directed by Norman Taurog.

MALTIN: Do you think anybody can learn comedy or do you think it's just something you've got in you? Do you think it's instinctive?

TAUROG: If it isn't born inside of you, somehow, some way, you can't learn it by reading a book. You can't learn comedy by being around it. If it rubs off on you, it's inside of you and it's by association. I have yet to ever see a comic that was created and made that has lasted. I think you can go and learn how to become a dramatic actor, but to become a comic, it must be somewhere down inside of you and somehow or other you just find it and little by little it comes out and all of a sudden, bam! There it is.

MALTIN: Can you remember the first time you heard about talking pictures?

TAUROG: Sure, I was working for Larry Semon and I started to hear a rumbling of sound. The minute I heard it, I went up to the Academy and started to find out all about it. I took the course of twenty-two weeks at night and did everything. And I said, "Larry, sound is coming in." Well, you never heard a man laugh so in your life. "What are they going to do, put it on records?" I said, "That's right, how did you know?" He said, "Yeah, they're going to put it on records and the people are going to mouth to it." I said, "No, it's going to be just the opposite. They'll put it on records and then play it back and the people will mouth it." He said, "You've gone crazy." I said, "No I haven't and I have an offer to do a sound picture." He said, "If you've got an offer to do a sound picture, don't wait for me."

MALTIN: How did you come to make those talkie featurettes with Clark and McCullough? They were longer than ordinary shorts, but they weren't quite features either.

TAUROG: Fox was crazy about Bobby Clark and they wanted to get him out [here]. And Bobby would never come without Paul McCullough because that was half of his act. I was at Fox at the time, and they wanted to know if I'd direct them. So I went over and talked to this little man who used to paint on [his] glasses, and we had quite a conversation. He was a funny little geezer, great with dialogue. So, I made *In Holland* and I made another three. They were great to work with.

MALTIN: Did they adapt well to films?

TAUROG: Bobby did; Paul never could quite make it. He was a straight man but he was always talking to the gallery. Eventually, on the last one, he finally found out that there were microphones right over his puss and you didn't have to talk loud. But they were funny.

MALTIN: Didn't Bobby write a lot of his own dialogue?

TAUROG: And Paul did, too. Paul wrote an awful lot of Bobby's stuff. The next thing [I knew], somebody at Paramount saw one of the pictures I had made for Rex Lease, and they called Walter Wanger at the New York office and said, "If you're going to do that feature with Ed Wynn, we just saw a picture a man made by the name of Norman Taurog. He's been a great guy for short two-reelers and slapstick comedy and he would be ideal for you." Walter came out and we had a talk and he said, "Would you do the picture?" I said, "Well, I have an agent." They made a hell of a deal for a man's first picture with a big company, with the option of a five-year contract. That's how I went into sound.

MALTIN: What did you think of Wynn when you directed him in *Follow the Leader* (1930)?

TAUROG: I was a great booster of Ed Wynn's from the beginning, I liked him. He also loved the business and he always wanted to be good. But he couldn't understand why he couldn't walk out of one frame and come into another with another outfit on. He wanted to keep changing his clothes all the time. So I explained that people wouldn't know who the hell you were. Finally, after about four weeks on the picture, that cleared up. But he was a funny man.

MALTIN: Did comics like that have a problem because suddenly they were not playing to an audience?

TAUROG: They had a bigger problem than that, [because] suddenly they weren't their own boss. And you had to be very careful and not hurt their feelings. You were talking to very talented and creative men, so you would have to explain if you wanted to keep a good performance going on, because [film] was an entirely different medium, completely.

When you say, "Be sure you hit that spot," you want a man to be funny, but [you have to] be sure he hit that spot. So what I used to do is take a little piece of rope and stretch it across, way low between the knee and the ankle. When they'd walk, the minute they felt that they knew they were there [on their mark].

MALTIN: Were you pleased with that film, *Follow the Leader*?

TAUROG: I was for myself because remember it was really my first big feature. It was [one of] Ginger Rogers's first pictures. It was Lou Holtz's first picture. I thought all and all we did a pretty good job. And what with changing the bloody title nine million times. One bunch of people called it on one side of the country, *Follow the Leader*, and in the others it was released under the title *Manhattan Mary*. They came out pretty good on it. I mean I stayed there [at Paramount] for five years.

Clark and McCullough with Marjorie Beebe in *In Holland* (1929).

MALTIN: Then you made *Finn and Hattie*.

TAUROG: With Leon Errol and ZaSu Pitts.

MALTIN: Tell me about Errol. He is somebody I admire very much.

TAUROG: Well, of course, [he] was one of the great comedians. Nobody could ever deliver like Leon. One of the great talents of the world. And that bum leg that he would never stand up straight on, he would always bend when he was in trouble. He and ZaSu got along very well. They complemented each other, they had respect for each other, and they worked well together.

MALTIN: The film credits Norman McLeod as co-director. How did that come about?

TAUROG: Well, because Norman McLeod was a writer and I wanted to keep him on all through the picture. They wouldn't let him stay as a writer. I said, well fine, let him co-direct with me. I wasn't after credits in those days, I was after getting good pictures under my belt. So I went to him and [asked if he'd] like to co-direct with me. He said, "I'd love to, but I won't interfere." I said, "What do you mean you won't interfere. You're going to be listed as co-director and [if] you see anything, come to me and we'll both go to the talents and talk." We got along beautifully. And then he became a damn good comedy director.

MALTIN: Wasn't he a cartoonist originally?

TAUROG: Yes, he used to draw that one line with the face and the skinny little legs. He made a lot of money with that.

MALTIN: When you had comics in pictures who had ideas of their own about what was funny or how something should play, how did you handle that?

TAUROG: All depends who the comic was.

MALTIN: Wynn and Errol were the kind of people who'd been on the stage for years and they had established routines that I'm sure they felt were sure-fire.

TAUROG: Well, if it did interfere with the story, you told them the truth. You say, "It's funny, there's no question, but it's a [bit] that you do and it won't be funny because they're waiting to find out about Ginger and the other people."

MALTIN: Did you usually win?

TAUROG: Sometimes it worked out. Sometimes you would do both if it's starting to build up into a tantrum. You would just say, "All right, let's do them both and we'll look at both." And once they saw it and you knew there was a lull, they'd say, "I guess yours is faster, so you'd better use yours."

MALTIN: Having worked with all these comics, why did Paramount think you were the right man to direct *Skippy*?

TAUROG: I had made a lot of comedies with Big Boy and [other] great young kids. I'd worked with Mitzi Green, who was a great talent. So Paramount and producer Buddy Lighton asked me if I would do it and I said, "What is it, a series of cartoons?" They said, "No, we're writing this story because Percy Crosby [creator of the *Skippy* comic strip] doesn't want anything to do with it except the money."

MALTIN: I've heard several versions of how Jackie Cooper got that part. What do you recall?

TAUROG: Well, tell me what you heard.

MALTIN: One was that Paramount had seen him in the Hal Roach Our Gang comedies and asked to borrow him. Another was that he just happened to test for it.

TAUROG: Anybody tell you he was my nephew?

MALTIN: Yes, I know that, too.

TAUROG: A man by the name of Ed Montagne was the scenario editor. When *Skippy* came through, he said, "There's only one person to play this, a boy by the name of Jackie Cooper." So [we do all the tests] and they asked Mr. Zukor would he [watch them]. He looked at all the tests [and] said, "I don't know what the problem is. There's only one person to play Skippy." [Zukor sent for me] and asked, "Who do you think should play Skippy?" I said, "Mr. Zukor, I have to tell you the truth, I'm Jackie Cooper's uncle and I don't want to put him in a spot." He said, "You don't put him in any spot because if they pick anybody else but Jackie Cooper after my seeing the test, we won't make the picture." That's how it was decided. Jackie Searl was magnificent in his part, but he could have never played Skippy.

MALTIN: Was Jackie Cooper an instinctive performer at that age or did he just have a mature understanding of things beyond his years?

TAUROG: He play-acted. When I gave them each that dog, Penny, at the beginning of the picture, I knew what I was doing. They didn't. Jackie Cooper said to me, "But this dog belongs to the studio." I said, "No, Jackie, they are giving the dog to you for the picture." He said, "Then he is our dog during the picture." I said, "That's right," and he said, "That's fine, we'll love him."

Robert Coogan, Jackie Cooper, and Jackie Searl in a publicity pose for Skippy (1931).

Robert Coogan didn't ask any questions. All he knew was that he had words to say and he said them well. Everybody said that was so marvelous each time Robert Coogan saw Skippy and he always said, "Hi Skip," his body moved and his little legs moved. [I'd say] "You know why that happens? The first time he saw Skippy in the picture he had to go to the bathroom and he didn't tell anybody, so I used it all through the picture," and that's the truth. It wasn't written in the script. I saw this kid having one hell of a time and I thought it was funny.

MALTIN: Did you expect it to be as big a hit as it was?

TAUROG: About the middle of the picture.

MALTIN: You saw it was working.

TAUROG: Yes, I felt the people coming together and I felt that everybody cared about one another.

MALTIN: What was it like to win an Oscar?

TAUROG: The way I won mine?

MALTIN: Yes.

TAUROG: There have been better ways.

MALTIN: How do you mean?

TAUROG: I was sitting at home with a broken leg and no one even thought I had a chance till it was voted. I knew the picture would get an Oscar. I didn't know whether I would or not but I was positive that they would mention Cooper. [So] I was at home with a broken leg [and] all of a sudden I got a phone call saying, "Can you get down here right away? We think you're going to win the award." I said, "How do you know?" They said, "The feeling in the audience, the different people who have gotten awards, and Cooper's been mentioned. [Studio chief B. P.] Schulberg wants you to come down right away." I said, "I have a broken leg; it's in a cast. But, if you want me to come down I will the way I am, no dinner clothes." They said, "That will be great."

There was a mob out to meet me; this was at the Biltmore Bowl downtown. And sure enough, when it came to the voting, I got it over Von Sternberg.

MALTIN: Was it a problem that you kind of got typecast for a little while directing kids? Did you mind that?

TAUROG: No, I loved it because I enjoyed it. But then I said to myself, "I've got to cool off a little bit and get back into grownups for a while, or musicals, or anything."

MALTIN: And you wound up directing Wheeler and Woolsey. What do you recall of them?

TAUROG: I had a ball with them. They were both two funny men. Bert was the cutest guy that ever lived. And Woolsey with those big glasses and everything and that frown always as if he had a pain in the belly. We had a lot of fun making that picture (*Hold 'Em Jail*, 1932). The funny part about it is that we shot it mostly at Metro.

MALTIN: Really? How did that come about?

TAUROG: They had that big jail set [constructed for 1930s *The Big House*] and we used that; then they built the exterior out on the RKO lot.

MALTIN: The leading lady in that was a very young Betty Grable. Did you see anything special in her then?

TAUROG: No. I missed her completely, absolutely. I got to know Betty later and I thought she had a lot of talent. But remember, in that one she was very young and scared of her life, and I was only worrying about two comics and loving it.

MALTIN: Your next film was quite different, *The Phantom President*.

TAUROG: Yes, I did that with George M. Cohan and Jimmy Durante and Claudette Colbert.

MALTIN: What was Cohan like to work with?

TAUROG: He liked me. I liked him but I couldn't understand him off the set. He was so used to being his own boss and making all the decisions. He felt hampered that he couldn't, because he didn't know this business. But he was always a good actor. I worked with him [on the stage] when I was a kid.

I think basically that Jimmy Durante just killed him, because he made a crack to me one day. He said, "I wouldn't be surprised when I went back to New York if they changed the name of this picture to *Noses Feathers*." I said, "Now George, that isn't nice and you know you don't mean that." He said, "No I don't, I really don't."

Jameson Thomas, George M. Cohan, and Claudette Colbert in The Phantom President (1932), which featured rhyming dialogue by Rodgers and Hart.

MALTIN: How did you get along with Durante?

TAUROG: Jimmy, whatever you wanted him to do he'd do. One of the most wonderful comics I've ever worked with in my life, and one of the sweetest men I've ever known. He'd say, "Tell me what to do, I'll do it."

MALTIN: Was it difficult doing a picture with all that rhyming dialogue? Did you feel awkward about it?

TAUROG: No, I really didn't. It was tough to do; you'd always have to go back and play back half and then get into it. Claudette was wonderful. She was great; a lovely lady.

MALTIN: How did you—or Paramount—talk W. C. Fields into appearing in *Mrs. Wiggs of the Cabbage Patch* when he wasn't the sole star?

TAUROG: My introduction to him I think fixed everything. We very badly wanted him to play this part, but the company wouldn't do anything about it. They said, "If you want him, go and get him." So I called one day and the butler answered the phone. I told him I wanted to come over and talk to Mr. Fields about *Wiggs of the Cabbage Patch*. He said, "Tell the young man to come over here tomorrow morning and I'll meet him at 9:30 for breakfast." So in the morning I went over and he was at the breakfast table. There was a pitcher of martinis on the table. He said, "Would you like a little something to start your day off?" and I said, "No sir, I don't drink in the morning." He said, "Don't know what you're missing." [Then] he said, "Would you like a little orange juice?" and I said, "Yes, I'd love some." "Some orange juice for Mr. Taurog!" The butler took the orange juice and then got the bourbon and filled it up to the top a glass. I put it down in front of me like you would do at a cocktail party and left it there.

I said, "Mr. Fields, I came over to see you about the part. It's a great part and it has tremendous laughs in it if it's played properly and I'm sure you're the man." He said, "That part is great, huh?" I said yes. He said, "Sure-fire, positive part?" I said yes. He said, "Then what the hell do you need in me?" I said, "That's with you playing. I'm taking for granted that you're going to be in it." He said, "Don't take anything for granted." He said, "I want a full-picture price (I think his price then was $150,000 or $175,000), all in cash like I always get it, and then I'll read the script. If I like the script I'll do it, and if I don't I'll return the cash." He said, "You're sold on this picture?" and I said, "Very much so." He said, "Fine, leave it with me and I'll let you know whether I'll do it or not." I said okay and got up to leave. He said, "Aren't you going to have any breakfast?" and I said, "No thank you, the orange juice was plenty." He said, "You didn't drink it," and I said, "That's right."

I left, figuring to myself no deal, what the hell, he's just a mean old grouch. About three days later I got a call. "Mr. Fields would like to talk to you." "Say," he said, "I doctored this thing up and I made it playable," which he did, I will say. Not that it was bad, it was a hell of a part. He said, "I played around with it a little bit and I'll be glad to play it so I'll keep the money." I said, "That I have nothing to do with, Mr. Fields." He said, "Chrissake, will you stop calling me Mr. Fields? I feel like your father or something and God knows I don't want you as a son." And I said, "God knows I don't want you as a father." He said, "That makes us even," and I said, "Yep," and he said, "We're going to get along fine."

So, I got a hold of him and introduced him to Pauline Lord, who he immediately took a very big dislike to; they developed a slight feud. Came the day [we shot] the death of the horse, the horse is lying on the ground dead out in Buffalo Flats, where we were working. Fields didn't have to come in until about 1:00. All of a sudden we heard his car drive up and he got out. Everybody is waiting for him to step into the rehearsal. He walks up and looks down at the horse and he said, "Good morning, Pauline my darling. Never saw you looking better."

She got into her car and headed for Pasadena, where she was going [to catch the train] back to New York. We sent for her and explained that that was his sense of humor. She thought it was a lousy sense of humor but she said she was an actress (which she was) and she'd see it through but, "God help me if I'm ever called upon to do another part with him." So it worked out.

MALTIN: Would he take direction?

TAUROG: Yes. In this way. He'd say, "How did that look to you?" I'd say, "Well, Bill, I think you're stalling getting under the two barbed wires a little bit. It's too long getting through." He said, "Did you ever try going through two wires?" and I said, "Yes, if I hadn't tried going through two barbed wires I wouldn't know that you're going through too slow." "Well, all right, see how this suits your highness." So he'd come through, then he'd drop the hat and put his arm up through the barbed wire and try and put the hat on and then it began to be funny, so we'd keep grinding and he'd say, "When are you going to quit grinding?" and I'd say, "When you exit." And he said, "All right, I'm getting out now." And he'd get out underneath the barbed wire and he'd start to go and by God he got his coat caught on it. He'd get the coat off and then his sleeve would get caught on it. Then he'd get the sleeve off of the thing and he'd turn around and put his hat on, which had fallen off and it went on the back of the post. He turned around and saw the hat, got the hat, put it back on, and ex-

ZaSu Pitts and W. C. Fields in Mrs. Wiggs of the Cabbage Patch (1934).

ited. He said, "Well, I gave you a pretty funny routine." I said, "That's what we were waiting for. You bet you did." That's the way you did it with Bill.

MALTIN: He would always put more into a scene than was there.

TAUROG: Yeah. So you'd always shoot the longer scenes with two cameras, 'cause you were protected. [You could] cut from the closeup into the long shot or cut from the long shot into the closeup, and take out anything you wanted.

MALTIN: What did you think of Eddie Cantor when you directed him in *Strike Me Pink*?

TAUROG: I liked Eddie very much. Eddie and [Samuel] Goldwyn weren't talking at the time I made the picture. So Goldwyn would come on the set and Eddie would say, "Norman, would you tell Mr.

Goldwyn that I'm very unhappy with the song?" I'd say, "Mr. Gold-wyn, he's very unhappy with the song." He'd say, "Norman, would you tell Mr. Cantor that I don't give a damn?" "Mr. Cantor, Mr. Goldwyn says that he doesn't give a damn." Cantor would say, "Tell Goldwyn I won't be in tomorrow; I'm going to have a terrible cold tomorrow." I said, "Mr. Goldwyn, he won't be in tomorrow; he's going to have a terrible cold." He'd say, "Norman, I have but one word for Mr. Cantor. Tell him *I'll sue him.*" I said, "Mr. Goldwyn said that he will sue you, Mr. Cantor." He'd say, "Norman, is this getting a little boring talking back and forth like this?" I'd say, "No, I'm having fun because we're just now two hours behind schedule so we'll be all right." And Goldwyn said, "Good-bye, Mr. Taurog," and I'd say, "Good-bye, Mr. Goldwyn."

MALTIN: Cantor was a worrier, wasn't he?

TAUROG: Oh God, was he a worrier. "Is this the same pair of pants I wore yesterday?" "Yes, same pair, Eddie." "How do you know?" "Wait a minute, I'll check it. Wardrobe man, is that the same pair of pants?" "Well, certainly, he's only got one pair." "You only have one pair, Eddie, and that's the pair." "Oh fine, fine. I just didn't want to be out of line on anything, you know. They are cleaned every night aren't they?" I said, "That I don't handle, Eddie, that's his job." But a worrier, oh God. [Ethel] Merman used to drive him crazy. "Eddie, you have anything to worry about today?" He'd say, "No, thank God, not today." She'd say, "Well, I've got a couple of problems I'll give you."

MALTIN: Was there a case with somebody like that where you'd shoot a scene and be perfectly satisfied but he wouldn't?

TAUROG: Sometimes.

MALTIN: Would you do it again?

TAUROG: Sure. And it would never be as good. He'd finally say, "I don't know, what the hell, I've lost something in it." And I'd say, "I think you lost it after the first take. It was spontaneous, it was good, it all worked; everything turned out fine. You're fishing for something and I don't know what it is. Maybe I could help you if I knew." "I just felt I could do it better." And I'd say, "Well, you haven't." "No, I don't think so, let's go on to something else." "Okay."

MALTIN: In *Rhythm on the Range* you presided over Martha Raye's debut.

TAUROG: Yes I did. I found Martha in the old Trocadero, and Bob Burns [too].

MALTIN: What kind of an act was she doing?

TAUROG: Martha, a hot singer—and great comedy, a good line of chatter. But she had more than that to me when I saw her. She had everything. Great talent, that girl.

MALTIN: When you had somebody like that who'd never been on the screen before, how would you try to make the best use of her talent? Would you work with her or would you work with the writers to concoct something special for her?

TAUROG: Always work with the writers. See, we had a part similar to Martha Raye's set already, but we had to rewrite it for Martha Raye. It was [written for] an entirely different looking girl, a blond girl who was a little nervous, which was not Martha. Martha would face a bear. And Louis Prima. I think that's the first time Louis Prima was ever in a picture. I'd seen him at the Open Door in New York, his own nightclub, and I'd always threatened to use him. I asked him if he'd do it and he said yes.

MALTIN: When you hired supporting players and character comedians, did you leave them alone or did you have certain things you wanted them to go after?

TAUROG: I had certain things that I knew I could get from them and that they fit a certain idea that I had. Most of those fellas get into the part themselves when you tell them the story and what they are to the story—what they are to the leading man and the leading woman. They will contribute if you want it. If you don't want it, you don't do it. I always loved good character actors and good second comics.

MALTIN: Did you enjoy working at one studio for a long period of time or did you prefer it when you freelanced for a while?

Taurog (center) strikes a mock-serious pose in this cast-and-crew photo for Rhythm on the Range (1936). Seated with him in the front row are actors Samuel S. Hinds, Martha Raye (in her feature debut), Frances Farmer, Bing Crosby, Bob Burns, and Lucile Webster Gleason. Standing behind, at extreme left, is Leonid Kinskey. Behind Taurog at right is Charles Williams, and over Taurog's shoulder the tall, well-dressed man is master cinematographer Karl Struss.

TAUROG: I loved freelancing after a while. Being you got the kind of money I got and being under contract, if you turned down a picture you always felt, Maybe they just think I'm turning it down because I want a rest. I loved to work; it didn't bother me. When you freelanced, you'd read a script and say, "No, I'd rather not do it," and you didn't feel under any obligations. And yet I always made two pictures a year even when I was freelancing. Sometimes, when I was working for a studio, I'd go as high as two and a half.

MALTIN: Back to comedians for a minute: what did you think of the Ritz Brothers?

TAUROG: Oh I love them; I loved Harry. Great talent. Jimmy was cute and his brother was a good talent. What Harry had as a comic, they had as dancers, and they were a great trio.

MALTIN: *You Can't Have Everything* is one of my favorite pictures with them, because you show them in a nightclub and that's where they really belonged.

TAUROG: That's right. That's the only way. There was another picture that they made right afterward that I turned down and that's what made Zanuck get angry at me.

MALTIN: Was it your idea to add slapstick to *The Adventures of Tom Sawyer* or was it there in the script?

TAUROG: Some of it was there and some of it I put in. I made *Tom Sawyer* twice, you know: once for Paramount in black and white and once for David [Selznick] in color, with Tommy Kelly.

MALTIN: Is that the first time you worked in color?

TAUROG: Oh no. First time I worked in color was way back when Mrs. Kalmus [Natalie Kalmus, wife of Technicolor founder Herbert T. Kalmus, who insisted on supervising use of color in "her" movies] used to come on the set, put red things on, and I used to go behind her and take them off and throw them down. Color was awful tough because they wanted to put as much color in, and I never believed in that. I wanted to take as much wild color out as I could and put in pastels, which didn't interfere with the goings-on on the set.

MALTIN: I recently saw a movie that I think is one of your best, *Broadway Melody of 1940*.

TAUROG: Oh really!

MALTIN: It's such a good film—such a good musical—and the performances are excellent. Astaire is wonderful.

TAUROG: Isn't he great in that?

MALTIN: He gives a good, rounded performance and has more of a characterization than in a lot of his other films.

TAUROG: A very peculiar thing about that picture. Jack Cummings produced that picture and it was the best thing, I think, that Eleanor

Powell ever did, because she believed in the picture, and if Ellie believed, she worked. I'll never forget this: [one] Monday Cummings came out on the set and said, "I'm stopping the picture." I said, "You are?" He said, "Yes. Meet me in Mr. Mayer's office at two o'clock." I said, "Jack, I'm sorry, but I'm going to call Mr. Mayer because I don't work this way." He said, "I wouldn't if I was you." The first thing I did was call Herman Citron, my agent. He said, "By all means, call Mr. Mayer." So I called Mr. Mayer and

The Ritz Brothers (Harry in the middle) in You Can't Have Everything (1937). Louis Prima is on the bandstand behind them.

he said, "Norman, you know me, I never hide behind anything but Jack's very unhappy with the first reel and a half of the picture." I said, "Is he? Well, that's too bad. How did he come to run the first reel and a half of the picture?" [Mr. Mayer] said, "He heard that you had it together. Norman, he's very unhappy." I said, "Mr. Mayer, are you going to look at the picture?' He said, "At two o'clock I'm going to look at it with you."

At two o'clock, we met down at the projection room and ran the picture. The lights went up and Mayer looked at Jack Cummings and said, "What is the matter with that film?" Jack said, "Well, it's slow and the characters don't relate." Mayer said, "My God, they're all playing practically themselves. [These actors] have never been better in their lives. Fred Astaire is magnificent, he's wonderful." I said, "That's thanks to the people, they really love what they're doing." Mayer said, "Jack, with Norman directing it, I'm sure you want to leave the picture." He said, "No, I don't, would it be all right if I stayed on the picture?" Mayer said, "That's up to Norman. Just like you wanted him taken off, he could ask to have you taken off." I said, "No, I don't want him taken off. I'll just go on and do the picture the way we had talked about it," and we finished it. Jack is a very talented man, don't misunderstand me. Jack did *Seven Brides*, a hell of a picture with a damn good director. But, probably he couldn't see where we were going to edit it.

MALTIN: I guess it was a different kind of approach because the characters are more interesting than you might expect in a musical.

TAUROG: That's why I wanted to make the picture, that's the only reason I would make the picture. I'd made musicals until they were coming out of my ears; I thought, wouldn't it be great if Ellie and George could come off good and if Fred could just once be a man, feel like he's a somebody, not just a nice guy who's a hoofer. I thought some of the scenes he did were delightful. And I'm giv-

Taurog makes a point to an attentive Mickey Rooney on the set of Boys Town (1938).

ing Fred the credit, too, because if he hadn't believed, he couldn't have done it.

MALTIN: Jumping ahead a bit, when was the first time you saw Martin and Lewis and what did you think of them?

TAUROG: First time I saw Martin and Lewis was in a nightclub called Slapsy Maxie's, and I thought Dean Martin was one of the best straight men that I'd ever seen and I didn't think that he had too much of a sense of humor. And I thought Jerry was a complete idiot. I loved him, loved the way he worked. The next time I saw a picture called *That's My Boy* and I thought they were just great in that. I hadn't seen *At War with the Army*. Then I got a call from Hal Wallis. Would I like to do a picture with Martin and Lewis? I said, "Would they like to do a picture with me?" I walked on the Paramount lot and Martin and Lewis were waiting in the parkway. I had a hunch that this was a planned thing. I walked up and Jerry Lewis came running over and got down on his knees and kissed my hand, kissed me on both cheeks, and said, "Oh, great filmmaker..." and he goes on with a big *megillah*. I took it very well. Dean is standing there, looking at him, and finally walks over and puts his middle finger in Jerry's mouth, like he did on the screen all the time, moves him around and says, "That will be about enough." I said, "I just have one thing to do," and Wallis said, "What's that?" I got down on my hands and knees and I took Jerry's hand and kissed it. And he said, "What's that for?" and I said, "For the amount of money that you people are going to pay me, 'cause it's fabulous." And we became pals right then.

MALTIN: Did Jerry Lewis aspire to become a director at that time?

TAUROG: Not at that time. Somebody made the mistake of telling Jerry that he was like Chaplin and I think that's what ruined Jerry.

MALTIN: Whose idea was it to do a film like *The Stooge*, which had so many serious moments in it?

TAUROG: Me. That was the first picture I made with them and that's when I found out that Dean was a funny man. That was my screen test for the two boys because I never made anything like it afterward.

MALTIN: Do you feel it worked?

TAUROG: Oh, it worked. I think Dean developed into a terrific light comic, and I think Jerry was the little guy and as long as he was that, he was very successful. The minute you take the belt off the back, take the cap off, the sneakers, and the little tight-fitting clothes [it didn't work any more]. Jerry was Bob Hope in one picture and Cary Grant in another. He's been everybody but Jerry Lewis, that's the whole problem. And Jerry is a great, great comic. But he's covered it all up. And Dean, I think, is a great light comic besides being a hell of a straight man.

MALTIN: Which is your favorite? You did about five or six.

TAUROG: Well, the one that I liked very much of course was *The Stooge*, because it had people in there that they had never worked with in their whole lives. The other one was *Pardners*, where they were cowboys.

MALTIN: There are some people who feel they were never as funny in films as they were live, or even on early television.

TAUROG: I think the box office would cancel all that out. My God, the money those fellas made with those pictures. Number one, they had an audience from the age of five years old up to sixty, sixty-five, seventy.

MALTIN: Did Lewis become difficult to direct as he got more interested in the filmmaking process?

TAUROG: He never became difficult but once with me, only once. We had it out, we straightened it out. I said to him, very honestly, "Jerry, any time you get the feeling you can do it better than I can, I work for you, you tell me, and I'll be on my way." He said, "Oh no, that isn't it, but I'm dying to learn." I said, "You don't do that forgetting who you are. You're a great comedian." You know, he's a damn good actor too. I've seen some of it and I know.

MALTIN: Why do you think he doesn't seem to have the filter that worked as it did when other people were directing him? He has the talent, but he can't see when he's going off the deep end.

TAUROG: Taste. If you have taste, that covers everything. He tried to prove a gag to me three times and each time it never worked. And I told him the first time, second time, third time. A little old lady comes up to him, he looks at her and says, "You're beautiful," takes her and bends over away from the camera and looks like he's giving her the greatest soul kiss in the world and straightens her up. I said, "Jerry, it's distasteful, it's rotten, nobody will laugh at it." He tried it three times and the third time he said, "You're right; they ain't gonna laugh at it." [But] it had to take three times to tell that. And yet he has magnificent taste in things about himself.

See, he went down in the gutter and we always tried to pick him up. If you dressed him, either his tie was off or the gloves were too big or he had the wrong shoes on, so that you said to yourself, "Poor guy!" but you didn't turn around and say, "Gee, what a slob." You never said that about Chaplin, what a slob; you always felt sorry for him. There was a wistful feeling.

MALTIN: Is there such a thing as the care and feeding of comedians? Do you feel comics have more delicate egos?

TAUROG: They're young babies, they're children. I've said I've directed children from the age of Big Boy, from three years old to Martin and Lewis who were thirty. Jerry was a baby. He'd pout. So I'd pout with him. When it was their own company, I'd just reach in my director's chair that had a pocket in it, bring out, and hold up a sign that said, "It's your money, take your time." Boy, they'd get in quick.

STILL LIFE

Florence and Arthur Lake came to Hollywood in the 1920s with their vaudevillian parents. Arthur starred in two-reel comedies for Universal from 1924 to 1929 and continued playing juveniles in talkies until he won the role he was born to play, Dagwood Bumstead, in 1938. Famed photographer Maurice Seymour took this picture of the two siblings early on.

Florence Lake made her screen debut in 1929 and just two years later was cast as Edgar Kennedy's sweet, dumb, talkative wife in his short-subject series. When this RKO publicity photo was taken in 1932, Edgar was already well-known to audiences, Florence was a relative newcomer, and studio contractee Ginger Rogers was just on the verge of true screen stardom. Florence had small parts in two of Rogers's starring vehicles at RKO (*Having a Wonderful Time* and *Bachelor Mother*) and continued acting, often unbilled, well into the 1970s. She died in 1980.

SHOOTING THE
SHOOT-EM-UPS

Going to the Source: EDWARD BERNDS

One of the relationships I will always treasure was my friendship with Edward Bernds. He was never a household name, even in Hollywood, but I defy you to think of anyone else who worked with both Mary Pickford and Sam Peckinpah, wrote for Shemp Howard and Elvis Presley, and who directed Hugh Herbert and Zsa Zsa Gabor. He spent the first fifteen years of his career as a sound recordist, and the rest of his career as a writer and/or director of B movies, but the breadth of his experiences was prodigious. What's more, he was a packrat and a diarist: when his memory failed, his paperwork could fill in the blanks.

When we first made contact, by mail, I never thought it would lead to a warm, thirty-year friendship, or that I could turn to Ed as a firsthand source on so many varied movie subjects. One example: I wrote a biography of Carole Lombard in the mid-1970s, and mentioned the project in a letter to Ed. He responded with a vivid recollection of the star:

"We were on an 'Eddie' and 'Carole' basis, although I usually called her, 'Hey, gorgeous.' I worked with her on Columbia potboilers as well as her later A pictures. She was completely uninhibited, in language and behavior. A couple of examples:

"In September, 1932, we were making *No More Orchids*, with Carole and Lyle Talbot. On September 29, my daughter Elsa was born in Cedars of Lebanon Hospital. My wife's roommate was the wife of Sam Nelson, our assistant director; I believe it was their son, Gary, who was born the same day. At another hospital, also on the same day, our prop man, Charley Granucci, had a child—a daughter, I believe. You should have heard Carole shriek when she heard about it. As nearly as I can remember, it went something like this: 'Why, you no-good bastards!

Ed Bernds at his recording console.

Carole Lombard.

Three kids on the same day! Jackpot!' And, in a reference to the brutal hours we worked at Columbia, 'When the hell did you guys find time to do it?'

"I was the sound man on Twentieth Century. I have never worked on a picture in which the scenes commanded such rapt attention from the crew. Crews can be pretty blasé even about blockbuster pictures. But Lombard and Barrymore were dynamic on the set. Anything could happen. We, the crew, were fascinated—more, I think, than we were even on Capra pictures."

I never ran out of things to discuss with Ed. In failing health, but still sharp and alert in his nineties, he loved to talk about his experiences; in fact, his caregiver told me that our conversations perked him up.

One day in 1998 I realized I'd never talked to Ed about making grade-B westerns at Columbia in the 1930s, so I took my tape recorder to his home in Van Nuys, and asked about the nuts and bolts of making cowboy movies. Edward Bernds died in May of 2000 at the age of ninety-four, but he's never far from my thoughts.

MALTIN: You worked on all the A pictures. What would happen when you finished a big assignment? Say you finished a picture on a Wednesday. What would happen Thursday?
BERNDS: Well, I wouldn't be put into another film in the middle of it, but I'd be put to work, no matter what it was, a two-reeler, a western, even a serial. Cameramen were choosy. They would not work on cheap stuff; [Frank Capra's ace cameraman] Joe Walker wouldn't touch a B picture. But if we turned something down, we'd be off salary and we

couldn't afford that. So, say a western was starting Monday, I'd be handed a script and there we go. They generally started on a Monday.

MALTIN: What were the most frequent locations that you'd go to for westerns?

BERNDS: Iverson's Ranch, good old Iverson's. I got to know every rock there. When I became a director, I'd use it; I knew where the locations were that I wanted. When I did science-fiction films, I shot them there. Yes, good old Iverson's. But it's destroyed now, you know, by the freeway. From the freeway, you can see the Garden of the Gods, which was the most spectacular rock formation at Iverson's Ranch. It had a lot of things going for it. It had a nice level place where you could make posse chases with the camera on a camera car, and they had a run of pretty near a mile where they could dash along at high speed in front of the posse and get close shots past the posse. It wasn't particularly easy to get to. Some of our trucks, the heavily loaded trucks, had to grind up Santa Susannah Pass in low gear, and then there were even more difficult roads in Iverson's Ranch, but we'd get there.

MALTIN: What time would you have to get there, when you were a sound man?

BERNDS: Usually, if we were going to go on a western, we'd report for work about 6:30. And in winter, it was still dark, but by the time we got there, there'd be light and we'd be able to shoot. Yes, it seems to me that we'd set out from Columbia . . .

MALTIN: You'd have to report to the studio first?

BERNDS: Generally, yes. I liked to drive my car on location because I could sleep a little longer. But the teamsters' union didn't want a lot of people using their own cars, and they put pressure on the sound men, on all the IATSE union members, to forbid their members to drive their own cars. So it's pretty hard to hide a car at Iverson's, but on other locations we'd hide the car blocks away from the location and walk the rest of the way, just so we could drive straight home and save maybe as much as forty-five minutes. They had a checker that was very much feared. He was reputed to be a Chicago mobster, and his title was checker, and he would snoop around, trying to find cars that had been driven on location.

MALTIN: Now there's an occupation!

BERNDS: Yes. [*Both laugh*]

MALTIN: So when you'd get there, how long would it take to get prepared?

BERNDS: Oh, probably from the time the sound trucks stopped rolling, we'd be ready to shoot in fifteen minutes. Camera probably took a little longer. Yes, we could set up and wrap up pretty quickly. Sometimes we'd have to run out a lot of cable to the mixing panel because the sound truck couldn't get there, that would take just a little longer. But if the sound truck could go near the place we were shooting, it was very, very quick.

MALTIN: How many setups a day would they do on a western? Do you have any recollection?

BERNDS: An awful lot of them. One of the first westerns I worked on, I marveled at the speed that it was done. Some directors were fast without being sloppy; others were pretty sloppy. Setups [that] would be done outdoors, of course, didn't need much—a few reflectors and that was it. Unless there were closeups, and every cameraman at any level took some pains with [the actresses]; women were supposed to look good. But I'm reminded, Columbia would often send starlets, little girls under contract, to get some seasoning on westerns, and I remember well, it happened many times, the little girl would come out cold and bewildered [the first thing in the morning] and be required to react to some terrible event. Here was a little girl trying to react to nothing, you know. The newcomers also had trouble with reflectors. The light that they used was pretty powerful, and the newcomers, like the starlets, had an awful time just keeping their eyes open. Sometimes when I see old westerns, ours and Republic's, you see people straining to keep their eyes open, if you look closely.

MALTIN: What were your impressions of Tim McCoy?

BERNDS: A gentleman all the way. Kind of aloof with the crew. Our crew was pretty rowdy. When we had Ross Lederman as director, the atmosphere was wild then. He was wild and the crew followed suit, but Tim was an officer and a gentleman, did his work; very quiet. I worked with him not only in westerns, but then tried to use him on B action pictures. He tried, but he was a little bit stiff.

MALTIN: What about Buck Jones?

BERNDS: Oh . . . Buck was the real thing, you know. I wrote about this in my memoirs, how Joe Bonomo nearly killed him. Hit Buck right in the back with this non-breakaway chair. That was a scary moment. It was the first time I'd seen a three-hundred-pound strong man cry. He (Bonomo) did.

MALTIN: Was there a special camaraderie making westerns? You're all out there together in the outdoors for the day. Was it different than making other kinds of films?

BERNDS: Yes, I think so. Everything was relaxed when Ben Kline was the cameraman, he was like Ross Lederman—loud, profane, relaxed. Good cameraman, very good cameraman. But he'd tell Ross Lederman if it were on a western, "Hey, Ross, that's a lousy idea." You know, I mean none of this kowtowing to the director. So if you were on a picture with Lederman and Benny Kline, it was camaraderie, yes, a lot of fun. A lot of ribaldry.

MALTIN: Did you work with Lambert Hillyer?

BERNDS: Hillyer was more businesslike. He was an intense little man. Charlie Granucci, a prop man, made a mistake, and Lambert Hillyer was gonna beat him up for it, he really lost his temper, and Charlie ran for his life. What it was: a dispatch rider was supposed to dash up, do a dismount, and hand a dispatch to somebody. Then take after take it didn't work right. Finally, it worked to perfection and the dispatch rider reached in the pouch, [and there was] nothing, you know, he had nothing to hand. And that's when Hillyer wanted to beat up Charlie Granucci.

MALTIN: When you were out at Iverson's, how late would you go?

BERNDS: As late as there was any light. You've heard the expression "chasing the sun"? The Santa Susannah mountains would cast a shadow where we were working, so we'd go to higher ground, shoot a few scenes until finally the light was completely gone. Then we had the wearisome task of taking all the equipment down the hill and loading up. We'd gone up in stages, but it was particularly tough on the cameramen, because we used cameras on tripods; of course, you couldn't use a crane on that kind of shooting. But going up is tough on a cameraman; going down is murder. They usually had a couple of grips right handy, so if the camera stumbled, they'd catch them. Downhill was rocky and slippery, you know, with sliding terrain; if you ever stumbled downhill, he and the camera would be badly injured.

MALTIN: What about rain? Would they schedule an outdoor shoot for a western during the rainy season?

BERNDS: Oh, yes . . . If the weather report was very bad, they might cancel it. You, of course, are familiar with the term "cover set." The nightmare of an assistant director or production manager is to run out of cover sets, to shoot all your cover sets, and still have exteriors to go. But the schedule was important. We'd go out even if there was a threat of rain or a prediction of rain, and if it rained, we'd come in.

MALTIN: Come in to the studio?

BERNDS: Yeah. We wouldn't be through for the day. We'd come in, unpack, and go into a cover set.

MALTIN: So if it was two in the afternoon, you'd still do that.

BERNDS: Yeah. Probably shoot until 7:00 at night to not lose much time. The hours in the old days were really grinding. I remember everybody would get short-tempered when we went past dinnertime. Knock off at 7:30. You got a reputation for making a lot of money, but it was a custom to subject the crew to long hours.

MALTIN: Would they serve you a box lunch out on location?

BERNDS: Oh, yes. But after a while, they began serving hot lunches. The trucks would drive up to Iverson's, set up some tables, and we had some pretty good noontime meals. They tried to feed us well out on location.

MALTIN: I'm trying to think who else was at Columbia . . . Charles Starrett?

BERNDS: Oh, my goodness, Starrett made a tremendous number of westerns. Columbia decided to make a cowboy out of him. He was a socialite, had been at Dartmouth, I think, graduate, had been a football star, but in spite of all the westerns he made, he never really bonded with the wranglers and the other people. They didn't like him, because he didn't take the trouble to really learn how to mount a horse and so on, and he'd blame the horse and he was rough with the horses. In other words, he just didn't please the wranglers, who were westerners, or at least, you know, real horsemen. Wranglers were a great bunch. When I directed westerns, I loved the people I had to work with.

These snapshots from western locations—including a Charles Starrett feature—came from Ed Bernds' scrapbook.

WOMEN OF INK & PAINT

Conversations:
BETTY KIMBALL & MARIE JOHNSTON

At various times in Hollywood history, women dominated certain aspects of film production. In the silent era, many of the leading screenwriters were female; later, they had a strong presence in the field of editing. But there is one neglected area of moviemaking that was populated exclusively by women in the 1930s and forties: the ink- and paint- departments of the cartoon studios.

Long before computers took over the painting process, and decades before the invention of xerography made it possible to transfer an animator's drawings directly onto cels, the unsung heroines of animated cartoons were those women in the ink and paint departments.

An animator would work with paper and pencil, and his assistant would refine the often-rough drawings. Then an inker would lay a clear piece of celluloid over the drawing and trace it as carefully as possible, trying to retain as much of the nuance of those pencil lines as possible. Later, the reverse side of the cels would be painted. The finished cels would then be photographed over painted backgrounds to create a finished scene. (Unlike fans, most animators have little use for cels; they sometimes saved drawings, because that represented their work in its purest form, before other hands got hold of it. Even so, no one involved with animation had any clue their artwork would some day be worth a fortune.)

At the Walt Disney studio, located first on Hyperion Avenue in Los Angeles, then in a brand-new custom-built facility in Burbank, two women found steady employment and lifelong mates. Betty Lawyer was hired on March 25, 1935, at $25 a week; several years later she married one of Disney's star animators, Ward Kimball. Marie Worthey joined the studio on August 8, 1940, at $16 a week (possibly a trainee wage) and three years later married Ollie Johnson, who would become another of Walt's fabled "nine old men."

Although I was lucky enough to know both animators, it wasn't until 1997 that I realized I should interview their wives to gain some insight into their careers; they were happy to oblige. Their memories help flesh out our knowledge, not only about the day-to-day workings of the Disney studio, but the practicalities of life at that time. Betty reveals that it was the crunch of making Walt's first feature film, *Snow White and the Seven Dwarfs*, that required staffers to work at night—and finally broke down the social barrier between the ink-and-paint girls and their male colleagues. Marie left Disney because she didn't want to cross a picket line during the bitter studio strike of 1941, then remained at Warner Bros. because the studio, affectionately nicknamed "Termite Terrace," was within walking distance of her home in Hollywood!

Incidentally, both women repudiated the nonsensical "urban myth" about lewd frames finding their way into Snow White, for purely practical reasons: no one could "sneak" a frame into a finished film without it being inked and painted first, by women, in a department supervised by yet another woman—Walt's sister-in-law Hazel Sewell!

I am only sorry I didn't get to publish this interview during Marie's lifetime; she died on May 20, 2005.

MALTIN: Betty, when did you go to work at Disney?

KIMBALL: January, 1935. My brother came home at Christmas time and a friend of his told him that they needed inkers and painters at Disney's studio. I had a little theater group that I was directing a play for, and the WPA was paying me something, but here was a chance for a real job. I never went to art school so I didn't really have much of a portfolio, but I had botanical prints that I did in my botany class and they hired me. No, first they had me work for a week for nothing while they were training me. They had a class that met from 6:00 to 9:00 in the inking- and painting- department, which then was just a little place that faced Hyperion [Avenue]. And I took a training course for four days.

MALTIN: Was that in inking or painting?

KIMBALL: Both. I flunked inking completely. The celluloid is slippery and the hand just goes sliding all over it and I couldn't do that at all. So after one evening of trying to ink they had me painting the backs of the cels. Then on Thursday they said, "Okay, you can come back and work Monday morning."

I didn't work very long in that little place where the inking and painting was because the new building was finished. I worked mostly in black and white in the old building and I'd been painting in shades of gray—gray number one, gray number two, gray number three, depending on what cel level it was on—and black and white. It seemed that when I moved into the new building, I moved into this bright color. I started working on *Silly Symphonies*; everything was brilliant and light, and the paint lab was right next door.

MALTIN: How old were you when you went to work there?

KIMBALL: I was twenty-two. I was out of school and I had majored in drama. I had no intention of being an artist.

MALTIN: Where did you go to school?

KIMBALL: I went to Pasadena City College and then took some extra courses at Pasadena Playhouse.

MALTIN: Marie, how did your Disney job come about?

JOHNSTON: Well, the mother of my friend June Walker worked at the studio as one of the secretaries. June got a job there and she called me and said, "They're hiring at Disney; can you get a folder together with some of your stuff?" So I went out with my folder and they called me the next day and I was hired.

A row of inkers at Disney's Hyperion Studio in 1939; the shelves were used to store finished work.

MALTIN: So how old were you then?

JOHNSTON: I was probably twenty-two.

MALTIN: What were you hired specifically to do?

JOHNSTON: It started out with the painting, and then you worked in inking if you wanted to; I liked both of them.

MALTIN: Who taught you how to do what they needed you to do?

JOHNSTON: The head of ink and paint. They believed in quality, not quantity, and I've never forgotten that. She would come around to your desk and say, "I want you to stop and just look out in the distance; look out the window." Because it's bad for your eyes, to keep going with that light under [the lightboxes]. So they cared about you. It wasn't just, "Get it out." It was very different from a lot of places.

MALTIN: When you arrived in the morning did you have a day's work to do?

JOHNSTON: Well, you sometimes had carryover. You'd do one whole scene, so sometimes you'd have leftover work from the day before.

MALTIN: Did you work on both shorts and features?

JOHNSTON: Whatever they needed to have worked on.

MALTIN: And when you were done with a cel, would you just put it aside to dry and then work on the next one?

JOHNSTON: You had to be very careful about that. We had shelves and we put it with the paint side up, of course, and paper under it to let it dry. I can't remember how long it took. You had to keep things numbered; the numbers were in the corner so you had to keep it in order, so that when you did collect them all, to turn them in, they were the way they were supposed to be. I'd kind of forgotten all of that and you bring it all back to me. Goodness. I do remember something funny: we had to wear cotton gloves and for the right hand that you hold the paint brush in, the thumb and index finger were cut out; your left hand had the full glove on it. I'm kind of ambidextrous, so if I'd find that I could get into [a] point easier with my left hand, I was changing hands, but not gloves. The supervisor came along behind me and was standing there watching me switching back and forth. Then she said, "It's marvelous that you can do this, but you're getting fingerprints on the cels and that'll photograph." Oh my gosh.

MALTIN: Oh, no . . .

JOHNSTON: I was so embarrassed. She said, "No, don't be. Normally I wouldn't have to say that, because most people couldn't do that." So then I had to remember that if I was going to switch. Well, then I didn't switch that much, because it was a pain in the neck to have to change your gloves right in the middle.

MALTIN: Did it seem like the time went quickly, or was it laborious?

JOHNSTON: No, it didn't drag at all. We were busy.

MALTIN: How were the paints to work with? Did they dry quickly, did they react to the weather?

JOHNSTON: They didn't dry too quickly. They could if you weren't careful, but I don't remember that they dried that quickly. They had their own department there where they made all their own paint colors and everything, which was a big, separate room, I remember.

MALTIN: Did you ever have any interest in inking?

JOHNSTON: I did inking all the time at Warner Bros.

MALTIN: Was it considered "graduating" when you went from painting to inking?

JOHNSTON: I suppose. I hadn't thought about it, but I suppose it was.

MALTIN: Because inking was more difficult.

JOHNSTON: Well, yes. It's a technique that takes a little time to master.

MALTIN: What was the greatest challenge of inking over a pencil drawing?

JOHNSTON: You have to figure it out ahead of time when you first look at the thing which line you're going to start with.

MALTIN: Did the line have to be done in one stroke for it to work?

JOHNSTON: Pretty much.

MALTIN: I'm guessing that in inking, if you made a mistake, you could always start over again. No harm was done.

JOHNSTON: You'd have to have a new cel.

MALTIN: You'd have a new cel, but that's the worst of it.

JOHNSTON: Mmm-hmm.

MALTIN: In painting, what would happen if you made a mistake?

JOHNSTON: Well, I never made one . . . [*Laughs*] I'm trying to remember. If you hadn't done too much, it seemed to me that you could wash it off with water and maybe cotton. We were able to clean a cel up without hurting the ink line which is on the back side.

MALTIN: Were fumes ever a problem?

JOHNSTON: No. The paint was water-based. It had to have been, or we wouldn't have been able to clean it up.

MALTIN: Did you enjoy inking? I would think it would be a really interesting challenge to try to capture that drawing.

JOHNSTON: Oh, yes. You need to get the flow of the artist's drawing, but you can't have all the [rough] lines coming out, so you have to ignore some of their lines.

MALTIN: What was the challenge or the knack of painting a cel? What kind of things did you have to learn how to do?

JOHNSTON: Well, it's hard to explain it, but if you have a shape that [tapers off] to a point, you start out with a lot of paint on your brush and you never leave an edge, you've got the ink line in back of you, so you never let that dry. You have to float up to it and then bring this paint down and lift your brush in a hurry and it comes to a nice point. But if you don't, if you let it dry, that streak of dry will show when it's blown up on the screen. And if you dig in too much with your paintbrush, if you don't float it on, those dig marks are a paler color and they'll show up.

MALTIN: So one of the things was to try to make one continuous motion with the brush.

JOHNSTON: Yes. You couldn't make it one motion, but to float and not dig in with the brush.

MALTIN: Did it come easily to you?

JOHNSTON: Well, it was fun. I enjoyed it. So I suppose it did, but I wasn't thinking about that at the time.

MALTIN: Betty, do you remember how long it would take to paint a cel of a character?

KIMBALL: You went through one color at a time and you would paint on the back of the cel. They were beautifully inked, and I'll have to tell you the inkers are geniuses. They followed the animators' pencil lines and did it exactly where the pencil line was but made it a free line. And it was on that celluloid that the pen would just go scooting every which way if you didn't have perfect control. They would follow those pencil lines [and] get it right on the nose because if it went [beyond the line] it would be magnified on a big screen. And they were working on celluloid, which is slippery.

MALTIN: How many cels would you be handed at one time?

KIMBALL: You would be handed a scene from start to the end.

MALTIN: Would you paint the one color on every cel first and then go back and do it like an assembly line?

KIMBALL: Yes. It would come from the inker and go into the paint lab, where they would mark up the [color] model with the colors that you'd use. (I still remember Candy Red, because it was used for candy cane stripes.) That color model would be given to a painter with a stack of inked cels. Then, she would paint the colors that were indicated.

MALTIN: So would you do it like an assembly line, where you'd do the one color on every cel first and then go back to the second color on every cel?

KIMBALL: Yes, that's the way you did it. And you had to judge painting something small to begin with and then something large because you could slop over the small thing, so you had to judge which color to put on first. That was really the only brain work in the painting department—and keeping within the line. There was no headache in that; it was just automatic painting. The colors were labeled, and the whites came in number one, number two, and number three, whether it was on the first level of the cel or the second level or the third level because you had to compensate for the color of celluloid.

MALTIN: So if a character was standing still in part of a scene, he might be on the bottom cel level, and the camera would "read" his color differently than when he was on the top level?

KIMBALL: You don't notice it when you look at it but if you put several layers together, it changes the whites. So the whites were listed according to cel level and the other colors all had numbers on like Candy Red number one, two, and three. You usually had a whole scene but only one cel level to work on. Sometimes you'd only be doing something that moves where something behind it moves slower and would be on a different cel level.

MALTIN: What would happen if you made a mistake? Was the paint washable?

KIMBALL: Oh yes, you either scratched it off very carefully or used something like a swab. If you made a horrible mistake and had to wash the whole thing off, that would take repainting the whole thing beginning with the first level that you used.

MALTIN: Would they remix the paints every day?

Here, a painter works on a Mickey Mouse cartoon in 1939; note the many varieties of paints, all custom mixed at the studio.

KIMBALL: No. If you had some left over and the weather changed, sometimes you'd say, "This is not drying," and you'd take it back to paint lab and they would change it.

MALTIN: What about the cels themselves? Would they ever stick?

KIMBALL: Yes, and you had problems with the paint not drying. That was because a medium was put in the paint so it would dry slower so you could finish painting and it wouldn't change color. Sometimes they put too much glycerin in and they would stick together. If it was a humid day in the paint lab, they had to use less glycerin, so paint lab was sort of . . . a chemistry lab.

MALTIN: Did the cels ever crack once they were finished?

KIMBALL: Yes. If you didn't have enough glycerin in, they'd crack.

MALTIN: Was there someone looking over your shoulder?

KIMBALL: No; you checked in a scene and then you checked it out when you were through with it.

MALTIN: Were you supervised when you moved into the color model department?

KIMBALL: You were on your own. Mary Weiser was in charge of it but she left it up to you if she figured you could do it. I never was supervised much. I was very good at matching colors and so I started working on color models almost immediately, because I was better at that. They tried to get a machine that would match colors. They brought a big machine in from Cal Tech, and it was called a spectrometer or something like that. It was a machine that took up a whole room, a little room that they sort of partitioned off. They would have me match colors and then they would have the machine match the colors. And I did it better with my eye; it photographed better than what the machine did. So they moved the machine out and they moved me in with an assistant and we did just extra special color models. [*Laughs*]

MALTIN: What would be considered extra special?

KIMBALL: Well, like splashes where you used a sponge or a dry brush; things that were extra hard. On *Fantasia* we did the special effects to make sparkles and the fairies dancing. We would do splashes by stippling on the top [of the cel] with a sponge to get foam.

MALTIN: How did you achieve some of those effects? Did you use luminescent paint of some sort?

KIMBALL: No, but we figured out how to get a special effect by highlights, sometimes on the top of the cel, and it just would sparkle. It wasn't special paint. Working on special effects was really interesting. I thought painting on the other side of the cel was dull, but figuring out how to get a sudden sparkle [was exciting]. In some of those [scenes] it really looks like a light going on. You did it with extra-light paint on the top of the cel and it really looks like a light goes on.

MALTIN: Marie, why did you leave Disney and go to Warner Bros.?

JOHNSTON: You know, the strike came on [in 1941] and I hadn't been there that long. [Someone] called me and said, "We have an opening at Warner Bros." I was fairly new there [at Disney], I might not get called back.

MALTIN: Were you laid off?

JOHNSTON: Well, no, it was the strike. I didn't feel that I could break through the [picket] line, so I thought [going to Warners] was the best thing to do. That was a terrible time. We had a guy called George who was the head of ink and paint [at Warners]. He didn't know a damn thing about inking and painting, believe me. He would stand at the back of the room and he'd be mad at one person, but he'd yell at the whole roomful. It was just terrible. I think I worked there a couple of years after we were married. I'd come home grumbling at something George had done or said, and it wasn't directed at me, it was just directed at everybody, the whole room, and Ollie said, "Why don't you quit?" But [the studio] was close enough to where we lived on Franklin that it was within walking distance.

MALTIN: Other than that onerous supervisor, what other differences were there working at Warners?

JOHNSTON: Well I hate to be saying [this just about] Warners, but it was [all about] quantity. To hell with quality. I met some nice people there, but it was a different atmosphere altogether. And they were doing, well, more like comic strips, that's what I call them. They didn't have any heart or character that Disney had.

MALTIN: Betty, what were your hours in those days?

KIMBALL: Eight to five, with an hour off for lunch.

MALTIN: Did you work Saturdays, too, or just Monday to Friday?

KIMBALL: We worked Saturday morning, eight to one. And then there was a law put into effect so the women could only work from eight to twelve.

MALTIN: Do you remember how many people were there when you joined up?

KIMBALL: No, I don't. There were two rooms of inkers and painters. But I was never good on figures so I can't tell you how many there were.

MALTIN: And were most of them young girls like you?

KIMBALL: Some of them worked during the summer that were still in school, but they were all ages.

MALTIN: And they were all female.

KIMBALL: Not one male. And we were discouraged from [going over to] the animation department.

MALTIN: So were you ever involved in anything outside of your area?

KIMBALL: I got into doing live-action for the animators, for the rotoscope [a tracing device]. I [even] did *Snow White*'s dialogue. I remem-

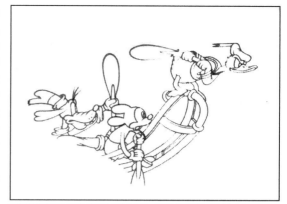

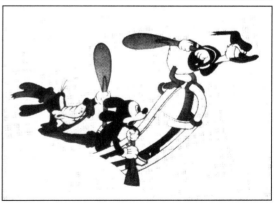

From top to bottom: inked characters on the top cel level in a scene from Moose Hunters (1937); inked water-effects from the second cel level; the first cel level, now fully painted. All illustrations © The Walt Disney Co.

ber the first scene I did for Ham Luske [a supervising animator on the film]; it was the scene of Snow White after she ran through the brambles and fell on the ground and talked to the little animals that came out. And (Adriana) Caselotti, who got the job a long time later after I did this test, had to match my timing. Because [by then] Ham had already animated it. They [also] called me in to do walk-throughs. I still have the black-and-white film that they took as I walked over a bridge, being Snow White, and looked to the right and looked to the left and talked to the little animals. [*Laughs*] I did a lot of moving back and forth.

MALTIN: What was the atmosphere like, Marie?

JOHNSTON: Very friendly. They had a lot of room outside in the animation building and the guys all played badminton, basketball, and all kinds of games. I don't know if they do that anymore, I doubt it.

MALTIN: Was the Hyperion studio a nice place to work?

KIMBALL: Oh, yes. It was like a college campus. And when the work got going real good on *Snow White*, it was really like a college campus, because then the inking and painting was no longer a nunnery. You got together with the guys and you ate dinner together and everything; it was like a co-educational college then. That was the period when all the romances started and the guys and the girls got together at dinner after work. You'd have a brief dinner across the street and then you would work until ten o'clock, and then you'd go to the Tam O'Shanter [a local restaurant that was—and remains—a favorite for Disney employees] and gripe about what was wrong with the work. There were a lot of marriages during the *Snow White* time because the inking and painting department kind of mingled with the rest of the place. And most of them lasted. I guess a few didn't, but most of them did.

MALTIN: When I first learned that it was all women doing inking and painting, I thought it had something to do with women having a more delicate touch. Then someone told me it was strictly a matter of economics; they could pay women less.

JOHNSTON: That's probably true. That's probably what it was.

MALTIN: Did you ever think about that?

JOHNSTON: No, I didn't at the time, but I have since then. I'm sure that's true. Well, that's changing slowly.

MALTIN: Why was this considered appropriate work for young women?

KIMBALL: As far as matching color, I think maybe they thought women were better than men. There were very few men that were good at matching colors, and you had to change the color with the cel level. The routine [job] of painting, I think, was because women worked for less money. They could get women for almost nothing then, because the Depression was really hard on them. That was undoubtedly it.

MALTIN: When did you have to start working nights? Do you remember there being a feeling of pressure?

KIMBALL: Yes. The one serious picture that they did was [the short-subject] "The Old Mill." Everything up to that time was in bright colors, but working on "The Old Mill" they went into subdued grays and it was a serious picture. And that was when you could feel that a feature was coming on and you began hearing about it. Then they laid off a lot of inkers and painters because the feature was starting and they kind of cut down on their shorts. And the animators were all doing tests and things on the feature. I remember I was laid off for a short while and then I went back and everything seemed to be tests for the feature. I really didn't do any straight painting on the feature; by then, I was doing color models.

Top: Here is the paint department's color model, indicating the numbers that correspond to colors for each component of the scene.

Bottom: A fully inked and painted composite of another frame from the finished scene.

MALTIN: Did you get to see the work in progress?

KIMBALL: That's another thing they'd call the girls in for: [they would] show us test reels to see what the reaction was.

MALTIN: Were there ever occasions when the director or an animator would have to come and give you a really specific idea of what they were after in a scene?

JOHNSTON: Not really. I think they'd go to the supervisor of our department and probably tell her and then she'd pass it on. No, I don't remember that ever happening.

MALTIN: Did you have a sense of what you were working on, a sense of the bigger picture?

JOHNSTON: No, and we should have. I think that's a good point. I don't know that it would matter that much, but it would be nice to have known, and I don't remember knowing the story. You kind of got into it, but it would have been good to know.

MALTIN: How did it feel when you'd see the finished film? Did you feel connected to it?

JOHNSTON: Oh, sure. That was fun. You know [*pointing*], "I did that! That's my scene."

ART CORNER

Joe Grant's place in film history is secure—as a character designer for *Snow White and the Seven Dwarfs*, story director on *Fantasia,* and co-writer of *Dumbo*, for starters. But in the early 1930s he drew wonderful caricatures for the Los Angeles *Record*, where drama editor Llewellyn Miller gave him a free hand. "I tried out every different technique I could imagine; that was the excitement for me," he recalls. "The most influential man for me was Ralph Barton, and also my father, George Albert Grant, who was an artist on the *Examiner*; in fact we were on competing papers." Walt Disney liked what he saw and invited Joe to the studio one day. "He said, 'How'd you like to work for me?' and I took a $10 decrease in my weekly salary, because I thought he had something." Grant stayed through the 1950s, leaving to create greeting cards and decorative tiles, but was lured back in the 1980s, and remains active there at age ninety-three. Seventy-seven of his original caricatures reside at the National Portrait Gallery in Washington, D.C. ("So I'm no bum," he says, in deadpan style) and plans are afoot to publish this exceptional work in book form.

Top left, the stars of Grand Hotel; at left, Charles Laughton and Claudette Colbert in The Sign of the Cross; upper right, Joan Crawford; right, Eddie Cantor, Lyda Roberti and friend in The Kid from Spain.

JOAN CRAWFORD
as caricatured by
Joe Grant at SARDI'S

JACKIE COOPER
as caricatured by
Joe Grant at SARDI'S

EDDIE CANTOR
as caricatured at SARDI'S

Here are some souvenir postcards Grant drew for the all-but-forgotten Sardi's of Hollywood, which was located on Hollywood Boulevard. The restaurant appeared in the 1936 movie of the same name. (Caricatures are still part of the tradition at Vincent Sardi's celebrated restaurant in New York City's theater district.) Had Joe not spent so much of his life making movies like *Fantasia, Dumbo,* and more recently, *Pocahontas, Mulan,* and *Fantasia 2000,* he might have had a pretty fair career doing drawings of Hollywood stars.

Conversations:
JOSEPH BIROC, ASC

Back in 1984, my friend Jeanine Basinger asked if I would interview cinematographer Joseph Biroc for *The* It's a Wonderful Life *Book*, which she was compiling from material in the Frank Capra papers deposited at the Wesleyan University Cinema Archive. I jumped at the chance to meet this celebrated cameraman, who suggested we get together at the American Society of Cinematographers' Hollywood headquarters, familiarly known as "the clubhouse."

Biroc was such an engaging man that I couldn't cut off our conversation after we finished discussing the Capra film, so we continued to talk, even though I wasn't really prepared for an in-depth career interview. This will explain why the conversation that follows touches on just a few highlights of Biroc's fifty years behind the camera. [For a detailed recollection of filming *It's a Wonderful Life*, I encourage you to seek out Jeanine's book.]

Born in New York City in 1903, Biroc started on the ground floor of the movie business at Paramount's Astoria, Long Island studio and worked his way up during the silent era, becoming a top camera operator at RKO in the 1930s. As he described the process of filming Fred Astaire and Ginger Rogers's dance numbers, I realized how little I appreciated the work of a camera crew. Just because Biroc wasn't listed onscreen in the credits of *The Gay Divorcee* or *Swing Time* didn't mean he and his cohorts didn't make a vital contribution to those extraordinary films.

Cameramen have a long tradition of mentoring members of their team. When Frank Capra's longtime cinematographer, Joseph Walker, had to leave *It's a Wonderful Life* before production was complete, he suggested that the director give his operator, Joe Biroc, a chance to move up the ladder and finish the picture. Biroc's work on that film launched

Joe Biroc, photographed at the ASC Clubhouse in 1984, with a Bell & Howell camera dating from the silent era.

him as a full-fledged "first cameraman" and from there he never looked back. Joseph Biroc photographed nearly one hundred feature films and countless TV series, made-for-TV movies, and miniseries until his retirement in 1986. (He died ten years later.) Directors ranging from Robert Aldrich and Samuel Fuller to Carl Reiner counted on him time and time again. His films include *Magic Town, On Our Merry Way, Johnny Allegro, Donovan's Brain, China Gate, 13 Ghosts, Bye Bye Birdie, Viva Las Vegas, The Flight of the Phoenix, Superman, The Longest Yard, Blazing Saddles, Airplane!,* and *Hammett.*

Even if I'd been better prepared, it would have been impossible to cover his entire career in one interview. Now I wish I could go back in time and ask him about photographing Arch Oboler's Bwana Devil in 3-D, or the original *Adventures of Superman* TV series, or . . . You get the idea.

His friend Roy H. Wagner, ASC, who provided the wonderful photographs for this article, recalls, "Joe Biroc was a great man who loved cinematography and the business until the very end. You could generally find him sitting right underneath the camera, smoking his cigar. As the smoke would waft up into lens view an assistant would reluctantly warn him. He would smile and simply say, 'diffusion.' I miss him and those great icons with such powerful personalities."

MALTIN: How old were you when you started working in the movie business?

BIROC: About sixteen or seventeen. My uncle Joe, who I was named after, had worked on the stage in New York for years. So when the motion pictures come along, he started working the pictures, because they needed people with stage technique. He worked as a prop man. He knew that I had been interested in cameras; he knew I wanted to get into the studio. So he went to the head of the camera department. That guy says, "Well, what does he know?" My uncle says, "He doesn't know anything about the camera, but for years he's worked in the lab." So the head of the camera department called the lab and asked about me. They said, "Yeah, he's one of our printers here." Then he says, "Send him over, let me talk to him." So I went over and I got the job.

MALTIN: And then you did a little bit of everything?

BIROC: They kept us around, playing around doing something. You know, maybe running a slate. They assigned me to George Hinners; he was one of the top operators and he got to go out here for a day, go there for a day. The head of the studio says, "My son is graduating. Go out and photograph the graduation exercise." Or, "There is going to be an air meet at Mineola Field. Go out there and get these guys going around, and see what you can get." So we would go out to Mineola, spend a couple of days there for the meet. I was there the day that it was either Doolittle or Williams set the world record, at two hundred and forty-four miles an hour, going around pylons. From then on he kept me busy when they went on pictures. Just like doing commercials and getting your feet wet [today].

MALTIN: And as you work with a lot of different people, you pick up ideas.

BIROC: Absolutely. Little by little.

MALTIN: What was the very first film that you worked on? Do you remember?

BIROC: I can't think of what the first picture was. I'm pretty sure it was a Richard Dix picture, because I made so darn many with him.

MALTIN: When did you move to Hollywood?

BIROC: I came here when sound first started. FBO was bought by RCA and they started Radio Pictures. The head of the camera department told the head of the production department that he wanted me as one of his operators. Well, I was only an assistant, so I went in to be interviewed by this guy, C. D. White his name was. Wonderful guy. He says, "Yeah, I know you want to be an operator; you are currently an assistant cameraman. I'll give you a week. At the end of the week if you don't cut it, out you go." I said, "Fine, that's all I want." I was there for twenty years. They were loyal to you in those days. There is no loyalty now; all they want is the money. It's just a rat race now, and I would say a tremendous amount of the people that are working now are not competent. They don't have the experience, so you have nothing to draw on.

MALTIN: How long were you an assistant before you became an operator?

BIROC: About seven or eight years. But I had the experience. At the [Paramount] Long Island Studio where I started they had a lot of real competent people, operators and assistants. The head of the camera department and the studio always believed in pushing people ahead. So what happens? Twice a year all the people in the studio, the high executives, if they had nephews, grandchildren, uncles or aunts, cousins who wanted to get into the business, the head of the camera department put them in. If they were competent, fine, they kept them on. If they weren't, twice a year everybody in the department got fired. Everybody fired. He kept bringing back all the people he wanted that were competent; the other fellows were all let go.

Then when we came to Hollywood [and RKO Radio Pictures], he brought in all of his own people that he knew, so he started on top by having all top people. As the studio grew, and we started making new pictures, we would draw on our knowledge from working at another studio and knowing somebody. All of the competent people that we had

Colleagues at RKO in front of the camera department building (1932): Joe Biroc behind the camera at left, George Barnes on the truckbed, Edward Cronjager with his hand on the horse's head, and Harold Wellman on the horse.

worked with over the years in different studios we brought in. So we had a better studio going in a couple of months than some of the others have that had been going for years.

MALTIN: This may be a difficult question, but was there one cameraman in particular who you learned the most from?

BIROC: No. Over the years you pick that up, but there was one cameraman that I worked with, the one who worked the early DeMille pictures . . .

MALTIN: Alvin Wyckoff was DeMille's first cameraman.

BIROC: Yes. I worked with him back in the Long Island studio. We went down to Florida on a show (this was when the big real estate boom was on, 1924–25) and I was working with an operator that always did the second units. And one day [they needed a camera] to follow Tom Meighan around a baseball field. To follow him, hitting the ball, taking him to first [base]. He talked to that guy, takes some papers out, tells the world about the real estate, goes to second, talked to that guy, and they go to the shortstop. He finally goes around. That was my job to follow this guy around the field. They didn't do that in those days.

MALTIN: That must have been quite a daring shot.

BIROC: It was. Wyckoff says, "Joe is going to do it." And that was it. I did it. When they started the union, the first twenty-five cameramen got together here, my name was one of them; we paid a buddy an initiation fee that went back to New York. Wyckoff at that time was president of Local 659. I get permission to work as an operator; now I have to go before the board, and Wyckoff was the president. He said, "Okay, I'll vouch for him." [*Laughs*] Al was a wonderful man. On the same picture, we photographed on a boat going down, and photographed on a boat coming back. They were coaching me. I was fairly new in the racket. But fortunately I had worked on the Aikley camera a lot. And in those days we could take a camera apart. That was our job: make sure that you could keep the camera working. Take it apart. Take every nut, screw apart and put it back together again.

MALTIN: And did you shoot some of the Wheeler and Woolsey pictures?

BIROC: I did part of the first picture that came out from Broadway.

MALTIN: *Rio Rita*.

BIROC: *Rio Rita*. I was one of the extra cameras on that. Then when they started making them on their own, I made several of them. They were wonderful guys.

MALTIN: Did you work with Clark and McCullough?

BIROC: Yes. [Bobby Clark] was a great guy for timing. I'll never forget, we had one [scene] that had a desk. The desk had to be a certain distance, a certain width. And he just rolled over that desk and came up sitting down on the thing, pulling the drawer out, and lighting a cigar. All in one movement. [Clark] was great to be around, every day he was there. His timing was great. That movement and form. You think that he is going to fall when he sits down into the chair, or trip somewhere [*laughs*], but he'd come up lighting a cigar. They were great people.

MALTIN: Did you work on the Astaire-Rogers pictures?

BIROC: Oh, yeah. Nearly all of them. The only one I didn't work on was the first one. when they weren't stars.

MALTIN: *Flying Down to Rio*.

BIROC: *Flying Down to Rio*. All the ones after that I worked on, 'til I left there.

MALTIN: You always read about how insistent Astaire was on getting a full-figure photograph in those dances. Most of them seem to be done in very long takes, so you must have really been kept busy.

BIROC: Well, the secret to everything is to keep them in the picture and have good composition at all times, so I would learn. You would hear the music over and over again, but I got the lyrics, and tried to memorize them. And he hit a spot [on] that note every time, so it got to be easy. The same way with the guy that was moving the dolly.

The floors are made in shiny blocks, in four-foot pieces, so we knew if he was on a certain spot, we had to be on a certain spot back there to keep the full figure. And we had people that were pulling dollies that were pretty darn sharp at it, you know. So we always had the full figures.

Biroc is sitting behind
the camera on an
enormous crane for
this setup from Shall
We Dance (1937)
with Fred Astaire and
Ginger Rogers.

His hands had to be in it if they were up here and his feet had to be in
it at all times. You finally work out a way.

MALTIN: Was there a lot of rehearsal?

BIROC: Oh, yes. He was great in that. He had to do it; he had to rehearse, because he was a perfectionist. That was why his shows were so
great. Everything is perfect, everything perfect, down to the taps. Most
of the taps were done after the show anyhow. He would just watch the
screen, and tap dance to the screen.

MALTIN: But there must have been more camera rehearsal? Not only
his rehearsal, but camera rehearsal, too.

BIROC: Well, fortunately, we had seventeen, eighteen, twenty weeks
on all of them. It only cost $425,000 for the first one. I think $450 or
$475,000 for the second one. So we were making it for peanuts. And
they could take time on it. Astaire's dancing we knew, and I had known
[Hermes] Pan on shows before I had got to work with Astaire.

He [Astaire] would always rehearse on the rehearsal stage in front
of big mirrors, so he could see everything he was doing. Then we would
go in there every once in a while, when they had most of the routine
down, and you would see it, the music would be playing. Pretty soon
you got the music in the back of your head. You couldn't think of any-

thing else. And you would drift right in with it. You knew exactly what he was going to do, when he was going to jump up; you were prepared for it.

The dolly guy would say, "Now when he gets over here on the beat . . ." He probably didn't know as much as I did, and I didn't know anything. He would say, "On the eighth beat they are going to do this." I would say, "The hell with the eighth beat, touch me when you want it to happen." Or, "Touch me before it happens." So Pan would say, "Watch me when he gets over there and the camera is going to pull back." When the camera pulls back naturally you are going to have more room. So the camera would go back and we'd get him jumping up in the air. And Pan would tap the guys and okay now we are going to do the regular routine. Even today, I don't know one note from another. I know what I like.

MALTIN: It's incredible stuff. That studio made a lot of interesting pictures.

BIROC: Yeah, they had excellent people there. It showed up later on, because all of the people that they brought in eventually went to MGM. Pan Berman went over to MGM and he brought over most of the people, because he knew they were talented people.

MALTIN: What was Mark Sandrich like?

BIROC: Mark was a wonderful man. Great guy. Great sense of humor. He's another guy that had a lot of confidence in me. It was a shame that he passed away so young. And his boy [Jay Sandrich] is very good. I made one or two *Richard Diamond* TV shows with him years ago. He was very good.

MALTIN: One of the best comedy directors in the business.

BIROC: That's the trouble. Most guys that direct comedies think they can direct drama. I worked with William Seiter years ago in the early days of sound. He was great at comedy, and he wanted to do a dramatic picture in the worst way. So he did this dramatic picture *Allegheny Uprising*. It had John Wayne in it. A lot of good guys in it. George Sanders. Brian Donlevy. But the picture laid an egg. Seiter didn't have it. But when he went back to comedies again, he was great.

MALTIN: When you went into the service, what branch were you in?

BIROC: I was an operator in the Signal Corps, doing the same thing.

MALTIN: Camera work?

BIROC: Exactly the same. Just took off my civilian clothes and put on the army clothes; took off the army clothes and was a civilian. Did exactly the same thing.

MALTIN: Were you at Fort Roach?

BIROC: Oh, hell no. I was in Europe. I was three years in Europe . . .

almost four years I was in. And I was assigned to Supreme Headquarters, so I was active nearly all the time. They knew we were from Hollywood. They had people in the higher-up echelon that knew our qualifications, and knew what we could do, and if anything really important came up they always came back to us. So I was pretty active. I went all over Europe. Many special assignments. Half the time I didn't know what the hell we were called.

MALTIN: Were you still an assistant?

BIROC: No, once I got into the service I was a full-fledged cameraman.

MALTIN: Shooting 16mm, or 35?

BIROC: Thirty-five sound.

MALTIN: Wow. In color?

BIROC: Oh, they didn't use color too much in those days. But the sound system was, well . . . they wanted as much of that as they could get. And the interviews we had, like Eisenhower, hell, five or six times we photographed Eisenhower with sound. The main thing that they felt the public would like to see him, hear him. And the WACs. There was a big thing on trying to get the WACs in. Well, I photographed that, trying to enlist everyone in the WACs.

MALTIN: Who did you work with? Any other Hollywood people?

BIROC: Yeah. A fellow named Holly [Hollingsworth] Morse. He was a director for TV for many, many years. And George Stevens, the George Stevens unit. We had the recognition there of being professionals.

MALTIN: So when you came back . . .

BIROC: So when I came back I had a year, presumably a year of work that the studio was supposed to give us after the service. And I went on to another picture as an operator. When the picture finished they put me on *It's a Wonderful Life*. As an operator.

MALTIN: You had a contract?

BIROC: No, no, I had no contract. Just working all the time with good people. RKO kept you on salary. All the studios were the same. If you were efficient and knew your business they just kept you going and hoped eventually to push you up a little bit higher.

MALTIN: I didn't know you had worked with Orson Welles in South America on *It's All True*.

BIROC: We went down on a special plane; it took five days to go from Miami to Rio. Five days. On a flying boat. We got our equipment ready in about a week. He got us together before the carnival and he says, "We're going to be working four days and four nights, twenty-four hours a day. When you get tired, go back to the hotel and sleep, then go out and photograph." We had brought down three Technicolor cameras, two or three big black-and-white cameras, and two 16 mm Eastman

Kodak cameras. So what happened was the other operator and myself went out as different units; we worked different parts of the town. A lot of times we would [wind up in] the same nightclub. The other cameramen would photograph me dancing with some of the girls, and I can't dance. I never could dance. Then I would get some footage of another cameraman doing the same thing at some other place that he was photographing. Welles would see some of the stuff and he'd say, "What the hell are you doing? You are not supposed to be in there." Then he'd laugh like hell. He got us altogether the next day, he said, "Okay fellows, take a week off. I'll need you back one week from today. "

We got back and he said, "Now that we photographed the carnival, what the hell are we going to do with it?" Everybody started getting ideas. Now we are back on salary, back on working on a picture. The idea came up, "Let's pick up some kid from the top of the hills, bring the kid all the way down to all these little places down here, and bring him into the main carnival." So that is what we did for the next six months. We were shooting the carnival in June, and the carnival was over in February! The people down there were getting sick and tired of us. [Laughs] We opened up all of the stages down there, and shot all the stages.

MALTIN: Was there a formal script?

BIROC: Everything was just off the cuff.

MALTIN: What were your impressions of Welles?

BIROC: Welles was a wonderful guy. He'd know exactly what he was trying to get. I always wanted to make a picture with him when we came back from down there. He was a wild son of a gun. He got into trouble down there. An apartment that he had, he started throwing furniture out the window, six-story windows. [Laughs] But he was great to work with. Talented man. He knew everything, explained everything to you, why he wanted to do something that was "wrong," and you're not supposed to do it. It's a "no-no." He said, "Now, you do it this way. Don't worry about anybody; I'm telling you to do it." When you'd see it on the screen, you would say Jesus Christ . . . From different persons you find out different things.

MALTIN: Did you know from week to week whether you were going to still be there?

BIROC: Oh, sure. Then when we knew we were getting to the end of the line and there wasn't that much more to do, they started shipping us back. I was the last one, because I had to ship all of the camera equipment back.

MALTIN: Were you privy to any of the problems that were going on with the studio and Welles at that time? They didn't understand what he was doing . . .

BIROC: How the hell could you? We had a script girl there. It was hard to tell what she was getting. Everybody knew their jobs, the studio picked them, and they knew he picked a crew that he was going to get along with. But the studio got pissed off with us, for not sending enough film back, and they wouldn't send us film. One time for two weeks they wouldn't send us film. Another time for three weeks. They didn't know the problems we had down there.

MALTIN: Was Welles good at keeping spirits up?

BIROC: Oh, yeah. He was a great man to work for, a great man to be with. He was the type of guy that knew talent. If you didn't have talent, he got rid of you right away. [Well, he] didn't get rid of you; he never fired anybody. Stanley Cortez was on *The Magnificent Ambersons* and Welles didn't like the way he was being photographed. Harry Wild came in, and took over the picture. He wouldn't fire Cortez; he just put him on something else, kept him the hell out of the way. Cortez was the type of guy that liked to take over; he wanted to be the big wheel. There was only one big wheel, and that was Welles. Harry Wild was just the opposite. He was a cameraman trying to get along; he could make a picture with anybody. He got along fine and everybody liked him.

MALTIN: Were you around when the drowning accident occurred? [Four poor fishermen, known as *djanga-deiros*, received international attention after they sailed a homemade raft some 1,600 miles in order to present their grievances to the president of Brazil. Welles asked them to recreate their story for *It's All True* and somehow, the unthinkable happened as they approached Rio de Janeiro.]

BIROC: I think I was the one who photographed it. I kept telling the Brazilians, "Why the hell are they so close to shore? Get them out a ways." What happened was that there was a log raft with a sail on it, they got into the waves close to shore, and it tipped over. And they were national heroes. For a week we stayed at the hotel and never left.

MALTIN: Because the resentment was so great?

BIROC: I mean they were national heroes; we helped to get them killed. They killed themselves. We told them what we wanted. We didn't tell them how to go about it because they knew. If this log raft had been out another fifty or one hundred feet it never would have happened. They were starting to get into the breakers, and you could see it happening.

MALTIN: I read an interview where Welles said that he thinks in a way his career never recovered from the bad publicity that came out of that.

BIROC: It wasn't his fault. The studio sent us down there on a goodwill tour. The carnival was so great, they said, "Make up a story." We never did get to the other countries. It was a goodwill tour. And it ruined a man's career.

MALTIN: You also worked with Katharine Hepburn . . .

BIROC: Hepburn was great. She thought I was great. She always called me Biroc. "Hey, Biroc."

MALTIN: From the start?

BIROC: Yeah. She was a wonderful gal. Wonderful person. And still is. She came in one day with a nice bonnet on the back of her head. And she had this nice thing on her back with a big gown on. She looked great. She did. Every time that she would look at me, she would say, "Well, Biroc, what the hell is wrong now?" So I would go to her and say, "Well, it's a nice outfit. It's a beautiful outfit. The hat is just sensational. But the only time that we are going to see the hat is when we shoot over your shoulder." That was it. She left. Next time she came back it was on the front of her head. She would listen; you could talk to her. But I was that way all the time, [an] eager beaver. If they want my help, fine. If they don't, I could care less. I get paid every Thursday, one way or another.

ART CORNER

The 1930s proved to be a golden age for movie caricatures. Even though newspapers and magazines had the ability to reproduce photographs, they often favored illustrations, as seen through the work of Joe Grant and others.

These comic renderings of Stuart Erwin and Jack Oakie by Sam Berman were presented in Paramount pressbooks which encouraged local theater owners to plant them in their local newspapers. The accompanying copy exhorted exhibitors to "Illustrate that story . . . with touches of art which will appear authentically newspaperish."

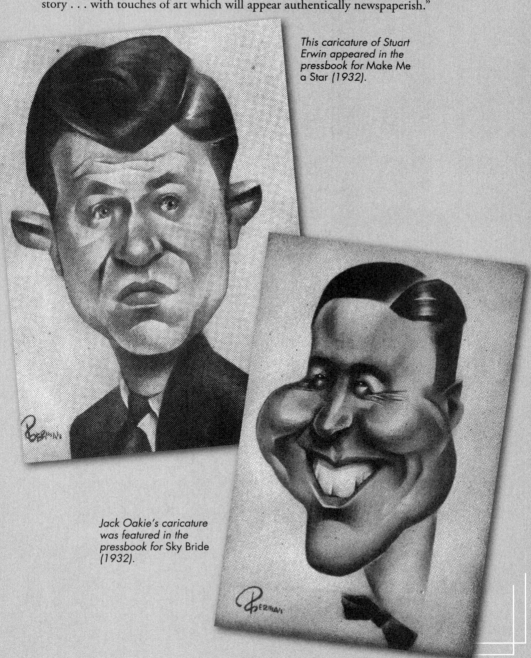

This caricature of Stuart Erwin appeared in the pressbook for Make Me a Star (1932).

Jack Oakie's caricature was featured in the pressbook for Sky Bride (1932).

Beginnings:
BLAKE EDWARDS

Blake Edwards's long and successful career as a movie director, writer, and producer tends to obscure the fact that he established his reputation in radio. I had the pleasure of speaking with him about the early days of his career, and the man who gave him his first big break, Dick Powell.

MALTIN: I've never had a chance, nor has anyone else, for that matter, to talk to you about the fact that you developed your writing chops in radio.

EDWARDS: This is true.

MALTIN: How did it come about?

EDWARDS: Well . . . [*Laughs*] Nothing terribly complicated. I had written a couple of low-budget westerns for films, and I was living with a young lady at that time who was an aspiring actress and happened to do a radio show. I'm trying to think of the name of it . . . *Hollywood Star Theatre*. And she came home and asked me what I thought of it and I told her I thought it was pretty bad. She got rather unhappy with me and said, "Well, you think you could do better?" I said, "Yeah, I think so." So she said, "Well, why don't you?" So I sat down and I wrote a piece using her radio script as a template. And she took it to the producer of the show, a man named Nat Wolf, who was also a fairly well-known Hollywood agent. He liked it a lot and gave it to Jack Webb, who was just breaking into some sort of stardom, and they did it. A short time after that, Nat took me to meet a man named Don Sharp, who was a radio producer and represented Dick Powell. I met Dick Powell and he told me kind of what he was looking for [in a show], and I said, "Well, you know, that's interesting because I've got something that's very similar to that." He said, "Let me read it," and I said, "Well,

I live at the beach, I can't get it for you now, but I'll bring it in first thing in the morning." And I went home and wrote it. And brought it in and that was the beginning of *Richard Diamond.*

MALTIN: Did he go for it immediately?

EDWARDS: Yeah.

MALTIN: So from a standing start you created a radio show with a big-time actor.

EDWARDS: That's right.

MALTIN: Not bad.

EDWARDS: No. [*Laughs*]

MALTIN: Did you have all the supporting characters figured out from the start?

EDWARDS: Yeah. Didn't take any shaking down at all. We just started and I started writing.

MALTIN: Were you the sole writer on the show at first?

EDWARDS: At first, yeah.

MALTIN: What distinguishes radio writing from, say, screenwriting?

EDWARDS: I don't know how you answer it, really, because writing is writing; you write character and you envision situations. And they either become totally verbal or they have another dimension to them. There's not that much difference writing [in either medium]—for me, anyway—it was certainly short form. You know, it was only twenty-three minutes or something like that of actual play. The rest was commercial.

MALTIN: Did you want to just soak up everything; did you go to rehearsals?

EDWARDS: Oh, yeah, I loved it. I was a big shot, all of a sudden. I just learned if anybody asked you, you've got something good. You say, "Yeah, I'll go home and fish it out," and you write that night. [*Laughs*] There were no great revelations, I just had a very good time. I was young and not particularly aspiring, I was just having a damn good time.

MALTIN: Do you remember what you were paid?

EDWARDS: Something like $750 a show. And, you know, it was quite a clique; there were just a handful of actors that everybody used. So, it was a family. It was the best sort of time for me because we all knew each other and we all had fun and it was secure-making.

MALTIN: Are there any radio actors whom you remember with a special fondness?

EDWARDS: Virginia Gregg . . .

MALTIN: Who could do anything, right?

EDWARDS: Yeah, she could do anything. Stacy Harris. Charlie Mc-Graw. Bill Conrad. See, usually about now in my life, my memory fails; it doesn't with radio. Sidney Miller. I could go on and on. [Ed] Begley was one of my close friends. Had a good time with him, kidded around a lot with him.

MALTIN: Tell me about Dick Powell. Obviously, he took a liking to you.

EDWARDS: Well, we took a liking to each other, as a matter of fact. He was a really sweet man. A terrible tightwad, at least where I was concerned. I didn't care so much [but] later on, when he put the television show on and did it without even checking with me, I went to him and I said, "Listen, Dick, this is [my show] . . . I originated it" and he gave me some sort of pittance with each show. But, other than that, we liked each other a lot, and had a good time.

MALTIN: He mentored quite a number of people; did you look upon him that way?

EDWARDS: I didn't then, so much. But I do now. He was quite a talented director in his own right.

Dick Powell and his
Richard Diamond
costar Virginia Gregg.

MALTIN: There must have been kind of a freewheeling atmosphere at that show, because I remember one episode where he was checking the directory of an apartment house and one of the tenants was Lillian McEdwards [the name of Edwards's mother].

EDWARDS: Yeah . . . [*Laughs*] I don't remember that, but I'm sure that's true.

MALTIN: And you got in a plug for his current movie, Mrs. *Mike*.

EDWARDS: Oh, sure, we did that all the time. And in those days, too, all you had to do was get a few products in there and you got some; he usually ended up with the product.

MALTIN: I know you also worked on *The Line-Up* on radio; are there any others I don't know about?

EDWARDS: Well, there was *Yours Truly, Johnny Dollar*. I was one of the important writers on that show. And *The Line-Up*. Those were the ones that I [wrote], and I was doing those three a week.

MALTIN: I know part of the answer is that network radio was on the wane at this time but was there a specific reason you didn't continue in radio?

EDWARDS: Only because I got a better job. You know, somebody called me up and said, "You want to write a movie?" And that was that.

MALTIN: I know you appeared in a number of films in the 1940s. Was that a part of an aspiring acting career, or was it just killing time . . . ?

EDWARDS: Well, I don't know whether you'd call it aspiring; I would have been delighted to have had a red-hot career as an actor, but it wasn't to be. At least, in the time that I gave it, it wasn't to be. And I was too anxious to be successful. So, if it wasn't gonna be there, it was gonna be somewhere else, and as it turned out, it was writing.

MALTIN: What made you sit down and try to write a western?

EDWARDS: Oh, I don't know, I guess I've always been a fan of westerns. And I went to see one one night, criticized it, and said, you know, "We can do better than that," [this other guy] and I did.

MALTIN: You're in *Panhandle*, which you also wrote.

EDWARDS: Oh, yeah.

MALTIN: Do you remember any of the details of how that all came together?

EDWARDS: Well, sure. It was a young guy that I went to high school with that was down for the summer from Stanford, John Champion, and we went to see a western. I think it was a Gary Cooper western and we played miniature golf afterward and talked about it, and I said, "Hey, let's write a screenplay." And that was that.

MALTIN: How did you sell it?

EDWARDS: Well, I hoodwinked him. I knew he'd been left some money. And I said, "Well, you know, if you don't want to put the money up, I'll go get somebody who will," and I kind of intimidated him into it. So, he backed it, got his money out of it, made a little, and we did another one, which wasn't as much fun.

MALTIN: Why?

EDWARDS: Well, because he actually began to become a Hollywood producer, overnight, sort of, and maybe I did, too. I don't know. But I got very resentful and said, "That's it; you go your way, I'll go mine."

MALTIN: When you started writing screenplays for those musicals at Columbia, how early on were you thinking, "I really want to be directing these?"

EDWARDS: Oh . . . my career wasn't like that, at least I don't recall it being like that. I just had a good time at the moment. I'm sure my aspiration was unnoticed by me at that point. You know, when the breaks came, I acknowledged them and made a move.

MALTIN: But you were happy getting paid, doing what you were doing. That's a nice way to live your life.

EDWARDS: Well, there were times when I didn't live it that way and I regret that I didn't. You know, when it became too important. Always when I had a really good time and it wasn't a matter of life and death, that's when I had a good time.

MALTIN: Just to wrap up what we were discussing, I haven't met anybody who worked in the heyday of radio who doesn't have warm feelings toward it. Can you explain why that is?

EDWARDS: Other than this family aspect, getting to know the people as intimately as you did, it was a little like working in a submarine. You'd better get along . . . and we did. It was too good a life. I mean, look at the hours, look at the pay. It was the best of all possible worlds at that time. Better than anything I know now.

STILL LIFE

When author Peter Benchley died in 2006, the fact that he was the grandson of humorist Robert Benchley rated barely a mention in most of the obituaries. How sad that the media world should have so little awareness of a man who was one of America's greatest wits and essayists, as well as a bona fide movie personality and actor. Robert Benchley's first short for MGM, *How to Sleep*, won an Academy Award in 1935; seen left is Benchley as Mr. Average Man, delaying a good night's rest by sampling leftovers in the refrigerator. Below, he poses with director Roy Rowland in a promotional still for one of the popular one-reelers that followed *How to Sleep* and endeared him to a generation of moviegoers who may never have read his work in print. Yet his influence is still felt. After reading Jon Stewart's hilarious book of comedic essays, *Naked Pictures of Famous People*, I got to ask *The Daily Show* host who served as his inspiration. He named several people—and one of them was Benchley.

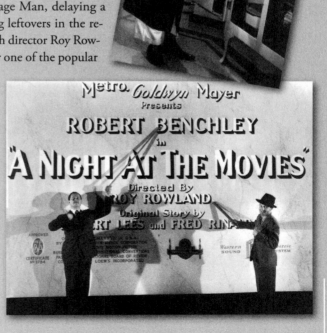

Conversations:
RICHARD KLINE, ASC

A conventional interview with Richard H. Kline, ASC, would cover his long and interesting career as a cinematographer, with such films as *Camelot; Hang 'em High; The Boston Strangler; The Andromeda Strain*; the 1976 version of *King Kong; Star Trek: The Motion Picture; Body Heat; All of Me*; and even *Howard the Duck* to his credit. One could even spend a fair amount of time discussing his family: his father was Benjamin H. Kline, who photographed countless B movies and short-subjects, and his uncles were cameraman-turned-director Phil Rosen and cameraman Sol Halperin. His brother Hank Kline was a busy and respected production manager for many years before taking a well-earned retirement.

But Richard had another, almost entirely undocumented career before he ever received his first screen credit as a director of photography. I only learned of this when I attended this year's ASC Awards, where he received a lifetime career honor from his peers at the American Society of Cinematographers. When I had the chance to meet and congratulate Richard, I asked him when he got his first job in the movie business. His response was my cue to ask if we could sit down for a formal interview. He was very generous with his time and even dug out some wonderful photos.

But it was only during the course of our conversation that I learned just how vast and varied his experiences were in the 1940s and fifties. I can't think of anyone else who can say that he worked with Orson Welles, Karl Freund, and The Three Stooges . . . not to mention the king of B movie producers, Sam Katzman.

Kline lines up a shot for director Carl Reiner on the set of All of Me (1984).

MALTIN: When you were born, was your father already in the business?

KLINE: My father got in the business, I believe, just after World War I, about 1921.

MALTIN: And how did he break in?

KLINE: His sister was married to the first President of the ASC, Phil Rosen. That might have been how he got in. When I was young I really wasn't prepared to ask, "How did you start, Daddy?"

MALTIN: Did you have a sense of movies growing up or was it just what your dad did for a living?

KLINE: Six days a week, Saturdays 'til midnight. It was tough work, a lot of hard work, and you didn't have the union protection. Meals weren't served every six hours and that type of thing. He was a very good father but I didn't see a lot of him. He worked those hours, and Sunday, he'd listen to the radio. How shall I put it? He didn't have time to be a great father.

I graduated from University High School in West L.A. when I was sixteen and a half. The war was on and I knew that I'd have to go in the service, [but] I had a year and a half to do something, and my Dad said, "Look, I can get you a job at Columbia as an assistant cameraman because everybody's away." Sure enough he did and that's where I started.

MALTIN: Timing in life is everything, isn't it? You had that year-and-a-half window before you turned eighteen, and at the same time, all the other men were away in the service.

KLINE: The openings were there and they needed to be filled.

MALTIN: Do you remember your first day on the job?

KLINE: Oh, unequivocally. The picture was *Cover Girl* and I came on as the new slate boy. We were shooting on Stage Eight and it was next to Columbia's camera department, so in between takes I'd go into the camera department and they taught me. We talked and I learned about the camera within a few months. *Cover Girl* was coming to an end and I was still the lily boy.

MALTIN: The lily boy? I never heard that.

KLINE: I'll tell you why. In those days, Technicolor controlled the set. After a take—"cut, print!"—they would go for what they called a lily. I would have to hold a chart, a tri-fold that was white on top and below it was the color spectrum. You'd do that after every print, or if there was a hold on a take you'd do it after; if you had to reload, you would do it after the reload. That was Technicolor's way of developing and printing, They would have that as an evaluation.

MALTIN: A reference . . .

KLINE: A reference, right. So I would do the slate for the scene, call out the number and marker. Then after, if it was a print, they would go for the lily and I would hold the lily. They were very strict about it; everybody had to hold still on the set when they opened the three-strip camera. Burney [Burnett] Guffey was the operator and Rudy Maté was the cameraman. I really started with great people. Stanley Donen was the choreographer with Gene Kelly. And, of course, [there was] Rita Hayworth and Phil Silvers and all the cover girls. Where I was it was really Hollywood at its best.

MALTIN: There must have been a lot of light on those sets in those days.

KLINE: Six hundred-foot candles—and they didn't have air conditioning like we have now, so it was very hot. All the arcs had to be maintained by a person, and it was all done from the scaffolding up above. It took a long time. Whenever I see *Gone with the Wind*, I say, "My God, how did they do it?" We didn't have nearly the sophisticated equipment that we have now.

MALTIN: Did you ask questions? Did you talk to Rudy Maté and Burnett Guffey?

KLINE: Oh yeah, it was a very friendly atmosphere; they were good people. [But] they were not teachers. Nobody gave away their secret, they just did it, so I would study them. I would find out what they were doing and I picked up what they were doing.

MALTIN: Do you remember how long you were on *Cover Girl*?

KLINE: Well, it had been in process before I started, I was on for about four months.

MALTIN: Would you have had occasion in your job to ever see dailies?

KLINE: I was not privileged or allowed to go into the daily room, but I'd go to the booth. A lovely man was the head projectionist and he welcomed me there and I'd look through the porthole 'cause I knew that was the best way to learn what was going on. I would hear what they would say: "It's too this, too that," [or] "Oh, that's good." And I learned from hearing different opinions of what they were saying. I remember one cameraman I worked with [as an] assistant and he knew when a bad shot was coming up. He would time it just right: he'd light a cigarette so that the match would warn everybody for a minute.

MALTIN: To distract the producer. That's a good one. After *Cover Girl*, how would you get your day-to-day assignments? Would you just show up in the morning not knowing what you were going to do?

KLINE: Oh no, in the camera department there was a call sheet that listed every production—the cameraman, the operator and assistants, the extra cameras and everything. I was carried because they wouldn't want to let me go at that time.

MALTIN: So you could be working on the biggest movie on the lot one day and the cheapest movie the next day.

Eighteen-year-old Richard Kline gets a send-off to the Navy on the set of Rough, Tough, and Ready *(1945) from the crew, director Del Lord (in hat), and star Victor McLaglen.*

KLINE: Yeah. They would carry you. The studio was very loyal, and that's why [I spent] roughly eighteen years there.

MALTIN: Do you remember what they were paying you?

KLINE: Sixty-four dollars a week, for six days.

MALTIN: Were you happy to get it?

KLINE: Oh, that was good money—are you kidding? When I went in the Navy and came out, they had had a raise and [it] was retroactive and I got a pretty good chunk of money, like $1,200 or something. I remember it went to $118 dollars after the war. That was a big, big, jump.

MALTIN: So you worked on a little of everything, then.

KLINE: The best and the cheapest. The Three Stooges comedies, and all those things.

MALTIN: By the time you were shooting those I don't think Del Lord was directing them any more, and he's my favorite.

KLINE: Oh, I worked with him a lot. In fact, the last picture I worked on before going in the service was with Del Lord. [*Rough, Tough, and Ready*, 1945] It was with Chester Morris and Victor McLaglen. In fact, my last day at work they gave me a [going-away present]. I even have a picture of myself [with] the crew. He was a wonderful man, Del Lord, just a very decent person. I really didn't know his background other than he just knew what he was doing and did it well. He was the antithesis of

Jules White. Jules White was excitable and [a] colorful guy. We always looked at him as the scene [would be] going on. We'd look at him, and he's going through all the facial expressions and everything. We didn't have the electric megaphones; we had just the Rudy Vallee type, and he'd be talking, then he'd forget himself and he'd start shouting around it. He thought he was doing Shakespeare. He really was a great character.

MALTIN: Tell me about working with the Stooges.

KLINE: I didn't work with Babe [Curly]. I only worked with Shemp. Shemp, Moe, and Larry. I didn't know Babe, I met him, that's all. He had had a heart attack by the time I started. Moe was the leader of the group. And Shemp was just there, he was a replacement and a nice guy. They were nice guys, really lovely guys. Then we had great characters; there was Vernon Dent, he [was] from the old school, and Richard Lane. He was a sportscaster and he was a great storyteller. All day long—great accents—and we would roar. I mean it was really fun to work on that set. I worked with Andy Clyde, too, a few [times]. There was Joan Davis.

MALTIN: Let's talk about the B unit for a little while.

KLINE: The Briskin unit. The main thing was to meet the schedule, because they were bread-and-butter pictures. They were [made to] fill a bill. Sam Katzman told

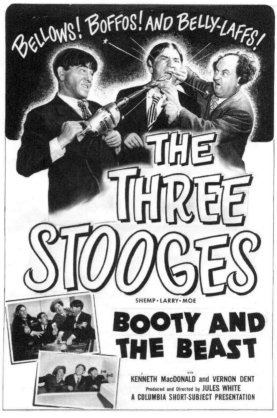

me, "I know I've never made a great film, but I never made one that went over budget." He was unbelievable. I remember once it was a Biblical film and somebody called the group to attention and said, "You know, there were twelve disciples but there's only ten in the script," and Sam said, "There might have been twelve in the Bible but there's only ten in my budget." I think if you [made] a picture [about] the making of one of those films, nobody would believe it.

MALTIN: Wasn't William Castle an assistant director there?

KLINE: No, Bill Castle came in as a dialogue director. Columbia brought five promising stage directors [to the studio] and made them dialogue directors just to see if they could do [it]. Henry Levin was one, Mel Ferrer, Bobby Gordon, and William Castle. They would sit on the set as the dialogue director and just observe; they all became directors.

MALTIN: Did you get to work on some of the Columbia westerns?

KLINE: Oh, tons of them, yeah.

MALTIN: Was the atmosphere different on a western?

KLINE: Maybe the only difference would be the wranglers. They were a breed of their own, they were terrific people. Unbelievable, [they'd] sit in the saddle all day long. We would start early, but they were very skilled—the crews, particularly the directors. I worked with different directors but on a lot of them the director was Ray Nazarro. Ray used to be an assistant director so he knew production well. He was the brother of a guy, very famous in his day, named Cliff Nazarro, a double-talk guy. And Ray's only direction was, "Nice and bright!" Nothing else. One day we were doing a funeral scene. He said, "Okay, nice and bright," and they all looked at him. And he said, "Oh, just do it anyway." He was a good guy, very sure, but the crews were very skilled. We didn't have lights in those days, we used reflectors only. Actors had to know their lines, and they never went for full retakes. In other words, if somebody blew a line on a take, "Okay, cut, pick it up." It was never, "'Let's start from scratch," like today. And they knew where to pick it up, they knew what to do. They were really very clever, and those B directors, most of them had a nickname. It was Roll 'em Sholem, a guy named Lee Sholem. There was Hurry Up Lou, that was Lou King. He was always, "Hurry up, hurry up." Then there was Choo Choo Landers. Nobody did more films than Lew Landers. He got the name Choo Choo because his wife divorced him, claimed that he would fall asleep over his little choo-choo track. Then there was Wagon Wheel. What's his name again?

MALTIN: Joseph H. Lewis?

KLINE: Right, Joseph Lewis—yeah, that's it. They called him Wagon Wheel 'cause every western he did, he'd shoot through a wagon wheel. They were great people, though. I loved them.

MALTIN: From your vantage point, did each one have a style or approach, or were they just getting the job done?

KLINE: Just shoot the schedule. Between sixty, a hundred setups a day. They had what was called Panic Peak at each of the ranches, [an] area that was higher than anything else, or the sun would remain there, so we would always "save it for Panic Peak," because we'd shoot until dark. They really knew what they were doing. Small crews, not a big crew.

MALTIN: Who were some of the cameramen you worked with in those days?

KLINE: George Meehan, he was like a father to me. [Charles] Bud Lawton, Jimmy Howe, Burney Guffey, of course, Henry Freulich, he did a lot of those B pictures. Bill Whitley did a lot of the Katzman pictures also. Then Kit Carson—his name was Fred Carson, they called him Kit. Bert Anderson was another one. They were not big time, other than Jimmy Howe. I'd go from a big picture to just filling in. It was great experience 'cause I could get the best, from being a sprinter to a distance runner.

MALTIN: Did you ever work in any of the serials?

KLINE: Yeah, a few. I did one of the Red Ryders. I did about four of them and one we did in Catalina [*Pirates of the High Seas*, 1950], I remember that one. They were fun to work on. They had two directors [and] they would alternate days. Tommy Carr and Spence Bennet, yeah. You shoot out of continuity, and the script girls were unbelievable; they kept everything straight. That was skill. It took about thirty days for each one. They were fun to work on and I enjoyed [it]. Hard work but I loved it.

MALTIN: Now let's talk about my hero, Sam Katzman.

KLINE: He was just a likable guy. He was a character; he had a stomach on him and he smoked the big cigar, but not a pompous guy at all. He came from New York and he started at Monogram before he came to Columbia. He was very nice to me. I liked him a lot.

MALTIN: Would you say that with him, what you saw was what you got? From what I've heard, he wasn't two-faced.

KLINE: No, not at all. Dead honest. We shot six days a week then and he'd say, "Okay guys." [There would be a] football game at the Coliseum; he said, "Finish by noon and there's a bus out there and I got seats on the such-and-such yard line for all of you." And sure enough,

Kline says shooting this Katzman production in 3-D was "no big deal" because "we didn't take it seriously."

boom, we would go to the game. He really was for the crew; the crew came first. The actors were of secondary consideration. He would get an actor on the way up or on the way down, and get them for practically nothing. I remember one of the final things I worked with him was *The Magic Carpet*. At that time Lucille Ball was having a problem with Harry Cohn and she had one picture to do on the contract and she didn't want to do it and Harry Cohn said, "Okay, I'm going to put you in Sam Katzman's pictures." She said, "I'd be delighted, he's your best producer."

I was going to mention one other thing, about how clever he was. We were up in Columbia, California shooting, and we had two prop-driven planes that were going to take us back after the day's filming. Something happened to the taillights of one of the planes and they wouldn't let us take off. We were going into all the meal penalties and Sam went up to the control tower and checked with people and he found that you could take off with one running light; you didn't need two. So, he took one from the good plane and put it into the other plane and we took off. Now, that's clever.

MALTIN: That's a producer. Solving problems.

KLINE: That's a producer. Right. That is a producer that stands by you and you appreciate him. I loved working for him. A lot of film went through the camera. I learned a lot of my skills from doing those films. There was no fooling around. The directors did not know the word "organic"—it was a business with them. Not that they didn't have talent, they did. Once Lew Landers was moaning, "Dammit," he said, "I get six, seven, ten days on a picture and they get thirty." They asked him, "What would you do if you had thirty days?" And he said, "Well, I'd probably shoot it twice."

MALTIN: Great answer.

KLINE: And Katzman had a writer named Robert E. Kent; as fast as he could type, that's the script. They were without any frills. I'd walk by the offices and say, "Hi," and he'd say, "Oh, hi Richard," and he'd keep typing. "How's everything going? Did you see the game last night?" He was unbelievable. I mean, he really was a skilled writer. Sam would come to him in the morning and [hand him] a headline [and say], "Let's get a script out [by six o'clock]." And they would do it; they'd knock it out in no time at all.

MALTIN: Talk to me about the relationship of the people on a set in the studio days at Columbia. Did the assistant director run the set?

KLINE: They ran the set, with the exception of the Katzman unit. Katzman had his own production manager, Jack Fier. He was the production manager on everything and the best, without a doubt. Unbelievable. And so, the assistant director would report to him. And anything went wrong, Jack would come right on the set and boy, he'd straighten it out [snaps fingers]. Jack was an old-time producer, I worked with him when he was a producer doing the westerns, and he knew filmmaking. He really was good. Gruff, but had a good heart.

MALTIN: Wasn't that an Orson Welles wisecrack? "The only thing we have to fear is Fier itself . . ."

KLINE: I worked on that one, yeah.

MALTIN: You worked on *The Lady from Shanghai*?

KLINE: Oh, yeah. When I came out of the Navy, in August of '46. *Lady from Shanghai* had started filming and I was waiting to start UCLA. I was going to become a lawyer. Columbia called me to say, "Look, we have a problem down in Acapulco. The assistant cameraman died and we need to replace him right away. We'd like you back at Columbia." They told me about Acapulco and I said, "I'll be there." I left the next day. I remember I left on September 30th, 1946, 'cause it was my sister's birthday. Anyway, I went down there and the movie shot down there for months. The best part was Errol Flynn. We were using his yacht; it was called the *Zaca*. He wasn't working, so he was the skipper and oh, what a man's man, a woman's man. He was the ultimate that I ever met in that category. Nobody was like him. He had so many women coming over the side of the boat to meet him and all that. They called the *Zaca* the *Cockzaca*.

Rita Hayworth in a dramatic moment from Orson Welles's The Lady from Shanghai *(1947).*

MALTIN: Who was the cinematographer on that?

KLINE: Bud Lawton. They had Sam Nelson [as assistant director] and Sam was one of the best, without a doubt. Always the last word with cleverness. [Once] we were shooting down in Acapulco and Orson got mad at Sam. He said, "Goddammit, Sam! A good assistant director is hated by the crew." And Sam said, "Okay guys, you heard the man. No Christmas presents for me." And Orson had to appreciate that, too.

MALTIN: Was the *Zaca* moored when you were shooting, or were you out at sea?

KLINE: Out a lot, yeah. Certain cuts we could shoot while it was close to the harbor. We were out quite a bit, but we had other parts of the island and land areas.

MALTIN: I assume with Mr. Welles and Mr. Flynn there, you ate and drank well?

KLINE: Oh, it was high living. Acapulco was just being built up then in 1946. And the main hotel was called The Reforma. Maybe it's still there, I don't know, and the eating area wasn't even finished; they were still working on it, so it was very primitive compared to what it is now. Which made it more interesting, because I've been a surfer all my life and surfing down there . . . It was the best.

This was really a honeymoon present to Orson and to Rita. But Harry Cohn didn't realize that [Orson] was going to cut her hair, 'cause she had that gorgeous, flowing, reddish-auburn hair. Orson cut it and made her a blonde without consulting Cohn and that started the nudging. Cohn would send Fier down to make certain. There was no script that I could see; I never read a script. It was all just thought of at the last minute or the night before, whatever. Orson had a midget; his name was Shorty. Shorty had a deep voice and he always wore a tuxedo and drove the limo. I mean, what a pair: here's Shorty and there's Orson's six feet.

MALTIN: Did you sense that Welles had a plan, or did he seem to be improvising?

KLINE: Well, he never stuttered, put it that way. He seemed to know what he was doing. Maybe it was pulled out of the air but he covered it well. I know that he was a man of great instincts. We went to San Francisco and shot for a month after Acapulco and then shot on the stage for about six weeks. One day on the stage, there was a film shooting next door—*To the Ends of the Earth*—and they had an FBI agent as a technical advisor. I got to know him because I'd walk over; we could go to different sets in those days, and we knew everybody, and between shots I might go over there. He came over on the set one day and I was talking to him. Orson spotted him and afterward he said, "Who was that man?" I told him, and he said, "Can you get him back over here?" I said, yeah, and Orson offered him a job. It was John Dierkes.

MALTIN: Orson just liked his look?

KLINE: Loved his look. And he hired him to do Macbeth. Just like that. He said, "I like that face." That's Orson. I mean, really . . . there was just nobody like him.

MALTIN: Did you ever think about returning to UCLA?

KLINE: Never, no. Let me tell you what happened. [After finishing *The Lady from Shanghai*] I had a low seniority and I couldn't work. So I took advantage of the G.I. Bill and I went to college. After three years of college, I got married. I went to the Sorbonne. I went to France and I got married over there.

MALTIN: How did that happen?

KLINE: Well, I could go anyplace. When I went to the Veterans Administration, they said, "Where do you want to go?" And I asked, "Where can I go now?" They said, "Any place in the world. You want to go to Paris?" I said, "Really?" They just kept opening door after door. I had six hours a day of French tutoring alone, for six weeks. I divorced myself of any English-speaking people; I moved in with a family and did nothing but concentrate on French, enough to get me started in at the Sorbonne for three years. Then I got married over there and by that

time, Taft-Hartley came in and I was able to go back to work [in Hollywood]. Again, the timing was just perfect. So no, I never thought of ever going into law at all.

MALTIN: What did you study at the Sorbonne?

KLINE: It was art history and fine arts.

MALTIN: Then you came back here in early '51, and TV was in its infancy . . .

KLINE: Nobody thought it would ever be anything in those days. How blind they really were. So I was able to work on the *I Love Lucy* shows, maybe ten of the *Lucy*s . . .

MALTIN: For Karl Freund?

KLINE: Yeah, Pappy Freund. He was very casual. A lovely relationship. They were the first of the three-camera shows. It was for a company called Al Simon Productions. And Al Simon did *Burns and Allen* [so] I worked on quite a few of those. Also *The Joan Davis Show* with Joan and Jim Backus. I also did just the pilot of *Our Miss Brooks*. But it was flat lighting. It was almost like they light today for the comedies. Just not very inspiring. But [Pappy] was good at it, he knew what he did and it was a tapering off of his career.

MALTIN: Apparently Desi Arnaz was very excited to get him.

KLINE: They loved each other; everybody loved each other. Desi was a bit frisky. There were times when he would pout, but not with us.

He was always good to us. They were fun to work on. Lovely people.

MALTIN: Even now people recognize what a revolution that was to shoot with multiple cameras.

KLINE: We all had our earphones on. A guy named Cam Rogers was the microphone guy [who] would talk to the director. Everything was wired and much more cumbersome than one would imagine. We had a day of rehearsals; they would block it, get a day of that, then we'd shoot the next day. We knew what we were going to do but they would keep reminding us. It was good experience. I really enjoyed that.

MALTIN: What was the next step for you?

KLINE: I was able to go right back to Columbia, where they hired me again, and within six or seven months I became a camera operator. That's when I went to work with Katzman for a six-year period.

MALTIN: Were there cases where he'd use standing sets from A movies?

KLINE: Oh, all the time. I remember I was doing a picture, I think something with Frank Sinatra, and Sam came in on the set. There was a huge boat they built, and he said, "When are they gonna finish in here? I want to use that boat and I'm gonna write a story around it." He'd snoop all over the place. That's why I said he was the best producer.

MALTIN: He'd fashion a script around a set?

KLINE: Right. Or he'd write a script from a headline. That's a producer. Really. God, he was good.

MALTIN: William Castle was doing a lot of directing for him then—

KLINE: Not as much as a guy named Fred Sears. [He] was the other guy I was trying to think of that was from the stage and became a director. Fred F. Sears. Fred was a very qualified director, he knew what he was doing. Cut, print, okay, pick it up, boom. That type of thing.

MALTIN: Did you have much contact, if any, with Harry Cohn?

KLINE: Never. Saw him a few times. I'd see him at lunch. He would come in at noon, so when we'd go to lunch I'd maybe pass him. Never talked to him. The only time he ever really came on the set was on a picture called *Pal Joey*. I was the operator on that. Sinatra was there, and we were working the European hours. We'd come to work at about eleven and work right through until eight o'clock and we'd eat a floating meal or something like that. [Cohn] and Sinatra were good buddies. I saw him a couple of other times in all the years I was there.

MALTIN: But his presence was felt, I gather.

KLINE: You're right. I used to hear stories about him, that type of thing. But I never talked to him, never met him.

I went to his funeral. We all went to his funeral.

MALTIN: How did you get out of the Katzman unit and onto A-pictures like *Pal Joey*?

KLINE: I think his unit tapered down. Because we did a hundred and eight features, that I know for certain, in six years. Then it tapered down and that's why I was on to other things and I was requested to work with Burney Guffey and Bud Lawton and people like that. They wanted me.

I'll tell you, one of the best cameramen probably [was] for many reasons, Joe Walker. I didn't ever assist him but I was like a second assistant or an extra camera with him. I knew him well, and he was the best female lighting cameraman ever; he was unbelievable. He had even some of his own lenses, his own diffusion. He was an optical engineer of sorts.

MALTIN: What film did you get to work with him on?

KLINE: Oh, many films. He started *Born Yesterday*; Bud Lawton took over. I worked on a couple of Roz Russell pictures. Just in and out but I was around him a lot and I'd kind of sit and observe. Charlie Lang was another, great with women, great with everything. Probably the two best cameramen I was ever around.

MALTIN: Some people complained that Lang was slow. Because obviously, he was very methodical.

KLINE: Extremely. Never stopped lighting.

MALTIN: How did that work on a set? Obviously a director hiring him knew his reputation, knew that he was not going to be speedy. But would there come a time when a director would say, "Hey, we've got to shoot?" Or would they just leave him alone?

KLINE: First of all, he had the attention of the star, and they wanted to look good. The same with Joe Walker. Joe Walker was not slow at all. But I do think the star power said, "I want him, he's my cameraman." And they knew that he would protect them. That's very important.

MALTIN: Walker's earliest films for Frank Capra are simply exquisite.

KLINE: They're magnificent, they really are. I agree. Real artistry. Charlie had a different kind of artistry, but equally as important. And he knew the value of making women look good. That's why he had a following, Joan Crawford loved him. I never worked with Audrey Hepburn. I only knew her casually, but he did a lot of her films and he did Marlene Dietrich. Charlie Lang has probably one of the best resumés of any cameraman of that time. He's one of my favorites and a nice, lovely man. Really good guy. He was not as bald as I am, but he was pretty bald [and] he had scars all over his face from bumping into kukalorises and all of his cookies falling on him. He was loaded with scars.

MALTIN: Kukaloris?

KLINE: It would be a piece of two-ply wood material. It was kind of cut out, it had a little opening, and you put it in front of the light and it would

Richard's father Benjamin H. ("Benny") Kline.

break up the light so it wasn't so flat on the person. I use them all the time. They're not used that much anymore but I used them a lot.

MALTIN: Did you also work with the great John Alton?

KLINE: He was a great guy. I was an operator for him on the one with Burt Lancaster, *Elmer Gantry*. Then I did *Birdman of Alcatraz* afterward. John Alton started the picture and so did Charles Crichton, the English director, who was a terrific guy. After about two weeks, he and Burt couldn't get along together, so they brought in John Frankenheimer who had done one Lancaster–Hecht film prior, *Young Savages*. Anyway, they brought Frankenheimer in and [he] didn't like John Alton. So one day, about three weeks into the picture, one week with Frankenheimer, I walked by the camera department, [and] I saw the sheet that I told you about before. It had the productions, who was working and where, and it had John Alton's name crossed off and Burney Guffey's name put on there. I went back to the set and I asked, "What's going on?" Frankenheimer said, "Well, he's being replaced." We went to dailies that night and I was sitting next to John Alton and Burt was [sitting] in front of me; Frankenheimer was next to him. A closeup came on of Burt and Burt turned to John Alton and said, "John, that's the way I want it to look throughout the whole picture." And I knew Frankenheimer was fired. About two hours later, John called me. "Guess what, I'm fired." I didn't want to say it but I thought something was up. "Don't worry," he said, "I want you on my next picture. It's *The Music Man*." He called me about two weeks before *The Music Man* was to start prepping. "Guess what? I was fired again even before I started."

MALTIN: What did you notice on the set that made Alton's lighting distinctive or special?

KLINE: Well, the very first time I worked with him, it was on added scenes to a Kim Novak film Richard Quine directed. Two weeks of added scenes, I forget the name of it; that's where I first worked with him. John just sort of sat back in the chair and he said, "Go ahead, go light it." Really? And he watched me [as] I worked with a gaffer. After about three or four days, I went back and I said, "John, you know, I really appreciate the freedom you're giving me, I'm learning and I'm getting great experience here. I know you're watching what I'm doing and all that. Really, thank you." He said, "I'll tell you what," his exact words, "Have you ever seen a famous chef peeling potatoes in the kitchen?" I said, "What do you mean?" He said, "I'm that chef. I don't peel potatoes. After everything is done, I come out and I put a little salt and pepper and season it a little bit." And he would do that. After I'd light it he'd come in with his cane and click a light . . . "Okay, we're ready." And that's what he would do. He'd salt and pepper it.

MALTIN: Were there actors who were especially camera-conscious in the old days?

KLINE: Everyone. They all were. I remember even Tony Quinn, I did several pictures with him, and he told me one day, "I don't like these long lenses. I like that camera close to me where I can feel it." [With] that great voice of his. They knew how to turn toward camera; they would work their way into the camera. My very first D.P. assignment was with Lillian Gish and boy, did she know how to find the lens.

MALTIN: What film was that?

KLINE: I did a TV series called *Mr. Novak* for two years and she was in the very first segment that I did. She played an elderly schoolteacher. What a wonderful woman she was. We were good friends for a number of years.

MALTIN: Did you ever get to work with your father?

KLINE: Only one day, when he [was] on a Sam Katzman thing, later on. I was an extra camera on *Rock Around the Clock*. Yeah, just one day, that's the only time.

Chapter 5
MUSICAL NOTES

PUT ANOTHER NICKEL IN ...

The Story of Soundies

When MTV came along and popularized music videos in the 1980s, a number of people (including me) seized the opportunity to resurrect Soundies, the three-minute musical shorts that were produced in the 1940s for use in jukebox-type devices. Those films have

been ubiquitous on television, in cable-TV documentaries, and on home video ever since.

Stars like Duke Ellington, Louis Armstrong, Cab Calloway, Fats Waller, Gene Krupa, Hoagy Carmichael, The Mills Brothers, Cliff "Ukulele Ike" Edwards, Count Basie, Jimmy Dorsey, Nat King Cole, and Spike Jones headlined these mini-musicals, along with scores of medium-grade and lesser-known performers. You never knew who you might see in a Soundie: 1930s leading lady Patricia Ellis singing, quite nicely, in a nightclub setting; Mary Brian, adding window dressing to a Stan Kenton number; nightclub legend Frances Faye; western music favorite Spade Cooley; Lina Romay, before she joined Xavier Cugat's band as featured vocalist; fan dancer Sally Rand; a young "Walter" Liberace; for-

Facing page: Duke Ellington and his orchestra.

Above: Former Our Gang kid Johnny Downs and Movie Crazy reader Jean Porter in At a Little Hot Dog Stand (1941).

mer leading man Buddy Rogers
doing his multi-instrumental
version of "Twelfth Street Rag."

A separate series of
Soundies were targeted to
black-owned establishments
and featured headliners from
Dorothy Dandridge to Pig-
meat Markham to Bill "Bo-
jangles" Robinson.

The Soundies also gave
work to comedians, including
vaudevillian Willie Howard,
standup comic Henny Young-
man, and silent-movie veteran
Snub Pollard. (One of my favorites stars the vaudeville team
of Low, Hite, and Stanley, three
acrobatic dancers of varying
heights. You just don't see acts
like that any more.)

From a film-buff point
of view, the most interesting
aspect of Soundies may be the sheer number of future movie stars who
appeared in them. Of that, more later.

There was a time when many people believed that "visual jukeboxes" would be an absolute sensation. The rivalry to gain predominance
in the field, and establish patents, was fierce. A story in the April 27,
1940, issue of *Motion Picture Herald* was headlined, "Nickel-in-the-Slot
Movie Race is On; 12 Making Projectors, Films."

The article went on to cite some of the challenges inherent in the
idea: "Chief among the problems are the technical developments to
facilitate the use of continuous projection of 16mm film, possible pat-
ent infringement trouble, which has been indicated already, the clearance
of music rights and setting up of union wage scales, decision on what
type of sound-sight subjects to present, and the possibility that obscenity and indecency will creep into the films."

The problem of projection was solved fairly simply in the Mills
Panoram machine, manufactured by the Chicago company already
known for its slot machines and jukeboxes, by using mirrors to rear-
project and "bounce" an image from a standard 16mm projector onto
a frosted-glass screen. (This is why so many surviving Soundies prints
are printed in reverse-image.) A sensor device turned off the projector

after each three-minute film was finished. The greater problem was that patrons couldn't choose which of eight films on a given program to watch; they had to select the next available film on the reel.

Obscenity and indecency were in the eye of the beholder. A majority of the machines were installed in bars and cocktail lounges, where men proved to be the main customers. Then as now, sex was the most effective sales tool, so Soundies almost always featured pretty girls in suggestive or revealing outfits. Other "spicier" reels featured burlesque stars and strippers, although the content would be considered mild by today's standards.

Shirley Gould, who worked for the chief legal counsel of Soundies Distribution Corporation of America, recalls, "I would have correspondence with some of the owners in places I had never heard of; when the war was over and years went on, I discovered most of those places were towns where military installations were."

Carl "Alfalfa" Switzer and other youthful performers enact Come Home, Father (1941).

Shirley also has vivid memories of the nuts and bolts of the Soundies business: maintenance of the machines, collection of nickels and dimes, periodic changing of film reels, and distribution of the prints, all of which made Soundies a more cumbersome operation than jukeboxes. "The office was in downtown Chicago and there was a workroom connected with it where reels were shipped from. When they came back, they had to be inspected and sometimes rewound, and then spliced. It was clumsy."

Among those hoping to establish a beachhead in this new field of entertainment was Sam Sax, the former head of production for Vitaphone in Brooklyn, who was partnered with top talent agent Frank Orsatti in a company called Phonovision. But the man who dominated this field was a songwriter with some entrepreneurial skills, Sam Coslow ("Cocktails for Two," "Learn to Croon," "My Old Flame"). Back in the 1970s, he told me about his involvement with Soundies.

"I got in at the very inception of the thing," he explained. "When I first heard about the new machine that had been invented to show musical films, I figured that with my background of writing songs for

the Hollywood musicals of the 1930s, this would be something that would be up my alley, so I contacted the Mills jukebox people in Chicago, who held the patents and were manufacturing the machines. At that stage, they were at a loss as to how they could get product for the Soundie machines, and after a series of meetings with them, we formed a film production company known as RCM Productions Inc., which held the exclusive right to produce these three-minute musical films. The RCM stood for Roosevelt, Coslow, and Mills, the Roosevelt being my friend Jimmy Roosevelt (son of FDR) who was associated with me in these productions." In fact, Roosevelt already had an agreement in principle with Mills to supply films, but Coslow had the ideas and the contacts to make the idea a reality.

"We leased offices and studio space [at the former Educational Pictures/Grand National studio] on Santa Monica Boulevard in Los Angeles, engaged a full-time production staff, and I spent the next thee years grinding out these three-minute Soundies at the unbelievable rate of about five or six every week.

"I acted as producer, script writer, casting director, and wrote a great many original song numbers especially for these films. I picked most of the artists myself, and let them use the same numbers that they had already recorded and performed, in most cases, and in other cases writing songs especially for them. We had very few problems with song clearances, as I made an arrangement with Harry Fox, who represented most of the U.S. music publishers, and we were allowed to do almost any number on the market for a nominal flat fee. To the best of my recol-

Marvel (later Marilyn) Maxwell in Tea on the Terrace (1942).

lection, this averaged somewhere around $100 per song."

Coslow continued, "I was quite amazed to find that we were able to get a great many of the leading pop music performers of the day for reasonable fees. I think we paid Louis Armstrong $5,000 for one week's shooting, which averaged out to only about $700 or $800 per Soundie.

"As I recall, it would cost us anywhere between $2,000 and $5,000 for the complete production cost per Soundie, which was about par for low-budget shooting costs on three minutes of film in those days. Most of them were profitable, as they were rented out to several thousand different locations [mostly cocktail lounges, hotel lobbies etc.] all over the country.

"When we found out that a great many of the artists were playing long engagements in the East and were not available in Hollywood, we set up a separate New York unit under Jack Barry, and acts I had signed up did their shooting in our New York studios." [Some of these films were produced under the banner of Minoco Productions, located on Decatur Avenue in the Bronx, but this wasn't exactly an outside contractor; Minoco was an acronym for Mills Novelty Company.]

"Aside from the big stars, we had to balance out these more expensive Soundies by making a number of less expensive ones with unknowns, and were constantly having musical auditions for new singers and bands that the agents were sending up for us to hear. Among these unknowns, I take great pride in the fact that the very first appearance on film was on our Soundies—by a lot of people who made it big afterward—people like Doris Day, Yvonne De Carlo, Marilyn Maxwell, Dolores Grey, Morey Amsterdam, Nat King Cole, Gale Storm, Cyd Charisse, Spike Jones, and dozens of others . . ."

Renowned film composer David Raksin recently confirmed that he conducted for Cliff Edwards in this 1941 Soundie, Jeannie with the Light Brown Hair, saying "I'm really delighted to think there was a time when I was so svelte."

The biggest problem with Soundies was the constant demand for new product by the bar owners who gauged the nightly feedback from their customers. "Their take was dependent on the terms of the leases and the quality of the films," Shirley Gould remembers. "It was common conversation around the office [as to] which ones were going best, and my impression is that the ones that went best (had) a lot of people in them and the most popular current numbers." But the Soundies couldn't hope to keep pace with the latest record hits playing in jukeboxes, often in the very same establishments.

RCM produced a two-reel musical for MGM called *Heavenly Music* (1943) which enjoyed great success and earned an Academy Award as Best Live-Action Short Subject. The company also kept the pot boil-

Donald Novis takes the hand of young Cyd Charisse in *Magic of Magnolias* (1942).

ing by making training films for the Armed Forces. At the same time, several competitors entered the field and began offering their own three-minute musical shorts for distribution.

The war affected the fledgling Soundies business in more ways than one. Says Gould, "It was very hard during the war to get the film supplies. You had to go through all kinds of hoops to prove that what you were doing was necessary to the war effort. I sat there for days on end and looked at old stuff, and put together [new] combinations from the old stuff. So there was already a lack of new [product]. They had probably spent inordinate amounts of money to get this launched, and I don't think it ever really repaid the investors."

At the end of the war, Coslow resigned as production head in order to take a position as producer at Paramount Pictures. His timing couldn't have been better.

World War II had delayed development and introduction of TV, and Gould, for one, is certain that this was responsible for putting the Panoram contraptions into mothballs. "If you had a bar and you could buy a television set that everybody could watch, and it had all the sports events, why would you want to continue to pay for this machine? I think television did it in."

One reason Soundies have had some afterlife in the consciousness of film buffs and historians is the presence of future stars in so many of these shorts, from Alan Ladd, who sings with Rita Rio (later rechristened Dona Drake) and her All-Girl Orchestra, to Ricardo Montalban, who appears in several entries but is most prominently featured as the subject of the deathless ditty "He's a Latin from Staten Island." Shirley Gould has a vivid memory of Betty (later Lauren) Bacall appearing in a New York–shot Soundie, but I have yet to nail down that title.

Prints of these films have circulated widely for years; the UCLA Film and Television Archive has a collection of more than 1,500 titles. Panoram machines were retrofitted with eyepieces and turned into peep-show devices, though they do turn up now and then, more or less intact. But it was quite by chance that I discovered that the negatives for the original eight-by-ten stills made to promote Soundies now reside at the Academy of Motion Picture Arts and Sciences. I don't believe these early photos of Doris Day, Cyd Charisse, and other future luminaries have ever been published before. They serve as a visual reminder of a valid—if unlikely—launching pad for a great many careers.

[*All Soundies photos courtesy of the Academy of Motion Picture Arts and Sciences.*]

STILL LIFE

Two great stars meet for the first time: Mickey Mouse and Spanky McFarland. The cartoon character was on loan to MGM for a guest appearance in Hollywood Party (where he was animated as usual, and not a costumed character). Five-year-old Spanky McFarland had emerged as the brightest star of Hal Roach's Our Gang comedies, which were also released by MGM, prompting a bright publicity man to stage this photo in late 1933.

Conversations:
ALEXANDER COURAGE

When I recently revisited the wonderful *Seven Brides for Seven Brothers*, I took note of the name Alexander Courage, who orchestrated the score along with Conrad Salinger, and realized that this Hollywood veteran had never been interviewed, to the best of my knowledge, about his work in the glory days of the movie musical.

A generation of *Star Trek* fans is certainly familiar with his name, as he composed the memorable theme for that durable television series, and the opening fanfare that has appeared in most of the Star Trek feature films as well. He wrote music for a number of other TV shows including *Daniel Boone, Lost in Space, Land of the Giants, Medical Center, The Waltons, Eight Is Enough*, and *Falcon Crest*, but he is better known as one of Hollywood's foremost arrangers, having worked for fifty years on movies ranging from *Annie Get Your Gun* to *Fiddler on the Roof*, and such A-list movies of recent years as *Jurassic Park, L.A. Confidential, Air Force One*, and Disney's *Mulan*. He shared an Academy Award nomination with Lionel Newman for adapting the score of *Doctor Dolittle* in 1967. His association with such composers as John Williams and Jerry Goldsmith dates back to the 1950s when they were all establishing their reputations.

Courage, whose nickname is Sandy, is a delightful man and a witty conversationalist. In this interview, we'll learn how a serious student from the Eastman School of Music found himself in Los Angeles writing for radio and film. For now, let's turn the clock back to the late 1940s, when MGM was still the Tiffany's of Hollywood studios, and a young man from Philadelphia found himself in the middle of movieland.

COURAGE: So I went to MGM and I started orchestrating for Adolph [Deutsch]. The first thing that I did there was on television the other night, I stumbled across it, *Luxury Liner*. It started off as one of those "hot Pasternak sandwiches." That's a quote from Billy Wilder, who was another friend. Adolph came in and they assigned him to do the score for the picture. The numbers had already been done.

MALTIN: Do you remember your first impression of MGM?

COURAGE: Well, I drove up to the main gate and stopped and said something to the cop and he laughed and he said, "You've got to be kidding. Go park over there in the [employees'] lot." That was my first day at MGM.

The first thing that happened, just about, when Adolph got there was a picture called *Julia Misbehaves*, with Greer Garson, in which she is an actress who [in one scene] has guys helping her come down the front of a burning building, and singing. So when they shot the thing, they cut this and they cut that and they had to break it all up in pieces. So Adolph looked at this thing and it was a mess. He had come from Warner Bros., which was a studio that was very sharp as far as cutting went. MGM was nonsense. The breakdown sheets that you composed to, with the dialogue, the action and so forth at MGM, there were no real timings. It said, "[She] goes through the gate." [*Laughs*] Now, how long does it take you to go through a gate? Do you want to start [the music cue] here, or when the gate is closed? Or when somebody smiles as they're going through the middle of going through the gate? It was ridiculous. So Adolph started looking around for a music cutter. And they said, "Why do you need a music cutter?" He said, "We have to redo this sequence and we have to know exactly where she puts her foot, and where the song is at that point. Somebody has to come here, put it on a movieola, and figure out where all these things happen." And they were just flabbergasted. They had never had anybody say anything like that to them at MGM. The other studios were way ahead of them, but MGM was kind of in its own world, so finally one of the guys came down and he was puzzled; he'd never had anything like this happen to him before. Adolph actually taught him how to measure these things on the film; you know a foot is two-thirds of a second and you go on from there and you work out some kind of a plan that he can work the music to. And then, I remember when he finally got it all cut, Greer Garson was great. She came over, we were watching the playback, you know, and she had to sing, so she had to redo some of the track, and she couldn't quite get in where she needed to at exactly the right time, so she said, "Adolph, would you goose me a little bit right there?"

MALTIN: And that was your first brush with movie stardom?

COURAGE: My first famous movie star. She was wonderful. Another great redhead.

[So I'm at MGM] and André Previn and I have become friends because I'm ten years older and he was living with his parents. I became a member of the family because his mother told me I looked like her long-lost brother. It was marvelous. I took André down to Brooks Brothers and got him some decent clothes.

And I got busy right away with Adolph. Adolph got his first musical, from top to bottom, which was *Annie Get Your Gun*. And a whole marvelous thing began to happen with Adolph. There was *The Band Wagon*. I don't think I'd ever seen anything that completely put together.

MALTIN: To a layman and a fan, just the name MGM conjures up all sorts of images from that period. But, of course, it was a business and it was your job. Looking back now, do you see it as a glamorous time?

COURAGE: Oh, yes. Very much so. My goodness, here I am, I'm working at MGM. Although I have to admit to you that if I ever could get out of having lunch there, I always went up to Fox because all my friends really were at Fox.

MALTIN: Was there a music table in the commissary?

COURAGE: Yes, but the one at Fox was round and it was right at the entrance to the studio so that any girls that came in were immediately seen. And in fact, that table later on became kind of a magnet because . . . What was the restaurant in Beverly Hills with the crazy Russian who ran it?

MALTIN: Romanoff's?

COURAGE: Romanoff's. Mike Romanoff used to come there and have lunch with us at the music table, 'cause he said it was more fun there than being at his restaurant. And Lennie Hayton would be there and several writers who liked being at the music table, because we were, I guess, a little more lively than most. That was just marvelous.

MALTIN: Describe the music table at MGM, then.

COURAGE: It was in a corner; it was long, oblong, sort of stuck in the middle of nowhere.

MALTIN: When you were working as an orchestrator, did you feel isolated at all from the physical production of a film?

COURAGE: We had very little to do with anything unless on a musical, you might be able to get in and see the number that's being worked on. I do remember very vividly a couple of times actually going over and watching Fred Astaire with his Greek dancing friend Hermes Pan. Very nice guy. Fred and his neckties tied around his waist. That was, to me, the greatest thrill of all. Here I am! My God, I'm working with Fred Astaire.

At that point, Johnny Green, dear Johnny Green, marvelous man [arrived at MGM]. I don't know how much you know about John but he was really something.

MALTIN: I'm a great fan of his piano playing. I always thought he was a fantastic pianist . . .

COURAGE: Oh, yes. Oh, he was a terrific musician. Up to a point. Anyway, he was now the head of the music department. And, of course immediately everything changed. There were more secretaries. Somebody said when the efficiency experts come in, the first thing they do is fire eight of John's secretaries. Now there are two pictures coming up. One is *Brigadoon* and the other one was *Sobbin' Women*, which was the original name of the story [*Seven Brides for Seven Brothers*]. Adolph, who was a great sports car nut, and I are driving to Pasadena to have some work done on one of his Astons (he had two of them), and he's furious, he's livid. I said, "What's the matter?" He said, "Dammit, Johnny Green has taken my picture and given me this goddamned hillbilly crap!" And I said, "Really, what's that?" He said, "Well, he's going to do *Brigadoon* because he thinks that that's the picture to do. Now I have to do this goddamn *Sobbin' Women* thing." And I said, "Gee, that's a shame." [*Laughs*] You know the ending of that story.

Well, you know, there's another person who fits in here and I have never, never figured out exactly what he did. And that's Saul Chaplin. Later on, of course, we became friends because he had an eight-hands piano-group, and I took over from John Williams. I never really had any truck with Saul on that or any other picture. But his name was always there.

MALTIN: When did you first meet John Williams?

COURAGE: I remember very vividly, exactly when it was. Two things. The first one was we were doing *Funny Face*, and we'd had pianist troubles for various reasons. We needed somebody to just play plain old cocktail bar piano for the show. We're all in the booth and there's a new guy out there and he starts to play and we all look around and say, "Gee that sounds absolutely [like] what we're looking for, who's that?" Somebody said, "His name is Johnny Williams, he just arrived from New York." And the other story is that the word got around that John had written a new main title for the *General Electric Theater* or something like that and it was so sensational, you know, 'cause Herbie [Spencer] had orchestrated it, that we all went out to Universal to the recording, just to be there and hear this. I still remember it; it was really something.

I've done a lot with John. We had a lot of fun, we did *Fiddler on the Roof* together. And he's a dear, dear man. In fact, I got him his only orchestration job, the more I think of it. He was just starting out and

I had done *Some Like It Hot* with Adolph, and now he was going to do *The Apartment* and I was stuck on something else, so I recommended John to orchestrate *The Apartment*, which John did. And he never did another orchestration job.

MALTIN: Adolph Deutsch was a composer. Did he also conduct?

COURAGE: Yeah, Adolph conducted. And he was the most nervous man in the world. One time he said to me before a recording in his bungalow, "You know, last night I woke up at 3:00 and I told myself that the second trombone in this bar is the wrong note." So he fixed it. And I said to myself, Is that going too far, really?

MALTIN: Would you attend the sessions?

COURAGE: Oh, yes. The only time I was ever late in my life and I would never be after that. [*Laughs*] Good God, on *Annie Get Your Gun*, we were just getting started and because of the switch between Judy Garland and Betty Hutton, the numbers had to be re-keyed, and I forgot to tell the copyists that this particular song had to be moved from A-flat to A. I got there something like seven minutes late because I'd been up all night in a hotel finishing something else in Culver City. So Adolph is absolutely flying up at the ceiling and I thought, Oh God, you know, I'm never going to work again. It turned out to be fine because the concertmaster of the orchestra said, "Adolph, don't worry about it. We can play it in A-major just as well as we can play it in A-flat." So it was no problem, they played the whole thing in the other key and that was it. Thank you, orchestra.

MALTIN: You mean the musicians just transposed it on sight?

Fred Astaire.

COURAGE: That's right.

MALTIN: That's impressive.

COURAGE: Well, they were incredible guys and they could do anything.

MALTIN: Because those musicians were of such a high caliber did that mean the sessions went quickly?

COURAGE: If everything was prepared, it should not take a long time. André (Previn), of course, being the kind of conductor he turned out to be, even then was an excellent conductor. We were inseparable back then.

MALTIN: Who else did you work with at MGM?

COURAGE: There was Bob Franklin, who orchestrated for Connie Salinger and Bronny Kaper. Then there was Al Woodbury. And Leo was really an arranger, Leo Arnaud. Mickey Rózsa had his own orchestrator who was a fellow Hungarian named Eugene Zador.

Courage (left) joins Miklós Rózsa, Alex North, Alfred Newman, Johnny Green, and David Raksin at a Hollywood Bowl concert for the Composer's Guild in 1964.

MALTIN: Did you have any dealings with Arthur Freed?

COURAGE: I had very little to do with Arthur Freed. He came down to the set on the number in *Show Boat*, and it's in two parts, so as you recall, the whole first part which is vocal ends up with "Life upon the wicked stage / Ain't nothin' for a girl . . ." So Arthur is there. Now, this is part one, we haven't done part two, which is the dance. Then he said, "You can't end that number that way. You can't end it, it's sad." He got all excited, you know, and everybody said, "Arthur, don't worry about it, that's the end of the first part. You see, after that, it's going to be terrific." Everybody is selling it to him. Finally, he just said, "Oh, yeah," and he left. Then we got back to work. You'd think after all those years of putting out the greatest musicals just about ever that he would have known that you do these things in parts. But in the beginning at MGM, they wanted everything done like a stage show. They wanted everything seen, finished, there was no nonsense about catching this or making an insert here or anything like that. And a click track? Not on your life.

MALTIN: Would you have anything to do with the playback recordings?

COURAGE: Do you know the process of taking down a number?

MALTIN: No.

COURAGE: Ah, well now we're getting down to it. What happens is this. Let's say it's Astaire. Fred is over there in his little space in the rehearsal hall. And he has his Greek, and he has his pianist. And maybe, possibly one dancing girl or something like that. And they're working on it, they've got the number, they're playing the thing on the piano and he's working out steps, with his dance-in, and they're now at the point where the number is set. So now we come in to look at this. Meanwhile, the pianist has written down musically just what's going on.

MALTIN: This rehearsal pianist's score then would indicate what? Accents? Movements?

COURAGE: Yes, what's happening: "Fred jumps," "Fred slides from here to there," everything is down, it's like a Mickey Mouse thing. And then you know generally what it's supposed to do.

MALTIN: So, that's your blueprint.

COURAGE: Exactly. It's a perfect way to put it. So, you take that home and you start writing it.

MALTIN: But you also see a demonstration of the dance, so you have some visual concept . . .

COURAGE: Oh, yes.

MALTIN: Can you give me any indication of how long it might take to work on a number of that kind?

COURAGE: First of all, it depends on how long and how complicated the number is. Could be anywhere between a week and a month, easily. And then it depends on what's happening and whether you're orchestrating it yourself or somebody else is. With Adolph, he would give me or anybody else a hugely complete sketch, down to the second trombone notes. And that was it. And all those things are still with MGM; why didn't I steal those?

MALTIN: So that was your last contact with the on-camera talent?

COURAGE: Well no, now comes the big contact, when you'd go on the recording stage and you start doing the number. One way to think about that is when we did *Seven Brides* the orchestra is in one huge room. And then the other very big room with the recording board and all the machinery that goes with it. But on *Seven Brides* they set up the saw-horses and the planks and everything else and the guys that were doing all of that stuff, you know, a lot of the flips and everything else, came in and did them because they had to make sure that the tempo that they were going to be filming to was the right tempo for them. So as long as we all knew that, everything was right. Who was it that used to do that . . . ? Gene Kelly came around with a stopwatch, and he's standing there, he's going through this whole thing, he gets to the end, and he said, "It's three seconds too long." He said, "The take before this one was three seconds shorter." That's Gene.

MALTIN: Another question for you, then. In the big courting number before the barn-raising, the dance music is the song we've heard early in the movie, "Bless Your Beautiful Hide." Was that a given or did that take some searching to figure out which theme would work if used in that way?

COURAGE: That would definitely be Adolph, or I have to say it, it could have been Saul Chaplin. Maybe that's something that he actually did on the movie. That's a possibility. And then the thing that's great about that piece of music is that there are oh, so many typical Adolph things. Adolph was a man who was so afraid that something might happen that he went around eighty times, to make sure that everything that possibly could happen could be taken care of immediately on the stage. So if somebody didn't like the fact that this was being played by a clarinet, they could easily have it played by a harmonica. And if the bass thing doesn't work, you can do it with the something-or-other, just in case and he was right, because the whole idea (he taught me this quickly) is that stage time with a big orchestra is very expensive and if you can be totally, totally overprepared before you get in there, whatever happens you can just say, "Don't play this, play that." And that's it.

MALTIN: Did you count on certain musicians who played in the MGM orchestra?

COURAGE: Oh, yes. For instance do you remember Jerry Goldsmith's score for *Chinatown*, that main title, with that tremendous trumpet thing going from Uan Rasey?

MALTIN: He was also in the MGM orchestra.

COURAGE: Yes. And where that happened before that—and I don't even think that Jerry even knew this—was that Uan was at MGM in *The Band Wagon* when they have that big ballet that they put together, you know, with Fred and Cyd Charisse. The key to that whole [private eye number] that they put together was the trumpet solo which was Uan Rasey doing the same kind of thing that he did later on *Chinatown*. That whole ballet was put together by Arthur Schwartz, who had written the original music, and Roger Edens, who was the great imaginer of the whole thing, and a great, a great fellow. And Adolph and Connie. So, you can't [get] better than that.

MALTIN: Any other musicians come to mind from that period?

COURAGE: Well, there was Lou Raderman who was the concert master, and his wife and his mistress, all in the string section. And Si Zentner who, after the studio system collapsed, had his own band. And it was just a tremendously great orchestra, too. Mel Powell, for a while, was one of the two pianists. They had a jazz pianist and a classical pianist, which was a good idea. I don't know if you know about the union situation. There were five or seven major, major studios, and the contract with them was higher than the others. The majors had signed a contract for fifty, count them, fifty players. Then it was up to you who played what. So, that was it. And Rózsa was furious all the time.

MALTIN: Why?

COURAGE: Well, we were all standing around outside the music department in the street and he was grumbling, Hungarian-style and he said, "They gave somebody this, that, and the other thing, and they wouldn't give me a third bass," for, I don't know, this enormous goddamn thing here on the desert with the pharaohs or something. [*Laughs*]

MALTIN: Could they negotiate? Could they wheedle for extra men for a certain session?

COURAGE: Oh, sure. It depended on who was negotiating. John [Green] was incredible. Every Thursday morning, a truck would pull up in the music department and a couple of guys would get out and start unloading those old-fashioned school chairs, you know, with the desk that you write on, and putting them in John's office, about a half a dozen of them. Then he would have a meeting of the composers in which he would talk to them about what was going on and what they should be doing and what they should not be doing—and who's John Green telling Mickey Rózsa, you know? I got all these things from André, 'cause he was a composer and I was an orchestrator and I wasn't allowed in there. Except when they had orchestrators come in and we were told what to do. Or not to do.

MALTIN: And yet you'd think Johnny Green would be the right person in the sense that at least he was a musician himself.

COURAGE: He was a super musician, he was a super executive, he was a super person, he was a dear soul, but he just was overdone. He got that one big picture, *Raintree County*, and I will give him credit because I have two big LPs of his score of that, and on the first one which is a plain old LP there is no mention of anything. The second one is a double LP in which he thanks all of us . . . because we wrote the score!

MALTIN: Alfred Newman must have been an exceptional person, a great musician, and apparently a great administrator as well.

COURAGE: Oh, yes. He was the best of the whole bunch. By a long shot. He really knew what he was doing, and if you did good stuff for him, he took good care of you. That was the way that department worked and it was much, much better than any place else. Fox was heaven in its way, oh, but watch out. You had to deliver.

MALTIN: There are some specific titles I want to ask you about. Did you do some work on *Show Boat*?

COURAGE: Yes. That was a marvelous, marvelous thing to do. In fact, that was the first time I ever got to do a number.

MALTIN: Which one?

COURAGE: Well, what happened was that "Life Upon the Wicked Stage" was supposed to be done by Adolph when his mother died in Buffalo. So he said, "I'm going to turn this over to you," and we went over it together.

MALTIN: Tell me about *Funny Face*, which started out as an MGM movie, I know and then went to Paramount . . .

COURAGE: One of the things that happened on that which was kind of wild was I did that number in the smoky cellar. And God, she was great, that lady [Audrey Hepburn]. They were rehearsing and Audrey had to do a slide under this guy's knee. He's supposed to pick up his knee and she slides under it. And doing it, he didn't get his knee out of

the way in time and she smacked right into it. And it knocked her out. Everybody picked her up and put her on a chair and gave her some water and in about, I don't know, three minutes or so, she was back on the floor again. She was great. That's one lady I have nothing but total admiration for. When I did *My Fair Lady* she walked into the room where we all

Audrey Hepburn and Astaire in Funny Face *(1957).*

were and she came over and said, "Nice to see you again, Sandy." I mean, that was what, however many years later. So, that's a total lady of the first type.

MALTIN: I love movies with a big finish, where the music ends with an oomph. My all-time favorite is the end of *Funny Face*, which, I think is Conrad Salinger.

COURAGE: That's Connie.

MALTIN: It segues from the final dance and it just builds and builds and builds. To me, that's a finale.

COURAGE: It's a dear, dear ending. Oh, yes. And considering what they were going through while they shot that, because they had drenching rain—so all the sod had to be taken up where that supposed church was. And then the drainage of gravel put down and pumped out and so forth and all, then new sod goes back in—and then it rains again. So, they were sinking into the turf and had a terrible time on that picture. They finally gave up and just started shooting in the rain. There are a couple of sequences in the picture where they're just with umbrellas. But that was fun, that was a great, great experience and I love that picture.

Somebody asked me one time about what was the greatest thing that I think I ever did. And as I said, as far as I'm concerned, the greatest thing I ever did was writing a *pasa doble* for Fred Astaire. Which is about as outré as you can get.

MALTIN: Were you blasé about seeing the stars when you'd walk in . . . ?

COURAGE: No . . . my God, I never was.

MALTIN: By the time you worked on *Gigi*, the MGM musical unit had pretty much fallen apart; but then it was pulled back together, it seems.

COURAGE: Well, actually, I did very little on *Gigi*. I was working somewhere else, so *Gigi* was done by André and Connie. Completely. And when I came in André said, "Listen, I've had it up to here with Beethoven and Schiller [his names for composers Lerner and Loewe]." [*Laughs*] He said, "I can't stand it any more. We all had a big discussion at the beginning of the picture about the fact that we were going to make it very French, very light, very soignée, very beautiful, Parisienne. Then we got through and Beethoven said to me, 'You have to have balls.'" He said, "Look, the big problem apparently is when they come into Maxim's. We had it nice and light and apparently, they wanted a brass band. Could you just do that over again?" So, that's what I did. I did the entrance to Maxim's and a couple of other little things and that was it.

MALTIN: Who hired you to work on *Oklahoma* and *Guys and Dolls*?

COURAGE: Adolph. I didn't really do that much on *Guys and Dolls*. I got a lot of great steaks out of it. That was the Fox group. What happened was they brought over Herbie Spencer and Earle Hagen and Sinatra's man, Nelson Riddle. I think that was maybe his first big picture. He did a hell of a great job on that.

You know, he really knew what he was doing, I didn't. I was a kid from a conservatory who had three different majors in four years. I didn't know what I was doing. I mean, I wanted to be a symphonic conductor. So I guess they had me hang around; I did some orchestration and Bobby Newman [one of the Newman brothers] was Goldwyn's assistant. And Bobby had a special refrigerator in the Chinese restaurant across the street.

MALTIN: The Formosa?

COURAGE: The Formosa Cafe. That's right. So he would take us all over there for dinner and they would bring out his steaks. It was marvelous.

MALTIN: I know you're from Philadelphia, and you attended Eastman School of Music. What made you come to Hollywood?

COURAGE: *Cherchez la femme.* When I was at Eastman, I guess my junior year, a girl suddenly showed up at school, the likes of which had never been seen at Eastman before. She was an absolutely ravishingly gorgeous blonde, very sophisticated, and from California. I said something to her once in the hall about *The New Yorker* and we became fast friends, to say the least. She'd never been in the snow, she broke her ankle and her parents came; we all got to be friends and she went back to California. She kept writing me letters, and said, "You have to come to California. All you need is a tennis racket and a tuxedo." I had earned (at fifty cents an hour) about $100, so as soon as I got out of school, I hitched a ride to California, because of this girl. Her name was Doris Atkinson.

MALTIN: That would have been what year?

COURAGE: That was 1941. And almost immediately, the war broke out. So because I had to prove to Mr. Atkinson that I wasn't some silly sissy musician, I was the second person downtown in line to enlist at 5:00 in the morning, the next morning. I enlisted at March Field; he lent me his big Packard Phaeton to drive down there in, and it was quite something. When Mrs. Atkinson found out that I'd gone down to enlist downtown, she said, "I'm going to give you a party for your birthday, so you'll have to wait until after that." Then at the party I met a man from the musicians' union who said, "Go down to the union and they'll put you in a band somewhere." So I did that and that was it.

MALTIN: What was your instrument?

COURAGE: I started as a horn player, which I'd always been. I did that as long as I could stand it, for just about a year and a half. It was quite a band, you can imagine. Joe Bushkin was part of it, and all the guys who were in name bands here before the war. I started writing while I was there and we had a little radio show on the Mutual Broadcasting System. There was a writer and an announcer and me.

MALTIN: What was the show called?

COURAGE: I can't remember, it was *March Field Salutes* or something like that. Bob Hope came to the *Field* several times for his radio show, and during one of those times, he was reading his monologue at the beginning of the show, live, and the lights went out, except for one beat-up old spotlight way up in the corner somewhere. He tilted his script up and didn't miss a word! It was incredible. I still can see that moment. He was incredible, that fellow.

MALTIN: Did you live out your Army career there?

COURAGE: Oh no, when I finally couldn't stand it, I took the exam and went to Washington and went through their music school and became a bandleader on my own, and came back to California where they sent me to Gardner Field and Taft. Have you ever been to Taft, California?

MALTIN: No.

COURAGE: Don't. It's sort of dirty oil company country. That was all right, it wasn't so far away, and there were some good guys there. I ended up near Phoenix, at Chandler, and we had a good colonel there who saw to it that the band got into Hollywood, to play at the Canteen, which is where we were on VJ-Day. So we led the parade with Mrs. Atkinson and the two girls down Hollywood Boulevard.

MALTIN: That must have been quite an experience.

COURAGE: Yes. Now in the band, to make the bridge, was a man named Maurice Crawford whose wife was the number two music copyist at CBS

A recent photo of Alexander Courage at home.

Radio. When I got out, I went up to see Harriet, and she introduced me to Bill [Wilbur] Hatch, who needed somebody to help him. I got a job with Bill, orchestrating his cues. He wasn't feeling too well [so] sometimes I would compose the show, and then he finally couldn't do it, so I was composing and conducting the show, which was *Screen Guild Players*. At the same time, through Doris I had met a man named Herbert Spencer, who was the chief arranger at Fox. He introduced me to Eddie Powell, who was the number one orchestrator at Fox. Eddie knew that there was a composer in town named Adolph Deutsch that needed an orchestrator who was a kid, and cheap. So I went to see Adolph, we had a little chat. Dear Hermina, his first wife, who was a darling lady, told me later that she said, "Doesn't he remind you of Connie Salinger in the old days of New York?" And he said, "Yeah, come to think of it, yeah . . ." She said, "Why don't you hire him?" So, I was then Adolph's orchestrator on the *Camay* show. That lasted, I guess, for about a year or two . . .

MALTIN: That must have been like a crash course, having to work on those deadlines. I imagine if you're smart, you absorb a lot in an experience like that.

COURAGE: Well, there were other people who were doctors [of music for whom] it didn't seem to work.

MALTIN: One of the things radio veterans say they liked the most was that everybody worked together as a group.

COURAGE: Oh, yes, very much so. The *Camay Soap* thing was with Hedda Hopper. There was a restaurant-saloon on the corner of Sunset and Gower, I guess; Hedda would go over there along with a lot of other people before the show and have a few. She came back and she always warmed the audience up, with one of her hats. So she's out there with her hat and the clock is ticking up to [air time]. And the director of the show, who was a furious man to begin with, was having absolute fits, he was screaming at her and banging on the glass . . . And Adolph, who was so nervous, hadn't been introduced, so he was still in the wings. Somebody pushed Adolph out and he realized what was going on; she was still talking. He started the theme, which got her into the show, and whew! But it was really something.

MALTIN: Did you work on *The Adventures of Sam Spade*?

COURAGE: Yes, with Lud Gluskin. Have you ever heard of the fact that somebody said that his name sounds like the last few drops of water going down a bathtub drain?

MALTIN: No. That's wonderful.

COURAGE: He was also known as "the worry with the fringe on top." And he was incredible. He was a businessman. He had three or four arrangers; he didn't write it all. Lucien Moraweck did *Suspense*, and *Sam Spade* was done by Rene Garriguenc, and every once in a while they'd get fed up with him and he'd go back to France. Now he was stuck, so he called me into the office and he said, "Hey, kid," he said, "You think you could do *Sam Spade*?" I said yeah, I guess so, why not? So I ended up doing *Sam Spade* for a few months at least and so I suddenly had three radio shows.

Now that I was sort of in solid with Adolph Deutsch's group, socially, one of them was Connie Salinger—Conrad Salinger—who was the chief arranger at MGM, and a very interesting fellow. The director of *Sam Spade* was Bill Spier, who was married to Kay Thompson. And Kay, of course, was a big friend of Connie's, because they worked together a lot. They were known for those long impossible endings that they put on all those numbers at MGM that went on forever. André [Previn] and I used to imitate them on the road when we were driving along. So now I'm doing composing and conducting *Sam Spade*, and because of the connection, they hired Connie to play his one and only radio role, as a queer dentist in "The Candy Tooth Caper." And he cries, he does everything; he had to join AFRA in order to do it. He got paid, I think, $75 and it cost him $85 to join AFRA. So we made our debuts, in a way, together. Adolph had been working at Warner Bros. forever, and he got all the crummy pictures, the big, bad tough pictures to do. Now, of course, he's on the list of angels because he did the greatest ones in their day. [*High Sierra, The Maltese Falcon, The Mask of Dimitrios, Three Strangers,* to name just a few.] Finally he just couldn't stand it anymore, so he quit.

And to show you the way Hollywood works, they were looking for a musical director for the musicals at MGM. L. K. Sidney remembered that in New York in the early thirties he had gone to see this show in which there was a number called "Heat Wave." He was so impressed with it, he remembered that the man who was the conductor of the show had written the arrangement for it, and it was great, so he said, "We've got to get this fellow Adolph Deutsch." So Adolph Deutsch, who had done nothing but the heaviest kind of pictures at Warners, was now, along with Lennie Hayton, the new musical conductor at MGM, and he couldn't get anything else. Couldn't get a dramatic [movie assignment] to save his neck.

So I went to MGM [with Adolph]. Then I met André and a very important fellow named Leo Arnaud who was one of the great arrangers there. Leo was very much in the American Legion and right after the war, the American Legion Post, the Musicians' Post had a band and he was in charge of it. So he made me his assistant and I did a lot of stuff, Sunday concerts all over the map with the Legion Post band, playing in the parks.

But in the meantime, one other thing happened, 'cause I've had a weird career, to say the least. My big friends were at Fox, [Herb] Spencer and Charlie Henderson, who was married to Lynn Henderson, who was a great Broadway dancer [known as] Mitzi Mayfair.

MALTIN: She was on that famous World War II tour, one of the "Four Jills in a Jeep."

COURAGE: Yes . . . And it just so happened when I was a teenager, my mother had taken me to New York, to see a couple of musicals, both of which featured her. So now at the Fox Studio Club, they decided they should put on a show. I used to do stuff at the piano and they said, "We don't have anybody else, so we have to use you as the lead." And it turned out that the other lead in the show was a young starlet named Marilyn Monroe. This is all true. I know it sounds weird, but it is actually true. We ran five nights in a rehearsal hall which was completely done over into a theater, with a revolving stage and everything.

MALTIN: Had you ever performed before?

COURAGE: I danced once when I was at school, just to prove to somebody that I could and I was kind of interested in a girl who was in the dance corps. Darla Hood [from the] *Our Gang* comedies [was in our show]. This was done just for fun by young employees at the studio. We had skits written by people like George Seaton, all original songs by Charlie Henderson. I had to do everything, because the guy who was supposed to call the square dance didn't show up, so I had to dance and call the square dance at the same time. And there were three guys from the legal department who came out and did a fan dance. It was really something.

MALTIN: So you weren't working there but you hung out there, you had friends there . . .

COURAGE: Yes. I worked there later, a lot. I have all these little funny tie-ups. One of the featured people in *Luxury Liner* [the first film he worked on at MGM] was Marina Koshetz, who later on became my neighbor; we lived next door to each other in Beverly Hills. My whole life has been this way. At one point when I was first out of the service and I was trying to get work (and my friend Doris had all kinds of social connections around town), one of the people was Lionel Barrymore, who lived in a tiny little shack, practically, in Hollywood. I gave him horn lessons because he was writing a piece for horn and he wanted to know what would work. I think that I got $10 for doing that. And another one was Eugene Zador, who wanted to learn how to drive. I tell you, I did everything under the sun.

That's another part of my life: Billy Wilder. You won't believe all this but it's all true. In the early 1940s, my parents were living in a little apartment in Beverly Hills and I see in the paper that there's a dance at the Beverly Hills Hotel. So, I go to the dance and I'm dancing with some girl and we get near a very elegant looking lady who calls us over and we have a little chat. She finds out that I'm a musician and she said her first husband was one of the great impresarios in New York in the time of Caruso, which was true; Coppicus his name was. We became fast friends and her older daughter Judith was married to Billy. I met Billy and he was very dear to me. I was in uniform, and he got me on the set; I watched that whole mouse coming out of the wall in *The Lost Weekend*. Years and years later, I work on *Some Like It Hot* and so I have two friends on the picture, Billy and Marilyn. I pass him going in and out of the commissary about three or four times and all of a sudden I hear him say behind me, "You think I don't know who you are?" And I turned around, he said, "You're Alexander!" I said, "Oh, thank you, Billy, thank you for everything that you did."

MALTIN: I guess you've had about as wide a circle of friends, acquain-

A sample page from Alexander Courage's work ledger, in which he faithfully recorded every music cue he composed or arranged during his long career in films and television. This entry itemizes the individual pieces he orchestrated for Seven Brides for Seven Brothers; the names of cues will be familiar to anyone well acquainted with the film.

tances, and encounters as anybody in this town. Tell me more about André Previn.

COURAGE: His girlfriend was Georgia Axt, the daughter of Harry Axt, who wrote "Dinah." She was a terrific pianist, so I would pick her up to go meet André to do something together, the three of us. She would be practicing in the dark in their apartment in Beverly Hills. Once in a while, they went downtown; near the old Bullock's on Wilshire, there was a big old house there with two pianos. So, they'd play a lot of Rachmaninoff together, sight reading it well. It was really something.

MALTIN: I read in Previn's book that Mel Powell played on some of those MGM soundtracks.

COURAGE: Oh, yes. Actually, Mel with his wife Martha Scott, and André and, I guess Georgia would go up to Big Bear and hire some kind of a cabin with a piano, and sit around and play four hands, Beethoven symphonies.

MALTIN: So if you loved music, you could be immersed in music all the time.

COURAGE: Yes, it was wonderful. [*Laughs*] One of the first things Adolph did was something called *Pagan Love Song*, and that's when I got sort of initiated into the workings of music at MGM. The man who was in charge of all the stuff for those big musicals was Roger Edens. Roger was a dear soul. So here we are, figuring out what to do about the music in this picture, which is in Tahiti. We're in the back room of the music department with a projector, projectionist, and the scene, and we have to get some music put to it, so I get all the records I can find of Tahitian music. (I still have them upstairs.) You know, old 78s, and we're sitting there: Roger is sitting at this little upright piano and he's banging out something, and Adolph is counting one, two, and I'm [making drum sounds] and finding drum patterns. [*Laughs*] So, that's the way we got this whole Tahitian nonsense going. It was a lot of fun.

MALTIN: What did you do on *The Band Wagon*?

COURAGE: I was allowed to do "I Guess I'll Have to Change My Plan," so I [can say] by God, I did a soft shoe for Jack Buchanan and Fred Astaire.

MALTIN: Pretty nice. Obviously, you had a facility—if that's the word —for the popular idiom, though you had been trained in classical music.

COURAGE: Nobody ever knew what the hell I was and I still don't. Really. For instance, did I mention the bullfight thing? Because I was, as somebody put it, the only composer around who had ever been to a bullfight. I'm a published photographer of bullfighting. I met Hugo Friedhofer, my dear friend, in the doctor's office and he said, "You know all about bullfights?" I said, yes. He said, "I've got to do *The Sun Also*

Rises. How would you like to do the Spanish music?" I said I'd love to do the Spanish music. In fact, I have a book of it; I saved that, one of the few I ever saved. And that was fun.

MALTIN: I think *Deep in My Heart* is an underrated musical. I mean, it's a mishmash, but there's a lot of good stuff in it.

COURAGE: Sure there is.

MALTIN: Do you remember which numbers you worked on?

COURAGE: I was the clean-up man. I orchestrated everything that Adolph did, like "I Love to Go Swimmin' with Women," and I did the number for the tap-dancing girl.

MALTIN: Ann Miller?

COURAGE: Miller, yes. What was it called? "It." And then when the picture's over, you know, you have all these scenes where they're sitting in some place and there's an orchestra playing. All of that, when there's some background music, I took all of that on myself. In other words, they didn't have to worry about that.

[Note: Although his orchestrating credits are far-reaching, including such films as *Porgy and Bess, My Fair Lady, Fiddler on the Roof, The Poseidon Adventure, Basic Instinct, Jurassic Park, L.A. Confidential, Mulan,* and *The Mummy,* Mr. Courage is undoubtedly best known for composing the *Star Trek* theme and fanfare. By now it should come as no surprise that a happy coincidence is attached to that assignment: the person who hired him for the job in the late 1960s was the music supervisor for Desilu: Wilbur Hatch . . . the same man who'd given him his first break at CBS in the 1940s.]

PHOTOS BY ALEXANDER COURAGE

Alexander Courage is an avid photographer whose work has been exhibited and published over the years. He has graciously allowed us to print these candid pictures of some famous colleagues.

Miklós Rózsa conducts his youthful musicians in preparation for a concert at the Hollywood Bowl; Previn is at the piano, his head turned to the conductor at this moment.

Miklós Rózsa and André Previn at a rehearsal for a youth orchestra in the 1950s: two greats of different generations who worked together at MGM.

Adolph Deutsch, Courage's mentor in radio and movies, plays four-handed piano at a party with Johnny Green, composer, pianist, and Courage's longtime boss at MGM.

STILL LIFE

Sammy Fain and Irving Kahal's song "By a Waterfall" inspired Busby Berkeley's production number of the same name in Footlight Parade (1933). It's amazing to behold onscreen and, judging from this rare photo, it was also pretty impressive to watch as it was being shot on a Warner Bros. sound stage. Photo from the Delmar Watson collection.

BIOGRAPHY of a SONG:
"DON'T FENCE ME IN"

Not every hit song has as long and colorful a history as "Don't Fence Me In," Cole Porter's cowboy anthem: commissioned for a film that never got made, it sat dormant for a decade, and then became a hit, with major exposure in three movies within one year's time.

The story begins in 1934. Porter was riding high with the success of his latest Broadway hit, *Anything Goes*, when he was hired to write a movie score by producer Lou Brock. A short-subject producer at RKO, Brock had hit the jackpot with the feature-length *Flying Down to Rio* in 1933, and a year later sold Fox Films on the idea of another South American–themed musical, *OK, Argentina!* (later retitled *Adios, Argentina!*). Porter was paid $15,000 for five songs, one to be "'Singing in the Saddle,' a Gaucho riding song," another to be "a cowboy song which ... must be written in such a manner that it can be sung as counterpoint against the 'Singing in the Saddle.'"[1]

Producer Brock had some doubts about Porter's ability to write in the western vernacular and remembered reading a poem called "Don't Fence Me In" in a collection of verse by Robert W. Fletcher, who made his living as a Plans and Traffic Engineer with the Montana State Highway Department. At Brock's suggestion, Fletcher added music to his poem, and on November 24, sent the completed song to Porter. On December 1, Brock wired Fletcher that Porter was sufficiently impressed to buy the title and "some characteristic words and phrases," and advised him to quote a price of $250.

The poem, which is published in William McBrien's biography *Cole Porter* (Knopf, 1998), bears only passing resemblance to the

Cole Porter with Ann Miller on the MGM lot during production of Kiss Me Kate (1953).

---

1   In her 2007 biography *Gene Autry: Public Cowboy No. 1*, Holly George-Warren reveals that the up-and-coming cowboy vocalist met and sang for Porter during a visit to New York in early 1935. The composer liked Autry enough to recommend his being cast in *Adios Argentina!* Had this project come to fruition, Autry would have been the one to introduce the song instead of his fellow cowboy crooner Roy Rogers.

finished song, although Porter used or adapted many of Fletcher's distinctive expressions, like "cayuse" and "I can't stand hobbles, I can't stand fences." Porter invented the verses about Wildcat Kelly from scratch, and rejected the poet's tune in favor of his own. However, the original manuscript of the song stated clearly, "Lyrics based on [a] poem by Bob Fletcher."

Adios, Argentina! was canceled in 1935 when Darryl F. Zanuck took over the newly consolidated 20th Century Fox studio; Lou Brock was apparently swept out along with the script, and the score was put into storage by Porter's music publishing firm, Harms Inc.

"Don't Fence Me In" remained in limbo until 1944, when Warner Bros. was looking for a western song for Roy Rogers to perform in the all-star musical *Hollywood Canteen*. Herman Starr of Harms suggested "Don't Fence Me In," which seemed like a natural.

The screen's number-one western box-office star, Roy Rogers, was borrowed from Republic Pictures for a weekly fee of $2,000 to appear in the film, which boasted a formidable array of talent, mostly from the Warners contract roster, including real-life Canteen co-founders Bette Davis and John Garfield. Separate memos were drafted to borrow Roy's famous horse Trigger and the singing group the Sons of the Pioneers. Roy was just one of many guest stars (from Jack Benny to Jimmy Dorsey) who appeared as themselves in the film, entertaining the troops at Hollywood's famous G.I. nightclub. The song is reprised in the film by the most popular vocal group of the 1940s, The Andrews Sisters.

Everyone was pleased, until one day in July of 1944, shortly after the sequence was completed, when publisher Starr made an unhappy discovery in his files: movie rights to the song still belonged to 20th Century Fox.

Starr immediately communicated with Jack L. Warner and laid his cards on the table: the studio had just filmed a song number that might have to be scrubbed! Starr then approached Fox's Darryl F. Zanuck, as casually as possible, to clear up the snafu. Warner was understandably concerned, as money had been spent and Roy Rogers and company had returned to Republic.

Starr then sent Warner a telegram to say that he had talked to Zanuck, who remembered that there was an unused Porter score in the Fox library; he even recalled that it wasn't very good, except for one song. The mogul then reassured Starr that he would cooperate and make a reasonable deal for the rights.

In the terse style of telegrams, Starr continued, "He was very nice about whole matter, especially after I told him *Wilson* [Zanuck's pet project] was one of the greatest pictures ever made and believe would hit jackpot. If I

The Year's TOP Song Hit...
The Screen's TOP Entertainer...
The Season's TOP Music and Action Hit!

ROY
ROGERS
KING OF THE COWBOYS
TRIGGER
THE SMARTEST HORSE IN THE MOVIES
in

"Don't Fence Me In"

featuring
GEORGE "GABBY" HAYES
and DALE EVANS
with ROBERT LIVINGSTON · MORONI OLSEN
MARC LAWRENCE · LUCILLE GLEASON
BOB NOLAN *and* THE SONS OF THE PIONEERS
A REPUBLIC PICTURE

THEATRE

lied God forgive me." Warners executives presumably breathed a collective sigh of relief, and prepared the movie for a December 1944 release.

There was one more snag for Harms, however: the company dropped Fletcher's name from the song credits when it was officially published. Porter was hospitalized and didn't learn about the gaffe right away. Although later there were charges of plagiarism over "Don't Fence

Me In"—as there often are with popular tunes—the poet who originated this song never had any dispute with Porter.

The song's continuing popularity, through constant radio play, inspired
Republic Pictures to build an entire Roy Rogers musical around it. The
studio paid $4,000 for rights to use the title and the song as well. *Don't
Fence Me In* went into production on July 12, 1945, almost exactly a year
after Roy first performed the song for Warner Bros. It took less than a month

to film, and was playing in theaters by October 10. The final cost for the western musical was $213,956, fairly generous by Republic standards.

Rogers fans agree that this is one of his most entertaining vehicles. Dale Evans plays a reporter who comes west in search of the fabled outlaw Wildcat Kelly (the character named in the verse of Cole Porter's song), and George "Gabby" Hayes turns out to be a crucial link to that mystery. Advertisements for the movie tagged it to "The year's biggest song hit."

Yet, ironically, it wasn't the King of the Cowboys whose rendition led the hit parade. (He didn't even record it until 1947.) Kate Smith introduced the song on her popular radio show on October 8, 1944, several months before the release of *Hollywood Canteen*. She didn't record it for another year, and enjoyed only fleeting success with that disc, which made the charts for just two weeks. Bandleaders Sammy Kaye and Horace Heidt also had modestly successful 78s, but it was the Decca record by Bing Crosby and The Andrews Sisters that cemented the song's enormous popularity: it was on the Hit Parade for twenty-one weeks, and spent eight of those weeks in the number-one position, according to music industry chronicler Joel Whitburn. (Roy Rogers's cowboy rival, Gene Autry, also recorded the song, and performed it on his *Melody Ranch* radio show.)

Roy was seen singing "Don't Fence Me In" for a third time onscreen in the 1946 biopic *Night and Day*, when Cary Grant, playing Cole Porter, watches a print of *Hollywood Canteen*. The song got another lease on life later on, in the 20th Century Fox submarine drama *Hell and High Water* (1954), where special lyrics took the place of Porter's.

In 2004, Kevin Kline portrayed Porter in a revisionist screen biography, *De-Lovely*, which celebrated the composer's life and work. "Don't Fence Me In" was supposed to be among the songs performed, but it didn't survive the final cut. Given some of the renditions that were included, this may have been the nicest gift the filmmakers could have bestowed on Porter's ageless cowboy anthem.

ART CORNER

Illustrators of the early twentieth century developed a wide range of techniques intended specifically for newspaper and magazine reproduction. The term "line art," still used today, doesn't begin to describe what these masters accomplished with pen and ink. Here are some choice examples, taken from newspaper and trade-magazine advertisements.

Bear in mind that, unlike artists who displayed their canvases, these professionals were keenly aware that their work was being reproduced in newspapers and magazines. All but the Barrymore portrait are reproduced here from original artwork salvaged from a Los Angeles newspaper morgue.

Three of these pieces are signed by Chris Marie Meeker, a prolific illustrator of the period whose work turned up in humor magazines and *Photoplay*, among others. The Horton portrait is by Henry (Hy) Goode, who was lauded by his newsroom colleague Joe Grant in an earlier issue of *Movie Crazy*. The Shearer profile portrait is initialed "JC." If anyone knows the name of this artist, we'd love to hear from you.

Norma Shearer
in profile

Norma Shearer again,
as she appeared in A
Free Soul

John Barrymore
on the cover
of a Universal
Weekly
promoting
Counselor at
Law

Gloria
Swanson

Edward Everett Horton in a
promotional portrait for a Los
Angeles stage production

George O'Brien as
seen in The Seas
Beneath

Chapter 6
SCREENINGS

Screenings:
I LIKE IT THAT WAY

The year is 2004, and I am taking Gloria Stuart to Universal Studios to see a film she made there seventy years ago. Talk about a time warp!

I cherish my friendship with Gloria, who is much too sharp, too aware, too politically active to be bothered with living in the past. But when Universal archivist Bob O'Neil told me he had struck a new 35mm print of the 1934 movie *I Like It That Way*, I couldn't resist asking its leading lady if she'd want to watch it. She practically shrieked, "That's the worst musical ever made!" but admitted that she'd enjoy seeing it again. It has never been on television, and apparently was never released on 16mm. Arriving at Universal's main gate, Gloria, my wife, and I had to show our photo IDs, as one does all over Hollywood in the wake of 9/11. The security stop made Gloria think of a time when she and her husband, screenwriter Arthur Sheekman, were traveling to Mexico with their good friend Groucho Marx. When a border guard asked Groucho his occupation, he immediately replied, "Spy." Needless to say, the entire party was routed from its automobile and searched.

Some films require extensive restoration, but the nitrate negative of *I Like It That Way* has survived in great shape. The print we watched was excellent, which is more than one can say for the film itself. As Gloria remarked, Universal dealt in chintz.

Roger Pryor stars in this breezy, grade-B musical about a super-salesman who finally meets his Waterloo. Having worked his charm on female customers galore, he meets absolute resistance from Gloria, whom he chances to meet on the stairway of her apartment building. She isn't buying what Pryor is selling: himself.

Pryor lives at home with his doting mother (Lucile Gleason) and kid sister (Marian Marsh), and orders sis to stay away from the brassy blonde across the way (Shirley Grey). He doesn't mind hanging around with her—this being a pre-Code movie, he even spends the night—but he doesn't want his sister picking up bad habits.

Gloria is different: aloof and unresponsive to his approaches. She finally agrees to go out on a date with Pryor, and even gets to like him, but when he makes a move on her she puts him off, asking if he wouldn't rather wait until she wanted to be kissed. This concept has never occurred to him before; he falls head over heels and renounces his womanizing ways. Little does he dream that Gloria, whom he now places on a pedestal, is the star of the sexy show at The Plantation Club, a nightclub and gambling joint where Grey works. The chorines' job is to entice suckers to part with their money; that's why they refer to themselves as "the chiselers."

Naturally, Pryor's sister persuades Grey to let her try out for a job at the club. Gloria befriends Marian that night and even protects her from the advances of club owner Noel Madison. But when Marian reveals Gloria's dreaded secret to her brother, he is crestfallen; he thinks she's been playing him for a chump. Of course, everything is sorted out for the inevitable happy ending.

The score for *I Like It That Way* was written by "Conrad, Mitchell, and Gottler," which is to say Con Conrad, Sidney Mitchell, and Archie Gottler, a trio of Tin Pan Alleyites who enjoyed success in the early talkie era. In 1933 they devised a series of eight rhyming-dialogue comedy shorts for Columbia Pictures, sharing writing and directing credit for *Um-Pa*. (Gottler directed seven of these Musical Novelties, including *Woman Haters*, which helped to launch the career of The Three Stooges at Columbia. There were no encores for the rhyming dialogue idea, however.) Con Conrad fared much better with another 1934 ditty, "The Continental," which won an Academy Award when it was showcased in *The Gay Divorcee*. Mitchell spent most of the 1930s at Fox, dishing up songs for Shirley Temple, Alice Faye, and other musical stars.

Musicologist Peter Mintun writes, "Archie Gottler was an old timer by 1933, having written some successful songs in the 'teens such as 'America I Love You,' 'I Hate to Lose You,' and the ever popular 'Would You Rather Be a Colonel with an Eagle on Your Shoulder, or a Private with a Chicken on Your Knee?' But his association with Sidney Mitchell and Con Conrad was an industrious period of his life. They wrote 'Big City Blues,' 'Breakaway,' 'Hittin' the Ceiling,' 'Doing the Boom Boom,' and dozens more. He later collaborated with George Meyer, veteran composer of 'For Me an' My Gal' and 'Where Did Robinson Crusoe Go with Friday on Saturday Night?'

"Con Conrad had been a vaudevillian around the teens, then became a manager and songwriter. He was the force behind the Russ Columbo phenomenon, and also wrote several of the biggest Columbo hits, including several standards."

Ron Hutchinson, who presides over The Vitaphone Project, adds, "Gottler wrote many tunes for Broadway revues, including *Padlocks of 1926*. I have a Columbia recording which shows it to be very much in line with the Musical Novelties. He also starred in the lost Vitaphone short *Archie Gottler, His Songs Are Sung in a Million Homes* (1928) and appeared as himself in another Vitaphone short, *Larry Ceballos's Crystal Cave Revue* (1928)."

The songwriting team of Conrad, Mitchell, and Gottler.

In *I Like It That Way*, Shirley Grey sings the movie's first (and best) song, "I've Got Two Little Arms," in her apartment. The remaining songs, "I Like It That Way" and "Good Old Days," are ostensibly sung by Gloria Stuart in the nightclub; she begins the first song with feathered fans, á la Sally Rand, although she is fully clothed. Her lip-synching is quite good, but the idea of casting her as a nightclub star when she could neither sing nor dance is one of those wonderful Hollywood absurdities.

The biggest production number revolves around "Good Old Days." It begins with Gloria and the chorus girls wearing, and singing about, bathing attire of their grandmother's era. Then we see them in modern swimsuits. And then, so help me, Gloria and company give us a glimpse of the future—at a nudist colony, where strategically placed shrubbery hides their personal assets. (I'd always wondered why Gloria had bare shoulders in ads and sheet music for the film; now I know.)

The film opens with the NRA symbol, heralding Hollywood's support of FDR's short-lived plan to help America out of the Depression. Then we see the Universal biplane and the main credits. The first thing Gloria remarked upon was the name of Lucille Gleason in the cast list, because "she is one of the founders of the Screen Actors Guild." People with just one scene in the film, like young Mickey Rooney and the ever-popular Mae Busch, get billing, in fact.

At the outset of her first musical number Gloria declared, "I may throw up." So how exactly did she find herself in such a film?

"I was under contract. I said, 'I don't sing and I don't dance,' and they said, 'Well, you just stand in front of the chorus and we'll take care of the rest of it.' I remember standing [there] and saying, 'I don't want to do this, I'm no good at this.' I'm standing there like a broomstick; they gave me no gestures, they didn't cover me at all. It's embarrassing."

She wasn't any too crazy about her wardrobe, either. "Polka dots! They couldn't have made me look worse."

Lucile Webster Gleason confers with some notable colleagues about the nascent Screen Actors Guild in 1934: James Dunn, Ann Harding, Boris Karloff, and James Cagney.

The young actress had loftier ambitions. Onslow Stevens, who appears briefly in *I Like It That Way*, had costarred with her in a production of Chekhov's *The Seagull* at the Pasadena Playhouse. Now she was caught in the Hollywood studio machine, turning out one potboiler after another. In 1933, her second year in movies, she appeared in nine feature films. One day Universal's production chief Junior Laemmle—they really called him Junior, she says—told her he was going to turn her into a female Tarzan, which prompted a violent reaction.

Of the would-be mogul, she says, "He was a nice little man with no talent; he just had his father behind him. He was not a moviemaker, that's all."

But if acting onscreen didn't give her the satisfaction she craved, political activism did.

"It was Melvyn Douglas who said to me, one night here at Universal about nine o'clock—when we'd been working since dawn—'We're forming a union; would you like to join?' I said 'What's that?' He said 'What's what?' I said 'What's a union?' We were working ten, twelve, fourteen hours a day and working Saturday into Sunday. For women, we had to be in makeup by six o'clock in the morning, [and] we'd get home by nine o'clock or ten o'clock at night. It was murder."

Gloria became a founding member of the Screen Actors Guild, and served on its board for many years.

As for her career, she was fortunate enough to appear in a handful of memorable films, including John Ford's *Airmail* and *The Prisoner of Shark Island*; James Whale's *The Old Dark House* and *The Invisible Man*; and two Shirley Temple vehicles that have kept her in public view for decades, *Poor Little Rich Girl* and *Rebecca of Sunnybrook Farm*. Even some of her lesser films are fun to watch.

I Like It That Way is not an undiscovered classic, sorry to say. But it was enjoyable to see it in the company of its leading lady, who concludes, "It's the worst musical I've ever seen. Maybe there were worse, but I've never seen them."

STILL LIFE: Hal Roach

Hal Roach had an immeasurable impact on the world of movie comedy (and his films continue to delight audiences in the twenty-first century). On December 7, 1933, five hundred guests gathered at his Culver City studio to celebrate the producer's twentieth year in Hollywood, including four of his top stars, Thelma Todd, Oliver Hardy, Patsy Kelly, and Stan Laurel.

This photo shows Roach returning to the role of director for his studio's first all-talking short, *Hurdy Gurdy*, in 1929. Behind the camera, partially hidden, is George Stevens; at right is Bones Vreeland, who was still on the studio payroll in 1963! Stevens later told me that he got his first chance to direct when his boss got restless while directing a two-reeler and turned the reins over to him. Roach, in turn, enjoyed telling the story about listening to a playback of his first talkie and getting annoyed at someone in the room saying, "That's good" at the end of every take. His anger mounted until someone finally spoke up and explained, "Mr. Roach, that's you." He didn't realize he was hearing his own voice on the movie soundtrack!

Incidentally, the title of the first talkie in each Roach comedy series made reference to sound: *Hurdy Gurdy* (An All Star Comedy), *Unaccustomed As We Are* (Laurel and Hardy), *Small Talk* (Our Gang), and *The Big Squawk* (Charley Chase).

Screenings:
JOHNNY DOUGHBOY

Consider these credentials, impressive for any film: songs by Sammy Cahn and Jule Styne; a story by Frederick Kohner (who later wrote *Gidget*, about his real-life daughter); cinematography by John Alton (who won an Oscar for photographing *An American in Paris*); musical direction by Walter Scharf (who earned an Academy Award nomination for his work on *Johnny Doughboy*); choreography by Nick Castle (renowned for the elaborate routines he devised for The Nicholas Brothers at Fox); and teenaged Jane Withers in a dual role. That's quite a lineup, especially for a lowly B movie produced by Republic Pictures.

Yet my longtime interest in *Johnny Doughboy* (1942) was mainly fueled by my interest in seeing Our Gang's Spanky McFarland and Alfalfa Switzer reunited onscreen, alongside such other juvenile stars as Bobby Breen, Robert Coogan (Jackie's brother, who starred as the adorable Sooky in 1931, and later played the oafish Humphrey in a pair of Joe Palooka films), Cora Sue Collins, Baby Sandy (all of four years old!), and the diminutive instrumental duo Butch and Buddy.

Thanks to a bootleg tape (ssshhhhh!) I finally had the chance to view this elusive title. While it isn't the first movie to examine the phenomenon of child stars who reach that "awkward age" (that distinction probably belongs to 1941's *Glamour Boy*, starring Jackie Cooper), it was still a novel idea, delving into subject matter that's still compelling today, judging from the endless supply of such fodder in current magazines and TV shows. Lawrence Kimble's script doesn't take full advantage of the idea, but *Johnny Doughboy* is still an interesting artifact.

The movie opens in Hollywood, "the end of the rainbow, where millions come—a few to find a pot of gold, others to find a cauldron

Tots no more: Bobby Breen, Carl "Alfalfa" Switzer, Robert Coogan, and Spanky McFarland in Johnny Doughboy (1942).

of disillusionment." Ann Winters (Jane Withers) is still a movie star at age sixteen, but is fed up with little-girl roles and the regimen of her life, which is dominated by her agent (William Demarest) and secretary (Ruth Donnelly). Rather than have to make a film called *Ann of Honeysuckle Farm*, she runs off, leaving her exasperated agent holding the bag. But when Penelope Ryan (also Jane Withers), who's won an Ann Winters lookalike contest, shows up, the agent asks her to step into Ann's shoes, for just a little while. She meets the members of the 20-Minus Club, a group of former child stars who plan to stage a Junior Victory Caravan to entertain soldiers, and they beseech her to join their troupe. Meanwhile, Ann is staying at the lakeside cabin of playwright Henry Wilcoxon, who has befriended her. Penelope brings the 20-Minus kids up to the lake, hoping to convince Ann to help the young entertainers . . . but what clinches the deal is Ann encountering her old boyfriend, Johnny Kelly. He wins her over, rekindles their friendship, and they appear together in a musical finale at a nearby Army base. (The number "Johnny Doughboy Found a Rose in Ireland" features an unbilled Arthur Q. Bryan doing a creditable brogue as the mayor of a village in Old Erin.)

Johnny Doughboy is a pleasant if unremarkable piece of fluff. Even in 1942, the trade publication *Film Bulletin* referred to it as "formula stuff." Jane is engaging, as always, and so is newcomer Patrick Brook, her personable leading man. But the most remarkable scene features a quartet consisting of Spanky, Alfalfa, Bobby Breen, and Bobby Coogan singing a Cahn-Styne song called "All Done, All Through" about being washed up! (". . . and we were only startin'.") Then Alfalfa steps forward to warble the ballad "All My Life" in his familiar, screechy style. The boys sitting behind him make faces during this agonizing vocal, and pretend to strangle him at the end. Alfalfa doesn't utter a word of dialogue, nor does Spanky, until we see him again later on.

Spanky's last Our Gang short, *Unexpected Riches*, was released to theaters just a month before *Johnny Doughboy*, so it's unlikely audiences would have considered him over-the-hill just yet. Alfalfa had bowed out of Our Gang two years earlier (his last short, *Kiddie Cure*, was released on November 23, 1940), but he was still in the public eye. *Johnny Doughboy* was his sixth feature film in 1942, including *There's One Born Every Minute*, which introduced the world to Elizabeth Taylor, and *Henry and Dizzy*, starring Jimmy Lydon. He also had a small, unbilled part with Bob Hope in *My Favorite Blonde*. Truth be told, the hard times still lay ahead for both fourteen-year-old Spanky and fifteen-year-old Alfalfa. (Jane worked with Alfalfa before, in her feature *Wild and Woolly*, and nearly worked with Spanky in 1934. She landed a part in the Our Gang short *Hi'-Neighbor!*, but just as shooting began, she won a plum role opposite Shirley Temple in *Bright Eyes*, left the Gang behind, and never looked back.)

Even the starry-eyed audiences of the 1940s knew that many child stars outgrew their cuteness. One article in the movie's pressbook, designed for planting in local newspapers, declared, "Hollywood is the Only Place Where One Is Passé at Twelve." Indeed, in the scene that introduces us to the 20-Minus Club, Bobby Breen tells Jane that he and the others are frustrated at being told they're too old. "If Hollywood doesn't want us any more, maybe Uncle Sam does," he says, explaining their idea for a Junior Victory Caravan. But it turns out that even the Army wants a little star power. "I guess Uncle Sam is a little like the movies—he doesn't like has-beens either, even young ones." That's why they need Jane to headline the show.

Breen handles most of the dialogue for the 20-Minus kids, but he doesn't have a featured song. The pressbook indicates that he sings "Ave Maria," but if it was recorded, it wasn't used, and Breen doesn't remember doing any singing for the film at all.

Bobby Breen, the celebrated boy soprano, was introduced to America by Eddie Cantor on his popular radio show and went on to star in eight movies, including *Rainbow on the River, Make a Wish,* and *Way Down South*. He had been off-screen for three years when this movie came along. "I never lost my voice," he recently told me in a telephone interview. "But there was a certain period, where they say you're in

between voices. My voice never broke, but they said to rest your voice so you'll have the voice later on, which was true. The voice developed, and while I was in the service, in the Special Services [during World War II], I sang then; we'd have these jeep shows. I still sing." Breen and his wife are still active running a talent-booking agency in Florida. He remembers Jane Withers as "really sweet, very friendly, a very warm kind of a gal."

Cora Sue Collins's career had petered out by the time *Johnny Doughboy* came along, but she appeared in almost forty films during the 1930s, including *Mad Love, Anna Karenina, Magnificent Obsession*, and *The Adventures of Tom Sawyer*. She was six years old when she was chosen to play Greta Garbo as a baby in *Queen Christina*. Her only recollection of *Johnny Doughboy* when I first mentioned it to her was how dismayed she was at the brevity of her costume. After watching the film again on tape, she found its treatment of aging child stars as interesting as I did.

"It brought back memories of my childhood and evoked the feelings that I'd had as a child growing up in the industry. All the time I was growing up, I kept thinking that the top rung was very slippery, and did I ever even want to be on the top rung . . . did I really want to be a Shirley or a Jane? There's very little way to prepare them for the adulation of stardom; I'm not saying I was a huge star, but there's just no way to prepare kids for that.

"But now I realize how blessed I was to know the incredible people in our industry that I knew as a child. In retrospect, I had this wonderful childhood growing up with the most famous people on the big screen. Jane is still one of my dearest friends, and what a wonderful friend to have."

Oddly enough, Patrick Brook, the young musical performer who was touted as a new discovery when he was cast opposite Jane, disappeared from movies. Where are they now, indeed.

The *Johnny Doughboy* pressbook includes an article, "Jane Withers Is Only Child Star to Grow Up on Screen," which states, "For the past seven years, from the time she was eight, she has been constantly in the public eye; there have been no periods taken out while she went through the 'awkward stage.' She has made thirty-two starring pictures in rapid succession."

In *Johnny Doughboy*, Jane Withers was able to share screen time with some of her peers who weren't quite so lucky.

[*Thanks to Cora Sue Collins, Bobby Breen, Marvin Eisenman, Richard W. Bann, and Jack Mathis*]

Conversations:
JANE WITHERS

Jane Withers is a remarkable woman who has never lost her zest for life, or her boundless enthusiasm for show business. What's more, she remembers her childhood experiences with amazing clarity. One interview could never do justice to Jane's long and colorful life; besides, she is busy dictating not one but six books on the subject. The living personification of the power of positive thinking, Jane was not discouraged when she left 20th Century Fox after eight years to go to work for B-movie factory Republic Pictures. She'd met Republic's chieftain Herbert J. Yates when she was fourteen, and decided she wanted to work with Gene Autry. Somehow she managed to get Yates and Fox's Joseph M. Schenck together to arrange a loan-out for the Republic cowboy star to make *Shooting High* (1940). Two years later, Jane moved to Republic—and charmed Yates into hiring friends and colleagues from Fox. This conversation centers on *Johnny Doughboy*, but when talking to Jane Withers, one topic naturally leads to another . . .

WITHERS: The kids that were in it [*Johnny Doughboy*], that was my idea. The only thing that hurt me, I said, "I don't ever want to refer to them as has-beens."
MALTIN: That's what I was curious about, because they do.
WITHERS: I'd forgotten that; I haven't seen it in fifty years. I know I fought like a tiger about that. I was so proud to have those kids; we had a big party on the set when they came in and did their stint. We had a wonderful luncheon catered that day and then we had a big cake and ice cream. It was just a glorious array of those kids. I didn't really know them, but I was so proud that we were all working together. I thought it was so neat. Patrick Doyle replaced somebody else that started out in

Jane and "Uncle Henry" Wilcoxon in Keep Smiling (1938).

Jane lunches with starlet Rita Cansino, who appeared with her in Paddy O'Day (1935), before changing her name to Rita Hayworth.

the movie and just couldn't cut the mustard; oh, I felt so badly about that. That had never happened before in anything I'd ever made.

MALTIN: The first scene of the film, you're swimming in a pool . . .

WITHERS: Yes, that's the old Doheny estate, and that's when I first met the Doheny family. We became very good friends because of that. I had to go inside a couple of times, because it was very cold when we shot that. They insisted I come in and get warm, and they had a painting there that I just loved. It was a little dog, of course; I'm such a sucker for animals, especially dogs. This little dog was very morose, with his body language. It said "Lost Playmate," and there was an empty cradle. I want to tell you, that picture just tore me apart. About ten years later, when they passed away, I couldn't believe it, they left me that painting. And that picture has been a very important part of my life and all of my children's.

MALTIN: How did you get to work with such top-flight talent at a studio like Republic?

WITHERS: Nick Castle always worked with me, so when I went to Republic, I said, "I just wouldn't think of doing anything without Nick Castle." And Mr. Yates was very kind to me. And they were so proud; they had a big party for me, "Jane Comes to Republic." I thought the songs that Jule and Sammy wrote for me were darling. I tried to use the people that I loved, any time I could get them. Henry Wilcoxon—I used to call him Uncle Henry—we did three films together. Oh, I adored him, what a lovely man he was.

MALTIN: What was it like playing twins?

WITHERS: I was so excited, I wondered, How in the world are we gonna do this? Mama said they broke the mold when they made me [*laughs*]. Of course, everything had to be timed, your marks and they way you looked at yourself.

MALTIN: You were a pretty savvy kid.

WITHERS: You know something I didn't find out until right before I left Fox? I was the only kid star that was ever called in to work with the writers. I did that because I would say, "You, know, I'm eight years old and you are an adult and we don't talk this way, so if you don't mind, I have changed this dialogue. Otherwise, the kids will laugh, and it won't be real to them."

MALTIN: Did you go to see Roy Rogers and Gene Autry or the other cowboy stars while you were working at the studio?

WITHERS: All the time! Oh good gravy yes, all the time. And of course, later, Roy and I were very close friends; he wasn't married to Dale then. He had [his first son] Dusty, and then his wife died, and he would come to our house a lot in the beginning, he was so upset. He felt comfortable with my dad and my mom and me. And then finally he called one day and said, "I've met a lady that I really like very much; I'm most anxious for you folks to meet her." Of course when it was Dale, I just fell in love with her, and I thought she was fabulous. We were neighbors for fifteen years. I bought Lucille Ball and Desi Arnaz's ranch, and Roy and Dale were just at the end of the block. That was in Chatsworth. Dan Dailey was out there, and Guy Mitchell. It was horse country, you know; we grew oranges for Sunkist Oranges and we had fifteen acres on Devonshire.

MALTIN: But you got to see them in their heyday at Republic, too.

Jane walks a couple of four-legged costars from her movie Pepper (1936).

WITHERS: Oh yes, I'd visit the sets all the time. Whoever was working there: I'd see John Carroll a lot, because he was in everything, and Vera Hruba Ralston. I loved her. You know, I'm such a fan, and they had all these movie magazines that wanted to do articles on me, and I said, "I've got an idea, maybe they would go for it." I said, "There are ten or twelve stars that I absolutely worship, and I've never met them. Could I write an article, interviewing my favorite stars, one a month for twelve months?" They said, "That's a great idea." I said, "I'll have to work it out with my teacher and get the time to do it . . . but there's a stipulation. I need a player piano for our Sunday school, and I need ten to twelve scholarships for kids that want to study music and dance." So I did ten or twelve interviews—Judy Garland, Mickey Rooney, Clark Gable. Of course I knew and adored Alice Faye, Don Ameche, Tyrone Power, and Cesar Romero; I wouldn't do anything filmwise unless I interviewed them. Oh, and Deanna Durbin. I was dying to meet Deanna Durbin! We had lunch together at Universal and I said, "You know, I haven't been here since I did extra work in *The Good Fairy*." She said "You did what?" I said "Yes, I did extra work." You can actually see me in the opening scene, the very first shot in the movie. In fact, Rock Hudson told me one night, "I've got a $1,000 bet on that that's you in *The Good Fairy*." I said, "How did you know?" He said, "Are you kidding? There's only one you!"

I think they cut the scene with me sitting up in the window when Margaret Sullavan leaves, but I was so proud to have been selected as one of the kids. I got in a fight; a little girl tried to push me out the window, because her mother got so mad that I was chosen instead of her. So she sent the little girl upstairs to go get in the window before I got there. I said, "I'm terribly sorry, the director told me to come and sit where you're sitting." She said "Oh, no, this is the one chance I've got to get a closeup, my mother said, and you're not going to sit here, I am." And we got into this terrible argument; she tried to literally push me out the window, and I was hanging there for dear life. Finally the assistant director said, "What's going on up there?" So they put her off the set, and I felt just terrible.

Jane as Vasthi Snythe in Giant (1956).

Now, time passed, and I had my own pictures, and they were looking for a little girl to be my stand-in. So they called in about sixty little girls and she was in the line. I wanted to help pick out my stand-in, so when we got to her, her eyes were down; she never looked at me, and I said, "Oh, we've met before; we had a nice time together on a film called *The Good Fairy*. We didn't really get to know each other, but maybe if she's my stand-in, we'll have that chance." And she had dark hair and wore the same size, and she was my stand-in for five years. Funny, but a true story, and we became very close friends; she only passed about five years ago and I knew her up till then.

MALTIN: You have such a good memory!

WITHERS: We've started talking about this, and I get this instant memory of all the different things that just come so quickly into my mind. So the only thing I can do, because I'm afraid I might not think of it again for another ten or twenty or forty years, I keep two tape recorders right beside me, wherever I go, so when these thoughts come I can talk about it, and think about it later on and write it better.

MALTIN: You've saved so many things from your career.

WITHERS: Oh, I always did. I had a Brownie camera. I've taken pictures my entire life, and so has my mother. When I was going to sign my contract for *Giant*, I was reading all the fine print and I said, "Uh-oh, I can't sign this contract." They said, "Why on earth not?" I said, "Well, it says in here that you can't take any photographs or movies. I have taken both 16mm movies and snapshots on every film I've ever made, even when I did extra work. It would break my heart, especially on this movie—I've waited my whole life to work with George Stevens—not to be able to take pictures." And he said, "I don't know what Mr. Stevens is going to do. Let me talk to him." So he came back and he was smiling. He said, "There's no problem at all. George has it all worked out." He had a gold card made for me and it said, "Jane Withers, Third Unit, *Giant*." And it says "Okay" down in the corner, signed George Stevens. Isn't that fantastic?

STILL LIFE

No one was more enterprising than producer Louis Lewyn, who originated the *Screen Snapshots* series in the silent era and continued making Hollywood-centric shorts for the rest of his career. His threadbare *The Voice of Hollywood* series of the 1930s caught the brass ring while covering the premiere of Charlie Chaplin's *City Lights* at the brand new Los Angeles Theater.

Yes, that's Albert Einstein in the company of the comedy genius, with child actor Leon Janney serving as host for *The Voice of Hollywood*'s mythical radio station STAR. Lewyn sent a copy of the short to Carl Laemmle at Universal, prompting this polite response—but no offer to distribute or take over the series.

Screenings:
REPUBLIC PICTURES
PRESENTS: MEET THE STARS

Imagine discovering, in the year 2005, unseen footage of Orson Welles taken at the time of *Citizen Kane* . . . unheralded appearances by John Wayne, Bette Davis, Anna May Wong, Abbott and Costello, and Rita Hayworth . . . or a rare onscreen encounter between cowboy stars Roy Rogers and Gene Autry. That's exactly what lies in store for the lucky film buff who reviews the contents of a little-seen Republic Pictures short-subject series called *Meet the Stars* made in 1941. *Meet the Stars* was produced, directed, and hosted by Harriet Parsons, daughter of the famed (and feared) Hearst newspaper columnist Louella Parsons.

Secure in its niche as a B movie factory, Republic had shown no interest in shorts (except for its weekly serial chapters) during its first years of operation, but the studio found this series—offering star quality at a bargain price—irresistible.

A Republic sales brochure called it "Box-office bait for millions of fans!" and went on to explain, "The popularity of fan magazines and the wide circulation they enjoy among motion picture fans prove the unlimited interest of a tremendous public in 'inside' stuff about Hollywood stars. Off-stage photographs and interviews are a potent factor in the large circulation of such magazines. It is this mass audience to which the *Meet the Stars* subjects have a tremendous appeal. Studded with star names of great box office magnitude, these Harriet Parsons shorts show intimate closeups of what Hollywood's greats do off-stage. They are choice entertainment for millions of fans, and offer exhibitors box office draw on which they can cash in."

Veteran and novice: Raoul Walsh and Orson Welles in 1941.

This, of course, was not a new idea. Fan magazines were created in the teens to satisfy the public's growing appetite for information about their favorite stars, and to provide a peek behind the scenes of moviemaking. It didn't take long for enterprising producers to realize that they could also provide "fan magazines" on film. The first such short subjects appeared in the teens, and others followed in the 1920s.

Most of those silent shorts were produced by entrepreneurs who realized that actors didn't mind getting free publicity by making casual appearances that didn't take long to shoot. They might be seen strolling on the studio grounds or playing with a dog in their backyard; the content was simple and straightforward. Even *Photoplay*, the premier fan journal, associated itself with a short-lived series of Hollywood featurettes in the silent era.

One such series launched an entire company. Jack Cohn was unhappy working for Carl Laemmle at Universal Pictures, and in 1917 conceived the idea for *Screen Snapshots*. It was this concept that inspired Cohn, his brother Harry, and Edward Small to form CBC Pictures Corporation, which became Columbia Pictures several years later. No wonder Harry Cohn had a soft spot for the series and kept it running until the late 1950s.

The man responsible for producing the CBC shorts was Louis Lewyn, who developed such an affinity for the genre that he never forsook it, piloting *The Voice of Hollywood* for Tiffany in the earliest days of talkies, *Hollywood on Parade* for Paramount, and a variety of behind-the-scenes shorts for MGM, including an elaborate series of Technicolor two-reelers and Jimmie Fidler's *Personality Parade*.

In 1933, the job of producing *Screen Snapshots* was awarded to Harriet Parsons, a Wellesley graduate who had been contributing articles to various fan magazines and living in New York, trying to stay out of the long shadow cast by her famous mother. A bout with pneumonia brought her home to Los Angeles, where much to her surprise, she received an offer from Columbia Pictures to produce the series.

"I couldn't figure out why Harry Cohn, head of Columbia, had offered me the job," she told Tricia Crane many years later in *Hollywood Studio* magazine. "Then I realized why he wanted me. It was a favor to Mother, who could help get him the stars he wanted." Louella frequently appeared onscreen to host the shorts, which were shown in theaters thirteen times a year.

Harriet was wooed away from Columbia by Republic with the promise that, along with a Hollywood short-subject series, she could produce feature films, an offer too tempting for her to refuse. She took along her trusted cameraman, Robert Tobey, and then proceeded to do what every freelance producer had done since the silent days to fill ten minutes of film: she scoured the town for events where Tobey would be allowed to set up his camera and shoot the stars in candid moments. Parsons also introduced each short on camera and read the narration. Some studios jealously guarded their talent while others were more lenient about permitting them to appear in such off-the-cuff footage. In 1991, Parsons wrote to Republic Pictures historian Jack Mathis, "It was originally planned to make one *Meet the Stars* each month. However, the climate was getting rougher and rougher for that type of 'publicity newsreel' with stars appearing for free. The Screen Actors Guild had been formed in '33 and from then on it became more difficult to get cooperation from the major studios. Toward the end of the thirties we had to rely for the most part on freelance actors, and by the time *Meet the Stars* came into being the handwriting was already on the wall."

Indeed, on May 13, 1941, a representative of MGM wrote to Republic complaining that "unauthorized photographs of our artists are being incorporated in short subjects released by you." The artists in question were two of Metro's biggest stars, Mickey Rooney and Judy Garland. Fees had to be paid for the use of songs performed on camera, although a music cue sheet from the sixth entry in the series reveals that money was saved on background music by using public domain songs like "Old Folks at Home" and "Sailor's Hornpipe," and existing library music like the main title cue composed for *She Married a Cop* by Republic's music department chief Cy Feuer. (Yes, the same Cy Feuer who later became a leading Broadway producer.) Other cues were credited to Walter Scharf, who succeeded Feuer, and William Lava.

Although Republic threw in the towel after only eight shorts, those eight contain some precious, even priceless, footage. Since the films are so difficult to obtain, I thought it might be worthwhile to describe their contents in some detail.

Episode one, referred to in a studio handout as "Chinese Garden Festival," focuses on a fundraiser for Chinese war-orphans chaired by Rosalind Russell and hosted by Mary Pickford at her legendary Pickfair estate. Framing this footage is a running gag in which Vera Vague (the screwball alter ego of actress Barbara Jo Allen) asks directions of double-talk comedian Cliff Nazarro, in various guises. These scenes, incidentally, were staged on Ventura Boulevard in Studio City, just outside the Republic studio.

Chinese war-relief charity hosts John Garfield and Anna May Wong.

At Pickfair we meet the event's co-hosts, Anna May Wong and John Garfield (always active in social causes) along with various Chinese dignitaries and personalities. A fashion show around the Pickfair pool, hosted by Dolores del Rio, features such models as Patricia Morison, Dorothy Lamour (wearing an outfit from her film *Disputed Passage*), Katherine Aldridge, Dorris Bowden, and Georgia Carroll. Others participating in the festivities include Jane Withers, Cesar Romero, 20th Century Fox ingénues Mary Healy and Mary Beth Hughes, Mary Martin, Walter Pidgeon, Rose Hobart, "Madame" Maria Ouspenskaya, Rita Hayworth, "old-timers" Beulah Bondi and Charles Coburn, plus Mary Pickford and her husband Buddy Rogers.

When I first saw this short it struck me how little has changed in Hollywood. Toward the end of the film, as Rosalind Russell and Mary Pickford conduct a charity auction, one person in the crowd hoists a camera over his head in order to grab a snapshot, while a reporter shoves his microphone toward the stage in the hope of getting some audio. My colleagues at *Entertainment Tonight* certainly know how A-list charity events can yield great photo opportunities and sound bites today.

The second release in the series, "Baby Stars," is built around a revival of the WAMPAS Baby Stars ceremony in which the Western Association of Motion Picture Advertisers chose the so-called stars of tomorrow from the current feminine crop. The event was staged from 1922 to 1934, then lay dormant until 1941. In this short, eight directors serve as judges: chairman Raoul Walsh, Edmund Goulding, Tay Garnett, Paul Sloane, John Brahm, S. Sylvan Simon, Theodore Reed, and, incongruously, Hollywood newcomer Orson Welles. How this varied group of filmmakers was chosen, we'll never know.

In attendance are eighteen former WAMPAS Baby Stars, including the then still-active Evelyn Brent, Dolores del Rio, Sally Eilers, Anita Louise, Joan Blondell, Fay Wray, Evalyn Knapp, Lois Wilson, and Jacqueline Wells (soon to change her name to Julie Bishop), as well as retirees Janet Gaynor, Claire Windsor, Helen Ferguson, Sally Blane, Sue Carol (by now an agent for, among others, her husband Alan Ladd), Carmelita Geraghty (married to MGM writer-producer Carey Wilson), Eleanor Boardman, Jobyna Ralston, and June Collyer. It's interesting to see some of these women ten to fifteen years after their heyday, most of them looking quite good. There's also a cameo by celebrated Hollywood fotog Hymie Fink.

Former WAMPAS Baby Stars Janet Gaynor and Fay Wray.

Finally, we meet the new parade of Baby Stars who alternately sing and perform monologues. They're not bad, but it's easy to see why none of them achieved stardom except one: Joan Leslie, whose personality lights up the screen performing a piece of special material designed to show off her versatility. (Of the others, Sheila Ryan and Marilyn—later Lynn—Merrick did become leading ladies in B movies of the 1940s.)

Episode three has four unrelated stories. "Kid Fashion Show" features young actors and children of the stars modeling clothing for charity, including Ann Todd, Joan Benny (whose mother Mary Livingstone is on hand), and Sandra Burns (with a beaming George Burns and Gracie Allen looking on). Among the spectators are John Wayne's children Michael and Toni, and sibling performers Juanita and Rita Quigley. "Between Scenes at Republic Studio" features a staged bit of tomfoolery with the stars of *Melody Ranch*: Gene Autry, Ann Miller, Jimmy Durante, George "Gabby" Hayes, Billy Benedict, and director Joseph Santley.

"Louella Parsons's Ranch" features the great lady herself (coyly referred to by her daughter as "L.O.P.") playing host to such Hollywood up-and-comers as Brenda Joyce, newlyweds Binnie Barnes and Mike

Frankovich (then a radio sportscaster, later a top producer), William T. Orr, Ilona Massey, and Alan Curtis (who married a short time later) as they rehearse a radio skit written by Edgar Allan Woolf. Orr steals the show doing his excellent visual impressions of George Arliss, John and Lionel Barrymore.

Finally, "*Redbook* Award at Ciro's" documents an award ceremony (not so different from today's trumped-up events) held at the famous restaurant and nightspot to honor *Our Town*. On hand are Greer Garson, K. T. Stevens (whose father, Sam Wood, directed the movie), Republic's own Judy Canova, Robert Stack, Glenn Ford, Edward Ar-

Bette Davis, left, presents the Redbook loving cup to Martha Scott.

nold, Shirley Ross, Walter Pidgeon, Donald Crisp, Gail Patrick, Mary Astor, Ann Rutherford, and Deanna Durbin, among others. The short uncharacteristically acquires live sound for the award presentation itself, in which Bette Davis (the previous year's *Redbook* magazine winner) extols the work of Martha Scott, William Holden, Guy Kibbee, Beulah Bondi, Frank Craven, Fay Bainter, producer Sol Lesser, and director Sam Wood.

Davis goes out of her way to praise Scott, saying "performances like yours make a true and living art of the screen." In spite of this sincere accolade, it's clear from both picture and sound that most of Ciro's patrons are too busy talking and eating to pay attention to the ceremony (another familiar note to one who's attended many staged gatherings in Tinseltown).

The fourth series entry, "Los Angeles *Examiner* Benefit," takes place in a stage setting with a giant front-page backdrop. (We never learn for whom the benefit is being held . . . but then, that's Hollywood, too.) Parsons explains that we're about to see outstanding acts from this year's benefit "especially staged for *Meet the Stars*," meaning with studio lighting but without an audience. The acts include the venerable Duncan Sisters performing their Topsy and Eva routine (blackface and all), the droll Reginald Gardiner doing his impersonation of a lighthouse (!),

The Andrews Sisters singing "Apple Blossom Time," Abbott and Costello in a brief but funny routine, and Arthur Lake and Baby Dumpling (Larry Simms). Master of ceremonies Milton Berle refers to Mary Martin having stopped the show, but we don't get to hear her sing; instead, she trades repartee with Berle, as does Mary Beth Hughes. It's exciting to see Abbott and Costello in action so early in their Hollywood career and the Duncans so late in theirs. Berle is in his element.

"Hollywood Visits the Navy," number five in the series, opens with that wry comic actor Charles Butterworth being invited to visit the naval air base at Long Beach, California. This prompts him to show off some of his wacky inventions, including a combination gasmask and stereopticon. The balance of the film is essentially a recruiting short, interspersed with Hollywood glamour, as when B-movie actress Anne Nagel is commissioned an honorary flight instructor—by her husband, an ensign. Others on hand include Henry Fonda, George Murphy, Richard Barthelmess, George O'Brien, Roger Pryor, and two ladies who easily capture the naval aviators' attention: Carmen Miranda and Carole Landis.

Episode six begins with "An Intimate Tour of Several Stars' Homes." First we visit fifteen-year-old Jane Withers, who opens her home to fellow teen-performers for sports, dancing, and horseplay. Then we move to Cesar Romero's "brand new bachelor home, a two-story, seven-room English farmhouse with a charmingly irregular roof line." Romero works out in his backyard before tackling a game of backgammon with neighbor Patricia Morison. Finally, Rita Hayworth reviews plans for a new house with her contractor and takes home movies of the carpenters at work. *Meet the Stars* purports to show the finished product through a lap dissolve, but somehow I doubt the house is really Hayworth's. (Bear in mind that 1941 marked a watershed in Hayworth's career, with the star-making release of *The Strawberry Blonde*, *Blood and Sand*, and *You'll Never Get Rich*; just one year later she might not have been so easily obtainable for this kind of folderol.)

The balance of the short takes place at Santa Anita Park, where stars gather for the running of the $10,000 San Antonio Handicap, including Randolph Scott; Fay Wray and her husband, screenwriter Robert Riskin; Lucille Ball and Desi Arnaz (pointedly ignoring the camera); Harry Ritz; George Raft; Jack and Tim Holt (the younger actor looking very sporty smoking a pipe); Edmund Lowe; Binnie Barnes; Gail Patrick; Bing Crosby; Gene Autry; Lana Turner on a date with Tony Martin; Annabella; William Demarest (who mugs for the camera); and Joe E. Brown. Two former actresses are shown with their sibling husbands: Judith Barrett and Andrea Leeds married Lindsey and Robert Howard, respectively, the sons of C. S. Howard, fabled owner of Seabiscuit. "Lin"

Bing Crosby enjoys a day at Santa Anita with Judith Barrett.

Howard was also co-owner with Bing Crosby of Bing-Lin Stables. One of America's most beautiful racetracks, Santa Anita was built with Hollywood money, and it's shown to fine advantage in this short.

It isn't until the seventh entry in the series that Republic takes full advantage of the self-promotional possibilities by devoting an entire short to one of its stars. "Meet Roy Rogers" allows us to see how Roy and Trigger tour the country in a special streamlined station wagon and trailer, then introduces us to his wife Arlene and their baby daughter Cheryl. Roy shows off his stock of homing pigeons and participates in some of his favorite sports: archery and bowling. The film winds up at his brand-new store in the San Fernando Valley, the Ranger Post, where friends and colleagues turn out for a grand opening event. Roy sings "Here on the Range with You" and introduces Judy Canova, Bill Elliott, George "Gabby" Hayes (acting less like Gabby and more like himself), Bob Baker, Billy Gilbert, Roscoe Ates, Republic's adolescent songbird Mary Lee (who sings a tune accompanied by Roy on guitar), and "the number one singin' western star" Gene Autry, who asks Roy about setting up a credit account at the store. Everyone is in high spirits, and the crowd packing the premises seems to enjoy every minute of the spontaneous entertainment, making "Meet Roy Rogers" an exceptional short.

The eighth and final chapter of *Meet the Stars* is informally titled "Stars—Past and Present." It opens at a backyard swimming pool, where such young actors as Brenda Joyce, the now-newlyweds Ilona Massey and Alan Curtis, William T. Orr, and Mike Frankovich have fun swimming, diving, and splashing. Parsons notes, "On the sidelines are Jane Russell and Jack Buetel, the two youngsters discovered by Howard Hughes and starred by him in *The Outlaw*." (That film wouldn't show up in theaters for several years, so this would be moviegoers' first and last glimpse of Russell onscreen for quite some time.) Cesar Romero and Patricia Morison are seen lawn bowling with tenpins shaped like penguins, before we move to the House of Westmore, where makeup expert Wally Westmore sets a custom coiffure for Mary Martin and Wanda McKay models some expensive jewelry.

Then the scene shifts to Republic Studios for the naming of a new soundstage in memory of the beloved silent film star Mabel Normand. (Republic was formerly the Mack Sennett lot, though not the facility where he famously worked with Normand in the early silent era.) Mack Sennett is there along with many of his colleagues and contemporaries: Louise Fazenda, Edgar Kennedy, Charley Murray, Chester Conklin, Minta Durfee, Eddie Quillan, Sally Eilers, Charles Ray, Dorothy Davenport, Mae Busch, Wesley Ruggles, Eddie Sutherland, and Eddie Gribbon. (Others who go unidentified include Heinie Conklin, James Finlayson, and Eddie Baker.) Three of Normand's leading men are on hand—Walter McGrail, Jack Mulhall, and Wheeler Oakman—as well as Richard Bennett, Walter Abel, and contemporary Republic stars Gene Autry, Judy Canova, John Wayne, Ann Miller, Mary Lee, George "Gabby" Hayes, and Smiley Burnette. William Farnum reads a tribute to Normand, in his best theatrical manner, as we see clips from her silent films, but the most moving tribute comes from Sennett himself, who is unexpectedly eloquent.

Top: Gene Autry congratulates Roy Rogers at the opening of his Ranger Post store.

Bottom: Mack Sennett waxes eloquent about the love of his life, Mabel Normand.

Even though Republic pulled the rug out from *Meet the Stars* after only eight of the twelve announced episodes, Louella Parsons's longtime rival Hedda Hopper sold a similar series to Paramount called *Hedda Hopper's Hollywood*, which resulted in six shorts for the 1941–'42 season, and RKO introduced its short-lived *Picture People* series in 1941.

For an old-movie buff, this material is catnip, to put it mildly, but the films are frustratingly difficult to locate. Hopper's shorts were later released to the home market on 16mm and then on videocassette, but the *Picture People* one-reelers are hard to find. I've spent several decades looking for a print of the entry in which Carole Lombard directs Alfred Hitchcock as he makes his cameo appearance in *Mr. and Mrs. Smith*.

Harriet Parsons's work, on both the Columbia and Republic shorts, is almost as hard to find. Only a handful of the hundreds of *Screen Snapshots* were ever distributed to the non-theatrical market, and most of those now reside in private collections. (Columbia's original nitrate-negatives reside at the Library of Congress.) Several attempts to use the films as the basis for a television series failed; one was to have been hosted by Milton Berle. Some choice *Snapshots* footage was licensed to Ken Murray in the 1960s for use in his Hollywood home-movies television specials, but it's high time someone made a serious effort to dig out these rare shorts and give them a showcase.

An unexpected couple: John Wayne and Ann Miller.

Meet the Stars has never been available on video and 16mm prints are quite rare. Perhaps, with Paramount now acquiring video rights to the Republic Pictures library, there's a chance they will see the light of day.

Harriet Parsons did not have happy memories of working at Republic. As she recalled in her 1991 letter to Jack Mathis, "You make no mention of the feature I produced at Republic after the series of shorts. It was a comedy about a hillbilly Mata Hari entitled *Joan of Ozark* and costarred Judy Canova and Joe E. Brown. But despite its success I got a royal screwing from Moe Siegel, Republic's head of production. I had written the original story idea for Joan and later came up with another original about kid stars called *Keep Swinging*, which Siegel proceeded to hand to producer-director John Auer while I still had writers working on the screenplay. He didn't even bother to tell me. So that is why I left Republic." *Keep Swinging* eventually became the Jane Withers movie *Johnny Doughboy*.

Republic's loss was RKO's gain. Parsons settled in at RKO Radio Pictures and over the next decade produced such films as *The Enchanted Cottage, I Remember Mama*, and *Clash by Night*. But it seems to me that her producing skills were already evident in *Meet the Stars*, the kind of project that required ingenuity, resourcefulness, and great powers of persuasion. If someone with Parsons's skills (and tenacity) arrived on the scene today, she could probably write her own ticket . . . with or without her mother's name to help open the door.

FAN MAIL

I started writing fan mail when I was a kid . . . and I was thrilled and surprised at the responses I got, often in the form of personal letters. As a result, I've always been intrigued by the concept of fan mail.

It's often been said that pioneering producers and distributors deliberately kept the names of their actors from the public, for fear that popularity would give performers bargaining power for higher salaries. That, of course, is precisely what happened, but once the floodgates were opened, there was no turning back. These postcards from the teens show just how early the concept of fandom established itself, along with the fan magazine.

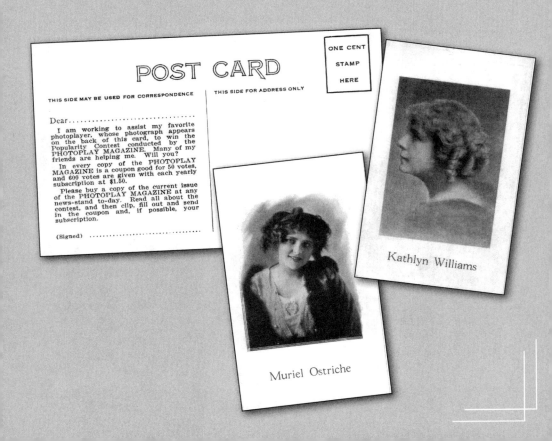

Kathlyn Williams

Muriel Ostriche

Imagine writing to a favorite star and receiving a personally addressed envelope with an autographed photo inside. Well, there's no need to imagine what that was like in the 1920s and 1930s: here are some choice samples. Note how studios even used the opportunity to advertise their stars' current and forthcoming films. Paramount's envelope for Clara Bow and *Wings* is the most elaborate we've ever seen.

By the 1920s, there were businesses that specialized in funneling letters to the stars, and working both sides of the street helping studios and stars process their mail and requests for autographed photos.

Studios and stars continued to grapple with ways to answer the enormous volume of fan mail that came to Hollywood on a regular basis. Studio publicity departments and independent fan-mail services came up with a variety of solutions, as you can see. Warners sent a printed postcard of Ronald Reagan's signed picture with an unsigned message on the back, while Paramount adopted a more formal response for Alan Ladd . . . along with a pitch for war bonds.

The signatures of W. C. Fields, Olivia de Havilland, and Henry Fonda are genuine—or genuine reproductions—on postcards that politely ask fans to defray the expense of mailing autographed photos. These similarly worded cards, from three different production companies, bear the telltale sign of a fan-mail service. Fox's response to a Lynn Bari fan provided a small photo free of charge, a rubber stamp implying that the picture was actually sent by Miss Bari from her Fox address . . . and an opportunity to plug the studio's latest picture on the postage-metered envelope. The one thing no one wanted to do was ignore the fans, who flocked to movies in record numbers during the 1930s and 1940s at the height of the studio system.

WALTER WANGER PRODUCTIONS, INC.
P. O. Box 671
HOLLYWOOD

Dear Friend:

Thank you very much for your recent letter. It certainly is appreciated.

I wish I could send you a photograph free of charge, but I feel sure that you will understand how impossible it is to mail them to the many who write and I hope that you will not mind helping defray the actual expense.

Again, my thanks to you, and best wishes.

Sincerely,

Henry Fonda

5x7" photo	10c
8x10" "	25c
	$1.00

"YOU ONLY LIVE ONCE."

WARNER BROS. PICTURES, INC.
Burbank, Calif.

Dear Friend:

I wish to thank you for your friendly letter.

However, owing to a motion picture industry ruling against sending free photographs, it is necessary to make a slight charge for the picture you requested. Herewith are the prices for photographs. If you will specify the size you desire and enclose the proper amount, I will be most happy to send you one.

Sincerely,

Olivia de Havilland

5x7" photo	10c
8x10" "	25c
11x14" "	$1.00
Foreign — International	
Coupons or Money Order	

PARAMOUNT STUDIOS, HOLLYWOOD

Dear Friend:

Thank you very much for your recent letter. It certainly is appreciated.

I wish I could send you a photograph free of charge, but I feel sure that you will understand how impossible it is to mail them to the many who write and I hope that you will not mind helping defray the actual expense.

Again, my thanks to you, and best wishes.

Sincerely,

W. C. Fields

5x7" photo	10c
8x10" "	25c
11x14" "	$1.00
8x10" hand-tinted	$1.00

Dear Friend:-

I wish to thank you for your friendly letter and to show my appreciation, am enclosing a snapshot for your album or wallet.

Due to the many requests I find it impossible to send larger studio portraits personally autographed, however, you may secure them by sending your remittance in coin or money order. Zone all mail.

10¢ for 5x7
25¢ for 8x10
1.00 for 8x10 Tinted

Lynn Bari
P. O. BOX 900
BEVERLY HILLS, CALIF.

WILSON

...THE MOST IMPORTANT EVENT IN 50 YEARS OF MOTION PICTURE ENTERTAINMENT!

SEC. 562. P. L. & R.

LOS ANGELES CALIF.

U.S. POSTAGE
.01
PB METER
P.B.103404

Chapter 7

STRANGER THAN FICTION

SORRY, WRONG MOVIE

Barbara Stanwyck was fiercely loyal to her friends—but she also knew how to hold a grudge, especially when it involved losing a good part. That's how it seemed to me the one time I met this legendary lady, in 1989.

I had approached her through her friend, costume designer Nolan Miller, to participate in a tribute to her favorite director, Frank Capra, on *Entertainment Tonight*. He told me that she was self-conscious about the way she looked because of all the cortisone she was taking for her ailing back. I said we'd be happy just to have her voice; he thought she would agree to that, and she did.

Miss Stanwyck and I had several lively telephone conversations before our recording date at her home in Trousdale Estates, a modern subdivision of Beverly Hills. We talked a lot about Capra, for whom she expressed "eternal gratitude," especially for helping to shape her career-boosting performance in *Ladies of Leisure*. "Nobody would have taken that much time" with a relative newcomer, she insisted. "I thought every director worked like that; I had a very rude awakening."

She soon learned that the success or failure of every movie hinged on the quality of the script. "I can't write the words, I'm not that talented," she said, but she had no hesitation in telling a writer, "I can't say that, 'cause I don't believe it, and if I don't believe it, I can't make the audience believe it, and that's my job."

"Honesty . . . that's the foundation of everything," she said, and it's that very quality that makes her performances so vivid.

She was also honest—perhaps the better word is blunt—when I happened to mention the name of Bette Davis, who had just made headlines after leaving a film one week into production. Stanwyck scowled, and told me the source of her still-simmering resentment toward Davis after half a century. It had to do with *Dark Victory*, the play she introduced to Hollywood—on radio, before it ever became a film.

Lux Radio Theater debuted in 1934 on CBS. After a false start in New York City, the weekly hour-long anthology program moved to Hollywood in 1936, named Cecil B. DeMille as its host, and quickly became the prime radio showcase for Hollywood stars. Stanwyck appeared on the show several times in 1936 and 1937 (in adaptations of Sinclair Lewis's *Main Street, Stella Dallas,* and *These*

Cecil B. DeMille, left, congratulates Madeleine Carroll and Herbert Marshall on the success of their Lux Radio Theater *adaptation of* Cavalcade *in 1936.*

Three), and after an absence of several months, the producers were eager to have her back. She told them she wanted to appear in a dramatization of George Brewer Jr. and Bertram Bloch's play *Dark Victory*, which had been a success on Broadway for Tallulah Bankhead in 1934. It's not surprising that Stanwyck was attracted to the property; the part of Judith Traherne, a spoiled socialite who learns that she has a brain tumor, fit her like a glove.

Lux had never presented a play that hadn't already been transformed into a successful movie, but Stanwyck was insistent. So, inquiries were made to David O. Selznick, who had optioned the rights to the play, and an arrangement was made to adapt the piece for radio. Melvyn Douglas played opposite Stanwyck in the hour-long production, which aired on April 4, 1938. (Cecil B. DeMille was ill that night, and actor Edward Arnold filled in for him as master of ceremonies.)

According to Stanwyck, director Edmund Goulding heard the show in his car that Tuesday night, and the next morning, urged Warner Bros. production chief Hal Wallis to acquire rights to the property. The next thing she knew, production of *Dark Victory* was announced in the trade papers—with Bette Davis as its star! The film went on to be a great success for all concerned.

But apparently, losing that plum part still bothered Stanwyck after all this time.

Some time later, I decided to check the validity of Stanwyck's story, and trace the history of *Dark Victory* in the Warner Bros. files at USC. (I also made use of Connie Phillips and Arthur Pierce's exceptionally well-researched book *Lux Presents Hollywood*, published by McFarland & Co., 1995.)

Brewer and Bloch registered their play for copyright on February 16, 1932, as *Days Without End*; its title changed by the time it reached Broadway almost two years later. On November 23, 1934, Warners staffer Harriet Hinsdale reviewed the play and registered her comments, but apparently did not recommend a purchase. Instead, just as Stanwyck remembered, David O. Selznick bought the screen rights on February 3, 1936, and agreed to allow the *Lux* production for a fee of $500, if the authors approved. He later transferred his rights to Warner Bros. on June 8, 1938, two months after the *Lux* broadcast.

Having first presented *Dark Victory* to the American radio public in April of 1938, with Stanwyck in the lead, *Lux Radio Theater* hosted a return engagement on January 8, 1940. This time, Bette Davis reprised her screen portrayal of Judith Traherne; filling in for the movie's leading man, George Brent, was Spencer Tracy. Davis and Tracy had worked together just once before, in 1933's *20,000 Years in Sing Sing*, when both performers were still on the cusp of major stardom. Later that decade they posed for pictures together as winners of the 1938 Academy Awards, for their performances in *Jezebel* and *Boys Town*. It's a shame their radio reunion didn't lead to another screen teaming.

Lux wasn't the first radio show to present adaptations of popular movies, but it soon surpassed its early competitor, Louella Parsons's *Hollywood Hotel*, which featured a condensed version of a current movie every week. By the 1940s there were a number of similar shows, all competing for the same limited pool of proven, recognizable properties. Two of them had an edge: *Screen Guild Theater*, which donated its stars' salaries to the Motion Picture Relief Fund, and *Screen Directors Playhouse*, which benefited the pension fund of the *Screen Directors Guild*. The studios granted rights to both shows without charge, receiving a plug for one of their current movies as compensation.

Other shows, like *Academy Award Theater* and *Studio One* (which later became *Ford Theater*) paid cash on the barrelhead to the studios for adaptation rights, usually between $500 and $1,000 per show. Playwrights Brewer and Bloch usually received the same $500 Warner Bros. did for radio productions of *Dark Victory*. The play turned up on such varied anthologies as *The Doctor Fights* (presumably because the leading male role is a sympathetic physician) and *Hollywood Players*. Bette Davis agreed to recreate her now-famous performance as Judith Traherne for *Hollywood Players*, but begged off twice due to illness, and was even-

Spencer Tracy and Bette Davis admire their awards at the 1939 Oscar ceremony.

tually replaced by Maureen O'Hara. Others who took their turns as Traherne include Sylvia Sidney (on *Philip Morris Playhouse*, August 15, 1941), Susan Peters (on *Encore Theater*, July 30, 1949), Madeleine Carroll (on the *United States Steel Hour*, February 15, 1948), Helen Hayes (on *Electric Theater*, December 5, 1948), and Joan Crawford (on *Screen Guild Theater*, March 17, 1949).

Lux pioneered the idea of bringing back stars in the roles they had made famous onscreen, but, like the other shows that followed, often had to "make do" with others who were willing and available to perform on a certain date. In many cases, the newly cast stars brought a fresh new approach to the parts.

Trading off "signature" roles from one medium to another was common practice. Indeed, Barbara Stanwyck inherited one of her showiest parts when she starred in the film version of Lucille Fletcher's famous radio play *Sorry, Wrong Number*, which Agnes Moorehead had famously introduced on the air in a tour de force performance. (Interestingly, the movie couldn't put a dent in the durability of the piece as a radio vehicle; Moorehead continued to play it, to great acclaim, in encore presentations long after the 1948 Paramount movie had come and gone.)

Other actresses made a habit of bringing Tallulah Bankhead vehicles to the screen; Bette Davis did it more than once, most notably with *The Little Foxes*, in 1941. On her early-1950s radio program *The Big Show*, Bankhead often made jokes about her supposed rivalry with Davis, but her "revenge" came on November 16, 1952, when she played the lead in the *United States Steel Hour* production of *All About Eve*.

Ironically, the role of aging actress Margo Channing, arguably Davis's best-known role today, became hers just weeks before shooting was to begin after a herniated disc forced Claudette Colbert to bow out

of the film. Hollywood history is filled with this sort of serendipity, and while it's always interesting to speculate about how a film might have turned out with different actors, I think most film buffs would agree that fate generally worked to the stars' advantage—and ours, as well.

John Loder and Bette Davis prepare for a broadcast of One Day After Another *on* Silver Theater.

Tallulah Bankhead was primarily a creature of the theater, just as Davis was the quintessential movie actress. And it's unlikely that Davis and Stanwyck would have been happy trading roles during their respective heydays. Davis would have been all wrong for *Union Pacific* and *Double Indemnity*, for instance, and couldn't have played a singing stripper as Stanwyck did in *Ball of Fire* and *Lady of Burlesque*. At the same time, it's hard to imagine even Stanwyck doing as good a job as Davis did in *Jezebel* or *Now, Voyager*.

As for *Dark Victory*, the medium of radio granted closure to two key players in the drama's long and checkered history. On a 1951 broadcast of *Screen Directors Playhouse*, Tallulah Bankhead returned to the part she created on stage seventeen years earlier.

And on March 6, 1952, *Hollywood Sound Stage* presented the now-familiar tearjerker one more time on network radio. Its star was Barbara Stanwyck.

[*Thanks to Jeanine Basinger, Jay Hickerson, Martin Grams Jr., and Michael Biel for their help.*]

Conversations:
JANET WALDO

Show business careers are seldom planned. As an adolescent in Seattle, Washington, Janet Waldo dreamed of performing on the Broadway stage. Instead, fate (and the fine hand of Bing Crosby) brought her to Hollywood, where she was absorbed into the studio system at Paramount. For many another attractive teenager this might have led to stardom, or at least starlet-dom, but she never felt comfortable in front of the camera, and as she readily admits, the studio didn't seem to know what to do with her.

Waldo did build a rewarding career in Hollywood, however: she discovered radio, just at the time when the major networks were operating in high gear on the West Coast and jobs were plentiful. Before long she established herself as the preeminent teenage actress in the situation-comedy field, working on all the top shows (with everyone from Orson Welles to Frank Sinatra), starring in *Meet Corliss Archer*, and, ironically enough, playing opposite many of the biggest stars in movies.

Like many of her colleagues, she did a fair amount of television work as radio drama faded from the scene (she and Richard Crenna, longtime friend and fellow radio juvenile, play teenagers in a memorable *I Love Lucy* episode of 1952 called "The Young Fans") but this was never her forte.

Fate smiled again when she agreed to audition to play the daughter in a new Hanna-Barbera cartoon series called *The Jetsons* in 1962. Doing the voice of Judy Jetson has brought her a kind of immortality, not to mention a loyal fan base. It also opened up an entirely new career which has kept her busy for decades, contributing voices to scores of television cartoons, including the lead role in *Josie and the Pussycats* and assorted other characters on *The Smurfs*, *Wacky Races*,

The New Adventures of Superman, and other series right up through *King of the Hill*.

Waldo also enjoyed another perspective on show business as the wife of Robert E. Lee, whom she met when he and his partner Jerome Lawrence were prolific radio hyphenates. They wrote, directed, and produced a variety of shows ranging from *Favorite Story*, a dramatic anthology hosted by Ronald Colman, to *The Railroad Hour*, a series of condensed musicals and operettas starring Gordon MacRae. Lawrence and Lee later gained greater fame as playwrights, with such enduring successes as *Auntie Mame, Inherit the Wind*, and *First Monday in October* to their credit.

Most recently, Waldo has been active in California Artists Radio Theatre, founded by actress Peggy Webber, and has played a wide variety of parts including a starring role opposite Robert Rockwell in her late husband's two-character play *The Lost Letters of Robert E. Lee*. Listening to this poignant drama, one can hear time stand still—the actress sounds just as girlishly endearing as she did on network radio in the 1940s. (Tapes and CDs of CART productions can be purchased at their web site, www.calartistsradiotheatre.org)

Janet Waldo would be the first to dismiss her movie career, yet I think you'll agree her experiences in Hollywood are as rich and varied as anyone's in show business.

MALTIN: When I called you today on the phone you said, "Oh, you must have worked in radio, you're so punctual." Was that one of the first lessons you learned?

WALDO: Oh, was that ever a lesson! When I first started in radio, of course, it was live, and I lived quite close to CBS. I got a call because the ingénue that was playing a role opposite Kirk Douglas on a *Silver Theatre* had panicked. She just panicked, she couldn't go on, and they said, "Can you get here in fifteen minutes?" I had just gotten my license, and I got in my car and I sped; I was going so fast and a policeman stopped me and he said, "Young lady, you're speeding . . ." and I said, "But I'm late! I'm late! It's radio, I have to be there on time, they're going to go on the air without me, I have to be there," and he said, "Oh—I'll escort you." So he blew his siren, escorted me to the studio, and I got there and did the show without having seen it at all. I can't believe I wasn't terribly nervous but I wasn't. And opposite Kirk Douglas, you know . . . It went beautifully. In fact, Harriet Nelson heard it and she said, "That's the way you should sound all the time," 'cause I did Emmy Lou on her show as a teenager. So the policeman stayed and watched the show and after we finished he said, "Gee, that was great, I really enjoyed that. I just want to thank you. And here's your ticket."

I even remember my husband Bob chewing out an actress who was five minutes late. He said, "You won't work in radio if you're late. You can't do that." That's why I really can tell people who've worked in radio; they're never late.

MALTIN: Where did you grow up and how did you get started in show business?

WALDO: You really want to hear that? Okay. I was born in Yakima Valley, Washington, and I went to a little country school in a little town called Parker. My father was a railroad man and we moved from place to place to place. My parents were very concerned because my sister was a genius at the violin, and my father used to say, "I don't want my girls to grow up and marry some guy who's gonna take the eggs to market. I want them to have a good education." They had owned a ranch which they traded for a house in Seattle, Washington, and my sister and I got to go to school in Seattle. Then I got very interested in drama, all phases of drama. As a little girl we'd come home from some place and they'd put the headlights of the car on and I'd perform. I was doing a play and Bing Crosby had a publicity gimmick going where he was [doing] a sort of talent hunt. His scouts saw this play and they said, "We want you to enter a contest." I was fourteen, [and] I was scared of contests. My mother and my sister said, "You're going to do it," and I won it! They brought me to California with my mother, and Paramount put me under contract, but the problem was they did not know what to do with me. I was very young, and I was trying to compete with all of the glamour girls. To this day I know how to pose for a bathing suit picture because, you know, you stand on your toes, you don't ever let your heels go down. They taught me a lot of things like that.

MALTIN: So you were being groomed like a starlet at Paramount?

WALDO: Well, [I had] what they called a stock contract.

MALTIN: Who else was there at that time?

WALDO: Susan Hayward. She had been under stock contract. Let's see, who else was there? Interestingly enough, not much has happened to any of the girls who were there with me, but they were all gorgeous, they were all models, but they couldn't act. And I could act, because I had had really good experience in Seattle and I had done play after play after play. I was very comfortable acting and they didn't know how to act. They used to say that I was the best actress on the lot, but they didn't know what to do with me. They used to call me the little girl with the little boy's figure.

MALTIN: Did they give you bits in movies?

WALDO: Oh, yes, they gave me bits. I got to work with some wonderful people. I remember working with Fred MacMurray and they had me be a hat-check girl. I remember I was in a little outfit, he picked up his hat and gave me a tip. And I thought, being an actress, how can I make them notice me? So I did a double take on the tip. And they made a little bit more to do because they would like me to be inventive. But I wasn't glamorous and I wasn't sophisticated in any sense. They used to say to my mother when she brought me down, "Be careful of the wolves," and she didn't know what they meant. She thought they meant a wolf at the door. My mother was more naïve than I was, 'cause my parents were right out of Dickens, they were so sweet and so naïve and so gentle and totally unsophisticated. A lot of people said "Were you approached, did people try anything?" Actually, a couple of them did, but [laughs] I was so dumb and so young that I didn't know

Janet, Betty Moran, Virginia Dale, and Jeanne Cagney in All Women Have Secrets (1939).

what [was going on.] One young man, you probably know him, I don't dare mention his name, a big, big producer in the business took me in his office, locked the door, and—you've heard "chasing around the desk?"—that's literally what he did. I didn't know what his problem was! [*Laughs*] And he was a very, very big producer. You see, I was so dumb that I didn't know what they wanted of me and I didn't think I could deliver it. One producer said, "I have a part for you coming up in a picture, but you have to show me that you can kiss passionately . . ." And I'd say, "I don't know how to kiss passionately!" And he'd say, "Well, do you want to try it?" And I'd say, "No!" I didn't get the part.

MALTIN: Would you show up for work every day? Would they have things for you to do?

WALDO: What you did was what we called glorified atmosphere, just background stuff, and once in a while, they'd give me a little break. I was pretty fortunate but I was miserable. And that's why I have never felt comfortable doing on-camera [work], even though I've done a lot of on-camera and was working on a show when I got the cartoon. But I just have felt inhibited. I remember I would get so nervous doing on-camera stuff. That's why when I discovered radio, it was like a beautiful coming home to me. I'd done a little theater, never radio, but, I loved it, I felt secure, and I enjoyed it thoroughly.

MALTIN: So, how did it come about?

WALDO: Well, my option was dropped. I had an agent, actually Larry Crosby sort of took me under his wing and Bing was so sweet and wonderful to me; he'd give me a lot of little bits in his pictures, but Bing knew that I was not a happy person in front of the camera. And his brother Larry would take me to his show, *Kraft Music Hall* and my mother and I would walk to the studio and they would arrange for us to sit right down front, and I just thought, "This is the most wonderful thing in the world, 'cause they had scripts, they didn't have to worry about lines and they were so relaxed; this is so great." As time went on, I got to work with Bing in radio and in fact, one of the shows that I got—I wanted to play the lead in it—they were auditioning for it and they auditioned ninety girls. Now, in radio days, that was a lot. But my mother and I knew the title of the script that they were doing. We knew that it was an old Alice Faye movie. My mother went down to Los Angeles with me to one of the faraway places where they showed old movies in those days, and I watched Alice Faye and I imitated her. I picked up every nuance that she had, I would take a little piece of paper with me in the theater and write down her lines and then I would listen until I heard it in my own head. I auditioned and I got the part.

Janet in costume for George Cukor's Zaza (1939), set in a Parisian music hall, and starring Claudette Colbert.

Bing was wonderful to me and very sweet. I worked with him several times [and once it was with] Charles Boyer. I have a picture of us together. Bing and Charles Boyer were standing and while we were waiting for them to take the picture, Charles Boyer said, "I'll wear mine if you wear yours." And Bing said, "Well, I'll wear mine if you wear yours…" I had no idea what they were talking about . . . and it was their toupees.

MALTIN: Great! So at this point did you start going out on open auditions?

WALDO: Oh yes, and I was more aggressive in radio; I was so laid back in films, I would hide in the ladies room, you know, rather than run into somebody that I should meet and should say hello to. In radio, I would go to the lobby of CBS and sit around with all the other actors and wait for the directors to come by and say, "Hi! I'm Janet Waldo and I'd just love to work for you!" [*Laughs*] Then they'd say, "Well okay, come on, I'll give you a chance, I'll have you audition." But the real break came [because] my sister knew a man who was very close friends with Edward G. Robinson. The next thing I knew, Tommy Freebairn-Smith, the director, gave me a call to be on the show, not an audition. But I was confident, because I knew acting, I knew theater, and I loved radio. So, they gave me the script . . .

MALTIN: This would be on Robinson's show *Big Town*?

WALDO: On *Big Town*. And it was [the role of] a very emotional, very dramatic young girl. I read it and I realized later Lurene Tuttle was sitting right beside me and they were just going to let me try it. I was called for the job, but they were prepared to replace me in the event I couldn't deal with it. And I remember hearing Eddie say, "She'll be fine. She'll be just fine." And he called me many, many times after that and I got to do wonderful roles in *Big Town*. It was a wonderful experience because he was so wise as an actor and as a performer. He would rehearse all day long and I learned so much from working with him. He would give direction, but he was great, he'd give you wonderful ideas. And that really got me started in radio, because then I was kind of a biggie, because I'd worked on Eddie Robinson's show. After I did *Big Town*, I started getting lots of calls and then, very early in my career I got the call to audition for *Meet Corliss Archer*. I didn't want to do a teenager, because I always wanted to be a Broadway actress and theater was what I really loved, next to radio. And I thought, "I want to be the world's greatest actress," and I thought, "just a teenager," that was too easy. So I [auditioned] and they chose me and I did it for ten years.

MALTIN: The original show that introduced Corliss Archer, *Kiss and Tell*, had been a success on Broadway, right?

WALDO: Yes.

MALTIN: Was the playwright F. Hugh Herbert involved in the radio show at all?

WALDO: Yes, he was my mentor. I just loved that man, he was so good to me. He wanted me and no matter what I did, it was perfect as far as he was concerned. He was the most sentimental and adorable man and his family—his daughters, I always felt—resented me because they wanted to play Corliss. Hugh was wonderful. He hired my husband—who was not my husband then—to do ghost-writing of a couple of scripts. Bob never liked to admit to this [*laughs*]; he'd be mad at me for telling. In fact, on the *Meet Corliss Archer* show he invented the fact that Dexter had an old jalopy car, and they got more gags with that car doing all the different sound effects; Bob invented that. Hugh liked Bob very much and encouraged him and he was just a wonderful man. I think he considered me like one of his daughters. I had a fan club and he let me have my whole fan club come out and have a pool party at his place; they had a beautiful home up in Bel Air, which Casey Kasem bought later. But doing Corliss was both good and bad for me; it was easy for me, I just loved doing it, but there was no challenge as far as acting.

I also did Emmy Lou on *Ozzie and Harriet*. As much as I loved Corliss, there was no teenager written as well as Emmy Lou. Sherwood Schwartz wrote most of the spots; they were little cameos, and they were always after the first act. Emmy Lou, their little girl who lived next door, would come breezing in and say, "Yoo hoo, Mr. Nelson! Hi, Mr. Nelson!" and then she'd come in and do this little bit with him and she would have an imagination that would just go crazy and then Ozzie would connect with her imagination and he would get all steamed up and then she'd say, "Well, goodbye Mr. Nelson!" and she'd go. It was just a little gem; it was just the most fun to do. In fact, Bing Crosby wanted me to do a radio show of his and he wanted me to do the squeals which I invented—well, Ozzie and I invented—on *Ozzie and Harriet.* I was very gullible and very naïve; Ozzie would tease me all the time and I never knew when he was teasing or when he was real. I said, "Bing wants me to do this Emmy Lou character in his show and we'd have to go to San Francisco to do it." He said, "I don't know about that, Janet . . . Well, if he wants you to do the squeals, he has to say 'squeals courtesy of Ozzie Nelson.'" I believed him and I said to Bing, "Ozzie Nelson thinks that I shouldn't do the squeals unless you can give him billing," and Bing says, "Well, I'll give him billing, what the heck?"

Janet Waldo recording with Alan Young and Keye Luke on the animated TV series Battle of the Planets (1989).

MALTIN: Who directed the *Corliss Archer* show?

WALDO: Tom McAvity was the original director. Later on, his wife, Helen Mack directed it, and later on, Edna Best directed it. When Edna Best directed it, it was the only time that Corliss [*using accent*] was just a little teeny bit British . . . because Betsy would say, "Janet, darling, you're not sounding quite right in that line, now you'd better just give it a little more oomph, you know?" And I'd say, "Okay!" and I was just a tinge British as Corliss, during that phase.

MALTIN: Very funny. Was she a good director?

WALDO: Wonderful director. Edna Best was a very good friend and her husband, Nat Wolf, was an agent and was my husband's agent. Her daughter, Sarah Marshall, is still very much around. She was also a very fine actress.

MALTIN: Tell me about Helen Mack.

WALDO: I loved her dearly. She was a pixie. Very much of a pixie, a very cute little lady who was always playing sort of the little girl. She was always the little girl, and I should know about that, but she was a wonderful director for *Corliss*, very easy, very relaxed. A beautiful lady.

MALTIN: Of course, I only know her as an actress in 1930s movies like *The Son of Kong.*

WALDO: She was beautiful, but she liked to direct and she had one of her first chances with *Corliss Archer*. I think she also directed *Date with Judy* on occasion. She was excellent, and she had a great sense of humor and timing.

MALTIN: What other roles did you enjoy performing on radio?

WALDO: Bob, my husband, did *Favorite Story* and he really saved the day for me in radio because he cast me in all sorts of wonderful acting roles. I met Bob in the halls of CBS, and he cast me as Cathy in *Wuthering Heights*, with Bill Conrad, which was one of my favorite roles of all time. He cast me as Roxanne in *Cyrano De Bergerac* opposite Ronald Colman. Then later he had me do it again opposite Howard Duff. He also cast me as the Bird Woman in *Green Mansions* which is one of my favorite roles of all time; he gave me wonderful opportunities. And I'll tell you a story: shortly after we were married, I did *Green Mansions* for him. It was three days after we had been married, and I came to rehearsal and, of course, this was very exciting for me, and he said, "Jan darling, you're sounding a little too much like Corliss Archer." Oooh, I was angry. I was furious. I thought, "How dare you say that to me!" An old-time actor, Norman Field, who worked in radio a lot, said,

Janet as Corliss and Sam Edwards as Dexter, in a publicity photo for the popular radio series Meet Corliss Archer.

"Come here, I want to talk to you a minute. Janet, you want to keep a happy marriage?" And I said, "Oh yeah." And he said, "When he's your director, you're an actor; never let your marriage or your relationship with him interfere with your job. You do your job and you don't get personal about it." I never forgot that lesson. And actually, it was one of the best jobs I ever did, because I didn't sound like Corliss Archer!

MALTIN: Was there any other downside to doing a long-running show?

WALDO: You could get lazy because it [became] routine. The trick in radio was to try to come up with something interesting with an uninteresting or rather dry piece of material. I remember one time with Bob

Hope—I don't know whether it was a Bob Hope show or another show that he was on—I was supposed to be selling Girl Scout cookies. I had to give this big pitch to Bob Hope and I decided, instead of saying, "Hello Mr. Hope, I have these cookies and I hope you'll be interested," I did the whole thing really bored. I talked very fast, like I'd said it a thousand times, and it just went beautifully and it was a different approach. But if you get lazy and think, oh, well I'll just read what's here it doesn't work. The real challenge in radio for me was working in front of an audience. Because the audience literally times things for you. I miss that now so much because you would know how to play to the audience.

[Also, in radio] you have to play it opposite each other, that's what makes it so real. You can't do radio if you aren't real and if you don't listen. Listening is the most important thing that we did in radio; we had to, because [there was so little rehearsal].

And we were all very good friends; everybody helped everybody. I remember when I first started in radio, I was very nervous and scared, and Elliott Lewis was on a show, we were doing a *Silver Theatre* or something and he just said, "You know what you do? Go and put your hand against the wall and it'll steady you," 'cause I was really shaky. I put my hand against the wall and he'd sort of lean up against me and say, "You can do it, you can do it, kid. You can do it." They were just so helpful to each other and if I couldn't do a part, I would always say I'm not free to do it, but why don't you call so-and-so? We all did that for each other.

MALTIN: Today there are professional cartoon voiceover performers, but in the first generation of television cartoons everybody came out of radio.

WALDO: I was so thrilled when I discovered cartoons because I was doing an on-camera show with Tony Franciosa and I had never done a cartoon. My agent sent me to audition for *The Jetsons* and I thought, "Oh, cartoons . . ." And when I started working, I knew most of them from radio: Daws Butler, Don Messick, Casey Kasem. Mel Blanc of course I had worked with in radio. He was a very good actor.

MALTIN: But people don't often realize just how good they were as actors.

WALDO: Daws was a born teacher, and if you worked on a show with him, he could hardly resist teaching. In my case, it was very gratefully received. He'd say, "Hey Janet, you don't want to just make that an ordinary character. Give it a little something extra." And he'd give me some ideas. He taught many of the current people in cartoons. Nancy Cartwright [who plays Bart on *The Simpsons*] studied with Daws and gives him full credit for her ability as a radio actress, certainly. By the way, Nancy and I did *Little Women* for Peggy Webber's *California Artists Radio Theater*; I played Amy and Nancy played Beth.

That's one thing [about] cartoons: you have to have a different voice and that's what I thought was such fun. Joe Barbera would always say, "Now that's a good voice Janet, but can you sustain it? Can you hold it? Can you remember what you did?" And that is the real challenge, because you can come up with something on the spur of the moment—

Bing Crosby in a 1945 candid photo taken at radio station KFI (probably during a rehearsal).

I remember I did a character, she was from *Good Cavekeeping Magazine*, her name was Hedda Rocker, and she was sort of a blustery lady. I did it and he said, "Mmm-hmm, well that's okay, but now can you do it again?" And sometimes he would have me do it again to just be sure before he would let me have the part.

MALTIN: Very interesting. Very canny, too.

WALDO: Joe was a wonderful director.

MALTIN: Who did you most enjoy working with in radio?

WALDO: Bing. 'Cause I loved Bing and he changed my life. You know, if it hadn't been for Bing, I would never have come to Hollywood. Even though he was a very reserved and, some people think, cold man and hard to get to talk, I felt such gratitude to him.

MALTIN: Why do you think some movie stars were so nervous when they appeared on radio?

WALDO: I think that movie actors were intimidated by the fact that "this is now," and live. [When tape came in] they all relaxed a lot more and they blew [lines] like crazy. But in live radio shows, they couldn't afford to blow; they knew that and they were feeling that their life was at stake, that they could ruin their career by being really bad. I worked with Clark Gable and he was terrified. He was trembling, his whole body was just trembling when he was doing it. I couldn't believe that this brilliant Rhett Butler was that scared. It just fascinated me 'cause I thought, What does he have to be scared about? He's Rhett Butler!

I worked with Abbott and Costello and that was a time that I was mortified because I made a boo-boo. They talked so fast, you never could keep track of how fast they talked, and I was just reading; we'd had maybe one read-through and they had given so many instructions to the audience about "when we want you to laugh," he would take his pant leg and jiggle it, you know? I was playing a very young girl who was talking to them and saying, "Oh yes, Mr. Abbott, Mr. Costello," and there was this silence. It was my cue, but it was dead air—well, forever is ten seconds, five seconds, but I hadn't realized they'd gotten to that place that fast. That was pretty mortifying to me.

Oh, so many stars that we worked with. And we learned from them. You know, working in radio, that was a thrill. You could work with these big stars and you could see what they did right and what they did wrong. And you could see why they were stars. Claudette Colbert was just wonderful, brilliant, a very good radio actress. She wasn't intimidated by it at all. I played her daughter on *Secret Heart*.

MALTIN: Did you work with Bette Davis?

WALDO: Yes. She was not temperamental, very nice, very businesslike. You know, it was very short, I mean, we didn't have a lot of time together. I worked with Laurence Olivier and Vivien Leigh, and Laurence Olivier said to Vivien, "Darling, that line, you're reading it a little wrong. That line should be read this way." And he read it and she looked at him and she said, "It's *my* line, dear."

STILL LIFE

Spontaneous, candid photographs of radio broadcasts (or even rehearsals) are rare; for the most part, the network publicity departments sent out posed pictures of the stars at microphones all the time. But here is a gem from October of 1943, showing a mustache-less Groucho Marx, an animated Orson Welles (with stogie), actress-singer Fay McKenzie, and bandleader Robert Armbruster at work on a *Pabst Blue Ribbon Town* program. That looks like busy character actor John Brown at the extreme left. The cameraman is obviously planted in the studio audience at Columbia Square in Hollywood.

EXTRA! EXTRA!

Autograph Hound Makes Good

Long before movie star signatures became a marketable commodity on eBay, people were collecting autographs of their favorite stars. Photographs with printed signatures were mailed to fans in the earliest days of silent films. In King Vidor's silent comedy *Show People* (1928), Charlie Chaplin asks Peggy Pepper, played by Marion Davies, for her autograph after a preview of her latest film (and Davies doesn't recognize him—a very amusing gag). When Walt Disney made a cartoon called *The Autograph Hound* (1939), there was no question that audiences would recognize the hobby Donald Duck pursues so obnoxiously at a movie studio. One equally assertive—but less obnoxious—participant in the hobby at that time was a teenaged Ray Bradbury.

Autograph collectors are a breed apart. Some are sincere, while others are annoying and even predatory. Today the sad fact is that many who pose as fans are in fact dealers who sell their signed photos online.

It was not always so. I once met a man in Cleveland who started his collection after being mustered out of the service in Los Angeles at the end of World War II. Thirty years later he was still at it and proud of his highly organized collection. Every autograph book was numbered, as was every page in every book. When Paul Newman passed through Cleveland on a campaign swing for George McGovern, the collector learned which hotel Newman was staying at and waited in the parking lot early one morning, certain the star would walk by. Sure enough, he did, a can of Coors beer in his hand. When approached for his signature, Newman begged off, saying he didn't like giving autographs and offering the man a beer instead. The man said he'd prefer an autograph and when Newman demurred

Marlene Dietrich poses with a teenaged Ray Bradbury across from the main gate of Paramount Pictures.

the collector responded, "Clark Gable signed for me and you won't?" Newman immediately took pen in hand. Later the same man had a chance to get an entire Cleveland ball club to sign for him before a game. One player, who happened to be black, declined. "Martin Luther King signed for me and you won't?" said the collector. The player signed.

When stars of the 1930s succumbed to the pleas of one bespectacled teenage boy, standing outside a movie studio or among the crowd at a gala premiere, they couldn't have foreseen that one day he himself would be world famous. Ray Bradbury was as avid a fan and collector as anyone, past or present, and remains an enthusiast to this very day. The author of countless books and stories, including *Fahrenheit 451*, says "I've never worked a day in my life."

After reading the last issue of *Movie Crazy*, Ray called to say that he had some material he wanted to share. I knew a little about his boyhood fandom but not the full extent of his history. When I went to see him a few days later, he was on the phone with his agent, Don Congdon. Ray later explained that Don has been his agent for sixty years; he's now ninety years old, while Ray is a boyish eighty-six.

He was an even more boyish fourteen years old when his family moved to Los Angeles from Waukegan, Illinois. "My mother was a maniac for movies, thank God," he recalls. "She went at least once a week, and my first film was *The Hunchback of Notre Dame*. I was three years old. I came out wondering if I was going to grow up and be hunchback. Then a year later I saw *He Who Gets Slapped*, again [with] Lon Chaney. And then I saw *The Phantom of the Opera* and it was pure love, pure love. That same year I saw *The Lost World*, which changed my life forever, 'cause dinosaurs dominated all my life from that moment on."

When the Bradbury family moved to Los Angeles they settled in an apartment building at the corner of Hobart and Pico Boulevard. "We were upstairs and from our balcony I could see the top of the Uptown Theater [at the corner of Western Avenue and Olympic Boulevard]. They had a red light lantern up there and when that was lit it meant they were having a preview. So I got all excited and I'd rush over to the theater and by God, there would be Norma Shearer in a silver lamé evening gown and Irving Thalberg in a tux. I would get their autographs and I'd wait for them to come out."

Eventually, Ray got to know the manager of the theater, a man named Roy Evans. "When he moved to the Paramount Theater in Hollywood [now the El Capitan on Hollywood Boulevard] I would roller skate there on Saturday night [some five miles!] and buy a Sunday paper, and he'd let me in the theater free. He'd take my roller skates, put them

in a closet, I'd go in and see the film; I'd come out at ten o'clock, get my roller skates back, and skate home."

A young Ida Lupino with an even younger Ray Bradbury.

There is a postscript to this story, as there is to almost everything in Ray's life. Thirty years later he was attending a reception at the Beverly Wilshire Hotel and he heard a man behind him greet someone as Roy Evans. Ray spun around and said hello but the man didn't recognize him and asked, "Who are you?"

"I said, 'I was that boy on the roller skates thirty years ago and you used to let me in the Paramount Theater free, and I've never forgotten, Mr. Evans.' I said, 'Give me your address and phone number. My film *Something Wicked This Way Comes* is going to be previewed at the studio next week and I want you to be there.' So the next week, Roy Evans, the manager of the Uptown Theater, came to Disney, and before the film went on, I introduced him and said, 'This is the man who treated me beautifully when I was fourteen years old.' So everything circles around beautifully, doesn't it?"

In the 1930s, during summers off from school and on Saturdays (in the days when studios worked six days a week), Ray's roller skates also propelled him to several prime locations for getting autographs and having pictures taken. By skating down Western Avenue and turning at Melrose, he could get to the main entrance to Paramount Pictures

Two more star sightings at Paramount: Grace Bradley and Henry Wilcoxon, both circa 1935.

on Marathon, opposite a legendary restaurant (now gone) called Oblath's. "I stood out in front of Oblath's every day for years when I was fourteen, fifteen, and sixteen and never went in because the food was too expensive. I went to the White Log Cabin down at the corner. They had nickel malts, can you believe that?

"I spent the morning there from 10:00 to 12:00, and then around 1:00, I skated to RKO around the block on Gower. Then I went up to Columbia. On Friday nights I went to Legion Stadium boxing matches, and at midnight I went over to the Brown Derby (on Vine Street) and hung out there. I was fourteen years old and my parents let me run 'cause they knew I was safe; nothing could happen to me. I'd roller-skate all the way to Western from the Brown Derby at midnight on Friday. That's how dedicated I was."

Recalling those days with photographic clarity, Ray mused, "You've never known anyone like me. I went to L.A. High School and there were three thousand students. Never once did I ever see another student in front of Paramount." Ray had adventures everywhere he went. When he was fourteen, he spotted Marlene Dietrich walking into the Westmore makeup studio on Sunset Boulevard and boldly followed her inside and up a flight of stairs. She actually obliged with a signature, but the Westmore staff threw him out. The next day he was in Louella Parsons's column. Dietrich even posed for one of Ray's snapshots, although she wasn't happy when he asked her to walk across the street from the Paramount gate where the light was better. She knew it wasn't as flattering as standing in the shade.

Some stars were friendlier than others. "Someone like Mary Pickford loved to talk," he recalls. "Victor Young, the conductor-composer, was very chatty. You could stand and talk to him for half an hour, 'cause he loved to talk about music. And George Gershwin was very nice. I got his autograph in front of the Vendome Restaurant, which was a very big restaurant in those days. If you're really interested and they see that, then they'll talk; they can see it in your face."

The starstruck teenager also roller-skated to a number of radio broadcasts. [His experiences with George Burns are recounted in my book *The Great American Broadcast*.] One night he went to see *The Shell Chateau* at NBC, and its star, Al Jolson, noticed him sitting in the front row with his roller skates in his lap. "He jumped down and grabbed my skates, jumped back on the stage, started to put 'em on, and I jumped on the stage and grabbed the skates away from him. Then I turned to the audience and said 'My transportation!' The audience roared and I got back in the front row; Al Jolson loved it, too."

Ray also had a nice relationship with columnist Parsons, whose *Hollywood Hotel* broadcast was just beginning. "I came up to her outside the studio over at Eighth and Dixon, up above a Packard [automobile dealership]. They didn't have a regular studio in those days. I said, 'Miss Parsons, can you take me in the studio?' and she took me in, sat me down by Gary Cooper, Sir Guy Standing, Richard Cromwell, and Franchot Tone [who appeared in an adaptation of] *The Lives of a Bengal Lancer*. Louella was kind to me, and I got to know her chauffer. He invited me to drive around town with him when he was running errands. When we'd come to a signal, people looked in the back seat to see who was there, and it was just old Ray with his roller skates."

When Ray first got published in *Weird Tales* magazine, he sent some of his stories to William Spier, the producer and director of the popular radio series *Suspense*. "And by God, he wrote back and said, 'Can you come up to the house and see me? I think I want to employ you.' So I had a friend drive me up there [Ray still doesn't drive], the door opened, and Kay Thompson was there. He was married to her, and she was fabulous, just as fabulous when you see her in *Funny Face*.

"I started writing for *Suspense* and I met all these famous people. I was there every Thursday night [and] at rehearsals when they did my shows. I went to the restaurant next door when I published my first book and I met Orson Welles and Ava Gardner there with Bill Spier."

One of Ray's stories was adapted as a *Suspense* play called "Summer Night" in 1949. It starred Ida Lupino, who had posed for Ray's Brownie box camera some fifteen years earlier when she was just starting out as a bleached blonde at Paramount.

He had other encounters that invoked memories of his fan encounters, as when he met legendary Columbia Pictures chief Harry Cohn around 1952. "They were considering doing *The Illustrated Man* there. Jerry Wald took me in; he did a script himself, then he introduced me to Harry Cohn, who called me Buck Rogers and Flash Gordon. That irritated me so much that I finally said, 'You know, Mr. Cohn, we have met before." He said, "What do you mean? We've never met before.' I said, 'Yes, when I was seventeen years old. You were making *Lost Hori-*

Ray and his wife Maggie with John Huston at a hunt wedding in Ireland during the 1950s. "Ten minutes after this picture was taken, we went out and hunted the foxes," Ray recalls. "John was on crutches; he had fallen off his horse the day before."

zon and I came here on my roller skates in front of the studio and got Ronald Colman's autograph, and at that very moment you drove up in your car and you left it at the curb in a No Parking place and ran into the studio to get something. When you came back out there was a policeman there writing you a ticket. You jumped in the car and tried to drive off and the policeman jumped on the running board, reached in, took the keys, put 'em in his pocket, and finished writing you a ticket.' And I said, 'You know what I did then?' He said, 'What?' I said, 'I laughed and I laughed.' And Harry Cohn didn't call me Buck Rogers after that. But we didn't make the film either!"

Ray remains a fan, first and foremost. His television is set to Turner Classic Movies most of the time, and he's happy to show off his hundreds of autographs from the 1930s, ranging from the biggest stars in Hollywood to such character actors as Claude Gillingwater, Ferdinand Gottschalk, and Nat Pendleton, whose names he rattles off with pride. But perhaps his proudest moment came fifty years ago when he attended the Los Angeles premiere of the film he wrote for John Huston, *Moby Dick*.

"Standing in front of Oblath's all those years I got to know all the other autograph collectors. There was a woman there named Constance; she was about forty, and she was there with her mother, who was sixty-five or seventy. At the premiere of *Moby Dick*, on the way in, I looked over and I saw Connie and her mother. They're still collecting autographs twenty years later! I said to my wife, 'Wait here, wait here,' and I ran over and said, 'Connie!' And she said, 'Who are you?' I said, 'It's Crazy Ray, remember Crazy Ray, in front of Oblath's, back in 1934?' And I said, 'Hi, Ma,' to the mother. She said, 'What are you doing here?' and I got embarrassed suddenly. I said, 'Well, I had something to do with this picture.' 'What did you do?' I said, 'Well, I had something to do with the script.' 'Did you type the script? Are you a stenographer?' And I finally said, 'No, I wrote the screenplay.' At which moment, the magic thing [happened]—the autograph collectors around, all their hands came out with autograph books. And I knew I had moved over to the other side of the wall."

COLLECTORS' CORNER: Games

There were apparently as many promotional gimmicks as there were movies way back when. Here is a card with a metal spinner that encourages recipients to play a game ("It's Fun in a Crowd!") inspired by RKO's *The Life of the Party* (1937). So which would you rather do, make three funny faces (in honor of Billy Gilbert) or try to imitate Parkyakarkus?

This is my kind of Bingo game: instead of matching letters and numbers, you try to fill in the names of popular stars of the 1930s. When two names are completely covered you shout out "Hollywood!" One can't help but love a game that includes not just the obvious names but comedienne Louise Fazenda! Perhaps someone was currying favor with her husband, Hal B. Wallis, then head of production for Warner Bros.

MONEY GIVEAWAY

Promotional giveaways have always been a part of movie ballyhoo, and that tradition continues to this day. Here are three prime examples of handouts designed to call attention to silent movies with money themes. Making a bogus dollar bill for star vehicles like Roscoe "Fatty" Arbuckle's *Brewster's Millions* (1921) or Bebe Daniels's *Dangerous Money* (1924) seems like a natural. (The idea has never died: I have similar giveaways for Richard Pryor's remake of *Brewster's* and Dana Carvey's *Opportunity Knocks*.)

It's a bit more surprising to find such folderol promoting a serious story like Erich von Stroheim's *Greed*. Note the reference to the source material, Frank Norris's novel *McTeague*, and that it's advertised as a Metro-Goldwyn picture. This was just before Louis B. Mayer managed to get his name appended to the company logo.

The coin of the Hollywood realm . . . the best (and most obvious) tie-ins in film history:

A cracked medallion to promote the 1915 serial The Broken Coin, *starring Francis Ford.*

1. And as recently as 1953, Rita Hayworth kicked up her heels on a golden coin advertising Salome. 2. Union Pacific railroad issued souvenir tokens for many years, but in 1939 one side promoted Cecil B. DeMille's epic film of the same name. 3. An equally impressive piece was created for Gloria Swanson's 1925 starring vehicle Madame Sans-Gêne. "We're in the Money" was sung in Gold Diggers of 1933, but the concept still worked for Gold Diggers of 1935, as you can see from both sides of this coin.

This April 1923 ad from the *Dubuque Times-Journal* heralds a promotional tie-in that took lighthearted advantage of a serious situation in Eastern Europe. In the aftermath of World War I, longstanding empires were overthrown and governments reduced to a level of chaos. Inflation was rampant and many countries' currency was literally not worth the paper it was printed on. But American entrepreneurs saw an opportunity for novelty giveaways like the one advertised here, which linked to a movie aptly titled *Nobody's Money*.

Another example: this 10,000 Reichmark note is overprinted to announce the showing of a 1923 Metro release at a New Jersey theater. These worthless bills were also sold by five and dime stores in small packs for use as play money for kids.

Thanks to *Movie Crazy* reader Mark Johnson for sharing his collectibles, and the story behind them.

GRAND OPERA HOUSE ·· Three Days Starting THURSDAY

JESSE L. LASKY PRESENTS

JACK HOLT
in
"Nobody's Money"

300,000 German Marks, Austrian Kronen and Russian Rubles to Be Given Away During the Run of "Nobody's Money."

a Paramount Picture

From THE DUBUQUE TIM...

YES, THIS IS REAL MONEY...
BUT TRY AND SPEND IT!
"Strangers of The Night"
(CAPTAIN APPLEJACK)
Will be after your money so keep a sharp lookout for they will be at the
Jackson Theatre   Week of Dec. 3rd

K 6820463
Reichsbanknote
Zehntausend Mark
zahlt die Reichsbankhauptkasse in Berlin gegen diese Banknote dem Einlieferer
Berlin, den 19. Januar 1922
Reichsbankdirektorium

10000

K 6820463

Conversations:
GRACE BRADLEY BOYD

Like so many young women of the 1920s, 1930s, and 1940s, Grace Bradley came to Hollywood's attention because of her striking good looks. Some of the starlets of that era worked hard, got the right breaks, and achieved success onscreen. Others saw their once-promising careers peter out.

Grace worked steadily through the early-to-mid 1930s in such films as *Too Much Harmony, The Gilded Lily, Six of a Kind, Rose of the Rancho, Anything Goes*, and *Thirteen Hours by Air*. She never did become a major star, but she succeeded in living a rich, full life. As a schoolgirl in Brooklyn, she'd pined over dashing silent-film actor William Boyd. In 1937 she married him. Theirs was a long and happy union, and a successful partnership as well: in the 1940s, they set out to acquire all the rights to the character of Hopalong Cassidy. Hoppy had rescued Boyd's faltering screen career in 1935; a decade later, he and Grace mortgaged virtually everything they owned in order to produce their own movies and own the character with whom William Boyd had become synonymous. Their gamble paid off handsomely when television made Hopalong Cassidy a bigger star than ever. He also became one of the first great icons of merchandising, with more than 2,400 products bearing his likeness. Bill and Grace traveled the world, greeting fans and making friends, until his death in 1972.

She has worked to keep her husband's image alive, and travels yearly to the Hopalong Cassidy Festival held near his birthplace in Cambridge, Ohio. She also spent many years entangled in a lawsuit over the rights to Hoppy.

As Grace's friend, the film historian Richard W. Bann, writes, "Has there ever been such a black-and-white issue? *60 Minutes* should have done a story. Here you have a huge insurance corporation, stonewalling her in a war of attrition lasting decades, hoping she would give up, or die, refusing to pay what they owed her in the matter involving these black-and-white films with their black-and-white values starring her husband in that black-and-white outfit and horse. This one little lady battling an army of attorneys for a huge company backed by money to stall her and deny her until they could crush her. Except that she won. She prevailed in the end, against all odds . . . just the same as in any Hopalong Cassidy movie!"

Even during this tumultuous period, Grace found comfort through helping others. She began teaching tai chi to senior citizens at a local hospital in Orange County, and she continues to work at the South Coast Medical Plaza to this very day. In 2003, she was asked to extend her volunteer work; she now helps patients with substance-abuse problems to regain healthy lives.

Grace is an ideal role model for such patients: she remains active, vibrant, and even glamorous at the age of ninety.

She still receives fan mail for her beloved Hoppy, but I was curious to know more about her own experiences. Her memories evoke an era in show business when youthful beauty opened doors, and starlets had to learn to fend for themselves.

I started our conversation by asking about Grace's childhood, which was certainly more eventful than most.

BOYD: I had grown up as a concert pianist. I gave my first recital when I was six, and when I was twelve, I played up at the Eastman School of Music. After grade school I went to a private girls' school where my mother had gone, and it gave me more time for my music. That was in Brooklyn. At fifteen, the piano teachers in the United States had an annual contest where the best pianist was picked from every state, and all converged on New York and played at Carnegie Hall before nine judges. I was picked as the pianist from New York, and when they finally announced my name as the winner, my teacher said, "You were absolutely inspired." But it didn't mean anything to me. When I came off my arms swelled up like balloons [from] the strain of it.

MALTIN: At what age did you become the breadwinner of your family?

BOYD: I started when I was fifteen. Two designers, a man and his wife, had this salon in New York and they wanted me for a model. They didn't know that I wasn't sixteen yet, because I went into high school at twelve. I started to work for them daily after school. We were still living in Brooklyn, and I would commute. I would do the modeling during the day. I had never had a manicure, I had never worn heels. And you can imagine, I was a nervous wreck. I'd get so tired because from what I

would do there, I would have a bowl of soup or something in a little restaurant right there and then I would go to dancing school at night. And then I'd go home, take the subway train to Flatbush.

I kept that up until I was sixteen with the school, and then I started modeling kind of full time. It was that same time when a producer saw me in dancing school and said, "I'm doing a play on Broadway and I'd like you to be in it, this fall." It was just Mother and me, because Daddy had died when I was ten, and I guess Mother thought that might be fun. Then I was in my first Broadway show, which was with Bill Fields; it was a revue, *Ballyhoo* (1930). I remember I was so impressed with him, I thought he was the funniest man in the whole world. Any time I wasn't having to change clothes for another number, I was in the wings watching him. When he would come off stage, he wouldn't pay any attention to me at all, like I wasn't there. But after a while, he realized that I was really there to watch him. And finally, he wouldn't say anything but he walked by and he'd pat me on the top of the head. He came out to Paramount just about the same time I did. So that's why I was kind of like a little good luck charm, I think, for him, because he used to try to get me in all his pictures, if it was just a walk-on, whatever. I just loved him.

MALTIN: Didn't you also work in nightclubs?

BOYD: The Paradise nightclub is where Eddie Sutherland saw me and called Paramount and said [they should] test me. Then the next night, I guess, another director saw me and did the same thing, called Paramount. So they notified me that they wanted to take a test, and they sent me a piece from *Red Dust* with Jean Harlow. And my friend then was Bill Frawley. He was in, I think, *Twentieth Century* onstage then. He was wonderful to me and when he saw what I had, *Red Dust*, he said, "That's not for you." He said, "I'll write a test for you," which he did, and I did it with another friend of his, Johnny Gallaudet. I knew nothing about acting. By the end I said something like, "Well, you can't blame a girl for trying." And they signed me to fifty-two weeks. I would not be making as much money as I was making killing myself in New York, but I decided that was the right thing to do.

MALTIN: Did your mother come with you?

BOYD: Oh, sure. We were always together. I was living with Mother when I met Bill [Boyd]. When I came out here, it was on the *Chief.* That was before the *Super Chief.* I came out on the *Chief,* they picked me up in Pasadena, took me right to the studio, off the train. I walked in the entrance, and Jack Oakie happened to be standing there and he put out his arms and gave me a big hug. And then Mother was sitting down outside and they took me right into [Cecil B.] DeMille's office. Just off the train and into DeMille's office. He was casting the picture where the young girl was coming into womanhood, *This Day and Age.* I'm sitting there and he's looking at me and the first words out of his mouth were, "You don't look like a virgin." What do you say to that?

MALTIN: Welcome to Hollywood!

BOYD: He said, "I see you on a leopard couch with a Nubian slave." That's the way he saw me. Okay, I didn't get the part. But the funny part about it was that [he cast] Judith Allen. She's the one that was really built, and she's the one that was married to the number-one wrestler in the country at that point. And she was the virgin in the picture! So that was my introduction to Hollywood.

MALTIN: What were your impressions of Paramount?

BOYD: God, when you think of the people all at one place. Carole Lombard and Claudette Colbert, Mae West was there. Freddy March attacked me . . .

MALTIN: Which apparently was a common occurrence.

BOYD: That's right, [but] nobody told me that. I was horrified. I went screaming up to makeup. Nellie, the hairdresser, who was there for all those years, said, "Oh you poor thing, you poor thing." Well, I was just glad to be alive.

MALTIN: Did they keep you working all the time?

BOYD: We didn't have [regular] hours then. So whether I was on a picture or not, I would do the P.R. stuff and all the cheesecake; we worked every day. I had the Al St. John house out in the Valley; there was a pool there, beautiful old grounds, I loved it. It was wonderful, 'cause the whole second story was the bedroom. And Sunday, I just wanted to do nothing, I just wanted to go out in the sun. I called in and I said, "I can't have a photographer come out today. I don't know what it is, but [I have] something on my cheek." Next thing I knew there was a cameraman at the door. He put a bandage across my cheek, took pictures, and the next thing that came out in the paper was "Hexed by a Hexapod." Anything to get a picture in the paper. It was a constant.

MALTIN: So they just used it for fodder for more publicity.

BOYD: That's right, exactly. Everybody went through the same thing. In 1934, I was doing *Come On Marines*, and it got to the point where they were working at night. Harold Lloyd was doing *The Cat's-Paw* and he wanted me; well, he was going to be shooting at the same time I was still on *Come On Marines*. At that time I was getting $250 a week; this was a fortune, my God, in 1934. But he paid $2,500 a week to Paramount for me; of course, I still got my $250 a week. And I worked for literally seven days and seven nights and never went to bed.

A 1935 photo of Paramount starlets Gertrude Michael, Gail Patrick, Wendy Barrie, Ann Sheridan, Katherine DeMille (C. B.'s daughter), and Grace Bradley.

MALTIN: You were doing two pictures at once?

BOYD: I was doing the two pictures at once. Lloyd started at about eight o'clock in the morning; he started early, and I worked until 6:00. Then I'd go back to Paramount and worked from 6:00 to 6:00 in the morning. I'd shower and change my makeup. I finished both at the same time. I don't remember any part of the Harold Lloyd picture—oh, I think I had a breakaway dress on, something like that. I know halfway through that picture, I was hallucinating and I was probably sleeping on my feet. After that, I kind of collapsed. I went to bed and I don't know how long I slept, I just died. And I awakened and my hand was paralyzed, just like that. Nobody knew about nervous tension [in those days], I guess. I had a constant fever. It took about three months [to recover], and Paramount paid my salary. Finally I decided if I didn't get out of bed, that's the way it was gonna be, so I got out of bed; I had Mother make arrangements to go to Catalina. I don't know how long I was over there, a couple of weeks maybe, and I got a call from Paramount. They had a picture they wanted me on, and I had to dance in it. I had two weeks or so to come

Publicity fodder: Toby Wing and Grace Bradley atop an airplane in 1934; Grace and Marsha Hunt two years later, definitely not wearing swimsuits. Grace and Marsha became reacquainted at the Lone Pine Film Festival some sixty-five years later!

back, and I did; I did the picture. From then on, it was onward and upward. But how you survive those things . . .

I left Paramount in 1936 to go independent, because I had an offer to go to England to make a picture with John Mills. I was getting $1,000 a week, and that was in 1936, so that was pretty damn good. I was over there about five months, and they loved me at Gaumont-British. They wanted to put me under contract, because Jessie Matthews, who was their top musical star, had tuberculosis. I think they wanted me probably to replace her. And I was in such a condition, I was wiped out. I finally got to another doctor there and he said, "Grace, if you were able to go to the South of France or get some sun . . . but I don't think you'll make it, if you sign this contract and stay here, because we're going into the winter." So I finally decided I'll go back. And all I could think of was the desert. Just the sun. A lot of the stress has been taken care of by the sun. I would have died, I think, if I hadn't had the sun.

MALTIN: So you went back to work in Hollywood as a freelancer?

BOYD: Republic had a picture for me [so I flew home]. And the plane was our first sleeper plane. The sleeper was right in back of the pilot's cabin; they closed it off with curtains and it was two seats put together. I got off the plane, I was picked up by Republic, taken to the studio wearing the clothes that I was wearing, and I did the picture with my own clothes. I had no idea what it was or what I was wearing . . . no idea. Then I went down to the desert and flaked out, and the next picture I think was *Wake Up and Live* with Alice Faye, at 20th Century. When I came back is when I got the call from Bill [Boyd] saying, "I'm giving a small party at my house in Malibu," and the third date he proposed. I remember he said he would have proposed the first night, but he didn't mention he was in the process of getting a divorce, and he was three weeks away from it. He said, "I was afraid of scaring you to death." At that time, too, everybody [was concerned] because of his reputation [he'd been married three times], the fact that he was older, and the fact that I had never been married before. But if it's right, it's right. And it was. We both were of the same opinion that it had to be together all the way; as I've often said, it's not fifty-fifty, it's 1,000 percent, that's the way it has to be. And it worked out, because when you think of thirty-five years and we were only separated for two nights . . .

MALTIN: How did you come to appear in those Streamliner comedies for Hal Roach in the 1940s?

BOYD: I stopped acting after we were married, except for a couple ones that I'd already signed to do, that I had to do. Then when I went back to Hal Roach for that series [*The McGuerins of Brooklyn*] with Bill Bendix, I did that because not only was I getting more money than I thought I would, I wanted to buy a tractor for Christmas, for Bill. But I got it in the contract that when Bill was working, they couldn't call me; I would only do it when he wasn't working, which worked out fine. I think we would probably still have been doing those silly things if the war hadn't [come along] and the government took over the [Hal Roach] studio.

Grace Bradley and William Boyd out on the town in 1942.

MALTIN: When you did that screen test back in New York, you'd never really acted before. What do you think they saw in you?

BOYD: I have no idea, except that maybe they thought I was a little sexpot or something, because I never got the good-girl role, until later on, when I really got serious about what I was doing and kind of understood. See, I had such terrible stage fright. I loved to dance, and that didn't bother me. When I was dancing, I was perfectly happy, I didn't get stage fright at all. But when I came out here, the stage fright was so horrible; it's a wonder I could do anything because I couldn't get it through my head that you could do it again. In other words, I had to be perfect. From the time I was a little girl, I had to play at recitals and I had to be the best one and I felt like I didn't have anybody to fall back on.

MALTIN: But you must have been a natural.

BOYD: I didn't understand acting, I had no idea about it, but I remember they had a coach on duty all the time. I think it was the second

picture that was with Charlie Farrell where I played a Russian. And every Russian in the business was in that picture—Gregory Ratoff, Mischa Auer, Leonid Kinskey. Now, not knowing anything about acting, I certainly didn't know anything about a Russian accent, and they sent me to the coach. The second time I went, she said, "Grace, you sound like you're repeating what I say. You sound like me. I want you to just sound like you." So it was probably the worst Russian accent, but actually it was a cute part. They never even attempted to teach me, so it was a learning process. But it grew on me. I played a couple of straight roles, but I don't think any of the films I did were very important. They weren't big things.

MALTIN: Were the directors patient with you?

BOYD: It's the strangest thing, when I think of it. No director ever gave me one word of direction. Not one. They just let me go. The only one I remember who took any time was Henry Hathaway. And I loved him. I remember, he did one scene silent, where I had to cry, and he talked me [through it]. Tears came out and I cried and he was delighted. They said, "He's hard to work for." Well, he was an angel as far as I was concerned.

MALTIN: And were your fellow actors understanding of you being a greenhorn?

BOYD: Oh, I always had a ball. It was fine, except when I'd have to get over that horrible stage fright, because I don't think I ever started a picture that I didn't have a cold. I walked on the set with a cold. And that, you know, feeling of having to be absolutely right all the time.

MALTIN: What do you think when you look back at all of those pictures you posed for in the 1930s?

BOYD: I did my own makeup, which was from my stage training, but once Wally Westmore did it for *The Big Broadcast of 1938*, I looked entirely different. It's soft and feminine, you know, and I think maybe if I had been made up [that way] I might have had a different career. It makes a difference. The first time I came on the set and the director, Mitchell Leisen, saw me, he said, "Now, that's the way you should look."

STILL LIFE

Stars, starlets, and contract players never had an idle moment in the heyday of the studio system. If they weren't working on a film, they were kept busy making personal appearances, giving interviews, and shooting silly publicity photos like this (which, we readily confess, we love). It was taken at the "world-famous" intersection of Hollywood and Vine, which doesn't look so very different today. The excuse for this 1933 outing? The original studio caption tells us, "Hollywood is indulging in a new form of an old game. Bicycle polo has been inaugurated by this team consisting of Kathleen Burke, Grace Bradley, Lona Andre, and Judith Allen, at the Paramount Studios."

WHEN HOLLYWOOD FOUGHT BACK

Imagine tuning in to a Sunday afternoon radio broadcast and hearing the familiar voice of a much-loved performer saying, with great sincerity, "For the past week in Washington, the House Committee on Un-American Activities has been investigating the film industry. Now, I have never been a member of any political organization, but I've been following this investigation, and I don't like it. There are a lot of stars here to speak to you. We're show business, yes, but we're also American citizens. It's one thing if someone says we're not good actors. That hurts, but we can take that. It's something else again to say we're not good Americans. We resent that!"

This was no rabble-rouser talking: it was Judy Garland. She delivered the first speech in a two-part broadcast called "Hollywood Fights Back" that is still remarkable even after nearly sixty years.

It isn't uncommon nowadays for stars to campaign for political candidates. Celebrities have also banded together for good causes, as in the fundraising efforts that followed the attacks of September 11, 2001, and in the aftermath of Hurricane Katrina in 2005.

But there has never been anything quite like the radio broadcasts that aired on October 26 and November 2, 1947, under the title "Hollywood Fights Back." Tensions had been building ever since the first closed-door hearing of the House Un-American Activities Committee on December 3, 1946, in Los Angeles. At its conclusion, it was announced that Communist activities in the motion picture industry would come under renewed scrutiny. More closed hearings were held in Hollywood during May of 1947, after which committee chairman J. Parnell Thomas declared, "We now have hundreds of names, prominent names, and they are mostly writers." Public hearings were then

Fredric March, Paulette Goddard, Edward G. Robinson, and the most decorated soldier of World War II, Audie Murphy (not yet a movie star) state their case on the first "Hollywood Fights Back" broadcast.

scheduled to take place in Washington that fall.

On July 20, Charlie Chaplin sent an unsolicited telegram to Thomas and made it public: "From your publicity I note that I am to be quizzed by the Un-American Activities Committee in September. I understand I am to be your single guest at the expense of the taxpayers. Forgive me for this premature acceptance of your headlined newspaper invitation.

"You have been quoted as saying you wish to ask me if I am a Communist. You sojourned for ten days in Hollywood not long ago, and could have asked me the question at that time, effecting something of an economy, or you could telephone me now—collect.

"In order that you may be completely up to date on my thinking, I suggest you view carefully my latest production, *Monsieur Verdoux*. It is against war and the futile slaughter of our youth. I trust you will not find its humane message distasteful. While you are preparing your engraved subpoena, I will give you a hint on where I stand. I am not a Communist. I am a peace-monger."

The Committee held its first public hearings on October 20, 1946, and heard from an array of so-called friendly witnesses, including studio chiefs Louis B. Mayer, Jack Warner, and Walt Disney, who defended both their movies and their American values. Screen Actors Guild president Ronald Reagan claimed that Communists represented "less than 1 percent" of his membership and that their efforts to gain control of the union had been thwarted. Others, including Gary Cooper, Robert Taylor, and Adolphe Menjou, gave much more damning testimony, citing a much broader and more insidious Communist presence in Hollywood. Names were named by these and other witnesses, with radio microphones and newsreel cameras present.

Simmering emotions in Hollywood then came to a boil. In response to these well-publicized hearings and the tarring of reputations by hearsay evidence, John Huston and William Wyler formed The Committee for the First Amendment and planned to generate headlines of their own by flying to Washington, D.C. to attend the next round of testimony. Meanwhile, a formidable array of stars, from Lucille Ball to Peter Lorre, Rita Hayworth to Groucho Marx, pooled their resources to buy a half-hour of air time on two successive Sunday afternoons in order to express their objection to the behavior of the Committee and its chairmen, Thomas of New Jersey and John Rankin of Mississippi.

With such stellar names as Gene Kelly, Myrna Loy, William Holden, Melvyn Douglas, Burt Lancaster, and Robert Ryan on hand, the star power was impressive (bolstered by politicians, statesmen, and even the most decorated solider of World War II, Audie Murphy, who had yet to appear in a movie), but it was imperative that their message be clear, direct, and pointed. The Hollywood troupe explained that while they respected the right of Congress to hold hearings, they questioned whether even those elected representatives had the right to question citizens about their political beliefs.

The first order of business was to ask the listeners how they felt about Hollywood movies they'd been seeing. Gene Kelly mentioned *The Best Years of Our Lives*, noting that its producer, Samuel Goldwyn, had been subpoenaed. He asked, "Did you see *The Best Years of Our Lives*? Did you like it? Were you subverted by it? Did it make you un-American? Did you come out of the movie with a desire to overthrow the American government?"

Added June Havoc, "Who is judging? Who makes charges about our pictures? Who is the committee?"

The program then proceeded to give the listening public a brief history of the House Un-American Activities Committee and a sense of its notorious reputation. Newspaper editorials and other sources were cited, as well as quotes commending the Committee's work—by such supporters as Nazi and Bund leaders and the Imperial Wizard of the Ku Klux Klan.

Danny Kaye said, "We found out that the committee has been making friends and enemies during all these years. Here are some of the people who didn't like it: as far back as 1938, when the committee began, Franklin D. Roosevelt saw what it was up to. He said, 'Most fair-minded Americans hope that the committee will abandon the practice of merely providing a forum to those who for political purposes or otherwise seek headlines which they could not otherwise obtain.'"

He was followed by Marsha Hunt, who said, "Of course, there are some of us who didn't happen to vote for Roosevelt. Some of us took the other side and voted for Mr. [Wendell] Wilkie. But Mr. Wilkie had something to say about the committee, too. He said, 'The committee uses methods that undermine the democratic process. They ruin reputations by publicity, inference, and innuendo, while denying the protection of counsel.' Well, that was in 1940, and apparently they haven't changed since then."

Hunt was also among those on the chartered aircraft flying to Washington when the first installment aired, so her remarks were recorded ahead of time. In introducing the first program, Charles Boyer explained, "The reason why parts of this program are transcribed [pre-recorded] is that fourteen of the fifty stars you are about to hear are at this moment on a special plane headed to Washington to carry on in person the fight for our rights as American citizens. If it were not for studio commitments, all of us here today and dozens more would be in the air as well as on it."

The committee's first round of hearings had gotten extensive newspaper, magazine, and radio coverage, especially with such major stars as Cooper and Taylor on hand. While the "unfriendly" witnesses of the following week were mostly writers and producers, the presence of major stars like Humphrey Bogart and Lauren Bacall made sure that the publicity continued apace.

The following Sunday many of the stars appeared "live" on part two of "Hollywood Fights Back" to report what they had witnessed in Washington.

Said Bogart, "We sat in the committee room and heard it happen. We saw it. We said to ourselves, 'It can happen here.' We saw American citizens denied the right to speak by elected representatives of the people. We saw police take citizens from the stand like criminals after they'd been refused the right to defend themselves. We saw the gavel of a committee chairman cutting off the words of free Americans. The sound of that gavel, Mr. Thomas, rings across America, because every time your gavel struck it hit the First Amendment to the Constitution of the United States."

A delegation of prominent New Yorkers, including Richard Rodgers, George S. Kaufman, Moss Hart, Clifton Fadiman, Leonard Bernstein, and Bennett Cerf appeared on the second show to voice their support of the Hollywood-based effort, as did novelist Thomas Mann (by then a Los Angeles resident), who proudly identified himself as a hostile witness before the Parnell committee.

Looking back on the broadcasts, Marsha Hunt marvels at how they were put together, describing the process as "last-minute and marvelously improvisational." In spite of that, "I was impressed by the research that had gone into some of the things we were given to say before they put them down on paper. There must have been exhaustive research."

Hunt's husband, Robert Presnell, was one of three writers who worked on the broadcast; the others were Millard Lampell and Norman Corwin. They holed up at the colonial mansion in Beverly Hills that was home to MCA, Music Corporation of America. "After hours, the place was theirs," Marsha recalls. "There they sat and typed out these inspirational short messages for a huge cast. I would grab them from the typewriter and take them to whoever was supposed to deliver that message. I do remember going back and forth."

Corwin was also charged with directing the show. An eloquent and impassioned dramatist, often referred to as the poet laureate of radio, he had written a widely praised anti-Fascist drama as early as 1939, *They Fly Through the Air.* "On a Note of Triumph," his one-hour program celebrating V-E Day and examining the cost of war (and the burden of peace that lies ahead) was carried simultaneously on all four radio networks, becoming a landmark in the history of broadcasting. It was the subject of last year's Oscar-winning documentary short, *On a Note of Triumph: The Golden Age of Norman Corwin.*

Gregory Peck, Dorothy McGuire, Myrna Loy, Danny Kaye, Fredric March, and Marsha Hunt in the ABC studio for their live broadcast on Nov. 2, 1947.

Corwin has vivid memories of the Committee for the First Amendment, and working on this program. "They asked me if I would put that show together and direct it, and I did." He adds, with some understatement, "It was done in a hurry." Corwin recruited a longtime CBS colleague, William N. Robson, to supervise the New York portions of the broadcasts.

These shows, however, were heard on the ABC Network, which was just a few years old at the time. Marsha Hunt says, "I remember the emphasis in the announcer's voice as he said, 'This is the American Broadcasting Company.'" Was this because ABC charged less for its air time than its bigger rivals—a reported $8,000 per half-hour—or because at that time ABC was the only network that permitted prerecorded content? It's difficult to know at this late date.

More importantly, could a pair of programs relegated to a Sunday afternoon/early evening time period really make a difference? Apparently they did. Says Corwin, "I think we had surprised HUAC by mounting such an attack. Nobody had risen to protest, not in any organized fashion. This was no small congress of people of no small consequence.

"It was a remarkable enterprise, and it stopped the committee, for a while," says Corwin. Indeed, Thomas hastily adjourned his hearings four days after the first broadcast. The follow-up show on November 2 cited widespread press and public support, and quoted numerous editorials in big-city newspapers condemning HUAC and its witch-hunting tactics.

"For a while the committee felt numbed by the program," Corwin recalls. "It was the first national rebuff that they had, and it had considerable force and influence with the listening public. All of that fine work was undone when the producers met at the Waldorf and decided they would honor the committee by firing anybody who resisted it."

That now-infamous gathering of movie industry movers and shakers at the Waldorf Astoria Hotel in New York on November 24 and 25, 1947, marked the turning point in what would become a dark era. Forty-eight industry leaders gathered behind closed doors. Apparently, few of them had any interest in fostering a blacklist, but after two days of meetings they came to the conclusion that it was the only way to call off the Washington bloodhounds and get back to business.

The New York Times reported the results of that meeting on its front page in a story headlined "Movies to Oust Ten Cited for Contempt of Congress," although an official statement by the group declared that it was "not going to be swayed by hysteria or intimidation." Four days later, a follow-up story was headlined, "'Safe and Sane' Films New Hollywood Rule: 'Social Significance' to Be Avoided Lest It Be Considered 'Red.'"

The following week, Humphrey Bogart was persuaded to distance himself from the all-star D.C. junket. "I went to Washington because I thought fellow Americans were being deprived of their constitutional rights, and for that reason alone," he wrote in an open letter, publicly recanting his position rather than risk his career by aligning himself with unapologetic radicals—and Communists. "That the trip was ill-advised, even foolish, I am ready to admit. At the time it seemed the thing to do."

In response to this announcement, the editorial writer of Massachusetts-based *The Berkshire Evening Eagle* opined, "The most valid criticism of American movies is not that they incite to vice, crime, or treason, but that the overwhelming proportion of them are trivial. For one picture like *The Best Years of Our Lives* there are ninety and nine devoted to phony psychiatry, cowboys and Indians à la Cecil B. DeMille, improbable whodunits, parlor comedies, or similar bits of fluff. The public asks for bread and Hollywood gives it marshmallows. Not that marshmallows are not very pleasant in moderation and at intervals, but they make inadequate as a substitute for meat and potatoes.

"The answer is not more and bigger spectacles. One of Hollywood's biggest illusions is that the worth of a picture is in direct relation to its cost. What our pictures need is something the best British pictures in the last year have had—stories that have realism, and the real touch of nature, characters drawn from everyday life, emotions displayed that are sufficiently comprehensible to be shared by the audience and a certain earthiness that is as recognizable as it is indescribable. A beginning toward the latter touch might be made by showing living rooms less than thirty feet square and kitchens without electric dishwashers and quick-freeze units. If the magnates will stop viewing with a disdainful smile the short and simple annals of the poor and get back to fundamental situations and emotions, they ought to be able despite all the restrictions of the Johnston Office, the Legion of Decency, and the Thomas Committee to put on some pictures that the American people will want to go to."

"It was a pretty high-pitched emotional time," says Marsha Hunt today. "What fascinates me is its lasting fascination with the public; the subject won't die. I'm kind of alarmed to realize that if I am remembered, it might be more as a victim than as a talent. It's only now coming out that I was among the people blacklisted, never having been subpoenaed, never having been called on that carpet—and I'm sure the reason I wasn't was that the FBI had searched me carefully and found me wanting as a threat to the government. It was never public; I just stopped working.

"Of course, I was given my outs and I just wouldn't take them. All I had to do was lie and swear to it, which came hard for me."

Hunt prefers to remember the excitement and idealism of the people who joined forces to fight against a committee they considered truly un-American. "I think we were still hopeful then that it would [do some good], which is why we all turned out so willingly."

She still has a copy of her husband's script, and says, "The charming thing about it is the name for which one given speech had been assigned was crossed out, another one substituted, that crossed out, and maybe a third of these superstars [written in]. I think the availability of people kept changing."

The results of the committee hearings and the Waldorf conference led to many years of anger, animosity, and frustration in Hollywood. Yet Marsha Hunt, like many others, not only endured that period but prevailed. Like Marsha, Corwin is not bitter. He remains as engaged and aware of political matters as ever.

And, at age ninety-six, he has one lingering memory of "Hollywood Fights Back" that is wonderfully human—and free of political implication. "There was a delivery of a script to me, or some component of the program, and the messenger was Ava Gardner. That's one of my fondest memories of that show!"

Chapter 8
LOST IN MOVIE LIMBO

LOST in MOVIE LIMBO

Part I

One day about twenty-five years ago, I ran into film scholar William K. Everson on West 79th Street in Manhattan, where we both lived at the time. "Have you heard about the Regency Theater?" he asked, referring to our neighborhood revival theater. "MGM shipped the wrong print of *Strictly Dishonorable*, and they're showing the 1931 version!"

I didn't need to be told twice. That afternoon, my wife and I went to the Regency to see a pristine 35mm print of a film that hadn't been screened for at least thirty years. Its claim to fame is that it was based on the first (and only) successful play by the great Preston Sturges, and, because it was made before the imposition of the 1934 Production Code, it retained most of its saucy sophistication onscreen.

What we saw was a Universal picture; the reason MGM had a print in its vault is that the studio purchased remake rights for a 1951 musical of the same name, which starred Ezio Pinza and Janet Leigh. (As with the first adaptation, Sturges had nothing to do with the MGM film.)

That New York showing was a happy accident for film buffs. However, there are scores of other desirable, often high-profile movies—from an all-star version of Antoine de St. Exupery's *Night Flight* (1933), starring Helen Hayes, seen pining for husband Clark Gable; to the only big-screen adaptation of Arthur Miller's *Death of a Salesman* (1951)— that haven't been seen in decades. Some may never see the light of day because of legal entanglements; others might still be pried loose if someone is willing to pay the right amount of money.

When the Museum of Modern Art mounted a major retrospective of Universal Pictures in the 1970s, it had to obtain special permission from MGM to screen a print of *Waterloo Bridge* (1931), directed by the great James Whale. Those of us lucky enough to attend that showing were

Helen Hayes pining for husband Clark Gable in Antoine de St. Exupery's Night Flight *(1933).*

thrilled to discover a long-buried gem with a great performance by Mae Clarke in the role of a prostitute redeemed by love. Vivien Leigh recreated the role in the popular 1940 MGM remake, as did Leslie Caron in a 1956 version called *Gaby*. Like *Strictly Dishonorable*, *Waterloo Bridge* benefited from the sexual frankness that was permissible in the early 1930s but no longer tolerated in 1940.

I never understood why MGM didn't own the Universal early talkie, as it did *Strictly Dishonorable*. In those days, it was common practice for a studio to buy—and bury—a film whenever it produced a remake. There was apparently something more complicated in the agreement for *Waterloo Bridge*, but I am happy to report that the roadblock has been cleared, and Whale's excellent film finally had an opportunity to reach a wide and appreciative audience on DVD.

Warner has also freed up *Old Acquaintance* (1943), the delicious story of lifelong rivals starring real-life acting adversaries Bette Davis and Miriam Hopkins. It's always been available on television, but it's taken eighteen years to secure home video rights. What's more, a new digital master is being made from the original nitrate negative. (It was remade in 1981 as *Rich and Famous*, but that had nothing to do with the disappearance of the original.)

At one time, buffs despaired over ever getting a chance to see the 1935 musical *Roberta*, the 1931 *Dr. Jekyll and Mr. Hyde*, the 1936 *Show Boat*, the 1939 *Love Affair*, or any number of other classics that were tied up because of outmoded ideas about competition between remakes. Enlightened thinking, especially by MGM and the company that purchased its library in 1986, Turner Entertainment (now part of Warner Bros.), helped turn the tide. Nowadays it's not uncommon to have two versions of the same film offered on a dual-DVD, as with *Gaslight, State Fair, Dr. Jekyll and Mr. Hyde*, and *Death Takes a Holiday* (available as a bonus with its quickly forgotten remake, *Meet Joe Black*).

Alas, for every one of those happy endings there are multiple instances of films trapped in a kind of limbo, depriving audiences of the opportunity to see good movies and failing to generate any income for their owners.

During a Cinefest excursion to the George Eastman House in Rochester, NY in 1992, a happy group of movie buffs watched a unique 35mm print of *Christopher Bean*, the 1933 MGM movie starring Marie Dressler and Lionel Barrymore. For me it was love at first sight. Dressler is perfectly cast as a housemaid for a spoiled Connecticut family whose only sensible member is the father of the household, a benign country doctor (Barrymore). It turns out that their one-time handyman, who died penniless, has become a celebrated artist posthumously. Several greedy Manhattan gallery owners race to Barrymore's home when they learn that one of Christopher Bean's paintings still hangs in his living room. From there the plot thickens, delightfully, with Dressler holding the key to the mystery of the late artist.

Sylvia Thalberg and Laurence E. Johnson adapted their screenplay from a 1932 Broadway play *The Late Christopher Bean* by the estimable Sidney Howard, who in turn based his work on a French play, *Prenez Garde à la Peinture*, by Rene Fauchois.

No one can see *Christopher Bean* nowadays except in Rochester, New York. It was never part of the MGM television library, which would imply that the studio had short-term rights to the play and didn't renew them. In those days, studios seldom thought about a future life for their movies. To-day, it has to be worth a lawyer's time to dig into the files and pursue a dormant title; if a company doesn't see immediate value for DVD sales or remake rights, the property sits on the proverbial shelf.

Sometimes, even money isn't enough to free up a film. It's no secret why Samuel Goldwyn's production of *Porgy and Bess*, directed by Otto Preminger, hasn't been available for so many years. As musicologist and performer Michael Feinstein confirms, "Ira [Gershwin] did not like the film, primarily because he felt that they made Catfish Row too 'prettified.' It did not look like a slum and lost the sense of drama in the process. When the music license expired in the early 1970s, Ira did not renew it so they could not further distribute the film. He felt that overall it was a major lost opportunity, but did like some of the musical changes they made for the picture." The Gershwin estate is said to be reconsidering its hard-line position after all these years.

It was presumed that a dispute or monetary stalemate with Irving Berlin was the reason MGM's splashy version of *Annie Get Your Gun*

Paulette Goddard
and Bob Hope
in their third film
together, Nothing But
the Truth (1941).

(1951) was out of circulation for twenty-six years. Film musical historian Miles Kreuger learned otherwise when he spoke to David Lahm, son of the musical's co-librettist (and co-owner) Dorothy Fields, who died in 1974. Lahm strongly disliked the film and refused to renew the license with MGM. He was finally persuaded to make a deal after the Broadway revival was set and the timing seemed propitious.

Creators of Broadway shows, musical scores, novels, and plays often granted limited licenses for screen rights to their work.

Jack L. Warner felt triumphant when he obtained the movie rights to Lerner and Loewe's *My Fair Lady* for an unprecedented price tag of $5 million. Yet Warner's deal obliged his studio to surrender all rights—and even the negative of the picture—after just seven years. The film has been owned ever since by CBS.

Novelist and playwright Edna Ferber was a forerunner in brokering this kind of deal, forcing producers and distributors to renew their rights to such works as *Giant* and *So Big* on a regular basis. Her frequent partner George S. Kaufman took his cue from her, as did his collaborator Moss Hart; their properties also require negotiations and payments. That's why Frank Capra's Oscar-winning film version of *You Can't Take It With You* was out of the public eye for a number of years.

Irving Berlin was the music world's equivalent of Ferber. He not only demanded—and received—billing above the title on most of his films, like Irving Berlin's *Blue Skies*, but when Hollywood underwent radical changes in how it made deals in the 1950s, he seized the opportunity, along with A-list stars and filmmakers. Paramount may have made *White Christmas* in 1954 but it was only one-quarter owner of the property: the other quarters went to Bing Crosby, Danny Kaye, and Mr. Berlin.

My favorite story about that period involves Crosby and Hope. Like everyone else in Hollywood, they were salaried contract players in the 1930s and forties, but by the time they made *Road to Bali* in 1952 they were partners with the studio. After completing a desert scene for the film, Hope was passing the Paramount soundstage and noticed workers shoveling pure white sand into a dump truck. He immediately recognized it as an asset for his private two-hole golf course at home and stopped the stage hands in their tracks, declaring, "Hey—one third of that sand belongs to me!"

Various partnerships launched for one-picture deals have made it difficult to see some of Hope's post-Paramount films like *The Iron Petticoat* and *Paris Holiday*, but one of his vintage studio movies is also in a kind of limbo. *Nothing but the Truth* (1941) is based on a novel by James Isham and a popular stage adaptation by James Montgomery. The premise is irresistible: a man bets a large sum of money that he can tell the absolute truth for twenty-four hours. Paramount filmed it in 1920 with Taylor Holmes and in 1929 with Richard Dix; it seemed a natural for their newest comedy star, Bob Hope, in 1941. (It was still a good idea when Universal made *Liar, Liar* with Jim Carrey in 1997.)

High culture: Ole Olsen and Chic Johnson flank a balletic Mischa Auer in Hellzapoppin' (1941).

Whether the absence of *Nothing but the Truth* from television or video release is a matter of an estate asking too much money, a studio with too many other fish to fry, or two owners who simply can't come to terms, I do not know. The fate of this, and so many other movies, is a situation studio legal-departments are loath to discuss. I do know that the UCLA Film and Television Archive has a 35mm nitrate print of the film, that it's very funny and ought to be seen. I did manage to show it as part of the American Comedy series I programmed for the Museum of Modern Art in 1976, but in recent years Universal Home Video had to retract an announcement of its imminent release on videocassette.

During that same eight-month American Comedy series, I also had my hands full trying to secure permission for a showing of Olsen and Johnson's *Hellzapoppin'* (1941). There was a private collector's print available to me, but I couldn't show it without someone saying yes; the question was who. An agent who represented the families of Ole Olsen and Chic Johnson indicated they had sold rights to the property to Broadway producer Alexander H. Cohen, who was mounting a major stage revival with Jerry Lewis. I threw myself at the mercy of Mr. Cohen, who wrote just the kind of letter I needed, which read (as I recall), "Insofar as I may have such rights to grant, I give you permission to show the film." We did, everyone had a great time, and nobody complained or filed suit after the fact.

Almost thirty years later *Hellzapoppin'* remains one of those titles that's in a frustrating state of legal limbo . . . but only in the United States. Universal's deal with Olsen and Johnson, which now extends to their families and/or estates, limited its rights for U.S. distribution only. That's why the film was licensed by TV Ontario for airing on Canadian television within the past decade, and could be given video release there and in other countries.

All it takes is someone who cares enough to do it.

Part II

I thought I'd never get a chance to see the 1940 version of *Swiss Family Robinson* until the late Phil Serling, founder of the annual Cinefest in Syracuse, New York loaned me a 16mm copy that had once been part of a rental library.

The film was made at RKO when Orson Welles was preparing *Citizen Kane*, and Welles's sonorous voice intones the opening narration. Special effects wizard Vernon L. Walker and his team supply some impressive production-values for the studio-shot adventure. Although Phil's print had seen better days, I was still grateful for the chance to screen it; having grown up with Walt Disney's lighthearted remake I was much intrigued with this darker, more thoughtful adaptation of the Johann Wyss novel. Thomas Mitchell plays the head of the Robinson clan, with Edna Best, Tim Holt, Freddie Bartholomew, and Terry Kilburn as his wife and sons.

Like many other currently unavailable titles, *Swiss Family Robinson* once was easy to see, but in time it became a genuine rarity. Although produced at RKO, using the studio's personnel and production facilities, it was made by Gene Towne and Graham Baker's short-lived company The Play's the Thing, which also made *Tom Brown's School Days* that same year, 1940. Towne and Baker had a seven-year distribution deal with RKO, and then sold theatrical rights to Astor Pictures, which (in its usual fashion) cut fifteen minutes out of the picture for a 1951 theatrical reissue. Although the film apparently was sold to television intact, no complete 35mm prints survived.

In 1958, when Roy O. Disney (Walt's brother and partner) wanted to clear a path for his studio's remake of the property, he purchased all rights to the 1940 movie and had it pulled from television release. Moreover, he was told that the camera negative had been destroyed in a laboratory fire and that no 35mm prints survived. (It had long been

standard Hollywood thinking that one shouldn't allow an earlier version of a title to remain in release when a remake was in the works.)

Several decades later, when Scott MacQueen was in charge of film preservation for the Walt Disney Company, he took it upon himself to attempt a restoration of the 1940 film, which proved to be a formidable task. A worldwide search yielded just one result: the British Film Institute had two 35mm prints of the shortened Astor reissue; MacQueen borrowed them and took the best scenes from each. Then he located two 16mm prints of the complete version, one belonging to Phil Serling, the other to the late John Foster, whose 1942 reduction print had been donated to Wesleyan University in Connecticut. Both prints were worn, but Scott took the best elements from the missing fifteen minutes and blew them up to 35mm. He rerecorded the soundtrack and produced a new 35mm fine grain negative, several generations removed from the original but at least complete and more than adequate.

Unfortunately, the Disney company has no plans for the restored 1940 *Swiss Family Robinson* at this time; it would certainly make an interesting companion piece to the 1960 version on a double-disc DVD.

As it happens, that's not the only "orphan" film now under Disney's control. When the company acquired the ABC Television Network, it also became owner of various motion picture properties, from the 1959 version of *The Bat*, starring Vincent Price (produced by ABC's ephemeral feature-film enterprise, Liberty Pictures) to most of the David O. Selznick library. While the Disney company has licensed almost all of

Tim Holt, Freddie Bartholomew, Thomas Mitchell, Edna Best, and Terry Kilburn, from Swiss Family Robinson (1940).

the Selznick titles (*The Adventures of Tom Sawyer, Intermezzo, Notorious*, et al.) it's made no use of the little-seen British film *Gone to Earth* (1950), produced and directed by Michael Powell and Emeric Pressburger in glorious Technicolor. Selznick disliked the film, which starred his wife Jennifer Jones, and ordered new scenes shot by Rouben Mamoulian in Hollywood to create a U.S. release version called *The Wild Heart. Gone to Earth* is a fascinating film, typical of the unique and quixotic work of Powell and Pressburger, and deserves to be seen outside of the handful of archival screenings it has received in recent years.

RKO was home base for a variety of independent producers in the 1940s, and distributed many films it did not own, from the Lum 'n' Abner comedies to Jean Hersholt's Dr. Christian dramas and Guy Kibbee's Scattergood Baines series, titles which never became part of its studio inventory. The company also allowed other studios to cherry-pick its library for remake properties on a regular basis. That's one reason such titles as *Rio Rita* (1929), *Holiday* (1930), *The Animal Kingdom* (1932), *Cimarron* (1930), *Girl Crazy* (1932), *Bird of Paradise* (1932), *Roberta* (1935), and *Love Affair* (1939) never appeared on television and were difficult to see for decades. (RKO also sold remake rights to its 1930 musical *Hit the Deck* to MGM, but it has seemingly vanished; no negative or print is known to exist on that early talkie, which stars Jack Oakie and Polly Walker.)

Other titles disappeared from the library for a variety of reasons. After serving as production chief of RKO in the 1930s, Merian C. Cooper purchased the negatives and remake rights to a handful of 1930s films, including *Double Harness, One Man's Journey, Rafter Romance*, and *Stingaree*, presumably with the thought of remaking them some day. In the process, he removed these films from circulation, although he wisely had them transferred to safety film in the 1950s. Cinefest screenings of these films in recent years haven't resulted in anyone hailing any of them as rediscovered gems, but *One Man's Journey* (1933), the story of a dedicated small-town doctor, does give Lionel Barrymore a solid starring vehicle. Incidentally, in 1938 a "whiz kid" from Broadway named Garson Kanin made his Hollywood directorial debut with a grade-B remake of *One Man's Journey* called *A Man to Remember* starring Edward Ellis, from a screenplay by Dalton Trumbo. (In 2007, Turner Classic Movies managed to untangle the complications surrounding these films and acquired the rights, putting them back in circulation on the movie network and even arranging for theatrical showings in New York and Los Angeles.)

Some films go into limbo because the studio "leased" the rights to the original properties instead of purchasing them outright. For instance,

RKO made two screen-adaptations of Harold Gray's popular comic strip *Little Orphan Annie*: one in 1932, with Mitzi Green as Annie and Edgar Kennedy as Daddy Warbucks; and one in 1938, with Ann Gillis. RKO also made two versions of Gene Stratton Porter's *Laddie*: one in 1935, with John Beal under the direction of George Stevens; and one in 1940 with Tim Holt. Apparently all four films reverted to the owners of the underlying properties years ago.

Irene Dunne and Richard Dix in RKO's Oscar-winning Cimarron (1931).

Other films have disappeared for a variety of reasons. *The Soldier and the Lady* (1937), based on Jules Verne's *Michael Strogoff*, uses footage from the 1936 French film *Michel Strogoff*, which may explain why it's missing in action. French law involving the rights of the original author François Campaux has kept *The Blue Veil* (1950), starring Jane Wyman and Charles Laughton, out of the public eye for many years.

MGM, Warner Bros., and 20th Century Fox seldom if ever sold off their properties, preferring to do remakes themselves, in sharp contrast to RKO (and to a lesser degree, Paramount).

As often as not, it is the transfer of rights that has placed films in limbo. In 1929 Paramount acquired the rights to Arthur Hopkins and George Manker Watters's popular play *Burlesque* and filmed it as *The Dance of Life*, with Nancy Carroll and Hal Skelly. Eight years later, the studio remade it as *Swing High, Swing Low*, starring Carole Lombard and Fred MacMurray. A decade later, Fox decided that this show business comedy-drama (about a successful partnership that runs aground when success goes to our hero's head) would be a good vehicle for its musical stars Betty Grable and Dan Dailey. In order to make a third screen version, retitled *When My Baby Smiles at Me* (1948) the studio purchased Paramount's rights to the original play, which meant Paramount could no longer exhibit the earlier films. Decades later, Paramount donated a 35mm nitrate vault print of *The Dance of Life* (with two-color Technicolor sequences) to the Museum of Modern Art when someone in the New York office realized that the company could make no use of it. That gesture has kept the film alive. Fortunately, a safety negative and print of *Swing High, Swing Low* resides in the AFI/Paramount collection at the Library of Congress.

In another instance, when Fox decided to film William Faulkner's *Sanctuary* (1960) it put Paramount's earlier version, *The Story of Temple Drake* (1933), on ice. Film buffs are fortunate that Paramount's West Coast library of 35mm nitrate prints wound up in the possession of the UCLA Film and Television Archive, allowing occasional screenings of this tantalizing pre-Code title starring Miriam Hopkins and Jack LaRue. (The Library of Congress also has a 16mm negative.)

Why wouldn't a studio automatically protect precious negatives, regardless of their origin? Remember that in the 1940s (and even beyond) many Hollywood executives saw no potential earnings in "old movies," especially really old movies. It was like outdated inventory that cost money to store. Warner Bros. evidently thought so little of *The Animal Kingdom* (1932), which it acquired from RKO to remake as *One More Tomorrow* (1946), that it allowed the original 35mm negative to languish in a mislabeled film can until the late, intrepid Ron Haver came upon it quite by accident in the 1980s while searching for footage to complete his restoration of Warners' 1954 version of *A Star Is Born*.

In the 1960s and 1970s, some extremely rare and desirable titles started turning up on the 16mm collector-market in bootleg prints when various entrepreneurs discovered that the films had fallen into the public domain. The 1934 RKO production of *Of Human Bondage*, with Bette Davis's smoldering performance, wasn't legally available because the rights to W. Somerset Maugham's novel had been passed from Warner Bros. (which produced a 1946 remake with Eleanor Parker) to Seven Arts Productions and MGM, which made the 1964 version starring Kim Novak. Such legal details didn't deter the purveyors of 16mm dupes, and no one prosecuted them; prints became commonly available, and in the 1980s, those copies begat videotapes, which in turn have found their way to public-domain DVDs.

On the one hand, this was good news for film buffs, who now had access to important movies that had been sidetracked. In hindsight, it has proved to be a stumbling block for the companies that own the original 35mm materials. Why should they invest money to restore or preserve a title when they've been scooped by low-priced public-domain distributors? What's more, if they release a perfect copy on DVD or license it to cable and satellite TV, they will only provide better source material for the dupers.

Thus, the copies we see of *The Front Page* (1931), *Our Town* (1940), and *Till the Clouds Roll By* (1946) are generally inferior because they don't derive from original negatives. The tide may be turning, however. Sony finally released a beautiful copy of *The Front Page*'s 1940 remake *His Girl Friday* on DVD, and simultaneously began squelching public domain copies of that comedy classic. Warner Home Video finally gave *Till the Clouds Roll By* an official release as well.

Charles Boyer and Joan Fontaine in The Constant Nymph (1943).

There are dozens of other films that are sitting on the proverbial shelf for a variety of reasons. If a film is out of release, odds are the studio hasn't bothered to negotiate a renewal with the rights holders, or those parties have an inflated notion of what the rights are worth. Sometimes the rights' owners are too complacent, too distracted, too wealthy, or too busy to deal with what they consider a low priority in their lives.

The hard truth is that even though DVDs have created a new revenue stream, there is limited interest—and profit potential—for older titles that don't have major stars or reputations. This is a sorry fact that diehard film buffs don't like to hear. It's even worse news for some rights holders who may not understand that the properties they've been sitting on are actually becoming less valuable with each passing year.

Film researchers and students can take heart in knowing that some of these disputed films do at least exist in film archives. Over the years, I've traveled to the Library of Congress, the Museum of Modern Art, and the UCLA Film and Television Archive, screening films that couldn't be exhibited to the public, often on flatbed editing machines.

That's how I finally got to see *The Constant Nymph* (1943), an enticing title starring Charles Boyer and Joan Fontaine that has never appeared on television. Margaret Kennedy's novel of the same name was filmed twice before in England, in 1928 and 1933; the silent version was even shown at Cinefest some years back. UCLA has a 35mm nitrate copy of the 1943 film in its Warner Bros. collection, and it lives up to its reputation as an emotional and intelligent romantic drama. The famous score by Erich Wolfgang Korngold is a joy to hear.

But in twenty-first-century terms this film has limited value. Would it be worth a corporate attorney's time to examine the original contracts and determine a course of action to clear this movie? I have no idea. Each case presents its own set of challenges. Sometimes it's a matter of money. Sometimes it's striking up a relationship with an heir or a representative. And sometimes it's a jigsaw puzzle with one of the pieces missing.

For example, Warner Bros. can show the 1953 version of the operetta *The Desert Song* any time it likes, but would have to enter into negotiations to release either the 1929 early talkie or the bastardized 1943 version (updated to incorporate Nazi villains) in any form.

I know it would require hammering out a deal with the Frank Loesser estate to take the 1952 Warner movie *Where's Charley?* starring Ray Bolger off the shelf. This adaptation of the stage hit, based on the venerable play *Where's Charley?*, allowed Ray Bolger to recreate his crowd-pleasing performance (and sing "Once in Love with Amy") onscreen, but since its last television airing decades ago it's been lost in movie limbo. That means it makes no money for any of the parties involved, and shortchanges musical fans of the opportunity to see a significant film with a famous starring performance. Let's hope there is some light at the end of this particular tunnel.

Part III

Some years ago my longtime friend, film teacher and scholar Jeanine Basinger, was on the trail of the 1952 Joan Crawford vehicle *Sudden Fear*. Jeanine was teaching a groundbreaking course about Hollywood's depiction of women, using Crawford movies from various phases of her career, but this woman-in-peril title had fallen off the map. RKO distributed the movie theatrically but hadn't retained long-term ownership.

Joan Crawford in
Sudden Fear (1952).

Jeanine did some detective work and eventually learned that the rights had reverted to producer Joseph Kaufman, who died in 1961. When his widow passed on she bequeathed those rights to a synagogue in Manhattan! It took many years for someone (namely, Raymond Rohauer) to make the right connections and acquire *Sudden Fear* and other Kaufman titles like *Pandora and The Flying Dutchman*. Eventually they came to DVD via Kino Video.

While this story has a happy ending for film fans, there are many other cases where heirs and estates remain intransigent, either because they place an inflated value on their properties or because they just can't be bothered. It takes patience and determination to wrestle with these problems and refuse to take "no" for an answer. In this arena, Kit Parker is a champion.

For several decades Kit ran the best independent 16mm rental-company in the country. In recent years he has acquired several vintage film libraries and has started to release titles on DVD through Oklahoma-based VCI Entertainment. The return of a 1957 black-and-white movie like *Portland Exposé* with Edward Binns, Virginia Gregg, and Lawrence Dobkin may not warrant major media coverage, but it's a surprisingly good racket-busting B movie, with Frank Gorshin as a hood with a weakness for underage girls. Parker even persuaded Lindsley Parsons Jr., who worked for his famous producer-father on this quickie, to provide a commentary track.

Neither Parker nor the Blair family that runs VCI is likely to get rich from such DVDs, but they happen to love these movies. "This distribution deal allows me to indulge myself in digging up, clearing, and releasing those obscure Bs that you and I, and hopefully at least some others, love," says Parker. "Most of the time I cannot afford the time and money to clear one obscurity, but if two or more are involved I'll put out what it takes.

"There are series and Bs that 'fit' into my collection, but a studio would prefer to keep them in a vault rather than identify, search for, and negotiate with the underlying rights holders. I can't blame them as they can't sell enough to make it worth their while even if they didn't have to go through the underlying rights hassle."

Despite this hurdle, Kit has had a number of success stories. Most recently he made contact with the three daughters of Phillips H. Lord, the mastermind behind such long-running radio hits as *Gang Busters* and *Mr. District Attorney*. They own the rights to some of the films adapted from his shows, including *Counterspy Meets Scotland Yard* and *David Harding, Counterspy* (both made in 1950), and a Columbia version of *Mr. District Attorney* (1947) starring Dennis O'Keefe and Adolphe Menjou. Lord's children are happy to honor their father's memory by helping to bring these movies back to life and providing personal memorabilia as well.

Normally, studios tried to purchase all rights in perpetuity when they optioned material as movie fodder. But, as we've seen, some smart authors, playwrights, and songwriters agreed only to finite license periods. This was especially true for films based on radio series and comic-strip or comic-book characters.

It was a longtime standoff between the owners of the movie negative (Columbia Pictures) and the owners of the comic book property (D.C. Comics, now part of Time Warner) that kept the 1948 and 1950 *Superman* serials out of sight for so many years. The same was true for the *Blondie* series until, in an unusual reverse move, King Features Syndicate purchased the negatives to all twenty-eight Columbia features years ago.

(In a further irony, the late Edward Bernds, who directed the final entries in the long-running *Blondie* series, told me that the reason it was discontinued in 1950 was that Columbia tried to strong-arm cartoonist Chic Young into re-signing his licensing deal, and Young wanted to withhold television rights. Producer Bert Kelly warned the studio that it was taking a big risk, and he was right: Young turned them down, and a profitable series ended prematurely. Columbia tried to rebound by transforming Frank King's beloved *Gasoline Alley* comic strip into a series. Bernds directed two B features with Scotty Beckett and Jimmy Lydon in 1951 but, he told me, studio chief Harry Cohn didn't support the fledgling series in spite of good reaction at the studio, and it died before it ever got off the ground.)

I never thought I'd live to see the 1939 *Mandrake the Magician* serial, but VCI made it possible after acquiring the rights from King Features Syndicate, the negative from Columbia, and by surmounting one final obstacle: the studio had a picture negative but an unusable soundtrack for all of chapter one and part of chapter two.

"We were fortunate to at least have the original track for reference and were able to lift a little sound from it; however, it was so badly decomposed that you could barely listen to it," Bob Blair recalls.

Undaunted, VCI hired a company called Movie Stuff in Houston, Texas to recreate the missing soundtrack! A Foley artist provided appropriate sound effects, and the director cast actors who could sound enough like the serial's stars, Warren Hull and Doris Weston, so it wouldn't be jarring when their actual voices took over in chapter two. (The same company filled in a missing track for one episode of *Terry and the Pirates*.)

Warren Hull brings Lee Falk's comic-strip character Mandrake the Magician to life in the 1939 serial of the same name.

VCI also made a deal with the estate of cartoonist Fred Harman in order to release a multitude of Red Ryder features and serials, and negotiated with the Edgar Rice Burroughs estate to release the excellent 1941 Republic serial *Jungle Girl*. They were then lucky enough to locate a 35mm print at the British Film Institute in London to use as a DVD master.

But even the experienced folks at VCI hit a brick wall when it came to untying the knots that bind the 1939 Republic serial *Drums of Fu Manchu*. I empathize with the Blairs (father Bill and sons Bob and Don) because I made a similar effort about fifteen years ago when I wrote and co-produced a special for Republic Pictures on their classic cliffhangers. Someone had told me that UCLA had 35mm nitrate material on *Drums*, widely considered to be one of the best serials the studio ever made. I did some research and contacted a literary agent for the estate of Sax Rohmer (Arthur Henry Ward), who created the character in 1913. She told me that the rights to the serial were owned by Republic, and when I responded that Republic didn't think so, she had no further information. Republic wasn't willing to take a chance on a property which, at least on paper, it no longer controlled.

Ultimately, VCI decided that if no one was going to claim ownership, it would release the serial on home video, and did. Score another one for the fans.

There is one more reason why films which once were commonly exhibited in theaters and on TV are now in a state of limbo. These films are referred to in industry shorthand as "Abend" titles.

Sheldon Abend was a rough-hewn New Yorker who worked as a tugboat fireman and reportedly tried his hand at boxing before channeling his energy and chutzpah into the acquisition of short stories, novels, and plays. In many instances he acted on behalf of the authors or their heirs; in other cases he scooped up rights and profited handsomely on his own. Some people think of Abend as the ultimate ambulance chaser, but like another notorious pursuer and purveyor of rights, Raymond Rohauer, he was persistent—and successful.

According to one obituary, Abend (who died in 2003) had his first taste of success when he sued RKO over a 1938 B movie, *Lord of the Underworld*, which was based on a little-known play called *Crime*. He represented the heirs of the playwrights and collected an $80,000 settlement, of which he kept half. This set him on a lifelong course ferreting out widows, children, and estates of authors who had sold movie rights to their work but hadn't paid attention to the issue of renewal.

LINDSLEY PARSONS SR.

There is little that Lindsley Parsons Sr. didn't know about making movies on a budget. He wrote John Wayne's first starring westerns for Lone Star Productions in the 1930s, and later became a top producer at Monogram Pictures and its somewhat more respectable successor, Allied Artists. When I met him toward the end of his life, he was working for a completion bond company, helping to rescue films that had production problems (and protect his company's insured investment). At the age of eighty-five, he was sent to New York to advise young filmmaker Mario Van Peebles, who had fallen behind schedule shooting his first feature, *New Jack City*. Parsons read the script, watched some rushes, and, falling back on his Monogram experience, told Van Peebles how he could make up time by pruning his script, combining scenes together, and making use of the same locations. The tyro director followed the advice and kept his job. When Parsons died in 1992, James Cameron and Gale Ann Hurd took a memorial ad in the trade papers thanking him for his wisdom. (Sorry to say, he never finished his autobiography, which I read as a work in progress.) Lindsley Parsons Jr. learned at his father's side and went on to become a major-studio production manager and troubleshooter in his own right.

Around 1970 he obtained the rights to Cornell Woolrich's 1942 short story "It Had to Be Murder" from the Chase Manhattan Bank, which had renewed the copyright in 1969. Woolrich left no heirs, so the bank happily transferred its ownership to Abend for $650 plus 10 percent of all future proceeds derived from the story.

He later sued Alfred Hitchcock, James Stewart, and MCA Inc. over continued exhibition of *Rear Window*, the film they co-owned that was based on "It Had to Be Murder." Since Woolrich died in 1968, two years before the original twenty-eight-year copyright term for the story expired, Abend contended that they were in violation of their rights because they hadn't renewed their license for the story. In 1974 he withdrew his complaint in return for payment of $25,000.

But Abend wasn't finished yet. Challenging a ruling by the U.S. Court of Appeals for the Second Circuit in a long-running battle between Raymond Rohauer and Paul Killiam over rights to *The Birth of a Nation*, he sued Hitchcock, Stewart, and MCA Inc. all over again, taking his case to the Ninth Circuit Court of Appeals, which overturned the Rohauer/Killiam decision. (This was based on Rohauer having obtained rights to Thomas Dixon's novel *The Clansman*, on which *The Birth of a Nation* was based. Rohauer once threatened Killiam over licensing an 8mm home-movie version of *Son of the Sheik*, claiming that he had acquired the rights to this property from the author's widow. The home-movie company asked William K. Everson to draft a reply, which I once had the pleasure of reading: Everson dismissed the claim, as author E. M. Hull couldn't have left a widow behind. She was a woman, first name Edith.)

The squabbling between two Circuit Courts led to Abend's case being heard by the United States Supreme Court, which, on April 24, 1990, ruled in favor of Sheldon Abend and changed the entire structure of movie rights.

When Kit Parker heard that Abend was going back to court yet again, "I thought he had lost his mind; it sounded so ridiculous. Next thing I know he's suing them, and then he wins! He pointed up to this big certificate that he had framed from the Supreme Court.

"He was a big guy, wore cowboy boots, and on the wall he had one picture that was stuck up with a thumbtack. It was Jake LaMotta, and next to it was a hole in the wall where he had hit it with his fist. He was very literate, well-read, and loved his tough-guy persona."

Abend painted himself as a defender of defenseless widows and children, but in fact Cornell Woolrich left no family behind, and Abend personally collected 90 percent of the money the *Rear Window* case dropped in his lap. As a result of the Supreme Court ruling, it was estimated that five-hundrend thousand songs and four-hundred thousand novels, short stories, and poems were freed up for the heirs of writers to sell.

The new ground rules were clear: if an author or playwright died during the first twenty-eight years of copyright, his heirs could tell a studio, "The deal my father made is null and void." This applied only to works created before 1978, by which time the copyright term was changed to the author's life plus fifty years, and only affected distribution of those works in the United States.

As a result of the Abend rule, Universal has had to put the Abbott and Costello movie *It Ain't Hay* on the shelf; it's based on a Damon Runyon story, which was filmed before as *Princess O'Hara* (1934). Abend himself represented the Damon Runyon estate and apparently couldn't make a deal with the studio. Other prominent movies went into temporary limbo, like William Inge's *Picnic* and two Paddy Chayefsky originals, *Middle of the Night* and *The Americanization of Emily*, until financial arrangements could be made. John Steinbeck's *East of Eden* disappeared for a decade, and *Viva Zapata* is still missing in action. *The Hanging Tree*, from a novel by Dorothy M. Johnson, has recently been cleared after many years on the shelf, but the 1937 movie of Robert E. Sherwood's *Tovarich* (1937) with Claudette Colbert and Charles Boyer can't be shown. Scores of other films fall into this category, both major and minor.

There are as many reasons for films disappearing from view as there are sprocket holes. Playwright Arthur Miller disliked the ending that was tacked onto the 1951 screen adaptation of *Death of a Salesman* with

Fredric March, and declined to renew his license. Reportedly the George Orwell estate felt the same way about the 1956 version of *1984*. The owners of the *Joe Palooka* series with Leon Errol and Joe Kirkwood Jr. haven't been able to find a buyer willing to pay their price. But what's the story with the 1943 Paramount musical *True to Life* with Dick Powell and Mary Martin, and the 1955 comedy *The Iron Petticoat* costarring Bob Hope and Katharine Hepburn? The answers may be "out there," but they're not easy to come by.

The good news is that DVD and cable and satellite TV channels offer a new revenue-stream for older films . . . and as long as there are movie lovers with determination and a few bucks in their pocket both at independent companies and at the major studios, there will be old movies for us buffs to discover as new, for many years to come.

Author of numerous books on the history of cinema and popular culture, LEONARD MALTIN is perhaps best known for his annual paperback reference, *Leonard Maltin's Movie Guide,* first published in 1969. Since 1982 he has been the resident film buff on television's *Entertainment Tonight*; in addition, he hosts the weekly program *Secret's Out* on ReelzChannel, and introduces movies on DirecTV. Mr. Maltin teaches at the University of Southern California and was previously on the faculty at the New School for Social Research in New York City. For six years he was film critic for *Playboy* magazine and his articles have appeared in *The New York Times, Los Angeles Times, The London Times, Premiere, Smithsonian, TV Guide, Esquire, The Village Voice, Modern Maturity, Satellite Direct,* and *Disney Magazine.* He has served as Guest Curator at the Museum of Modern Art, and was President of the Los Angeles Film Critics Association in 1995 and 1996. In 1997 he was named to the National Film Preservation Board to help select twenty-five films annually to join the Library of Congress's National Film Registry, and in 2006 was appointed by the Librarian of Congress to the Board of Directors of the National Film Preservation Foundation. In addition to writing television specials and documentaries such as "*Fantasia*: The Creation of a Disney Classic," "The Making of *The Quiet Man*," and "The Making of *High Noon*," Mr. Maltin is also active in the field of DVDs, hosting and coproducing the popular *Walt Disney Treasures* series and appearing on Warner Home Video's "Night at the Movies" features. Perhaps the greatest indication of his fame was his appearance in a now-classic episode of the animated series *South Park*. Recipient of numerous awards, among them citations from the American Society of Cinematographers, Anthology Film Archives, and The Society of Cinephiles, he recently received the Special Medallion Award from the Telluride Film Festival in 2007.

Mr. Maltin publishes the quarterly newsletter *Leonard Maltin's Movie Crazy* and posts his picks among current movies, DVDs and film books on his web site, leonardmaltin.com. He lives in Los Angeles with his wife Alice and daughter Jessica.